School Stories

Elinor M. Brent-Dyer

Trials for the Chalet School

Theodora and the Chalet School

PARRAGON

This edition published in 1995 for
Parragon Book Service Limited
Units 13–17 Avonbridge Industrial Estate
Atlantic Road
Avonmouth, Bristol BS11 9QD
by Diamond Books
77–85 Fulham Palace Road
Hammersmith, London W6 8JB

First edition published 1992 for Parragon
Book Service Limited

Printed in England

Contents

Trials for the Chalet School 9

Theodora and the Chalet School 161

Trials for the Chalet School

Dedicated to the memory of
my dear mother

First published in a single volume in hardback in 1959 by
W & R Chambers Ltd.
First published in paperback in 1983 in Armada

Chapter 1

"TRUST MARY-LOU!"

"REMEMBER that this is sickness term," Miss Wilson said forebodingly.

Miss Annersley, co-Head of the combined school proper and finishing branch with Miss Wilson, glanced up from the sheet of paper over which she had been frowning. "Why the gloom, Nell? Do you feel it in your bones that we're due for one epidemic after another this term? Not," she added candidly, "that I pay the slightest notice to any of your prophecies."

Miss Wilson shrugged her shoulders. "Trust you to be downright crushing! All I was pointing out was that when we *do* get epidemics, it's nearly always in the Easter term. I can't see why I should be jumped on in such a wholesale manner for such a mild observation." She decided to change the subject. "Hilda, why *are* you scowling like that at the letter you have? Who's written about what?"

"It's this new girl," Miss Annersley replied, picking up her letter. "I'm strongly tempted to wish we'd said a very firm 'No' when her guardian first wrote to us."

"Why?" Miss Wilson demanded, leaning forward and twitching the letter from her friend's fingers. "You told me the lady said the girl was slightly deformed as the result of an accident some years ago, but I don't see why *that* should worry you. The girls won't make remarks about it if that's what you're afraid of. They've all had it well dinned into them that that sort of thing isn't done in this school." Her voice died away as her eyes went down the page of small, neat handwriting. She looked up and the twinkle had left her keen grey eyes. "*Oh!* Yes, that certainly looks like being a drawback."

"What *is* all this?" Rosalie Dene, the school secretary demanded. "What does the letter say? Do remember, you two, that I only came up late last night and this is the first I've seen of any of the correspondence since the holidays."

"This came yesterday morning," Miss Annersley said. "Give it to her, Nell. Read it, Rosalie, and tell us what you think."

Miss Dene took the letter, sat back and read it carefully. When she had finished, she sat in a frowning silence.

"Well?" Miss Wilson asked with some impatience in her voice.

"I don't think it's 'well' at all. In fact, I don't like it. The good lady is vague, to say the least of it." She quoted from memory, "'Owing to the accident of which I have already spoken, I am afraid her mind has become slightly warped.' *That* doesn't tell you much. Does the girl tell lies, lose her temper for nothing, help herself to other people's goods—or what?"

"I should think it might be 'what'," Miss Wilson said thoughtfully.

"But, Nell, that may mean anything," Rosalie protested.

"How old is she? Is she our only new girl this term?"

"She is," Miss Annersley said, answering the second question first. "I may say I wouldn't have agreed to accept her, but this lady says that she must go to Nigeria to be with her own girl who is expecting her first baby and wants her mother with her—naturally. They are rather afraid of the effect of the climate on Naomi, and their own doctor advised Alpine air for her. Hence, she is coming to us. As for age, she's sixteen."

"*Hilda!* I thought we'd decided after Yseult Pertwee that

we would never again take a girl over fifteen? I'm sure that's what you all agreed on."

"I know; but it was difficult to refuse. You see, Peter Chester put them on to us. And he made sure by writing to Madge Russell and begging her to get us to make an exception where Naomi is concerned. They've been staying in St Peter Port in Guernsey and he was called in to prescribe for the girl when she had 'flu. He says that it must be a school of some kind, as they seem to be oddly minus relatives with whom she could stay. His own Barbara knows her, and so does Vi Lucy, and they would help her over the first few days. In the circumstances, Nell and I decided that we ought to stretch a point. I may say, nothing on earth would have persuaded me to do it if I'd known of *this* complication."

"No, but you can't exactly go back on your word now. We'll just have to take her and hope for the best," Rosalie said. "Only I do wish this Mrs.— what's the woman's name? —oh, Weldon, of course—had been rather more explicit. As things stand, we haven't a clue just what to look out for."

"Well!" A fresh, ringing voice from the doorway broke into their conference and they all turned with sighs of relief. "What's the matter with you folk? You all look as if you'd just heard that your rich old uncle had died and left all the money he had promised to leave you to form a society for the protection of household pests!"

A cry of "Joey!" rose from the three, Miss Annersley adding, "Don't talk such utter rubbish! Anyhow, you're the very person we want. Come in, take off that enormous wrap you call a shawl and sit down. We need your considered advice."

The newcomer laughed as she entered the room, tossing off the great grey shawl in which she had been closely muffled against the piercing cold of an Alpine January day. "You *do* sound as if you'd come to the end of your tether!" She pulled a chair up to the table and sat down. "Well, I'm all ears. Open your hearts and tell me all!"

The two Heads looked at each other, but Rosalie got in first. "Hilda's accepted a new girl who is slightly crippled as the result of an accident. She's just had a letter from the kid's guardian to say that her mind is also warped—though *how* warped, the lady doesn't condescend to inform her. She accepted the girl before this and now she's by way of regretting it."

"Well, that sums it up very neatly," Miss Wilson observed. "All right, Joey. Rosalie's put the whole thing into a nutshell and you know everything—except that the girl is sixteen, so will be among the Seniors."

"Where among the Seniors?" Joey demanded.

"VIb, to be exact, so I suppose it isn't quite so bad as it might have been."

"I see." Joey considered a moment. "In VIb, you say? Who does that consist of at the moment?"

"Your English!" Miss Annersley murmured with an air of deep pain.

"Never you mind my English. Much more important to try to solve this latest problem. Rosalie, you keep the registers. Who, exactly, is in VIb now?"

"Oh, Verity Carey, Barbara Chester, Josette Russell, Prunella Davies, Jessica Wayne, the two inseparables, Christine and Catriona. How many is that? There are twelve of them, all told. That lot, anyhow," Rosalie Dene replied.

"There'll be thirteen of them, if Naomi goes there," Miss Wilson remarked.

"Is that her name? Well, I don't see any reason to worry about any new girl warping the minds of any of that lot. Every one of them is a girl with a mind of her own."

"I'm not worring about that so much," Miss Annersley said slowly. "As you say, that crowd all have minds of their own—even Jessica. At the same time, they have important public exams ahead of them and I don't want them upset."

"It'll all depend on the kink in her mind, won't it? May I see the letter?"

Miss Annersley passed it over to her and she settled down to read it while the other three watched her anxiously.

When she had finished, she looked up. "Ye-es! It does leave you rather hung up, I must say. This may mean anything. What are you going to do about it?"

"That's what we're considering," Miss Annersley said. "Have you any ideas?"

"Give me a chance! I've just this moment heard your tale of woe. I'll give you one idea, though. Turn Mary-Lou on to her."

"How do you mean?" Miss Annersley demanded.

"Just what I say. Look, Hilda! Mary-Lou is the sort of girl you can take into your confidence. Furthermore, she may be only seventeen in years, but as we all know, mentally, she is considerably older than that." She glanced round them with questioning eyebrows and they all nodded assent. She went on; "She has her head well-screwed on and she *is* extraordinarily understanding. On top of all that, she is *kind*. If you take my advice, you'll explain things to her—a little, anyhow. At least give her some idea of what to expect. Then, you can leave it to her. She'll cope all right, or I don't know my Mary-Lou!"

"I don't think I like it," Miss Wilson said after a moment.

"What don't you like about it?" Joey demanded.

"This is Mary-Lou's last year at school. I know she's coming on to St. Mildred's for a final year, but it's not the same thing. Once she finishes here, she is no longer a schoolgirl. She's Head Girl this year, which gives her plenty to do in any case. I don't think it's fair to dump a heavy responsibility like Naomi on her at this stage."

"But, my dear Bill, you know as well as I do that May-Lou *thrives* on responsibility! Heaven knows she's butted in over and over again when no one asked her to!"

"Oh, we all know that Mary-Lou has inherited your mantle—"

"Rosalie Margaret Dene, may I ask what you are talking about?"

"Josephine Mary Maynard; you may. You, let me remind you, were the school's prize butter-in—still are, if it comes to that. Mary-Lou is just a chip off the old block in that direction."

"She's no such thing!" Joey said heatedly. "I suppose I *might* have been her mother, but I'd have had to start jolly early in that case! The girl's nearly eighteen!"

"So she is. But I didn't mean that way, but—well, *spiritually*. At the same time, I agree with Nell that it's rather hard lines to ask her to take on any special effort now. She told me at the beginning of last term that she meant to enjoy this final year at school. She has no exams to bother about and she's specialising in her own subjects. Ordinary Head Girl duties she can take in her stride. If we turn her on to a girl with warped tendencies, that's going to be an extra job. She'll take it on if she's asked, of course, but are we being fair to her?"

Joey looked thoughtful. "You know I'd forgotten how nearly Mary-Lou's school career was at an end. Oh, dear! There are times and seasons when I wish children didn't grow up so rapidly. Look at my triplets! Fourteen last November—into their fifteenth year and in the Senior school! And it seems only yesterday that they were tiny girls, trotting everywhere after Mamma."

"Bless me, you've plenty of babies to go trotting round after Mamma still, haven't you?" Miss Wilson demanded. "There are Felix and Felicity. Cecil's on her feet now. You aren't left babyless. And if I'm any judge of the matter, it'll be a few years yet before you have *that* particular loss to growl about."

Joey grimaced at her. "I hope so! I *like* long families!"

"Well, you've *got* one—nine is a long family all right!"

"Ten, when July comes," Joey said calmly. "That was my real reason for dropping in on you now. Only I may as well tell you that Jack and I are hoping for twins again, so that will make us eleven."

"Joey Maynard!" The shriek came from three voices.

"You're incorrigible!" Miss Annersley cried. "Anyhow, this isn't getting us any further with Naomi—"

"Yes, I was going to ask you," her co-Head interrupted her. "Are we to speak to Mary-Lou or not?"

"I shall have to consider it before I say anything. Oh, I daresay I shall agree in the end. For one thing, quite apart from her influence over other girls, I don't see anyone making much impression on *her* mind. Mary-Lou has a tremendous personality and she will stick to her own lines. But I can't say now."

Joey, her news announced and her advice given, stood up and picked up her shawl. "I must fly back. The family is making toffee and fudge and there's only the Coadjutor in charge, this being Anna's free day. As for putting Mary-Lou on the job, you must make up your own minds about that. But I'll say this. Whatever you do about it, if there's anything outstandingly odd about this new girl, you can trust Mary-Lou to spot it and wade in on her own. I think you might as well leave it at that, now I come to think of it. She'll see to it, whether you do anything or not. And what's more, if she does, you can trust her to make something out of the poor child. Now I'm going!" And with that, she departed and left them to make up their own minds as she had said.

Chapter 2

A Job For Mary-lou

THE Chalet School—or such of it as came from any distance, which means most of it—was arriving for the new term. As usual, they had left the train at Berne to pile into the big motor-coaches in which they made the last stages of the journey up to the Görnetz Platz, high in the mountains of the Oberland Alps. After a wide detour across the plain, there had been the long climb up the road which was originally built for the passage of motor ambulances to and from the great Sanatorium which stood at the far end of the Platz. Now they were running smoothly along, past tiny villages, perched among the mountain slopes and the pines, between the walls of the mountains, beyond solitary chalets and huts built here and there in niches.

The leading coach carried the members of the two top forms. As they were all girls of sixteen and over and had all the prefects with them, they were without any mistress. This was a much-prized privilege, for it meant that speech could be free. Even the best of mistresses, as Clare Kennedy of VIb remarked, could cramp your style on occasion. The Seniors and mistresses, especially the younger mistresses of the Chalet School, were on friendly terms as a rule, but it *was* a joy to be able to gossip as they pleased and not to have to pick and choose their English!

Seated at the back of the coach was the Head Girl, Mary-Lou Trelawney. She was a tall girl, very good-looking, with a mass of silky golden-brown curls clustered tightly over her shapely head, clear blue eyes and a glorious complexion. However, handsome though she might be, character was not lacking in her face. Her short chin was firm and there was a look about her finely-cut lips that told you that when Mary-Lou chose to dig her toes in, she was a very hard nut to crack!

On her right was Hilary Bennet, another tall girl, with a head of boyishly-cut wavy hair and a piquant face of her own. On her left was Vi Lucy who, so far as looks went, beat most of the others hollow with her bronze curls, deep violet eyes and perfect features. One either side of this trio sat Doris Hill, an ordinarily pleasant-looking girl, and Lesley Malcolm who had no claims to beauty, though her keen, clever face stood up well to the contrast with the centre three.

These five formed the backbone of the prefects and, as anyone in the school could have told you, Mary-Lou was their leader in most things. They had spent most of the long journey from England in exchanging news of their holidays. Now that school was so near, Mary-Lou saw fit to change the subject.

"Winter sports this term! And, thank goodness, they seem to have had plenty of snow."

"*And* a good hard frost," Doris Hill supplemented. "I'm aching for it. I was frightfully disappointed with last term."

"Oh, we hardly ever got much in the Christmas term," Vi told her. "January, February and March are the best months for winter sporting."

"I'm looking forward to a gorgeous term," Mary-Lou added.

"You'd better touch wood," Lesley warned her seriously. "It doesn't do to be too optimistic."

"Why, what do you expect to happen that's so awful?"

"Nothing in particular; but I don't believe in tempting Providence," Lesley replied, laughing. "And why more gorgeous this term than usual?"

"Well, think of it—no exams to worry about; I *think* I can manage the Head Girl business all right, now I've got into the way of it; nothing in the shape of out-of-school extras, since the Sale's been shifted to the summer term. The pantomime is St. Mildred's affair and won't affect *me* this year. In fact, I expect to be able more or less to sit back and enjoy life for once."

"Yes; it does look as if it might work out like that for us," Lesley owned.

"Apart from the usual bothers with the Middles," Doris warned them.

"Oh, surely we've got all that well taped by this time?" Vi said.

"You can *never* have Middles 'well taped'," Mary-Lou asserted. "They think up the maddest things that no one in their senses would think of forbidding until the little pests have done them."

"Well, you ought to know!" Josette Russell, sitting beside Barbara, told her with a grin. "I never heard that *you* crowd were a bevy of little angels when *you* were Middles. I know *I* wasn't!"

"Oh, Middles are all alike for that," Doris returned, rather sweepingly. "I'll tell you what I'm so thankful for and that is that we're all specialising now. I do find that a most terrific relief!"

"By the way," Vi observed, "didn't Biddy O'Ryan—I mean Courvoisier—say that she wasn't coming back this term? We'll have a new history mistress, then. I wonder who she is and what she's like?"

"She won't come up to Biddy," Lesley said positively. "It will be very difficult for anyone to take *her* place. I'm on the science side as you know, but I wouldn't have missed one of Biddy's lessons for anything you could mention."

"Nor I," Vi agreed. "Anyone else after her will be a fearful drop."

"There's Freudesheim!" Josette suddenly exclaimed. "Look! Auntie Joey at the gate to welcome us! Oh, I wish they'd stop the coach and let us have a word with her." Here, she waved wildly at the window. "I've heaps of messages from Mummy for her, and a whacking big parcel."

"The Head will let you go over tomorrow some time," Mary-Lou said soothingly.

"I know that." Josette sat down as the coach swung round the wide curve and the gate of Freudesheim was out of sight. "But I'd like to see the twins and Cecil for a moment. The boys will all be back at school now. They start earlier than we do; but I'd like to see the babies."

"The Trips will be at school and you can see *them*," Vi grinned. "You pipe down, Josette."

"She'll have to, anyhow," Doris said as she peered into the gloom. "We're turning in at the gate this minute."

It was a very short drive and they could all see the light pouring out into the darkness of the January evening from the wide-open hall doors. Lights gleamed in many of the windows, too. At the doors stood the two Heads to welcome them back, those of the staff who had not been on escort duty standing behind them, and further in, clusters of girls, mainly those who lived on the Platz or in the Swiss towns and cities, for the Chalet School, which had begun life as a cosmopolitan school but had lost it when it had been forced to leave Tirol, the place of its birth, was now regaining its old position and almost half of the girls there now were not British.

Another moment, and the motor-coach had pulled up before the four shallow steps which led up to the building. The girls hurried to claim their hand luggage and scramble out. The cases were all deposited on a big truck beside which stood Gaudenz, the man-of-all-work. Then the big girls swept forward and streamed into the house to be greeted warmly by the two Heads before they passed on to line the walls, standing in close ranks. Everyone must be squeezed in somehow, and already the girls from Vb and Inter V were following on their heels.

It was more than a squash, as Doris, standing next to

Lesley Malcolm, murmured; but they managed it. By the time the last Junior had been crowded in and the staff, laughing gaily, were standing on the stairs, everyone had been pushed into line somehow and the big doors were shut.

"Welcome back girls!" Miss Annersley said, her beautiful voice ringing clearly across the phalanxes of girls all looking at her as she stood on the bottom stairs. "I won't talk now. Abendessen is ready and I'm sure you are, too. Go off, form by form to your Splasheries and get rid of your outdoor things and change your shoes. When the entire form is ready and *not before*, march to the Speisesaal and take your places quietly. You may talk till the gong goes. Then be silent, please. Lead on, there, second form!"

The little girls marched off smartly at once, the rest following to their cloakrooms which were always called Splasheries. The prefects went last and as Mary-Lou passed her, Miss Wilson, standing near the corridor leading to them, touched her on the arm. The girl stopped at once.

"Yes, Miss Wilson?" she queried.

"When you are ready, Miss Annersley wants to see you in the study, so be quick, please."

"Yes, Miss Wilson." It was all Mary-Lou said, but her blue eyes were like saucers. This was *not* in accordance with the general rule.

"Tell Vi Lucy to take over for you until you return—but it won't be for more than a minute or two. Now fly!" Miss Wilson turned away with a smile and Mary-Lou scuttled off after the rest.

"What did Bill want?" Vi demanded as they hung up their coats and berets and fished in their lockers for the house shoes left at the end of the previous term.

"Not knowing, can't say." her friend replied airily. "I've to go to the study when I'm ready. The Head wants me. Am I decent?"

"You're all right—except your hair. That's a bit wild. Run

a comb through it and then you'll do," Vi said as she took a hasty look at her friend.

Mary-Lou obeyed and then with a quick, "Take over, Vi, will you?" fled to the study. She tapped at the door and went in quietly at Miss Annersley's summons, remembering to pause long enough to make her curtsy. When the school began, Miss Bettany as she then was—Lady Russell, these days—had adopted certain Tirolean customs and manners and the courteous salutation to the Head was one that had never been omitted.

Miss Annersley was standing behind her desk. She smiled at her Head Girl before she said, "You have been quick, Mary-Lou. I won't keep you, dear. I'm sure you're longing for Abendessen! We have a new girl this term—Naomi Elton. She is a senior and will be in VIb. I want you take charge of her for the moment. You know what to do." She turned to an armchair standing with its back to the room. "Naomi, come here, my dear. This is our Head Girl, Mary-Lou Trelawney. She will look after you for the next day or so until you begin to feel your feet. Mary-Lou, Naomi knows Barbara Chester a little, so put her to sit next to Barbara."

"Yes, Miss Annersley," Mary-Lou replied, inwardly wondering why Barbara had not been sent for in the first place.

"Thank you, dear. That's all I want now. Go with Mary-Lou, Naomi."

Naomi had been getting slowly to her feet and now Mary-Lou found herself looking down on a girl who was badly stooped with a crooked shoulder. But the face lifted to hers was lovely—almost as lovely as Vi Lucy's with cloudy fair hair framing perfect features. Dark grey eyes looked straight into hers as Naomi said, "How do you do?"

It was a musical voice, but there was a hardness about it which rang in Mary-Lou's ears at once. The perfectly cut mouth was set in thin lines and there was a crooked twist to the smile which accompanied the words.

"Hello, Naomi," she said, with her own delightful smile.

"Come with me and I'll see you through. So will Barbara."

She led the way to the door where she paused to curtsy, then she ushered the new girl out, thinking to herself that perhaps Lesley had been right to warn her to touch wood. She felt an odd repulsion to the girl mixed with the genuine pity that rose in her warm heart for anyone so terribly deformed.

Chapter 3

NAOMI

"THIS place is a regular rabbit warren for corridors," Mary-Lou said as she tried to match her swinging walk to Naomi's halting progress. "It used to be a winter-sports hotel, you see, and a bunch of chalets and pensions nearby. It's all linked up with covered passages on the ground floor now, but it does make it something of a day's march to get from one end of the place to the other. However," she added cheerfully, "you'll soon get to know the geography of the place. And while I think of it, this is first day when rules are more or less in abeyance. From tomorrow morning onwards, no talking in the corridors or on the stairs unless it's absolutely necessary—and you've got to satisfy the powers that be that it *is* necessary, or else!"

Naomi flashed a quick look at her. "Or else—what?" she asked, pausing a moment and leaning against a set of shelves as if she were tired.

Mary-Lou glanced at the stick on which she leaned, and stood still. "Was I going too fast? Sorry! Why didn't you yank me back before?"

"It's all right, I'm just a little tired. I flew here this afternoon," Naomi said, resentment plain in her face. "Go on and tell me about the rules."

Mary-Lou was wise enough to let it go. "Oh, if you talk out of turn, so to speak, you're fined, that's all."

The delicately arched eyebrows drew together in a quick frown. "I thought a breach of rules would mean an order mark or lines or something like that."

Mary-Lou shook her head. "Order marks are mainly for untidiness or cheeking the prefects and it's mostly Juniors and Middles that go in for that sort of thing. Talking in forbidden places and at forbidden times always means a fine."

"I see." Naomi began to limp forward again. "Certainly, I must avoid leaving my things about and cheeking people. One hardly wants baby punishments when one is verging on the adult stage, does one?"

Mary-Lou was, for once in her life, silenced. There was a nasty little undercurrent in Naomi's voice which made her wonder. When she spoke again, it was about the fines.

"Of course, you're fined, too, if you forget to use the set language for the day. That can mean that when the end of the week comes, you're penniless. *Not* a very pleasant state of things, for you mayn't borrow or anticipate your weekly allowances except for church collections or stamps. Here we are!" as they turned a corner. "Down this corridor. Here's our door. The staff use the one further up." She nodded towards a second door in the wall, then opened the first and led the way into a long, narrow room, bright with lights, gay cloths, coloured glasses and pretty tableware. There was a steady hum of laughter and talk mingled with the sound of knives and forks at work. Abendessen had begun already. Mary-Lou took Naomi to the table where the prefects sat in all their glory. Her quick eyes noted a vacant chair between Barbara Chester and Prunella Davies, and she led Naomi to it.

"You sit here for the moment," she murmured. "You'll have to say your Grace to yourself. We're too late for ordinary Grace." Then she left the new girl and made her way up the table to her own seat at the head, where she sat down and bent her curly head for a moment as she murmured her Grace.

Naomi stared, but she fell in enough with Mary-Lou's ideas to bow her own head in the same way. When she raised it, someone was setting a plate of meat before her and Barbara was pushing a dish towards her, filled with tiny golden potato-balls.

"Hello, Naomi," she said pleasantly. "I didn't know you were coming here. Have some potatoes and then give the dish a shove on to Mary-Lou, will you?"

Naomi helped herself and passed the dish on. Someone offered her a sauce-boat of rich, delicious gravy; her glass, after a question as to whether she would prefer milk or lemonade, was filled with rich, creamy milk and she was able to begin. Mary-Lou had not waited for her. She was tucking in at a tremendous rate, being, as she plaintively remarked, famished by this time.

Presently, when the edge was taken off her appetite, she smiled down the table at Naomi who was eating in much more deliberate fashion, and began introductions in the breezy way that seemed habitual with her.

"Everyone! Meet Naomi Elton who has come to grace our sixth forms. She's in VIb. Naomi, the person on my left is Hilary Bennet who is games prefect. On my right, our second prefect, Vi Lucy—"

"I know Vi," Naomi interrupted her. "We met when I was staying in Guernsey."

Vi nodded pleasantly at her, though her eyes were clouded. Mary-Lou glanced at her questioningly, but said nothing. She merely carried on with the good work. "Next to Vi—Barbara Chester, her cousin. You know Barbara, too, don't you?"

"Yes; we have met two or three times," Naomi replied distantly.

"And on your other side, Prunella Davies, who is your form prefect."

"When did you come?" Prunella asked. "I didn't see you on the train."

"I flew with Aunt Harriet," Naomi replied. "It's quicker

and, they thought, easier for me. I'm a cripple, you see." Her lips twisted as she spoke.

Prunella was silenced, but Hilary picked up the ball and tossed it back.

"Flew?" Her saucy, laughing face wore a frankly envious look. "Oh, lucky you! I've always longed to fly but Dad says he isn't a millionaire and I can wait for such luxuries until I can provide them for myself."

A tall girl with the face of a thinker who was sitting on the other side of the table, glanced at the Head Girl with a wicked smile. "Remember when you asked the Head if we should all fly to school, Mary-Lou?"

Mary-Lou hid her face in her table-napkin while the rest shouted.

"Lesley, you wretch!" she said when she emerged again. "Shall I ever be allowed to forget that historic occasion?"

"Never!" they assured her in a laughing chorus.

"And," Lesley Bethune continued in a meditative voice, "when the Head asked you if you had any idea what it cost, you replied, "Not a sausage!" Even Miss Annersley had to laugh on that occasion!"

"All the same," Vi interrupted her, "she sat very heavily on your little aspirations. And if you're going to give Naomi all our names, you'd better stop reminiscing and get on with it."

"So I had. The next one to Vi is Doris Hill, Naomi, and next to her," she projected a smile at the small, slight girl in that place, "is my sister-by-marriage, Verity Carey."

Naomi was taken off her guard. "Your what?" she jerked out in the ordinary tones of any schoolgirl.

"Sister-by-marriage. Her father married my mother when we two were Senior Middles. We aren't step-sisters, so that's what we call it."

"Oh, I see." Naomi looked across at Verity, whose smallness made her seem almost out of place among the elder girls.

"Welcome to our midst," Verity said in the silvery voice

that seemed to match both her size and her amazing fairness. Indeed, if it had not been for her eyes, she would have been almost insipid; but those glorious eyes of vivid gentian blue, with finely arched brows and long lashes of black prevented that.

Mary-Lou grinned to herself and went on with the introductions. The girls all spoke to the stranger pleasantly and when Mary-Lou had finished, she summed up the position with her usual clarity.

"Well, now you know our names. You'll soon learn which to fit to which person if you don't remember now. Barbara, you'll give Naomi a hand? She's in your form, so take her to stationery and the stockrooms tomorrow, will you, and see that she gets everything she needs."

Barbara nodded. "I'll see to it. I'll make out the list as soon as I can, Naomi, and come and help you collect them."

"Thank you," Naomi said. "I'm afraid I could hardly carry much myself. Being a cripple means that one is able to do so little of that sort of thing."

The girls glanced at each other uneasily. It was difficult to know what to say. Naomi knew it quite well and her eyes gleamed as she saw their discomfort. On the whole, it was as well that the maids arrived to change the plates and by the time they were all busy with a delicious creamy mixture, the moment had passed and Mary-Lou had changed the subject.

When the meal was nearly at an end, a bell sounded from the high table. At once the chatter and laughter ceased as the girls turned in their seats to face up the room to where Miss Annersley, very trim and attractive in her blue woollen frock, had risen.

"After Grace," she said, "clear the tables, please, and then go straight to Prayers. After Prayers, Juniors and Junior Middles go to bed. Everyone else will go at their usual time. That is all at the moment."

She sat down and the girls went on with their meal. When it finally ended, they all stood, each girl stepping to the left of her chair before pushing it in to the table. Naomi, slower than the rest because of her lameness, waited until her neighbours had moved before she fumbled for the stick she had laid beneath her seat. Mary-Lou, seeing her difficulty, was at her side in a moment, but her help was repelled freezingly.

"Thank you, but I can manage for myself. I am not entirely helpless," Naomi said as she slowly levered herself to her feet with the aid of the stick.

There was no more to be said. Mary-Lou, flushing, went back to her seat and the new girl stood behind her chair, her fair hair bent as decorously as anyone else's, while the Head, in the beautiful voice that Joey Maynard always declared was one of her greatest assets, repeated the short Latin Grace they always used. The staff followed her out of the room, but some of the prefects hurried to the back where several trolleys were standing and brought them up to the tables in turn. Others were already passing plates, cutlery, glasses and dishes up to the top. .

Meanwhile, the rest had seized on their napkins and marched off to place them in a drawer of a great armoire that stood at one side. Two other people, swept and folded the cloth and added it to the drawer before it was closed. Naomi, still standing by her chair, nearly gasped. The entire room had been cleared in exactly seven minutes and the girls were forming into two lines near the door. Then Mary-Lou was once more at her side.

"Prayers now," she said. "Are you Protestant or Catholic?"

"Why?" Naomi demanded.

"The Catholics have Prayers in the gym. If you are Protestant, you go to Hall." Then, as the new girl stared at her, she added somewhat impatiently, "Of course we separate for Prayers! What else did you expect?"

Naomi gave that curious, twisted smile of hers. "I can't really say *what* I am. Aunt Harriet could never make up her mind, so sometimes we went to the Church of England, sometimes to Chapel and sometimes to the Catholic church. It all depended."

"Depended on what?" Mary-Lou asked involuntarily.

"On what sort of music there would be or the preaching and so on. Some Sundays, we didn't go anywhere, of course."

"But what am I to do with you?" the Head Girl cried. "Weren't you baptized anywhere?"

"Not that I know of." Naomi replied calmly. "My people were agnostics, I believe, and Aunt Harriet thought it better to try everything before I made up my mind."

Mary-Lou stared at her speechlessly. This was a problem she had never run up against before. There *had* been girls who didn't care in the least about religion, but even they were nominally members of some form of Christianity. There was only one thing for it. She must go to Miss Dene who would surely have some idea as to which branch this odd girl was to belong—for belong to one or the other, she must, so long as she was in the school.

"We'd better go to the office," she said slowly. "I don't suppose you'll be allowed to run from one to another as you choose and you'll certainly not be allowed to stay away from either Prayers or church. Everyone goes. I expect your aunt will have told Miss Dene which she wants you to attend." She looked down at Naomi and added, "It's getting frightfully late. I think you'd better wait here, while I fly—" Miss Dene herself interrupted this speech, coming into the Speisesaal in search of her handkerchief which she had dropped.

"What are you two doing here?" she asked. "You ought to be at Prayers."

"I know," Mary-Lou said. "The thing is, which services is Naomi to attend?"

"Church of England, my child. Mrs Weldon said she had better attend them for this term, anyhow. Next term, she is to consider and decide for herself." She gave the new girl a curious glance. Already this fiat had caused a hubbub in the staffroom, for such an arrangement had never before been heard of at the Chalet School. Then she turned back to Mary-Lou. "You go ahead, Mary-Lou. You ought to be in your place now. I'll bring Naomi along with me. Off you go!"

Mary-Lou nodded and left the Speisesaal, going with long, swift strides. As she went, however, she wondered to herself what sort of home the new girl came from. In her experience, you definitely knew where you stood in religious matters while you were at school.

"It strikes me that Naomi is going to be a weird sort of problem," she said to herself as she turned in at the top door of Hall and went to take her seat. "But I'm awfully sorry for her. She has a big load to carry with her lameness and, apparently, she hasn't anything to fall back on but herself."

"Where on earth have you been?" Hilary murmured as she sat down. "Here's your hymn book and Bible and I've found the parable of the Talents for you. What have you been doing to be so long in coming?"

"Tell you later," Mary-Lou murmured back. "Thanks for finding my place."

There was no time for more, for the bell rang and instant silence fell as the mistresses came in to take their places. Miss Lawrence, head of the music staff, was already at the piano and had been playing softly. Now as the Head came to stand before the carved oak lectern, she struck a chord and the girls all stood to sing the beginning-of-term hymn. The clear voices rang out through the great room, for everyone who could sing, sang with all her heart. Naomi, standing listening, wondered a little. She wondered more when Mary-Lou stood out and read in a clear, steady voice, the parable of the Talents. For the first time in her life, the young pagan found herself listening and taking it in. Perhaps the shock the Head Girl had just received caused her to read it with more than usual emphasis. However it was, Naomi was struck by the fine old story and when they all knelt to pray, she was startled anew by the air of devotion around her. She realised that

Prayers meant more than a mere form to most of these girls. For the first time, she was moved to wonder what it was like to be so sure of help and comfort. Then she shook herself. She didn't believe in it and she could think of nothing that was likely to make her believe.

All the same, when the others rose from their knees and she sat back in her chair—kneeling was out of her power, of course—she found herself wondering about it all through the brief words the Head spoke to the assembled school when the Catholic girls and staff had come in and taken their places with the rest. She tried to laugh at herself for being so impressed, but it would not do. Already, she was feeling the influence of the Chalet School.

Chapter 4

A PUZZLE FOR VIB

BY Monday, the two Sixths were in a complete state of bewilderment over Naomi Elton. She was totally unlike any girl they had ever met before. Quite a number had been attracted to her at first by her face which, in both features and colouring, were almost perfect. They were sorry for her lameness and her crookedness, but they knew better than to say anything. Apart from the fact that it had been well dinned into them from Junior days that personal remarks were not only ill-bred, but also unkind, there was something about the new girl that forbade any show of pity or sympathy.

She had gone to Prayers with the rest without further demur. On Sunday, when the Protestants all attended their own service in the little chapel about a mile along the road, she had been drawn there by Mary-Lou and Vi, who had tucked her and her stick and the prayer-books of all three on a toboggan, and, themselves on skis, had pulled her along. It had been a gloriously fine day with a bright sun and no wind, but bitterly cold for all that. Naomi, well wrapped up in her fur-lined coat and big scarf, felt the keen air stinging her face. Everyone had been warned to wear tinted glasses against the glare of the sun on the snow. As Miss Annersley had reminded them at Frühstück, snow-blindness can be most unpleasant.

"What, exactly, *is* snow-blindness?" Naomi had asked.

She was answered by Emerence Hope from Vb. "Oh,

simply awful! You see everything through a red, swimmy mist. I know! When I was an ass of a kid, I took my glasses off one day and I had a sweet three days or so of it as a result. I've never played *that* trick again, and don't you risk it, either, Naomi."

"Not being an ass of a kid, I shall certainly not do it," Naomi said sweetly; and Emerence went red.

She sat through the service with a queer, half-amused, half-scornful expression on her face. Only when they sang did it vanish. Verity Carey was at one side of her and she was the owner of a really lovely mezzo-soprano voice. As her clear, larklike notes went soaring up, Naomi's eyes glowed unexpectedly. She was not singing herself, but she gave her full attention to Verity's singing.

Needless to state, her absorption had not passed the Head Girl. That eagle-eyed young person, sitting on the other side of the aisle, watched her in the intervals and nodded to herself shrewdly. "Music means something to her," she thought as they sat down after *Jerusalem the Golden.* "That may very well be a key to her make-up. I must remember that. For she really is the oddest creature I've ever come across!" Then she turned her attention to the sermon.

In the afternoon, most of them went for walks. Naomi was told that it was too cold for her and she had better find a book and stay quietly in the common room. Two Juniors who had complained of toothache the day before were also staying and so was Marie Zetterling from Va who had twisted an ankle during the holidays.

Mary-Lou was all prepared to go with the rest. There was nothing she liked better than a ski-run in weather like this. Then she saw Naomi limping along to the common room by herself, while everyone else in the Sixths was heading for the Splashery to get ready. She watched that proud, lonesome figure and a queer look crossed her face. The next moment saw her heading for the stairs.

"Where are you going, Mary-Lou?" Hilary demanded at the sight.

"To fetch my book and writing-case," Mary-Lou told her firmly.

"What? Oh, don't talk rot! You're coming out with us, aren't you?"

"Not this afternoon. I haven't finished my letter home and Mother will be expecting it by the usual post. I can't disappoint her."

"But you've plenty of time after Kaffee for that," Hilary protested. She was a nice girl, but she was lacking in insight. "If you come to that, I haven't finished my own screed home. Give it a miss and come along, do!"

"Not today. I have to write to Clem, too, and I haven't done much more than a page and a half to Mother. You trot off and leave me to go my own way."

Vi, who saw beneath the surface far more deeply than Hilary, glanced at her friend and then along the corridor where Naomi was making her uneven progess to the common room.

"I'm staying, too," she said quickly. "I've finished my letter to Mummy, but I've got to write to Julie and I want to send a line to Beth, as well. Hang on a sec, Mary-Lou. I'm coming to bag my things, too."

"Idiots!" Hilary commented heatedly. "Tomorrow we may wake up to a minor blizzard and there'll be no going out. Surely those extra letters can wait a day or two more? Oh, come *on*, you two, and don't be asses! It's a glorious afternoon for a run. Let the letters go hang!"

"Clem's can't!" Mary-Lou retorted. Then she added rather more gently, "It was this week that the news came that her father and mother were dead and she still feels miserable about it then. A letter from me full of school gossip helps her. She says so. I can't let her down in those circs, can I?"

Hilary flushed. "Oh, in that case, I'll say no more. Give

Clem my love and say I wish she was back here still. But *you* could let Julie and Beth wait, Vi."

Vi laughed. "And have Julie going up in the air at me for not writing? No, thank you!"

"Have it your own way! I think you're a fuggy pair. I'm off to enjoy myself in the great outdoors!" Shrugging her shoulders Hilary turned down the passage to the Splashery and wriggled into coat, scarf and beret and went off with some of the others. It was not until bedtime that enlightenment came to her. Then she wished that she had thought of it herself.

Meanwhile, the other two, having secured their novels and writing cases, descended to the common room where they found Naomi seated in a chair near the tall white porcelain stove, staring into space.

"Haven't you anything to read?" Mary-Lou said as she dropped her belongings down on a nearby table and began to lug it nearer the other girl. "You can take any of these, you know." She waved her hand in a lavish gesture towards the low shelves that ran round two sides of the room and were loaded with books to suit every taste. "These are our own—sixth form books, I mean. They don't belong to anyone else and only we may borrow them. Got any special likes, Naomi? Shall we help you find something before we get down to our letters?"

Naomi gave herself a shake and got up slowly and painfully. "I can manage, thanks," she said. "I know I'm lame, but I *can* get about. You go on with your letters and pray don't trouble about me."

The two prefects glanced quickly at each other and then looked away again. Neither knew what to say in reply to the bitter little speech. Naomi was at the bookshelves now, her back turned to them. Clearly, she meant what she said. They pulled up their chairs, sat down and began to write.

It was a silent party in the common room. Naomi, having chosen her book, sat hunched over it, taking no notice of the two prefects. They scribbled industriously but only part of their minds was fixed on what they were doing. They were all too conscious of the waves of dislike the new girl was spreading round them. What made it worse was that neither could think what she had done to deserve such feelings.

Later, at Kaffe and Kuchen, which on Sundays the two Sixths had in their own common room, more than one of the girls tried to talk to Naomi. She made little attempt to respond and her dry, nippy replies to their remarks made them draw off in the end, so that she was left to sit in silence while the gay chatter of the rest flew round her.

Most of the Seniors went to Evening Service and Mary-Lou, feeling that in giving up her walk, she had done her share for one day, departed with them. Only Naomi of the two Sixths was left, and Miss Dene, finding her sitting alone in their common room, promptly shooed her off to join the dozen or so Fifth formers who had also remained at home.

"You can't stay alone here," she said briskly. "Besides, there's no need to burn extra electric light for one girl only. Come along Naomi. You'll find plenty of company in the Fifth form common room."

Naomi went reluctantly. She would far rather have been left alone. Miss Dene handed her over to Richenda Fry of Vb who happened to come along the corridor at the same time, and then went to fulfil her promise to read some of *Swiss Family Robinson* to the younger girls.

"Come along in and sit down," Richenda said amiably to the new girl.

Naomi glanced at her with a frown, but she did as she was asked without comment.

"How do you think you'll like it here?" Richenda asked.

"I have scarcely been here long enough to find that out. Do *you* make up your mind to your likes and dislikes in three or four days?"

Richenda felt snubbed, but she was a good-natured girl, so she tried to find some other topic that would interest this very odd new girl. After having tried three or four only to have each wet-blanketed, she gave it up. Jo Scott, the prefect of Vb then took a turn, but she was no more successful than Richenda. It ended in Naomi being left to herself for a while.

Towards the end of the period, two more girls came to speak to her—Jocelyn Fawcett from Va and Joan Baker of Vb. Jocelyn was a girl who was curious about everything. Joan had proved herself a real problem for the school. Indeed, during her first term, she had come within an ace of being sent away. She had improved in some directions, but bad early training allied to a feather-headedness that was inborn, had made it difficult for anyone to have a great deal of influence over her.

These two began asking questions about Naomi herself. She endured it for a short space. Then she struggled out of her chair. Leaning on her stick, she looked them over with an expression in her eyes that made them feel queerly uncomfortable. At last she spoke.

"I had no idea," she said icily, "that in a school where the girls were *supposed* to be gentlewomen—at least, I imagine so—people would be so totally incapable of anything approaching real conversation." With which she limped off to the door and vanished, leaving them staring after her in consternation.

Monday saw the beginning of full school rules, among them, the one that made German the language for the day. Mary-Lou had carefully explained this to the new girl the evening before when they were sitting in their common room after Prayers.

"You see, we are all supposed to learn to be fluent in French and German when we come here," she said. "We speak German on Mondays and Thursdays; French on Tuesday and Fridays; English on Wednesdays and Saturdays. That gives us all a fair chance. When we first came, of course, most of us were English. Now, we have at least as many continentals—French, Swiss, German, even some Dutch and one or two Italians. This school is regularly cosmopolitan! Can you speak either French or German, Naomi?"

"Oh, yes," Naomi said carelessly. "We lived in Vienna for a year once, so I picked up quite a good deal of German then. French, I know even better. I shall get on all right, I expect. It's exceedingly kind of you to be so solicitous" she added with a drawl, "but really, there's no need, you know. I have a very good brain—perhaps to compensate me for my other disability."

It was just as well for her that this unpleasant speech was made in private. Mary-Lou was a tremendous favourite in the school and it would not have endeared Naomi to anyone if they had overheard her biting snub in return for the Head Girl's kindness. Mary-Lou took it in her stride. She did wonder what she could have done to set the new girl so much against her, but she merely replied, "Oh, then, that's all right. But if you get stuck and I'm anywhere in the offing, ask me. Or any of the others, either," she added.

When she was in bed that night, she thought it over. "Poor kid," she said to herself. "Probably she's frightfully sensitive about her lameness and is afraid of being criticised or laughed at. As if she need fear anything of that kind *here*! Just let me catch anyone doing anything of that sort and I'll make her wish she had never been born!"

Naomi came to lessons with a superior air that made everyone else in VIb ruffle up like a set of young turkey-cocks. They were not accustomed to that sort of thing in new girls who, as in most other schools, were expected to be on the *piano* side for the first few weeks, at any rate.

As the morning went on, they found that she had every reason for her superior airs. Her maths were as good as those of Virginia Adams and Jessica Wayne. Her German was excellent, even colloquial, and her accent drew a commendation from Miss Denny who taught it. She had been well taught in geography and when it came to history, the other members of VIb found that she could reason from cause to effect and vice-versa as well as they. A new mistress, Miss Charlesworth, had come to take the place of the beloved Miss O'Ryan when that lady discovered that she would be unable to go on teaching, now that she was married. Much to their relief, they found that Miss Charlesworth taught history along the same lines, though it must be owned she lacked the flow of picturesque language which had so enlivened the now Mme Courvoisier's lessons for them.

It was another fine day, so after Mittagessen and their afternoon rest, no one was surprised when Miss Burnett, the games mistress, arrived in Hall to announce that, apart from the art classes, everyone was to go out for ski-ing, tobogganing or generally playing about on the meadow they usually used.

"What about us, Miss Burnett?" demanded Len Maynard of Vb. "Have we to go to the art room as usual while everyone else is winter sporting?"

Len sounded deeply injured and Miss Burnett gave a chuckle before she replied blandly. "And why not? Herr Laubach has come up for your art classes. You surely don't expect him to forego them?"

Several faces fell noticeably at this dictum and the mistress indulged in yet another chuckle before she relieved their minds. "As a matter of fact, he is taking you to the meadow to practise snapshot sketches. Take your blocks, pencils and rubbers and the sketching-stools in case you need them." Then she swung off and they were left to pack up their deckchairs and cushions before heading for the Splasheries to get ready.

Chapter 5

Two Violent Tempers

MARY-LOU was on her way out of Hall after seeing to the stacking of the deckchairs they had been using for the half-hour's rest, when Barbara Chester went scuttling past her in search of her block and pencilbox. The Head Girl caught her arm and pulled her up short.

"Half a sec! Have you seen that Naomi has everything she needs? Or hasn't there been time yet?"

"Saw to it on Friday," Barbara replied. "In fact, I've made jolly sure she has everything—including all she wants for art. I say, Mary-Lou, how do you think she'll get on with Herr Laubach? I should say she has a nasty temper when it's roused, and you know what *he* is!"

"She may have a gift for it," Mary-Lou said hopefully.

"And she may not! In any case, no matter how much of a gift you have, he can always find something to rage about. Look at the way he raves at Vi!"

"We can't do anything about it, my lamb. We must hope for the best."

"And prepare for the worst. I get you. One other thing. How is she to get to the meadow? She doesn't ski, of course; and walking will be the edge today!"

"Oh, that's easy. Vi and I are tobogganing this afternoon. We'll park her on the toboggan and pull her there. No; don't go yet. Just see to it that everyone has all she ought to have with her, will you? We may as well keep the old boy as sweet as we can," Mary-Lou said with feeling. "Remember, you're art prefect and it's your job."

"O.K., Grannie! I know it all too well."

They parted on that note. Barbara went flying along to Vb's Splashery to demand a show of all art materials and find out that Mary-Lou's warning had been well justified. At least half the girls were proposing to go without some vital belonging. Mary-Lou scurried off to the prefects' Splashery where she dressed in short order, talking hard in German all the time to Vi Lucy. Then she left her friend to go and seek the toboggan they usually shared while she hunted up Naomi, intent on giving her the invitation.

Naomi was in VIb Splashery. Prunella Davies was helping her with the great shawl that was a *must* when they had to do any sitting or standing about in cold weather. Mary-Lou waited until it was properly folded, and arranged so that it covered back and chest. Then she nodded to Prunella, who went off to attend to herself.

"I was looking for you, Naomi," she said in her friendly manner. "I know you don't ski. Walking is appalling when the ground's frozen like this. Vi and I thought you might like to ride on our toboggan. We can pull you along and it would be doing us a good turn if you would. Your weight would steady the thing, you see. It's always more of a nuisance if you have to haul it light ship, so to speak."

Naomi's brows had been drawing together; but at the new expression, they straightened, and she said, "'Light ship?' What *do* you mean?"

"Oh, haven't you heard it before?" Mary-Lou said airily. "That's what they say of a ship that puts to sea without any cargo. Well, will you come, Naomi?"

"You will if you know what is good," Josette Russell, standing near, observed. "You wouldn't like a second passenger by any chance would you, Mary-Lou?"

"Not if it's a lump like you!" Mary-Lou retorted. "OK, Naomi. We'll be waiting for you outside the side door. I must fly!"

She left the Splashery, intent on seeing that the long lines of girls were in some sort of order. Naomi, left with the others, discovered that she was envied.

"Lucky you!" Josette said in Geman.

"Isn't she?" Christine Vincent chimed in. "Are you sure you're well wrapped up, by the way? Standing about doing snapshots isn't a very warming business on a day like this."

Naomi glanced at her. "I am quite warm, thank you," she said. Then she added, "You all seem to make yourselves very busy about other people, especially Mary-Lou."

"Well, that's one reason why she's Head Girl," Christine said.

"Really? How very interesting. She certainly seems to attend to that part of it *con amore*," Naomi said suavely, picking up the light bag containing her art materials and slinging it over one arm before she took her stick.

In their indignation at the covert sneer, no one noticed that she had taken the wrong one. She had two—one with a rubber ferrule for the house; the other steel-pointed for such times as this. The one she took now had the rubber ferrule. She limped off out of the Splashery, followed by Josette Russell, who was also ready. On the way, Josette wondered to herself if she ought to say anything about the new girl's attitude to Mary-Lou. Then she decided against it. It really was no business of hers, and it was hard to see how she could begin. Better leave it to Mary-Lou herself. Naomi would soon find that the Head Girl's kindness was genuine and not put on. "And that," thought Josette, "is more likely to make her think again than anything I or anyone else could say."

Miss Wilmot, head of mathematics was in charge that afternoon, though, as everyone knew, every single mistress who could manage it would be at the meadow. She was a plump, pretty young woman, easy going to a degree, though she had her limits as sundry people who had presumed on her knew all too well. She smiled at the two girls as they arrived in the doorway, and nodded at them.

"Naomi, I understand Mary-Lou and Vi are taking you

along to the meadow on their toboggan. Josette, if you and the rest of VIb who are here like to get off, you may. Go straight to the meadow, and mind you stick to the road until you're there. Herr Laubach will be waiting, and I know he wants to start you all as soon as possible.

"Oh, thank you, Miss Wilmot," Josette said, her face lighting up. She fell in with the half-dozen or so of her form who were already waiting, and they skimmed off gaily.

Miss Wilmot turned to Naomi. "Take my arm, Naomi, and I'll lead you to your chariot. The ground is like polished glass today." She tucked Naomi's free hand through a strong arm and brought her to where the two prefects, very trim and smart in their ski-ing suits of gentian blue with caps, gloves and scarves of crimson, stood waiting.

"Here's your passenger!" she cried as they came near. "Give me your bag, Naomi. And your stick. Ease her down, Mary-Lou. There you are! Here's your bag! All quite safe? Good! Then you three had better be off before the crowd come. Take her to Herr Laubach, you two, and see that she has a sheltered corner. *He* won't think of it, and the wind has a bite today, even though it was sunny all the morning."

"But there's no sun now," Vi pointed out. "Just as well, too, considering the art crowd. I can't imagine snapshotting through coloured specs."

"I know. But if the clouds break, be sure you put your specs on," Miss Wilmot returned as she left them for the next job, dismissing them from her mind.

"You all right?" Vi asked as she stood to her rope.

"Quite, thank you," Naomi replied.

"Then off we go! Ready, Mary-Lou?"

The two prefects set off at once. They were on skis at the moment, and Naomi, sitting helpless on the toboggan, fiercely envied their free, graceful movements as they skimmed over the glassy surface, drawing the toboggan easily and steadily. What would she not give to be able to move like that! Why should other girls be free while she must go limping through life, always heavily handicapped?

Her face became sullen as she sat behind them, scarcely answering their chatter. Why should she have suffered that horrible accident which had left her the twisted thing she was? Of course they pitied her, these girls! They dared to pity her, she who had as good brains as anyone in the school; whose beauty was unmistakable—and here, she spared time to hate her unmarred beauty and wish that the fire which had caused her lameness had rather scarred her face and left her to move freely.

"Why should they be so happy?" she thought bitterly as their laughter rang out at a quick sally of Mary-Lou's. "I hate them! I wish I could spoil their fun! I wish I could make them feel as miserable as I do! They'd know all about it then! They mightn't laugh like that if they'd ever known what it is to be so handicapped. And I'm young; not yet seventeen. I may live another sixty years, a crippled thing like this! Oh, I *hate* them!"

They reached the meadow, where they left the road, and the two prefects, after a quick glance round, drew the toboggan to the big bush where Herr Laubach, the art master, was already busy, instructing Josette in the need for economy of line in snapshot sketching. While Mary-Lou carefully helped Naomi to her feet and gave her her stick, Vi went up to him with a note the Head had asked her to give him. He scanned it swiftly and nodded his great head.

"Very well," he grunted in his native German. "I will remember. And what about you, hein? You do not sketch today?"

"It isn't our lesson today," Vi said hurriedly. She was one of the few girls in the school who usually escaped a bad tongue-lashing from him, for she had a real gift for art. All the same, she had no idea of giving up her fun for one of his lessons. She hoped Mary-Lou would hurry up with Naomi, or he was quite capable of sending her back for her materials and insisting that she join his lesson. For really gifted pupils, he spared no pains. For those who were mediocre or poor, he never spared his tongue. Vi was moved to hope that he would handle Naomi gently. Otherwise she could see sparks flying!

Mary-Lou, who had welcomed her release from all art lessons at the end of the previous summer term with cries of joy, put Naomi's stick into her hand, and then turned to Vi.

"We ought to be getting to the top of the run, Vi. I can see the others coming, and we ought to be up there before them. Otherwise, there's no knowing what mad things some of those young monkeys from the Fourths may do."

"I'm coming," Vi said, blessing her friend mentally for this tactful speech. "You'll be all right now, Naomi. Herr Laubach will look after you."

The master raised his eyebrows as he noted that she addressed the new girl in easy German. "You speak German, hein?" he rumbled at Naomi.

The prefects were already off before they could hear her reply that she could. "Das ist gut!" he grunted. Then he went on to ask what she had done previously and what her training had been. By the time he had settled her in the lee of a bush, the others were arriving, and soon the meadow was crowded with girls flying here and there or, in the case of the novices, finding that skis have an unpleasant habit of crossing their points before you have gone very far and sending you over.

Naomi was seated on a campstool, and having started her off on making—or trying to make—sketches of the others, he turned to attend to someone else. The other members of VIb had also arrived and were standing about the edge of the ground, doing their best to produce snapshots of the rest. Naomi saw that they were allowed to move now and then. Only she was glued to her stool.

Herr Laubach came to her now and then to criticise her drawing, and he found plenty to criticise. Clever in most other ways, Naomi was no artist, and before long the art master's hair-trigger temper betrayed him. Snatching her block from her, he ripped off the sheet on which she had been trying to reproduce something of what she saw, crumpled it up, and almost threw the block back at her with the furious comment, "Wooden—*wooden*—WOODEN! They do not move! They are blocks—puppets! Look you!" as Mdlle de Lachennais, doyenne of the staff and head of the languages, flew past with a lovely swooping movement. "Mark the curves of the figure! See how she uses the arms—the sticks! Begin again and drew me *people*, not *dummies*!" With a final furious grunt, he went off to reduce Heather Clayton to the verge of tears by even unkinder criticisms, leaving behind him a seething Naomi.

In her rage she forgot her helplessness. Seizing her stick, she forced herself to her feet. The rubber ferrule failed to grip on the icy ground. She staggered, made a wild effort to recover her balance and fell headlong, striking her head on the icy snow, and stunning herself completely.

Chapter 6

A TRIAL FOR MATRON

IN the end, though Naomi came to herself in the school San with an outsize in headaches and a lump like a cricket ball on her brow, it was poor old Herr Laubach who was the greater sufferer. He blamed himself bitterly for losing his temper with the girl, and finally demanded an interview with the Head during which he requested her to accept his resignation for the end of that term.

Miss Annersley was greatly distressed. Herr Laubach had been at the shool from its beginning. Joey Maynard always referred to him as "one of the more important foundation stones." When the Nazis had marched into Austria, he had delayed escaping only because he had an invalid wife. After her death he had seen her decently buried, and then left the country by a devious track, arriving at the school practically penniless. There he had been ever since.

"Oh, Herr Laubach," the Head said anxiously, "*must* you? Frankly, I do feel that Naomi herself is chiefly to blame for this accident. If she had not been careless enough to take the wrong stick out, it might never have happened. And you are one of us—have been with us so long. We can't spare you. Do change your mind and stay! I know Madame would say the same thing."

"If I had ever learned to control my temper, also it might never have happened," he said sombrely. "Listen, gnädige Fräulein! You must not disturb yourself for me. I am an old man, now—too old to change my nature. I have enough saved to live in quiet comfort. The school has been very good to me all these years, and now I have no one but myself to keep. Yes; I am old—sixty-six this year. It is time I retired and left the post open for a younger man. So, I will go."

"Sixty-six is *not* old nowadays," Miss Annersley said firmly. "And the girls do so well with you generally."

"Ah, well, let us say, then, that my age, he is not old, but I myself am. The old pepperpot is growing too old and too peppery to teach these present girls. So I will go. But not far. The school is my whole life now, and I will find me a chalet up here where I can see you all and visit you. Perhaps, even, some of you will visit me. But no longer will I teach. No, no; that is over for me when this term ends."

Miss Annersley argued in vain. She even sent Rosalie Dene flying across to Freudesheim to bring Joey to back her up. It was no use. He had made up his mind to retire, and retire he would. Between them the three got him to agree to finish the year, but when the summer term ended, his teaching must end.

"I could cheerfully take that wretched girl across my knee and give her a little of what she deserves!" Joey declared wrathfully when he had finally stumped off. "I'm raging mad! Poor old Herr Laubach!"

Miss Annersley had been thinking it over. "Yes; I know how you feel. But I'm beginning to think that perhaps he is right. He has worked hard all his life, and it is time he rested now." Then she smiled. "He has paid us a wonderful tribute, Joey. He says the school is his life and he will not go far. Think what that means, coming from Herr Laubach! Well, we must see about finding a chalet for him and as a farewell gift, the school shall see that he has every comfort."

"*Comfort!*" Joey echoed. "My good Hilda, we shall pretty well have to *furnish* it for him! He lost everything when he fled to England before the war. He's lived in rooms ever since. I doubt if he so much as owns a chair, a table, and a bed! But as for a chalet, short of *building* one for him, I don't know where you'll find one up here! Every hole and corner is chock-a-block, these days."

"You never know what may happen," Rosalie said hopefully. "We must keep our ears and eyes open, and, the first chance there is, snaffle the place at once. We have the best part of six months for it, Joey, and that should give us time to find something."

"We can *try*," Joey said sceptically, "but I doubt if we'll succeed." On which note she departed homewards, still very indignant.

Naomi remained in San four days. By that time her head looked more or less normal, and she was as well as usual. Matron, who never stood any nonsense, then told her that she was quite well enough to be at lessons, and returned her to school. But the Head sent for her, and gave her a sharp rebuke for her carelessness in the matter of the stick before informing her that, in future, she need not attend any more art classes.

Naomi remained expressionless during the interview, but inwardly she raged. However, she had enough sense left to keep her feelings to herself, and when she was dismissed, she went to VIb, outwardly her usual self. None of the other girls had been near enough to know exactly what had happened, and she kept her own counsel. Neither, of course, did they know that the episode was to be the reason for the severing of Herr Laubach's connection with the school as art master.

Herr Laubach himself made pitiful efforts to control his temper in lessons. He succeeded to some extent, thereby giving the girls a shock. Never had they known his criticisms of their work to be so mild, and Vi Lucy, for one, was certain he must be ill!

The next trial that came, however, was a very different matter and one that gave the entire school something to think about.

It began with Margot Maynard, the youngest of Joey's triplets. She woke up one morning in a bad temper, and throughout the day behaved as if she had a whole kennel of black dogs on her back. She even quarrelled with her bosom friend, Emerence Hope.

"What's eating you?" Emerence demanded when she had been flatly contradicted three times and snarled at into the bargain. "You're acting like a bear with a sore head today. Got out of bed the wrong side? Come off it, Margot, and be your own sunny self! You're like a thunderstorm and a blizzard rolled into one!"

"Oh, shut up!" Margot flared. "I'm sick of all your silly talk!"

Emerence got up from her seat beside her friend with some dignity, gathered her possessions together and marched off to another seat with her head in the air. Margot remained hunched up over the cane basket she was weaving—they were at a Hobbies meeting—and snapped at everyone who merely asked her to pass something. As a result, by the end of the evening everyone was giving her a wide berth, and she stamped off to bed at war with her entire world.

In the middle of the night Matron, sleeping peacefully, was roused by an agitated knocking at the door. She was out of bed and pulling on her dressing-gown and slippers, even as she bade whoever it was to come in. Emerence entered, looking alarmed.

"Please, Matron," she said, "will you come to Margot? She's frightfully hot and her eyes are all shiny and funny, and she's talking the most awful rot."

"No slang!" Matron snapped, opening a drawer and bringing out her thermometer. "And why, pray, have *you* come to fetch me? I thought Penelope Grant was dormitory prefect there? Aren't you in Daisy? Margot is in Pansy."

"I know; but Penny was sent for on Saturday to go to Berne to see her people, and she's not back yet. Carmela Walther is sub-pre, and she was scared and came for me as we are next door. She said Margot had wakened them all up with talking."

By this time, Matron was ready. She hustled Emerence out of the room, snapped off the light, and then led the prefect of Daisy down the long corridor until they reached the open doorway of Pansy. Margot's voice could be heard, pitched a full tone higher than usual and running on in an excited way which told Matron plainly enough that something was badly wrong. She paused before she went in.

"Have you been bending over her, Emerence?"

"Well, I had to," Emerence said apologetically. "I tried to get her to see sense, but she didn't seem to know me, and she was so frightfully hot—*burning* hot, in fact. I guessed she was running a temp, so I came for you."

"I see. You haven't been back in your own dormitory, have you?"

"Oh, no. I just came straight for you."

"H'm!" Matron thought a moment. "You'd better go straight to San and rouse Nurse. Ask her to get a bed open and a hot bottle in it, and stay and help her. Don't go anywhere else until I've seen you again. Run along."

Emerence "ran along", and Matron, with a strong feeling of coming trouble, stalked into the dormitory where all the lights were on and a mumur of voices told her that the girls were all awake.

"Everyone into bed at once!" she said. "Carmela, are you with Margot?"

The curtains of Margot's cubicle parted, and Carmela Walther, a gangling, mop-headed creature with eyes like blue saucers, appeared. "She was trying to get out of bed, Matron," she said anxiously. "I thought I'd better stay and try to keep her in."

"Very sensible of you; but now you may go back to your own. I'll see to her. Be quick about it! It's a cold night!"

She left Carmela to attend to the matter, and went on into Margot's cubicle, arriving just in time to see that young woman fling off the bedclothes and begin to get out. Most unexpectedly, Betty Landon from Vb was with her, and Betty was trying to push the younger girl back on her pillows.

"And what are *you* doing here, may I ask?" This was Matron at her grimmest.

Betty turned a frightened face to her. "I heard someone run past our door, so I got up to see what was happening. I didn't see who it was, but the light was glaring out of here, so I came along and found Margot like this."

"I see. Well, you'd better wait here. I shall need help, I expect. Let me see."

Betty stood back, and Matron stooped over Margot. There was no mistaking it. She was running a high temperature already, and rising almost every minute to judge by the signs. Matron opened her pyjama jacket and scanned her chest. What she saw there made her mouth come down. She buttoned up the jacket, and sent Betty flying to fetch Nurse and the light stretcher that lived in San.

"Matron, is it—is it something—infectious?" Carmela ventured.

"That's for the doctor to say when he comes. May just be tummy upset. We must wait and see," Matron replied. "Meanwhile—do you hear me, all of you?—no one in this dormitory is to leave it for any reason whatsoever until I've been round in the morning. Is that quite understood?"

"Yes, Matron!" It came in two or three languages and the meekest of voices. Matron on the warpath was not to be argued with. In fact, no one had ever dared to defy her for long, and Emerence Hope, who had tried it on in her very early days at the school, could have told them that the consequences were far too unpleasant for it to be worthwhile!

Meanwhile, Matron was continuing her examination. Margot's pulse was racing and her rapid mutterings never ceased. Her skin was dry and her blue eyes were brilliant with fever. Matron finally drew back just as Betty returned with Nurse and the stretcher.

The two people most responsible for the health of the

school conferred briefly. Margot was rolled in blankets, laid on the stretcher, and Betty summoned to help Nurse carry her along to San. Matron remained. She had something to say to the people in Pansy.

"Girls! Which of you are in Margot's form? And which sit near her at table?"

"Me," said a meek voice from the next-door cubicle. "And Zita, and Penny, when she's here."

"Oh, yes; Penny's in Berne, isn't she? H'm!" Matron said, speaking more to herself than the girls. "That's a nuisance!" She raised her voice again.

"Prudence—it *is* Prudence Dawbarn, isn't it? I thought so!" As Prudence assented, "Well, can you tell me if Margot has been off her food at all?"

There was a pause. Then Prudence said, "Well, she played a lot at Frühstück. I did notice that."

"Why didn't someone report it to me?" Matron askcd sharply.

"We thought she was just in a bad temper," another voice replied in Italian.

"Is that Zita Rincini? What do you mean—in a bad temper?"

"Well, she was," someone said from the far end of the dormitory. "Most of us have had our noses snapped off today by her. And she didn't do a thing at lessons."

"Janet Kemp, is that you? How was she during Hobbies this evening?"

"Worse than awful!" Janet replied fervently. "She even fought with Emmy Hope."

"She has been cross—oh, but *so* cross all day." This was a French girl, Marie Lemprière. "Truly, Matron, we have left her to herself she was so cross."

"I see. Then that is all. Lie down now, all of you. I'll send some hot milk round presently and then you are all to go to sleep and no more talking. I shall come back later, and I'll see anyone I catch talking or out of bed in the morning."

With which dire threat, she rustled out of the dormitory and left them to obey her.

She went straight to the school San, where she found Margot already in bed. Nurse glanced up as Matron came in and gave her a look which brought the elder lady swiftly to the bedside. Margot's jacket was open again, and already a telltale rash was beginning to show on her chest. Matron inspected it, and then, as Nurse tucked the patient up firmly, she moved away from the bed to the window where Nurse joined her a minute or two later.

"Scarlet, I'm afraid," she said softly. "I've sent Betty to ring up Dr. Graves and Carmela to the extension off this room to get Mrs. Maynard."

"What? Joey can't come here! She has the twins and Cecil to consider."

"I know that; but she ought to know. Wasn't Margot the delicate one of the triplets?"

"She was; but that's a thing of the past, thank goodness! What have you done?" She nodded at the bed where Margot seemed to be quieter at the moment.

"Gave her a cooling mixture. That won't hurt, whatever it is. But it strikes me we'd better face the fact that we're more than likely in for a raging epidemic. Scarlet can be infectious, you know, in the early stages."

"Don't I know it!" Matron groaned. "And where she's got it from, I can't think."

However, that problem was solved by Dr. Graves when he arrived, which was an hour later. He had been out when Betty put her call through, summoned to the small son of a visitor, who was undoubtedly down with scarlet fever. The children at the Görnetz Platz were apt to be together a good deal during the school holidays, and Matron, answering a call from a frantic Joey, soon learned that the boy had played most days with her family.

"And do you realise what *that* means?" Joey wound up. "My own three lads are back at school, and ten to one they'll hand the wretched germ all round. Jack must ring up first thing in the morning to warn the folk there. And Matey, when can I come and see Margot?"

"Not at all," Matron returned promptly.

A loud wail answered her. "Matey! I simply must!" Then her tone changed. "There's Cecil again! She's cutting one of her double teeth, poor pet, and having a bad time of it. And Felix is inclined to be whiney. Tummy, I think—"

"Where's Jack?" Matron cut her short ruthlessly. "Felix whiney? Use your sense, Joey! Hasn't he been exposed to infection as much as the boys or the triplets? You dig Jack out and ask him to look at Felix at once! I'm going. You can ring me after Frühstück. But unless I'm much mistaken, Felix is starting scarlet as much as Margot." With which she rang off.

So she never heard till next day that Jack Maynard was at the great Sanatorium at the end of the Platz and not available when Joey heard the news. However, that young woman took no risks. She rang up until she got hold of a doctor, and for her pains was told that in all probability Felix was infected as badly as his sister, and she must keep an eye on Felicity and Cecil into the bargain.

"And considering all things," Miss Annersley remarked when she heard the news. "I think we'll have to do something about it. Joey must *not* be left to cope unaided with anything like that. I'll go and consult Matey and Nurse."

Chapter 7

SCARLET FEVER

THE awful news had to be broken to the school next morning. Dr. Graves had diagnosed Margot's illness as scarlet fever almost as soon as he set eyes on her. By the time day was breaking, the rash was coming out all over, though her temperature had dropped a point or two, and when she roused from an uneasy sleep, she was sensible enough. He warned both Matron and Nurse, however, that she would probably go up again as the day wore on, and they were in for a hard two or three days of it. Her throat was badly inflamed, and when Nurse asked if it had been sore at all, she croaked that it had felt "rough" for a day or two, but she had said nothing as she didn't want to miss any fun.

She was in no state to be scolded, but Nurse afterwards owned that it would have been a relief to give her a good shaking! Jack Maynard came home at last, and once he heard Joey's news and looked at Felix who was decidedly cross and complaining that it hurt to swallow, he bounded across to the school to interview the authorities.

"We're in for it," he told the three who organised affairs. "That wretched Johnson child is well away with it, and he's spread it—not a doubt!"

"Then," Matron said firmly, "there's only one thing to do."

"What's that?"

"We can isolate properly, now we've built on to this place. I propose that if any of the outside children—including the

Johnson boy and your own Felix—start, they come to us. You must get us nurses up from Berne or Lucerne or somewhere. We'll turn the San into an isolation hospital. If need be, we can use one of the houses—St. Hild's would be best as it's next the San—and with any luck we ought to be able to confine it fairly closely to the Görnetz Platz."

"She's right," Miss Wilson said. "What's more, once any of the two Sixths can be released from quarantine, they can come along to St. Mildred's. I hope we shall escape altogether and it would make things easier for you folk. Now, what's the next item on the programme? Find out who has had it before, I suppose."

"I doubt if more than a dozen or so have had it," Miss Annersley said gloomily. "I thought it was almost wiped out, these days. Well, we'll just have to face the fact that practically the whole school may go down with it. All right, Gwynneth." She turned to Matron. "We'll ring the bell and get them all into their form rooms, and you and the other matrons can go the rounds. What will you do?"

"Take temps and look out for sore throats and general poorliness. Jack, you'd better get off and let the outside families know what we have decided. And above all things, do what you can about getting us extra help. We'll *need* it!"

The staff were interrogated first. Only three knew that they had had it in their extreme youth. Miss Ferrars acknowledged to a sharp attack when she was a Kindergarten baby; and Miss Andrews and Miss Wilmot had also been victims. The rest were sure they had never met it or else had to find out from home.

By the time the girls had all been examined and had replied to the question, "Do you know if you have ever had scarlet fever?" the school hummed. The Juniors were examined, but not questioned, older sisters answering for some while parents had to be asked about the rest. By the time the last reply had been received, there were two rooms full of cases in San, among them Joey's twins, Hilary Graves' small

Marjory, and the two elder children of Dr. Morris, who was on the Sanatorium's staff. Forty-one out of the almost three hundred girls had definitely had it. Twenty-seven more were doubtful. The rest all had to be closely watched.

Joey Maynard, arrived three days after Margot began, and held an anxious conversation with Miss Annersley through the study window, having been forbidden to set foot inside the school buildings.

"Cecil seems all right so far," she reported. "*And* the tooth is through, thank goodness! How are the rest of my family?"

"The twins are cross and whiney, but theirs are light cases. So far, Len and Con are all right. Margot's temp is down and *staying* down at last, thank goodness! But she's very weak, poor little soul, after all that fever. Any news of the boys?"

"Oh, Mike's got it." Joey said resignedly. "I expect Charles and Steve will follow suit. What the school must be saying about us, I shudder to think!"

"They'll get over it," Miss Annersley said philosophically. "There's one mercy."

"Oh? Whats that? So far, I don't see any mercy about it at all."

"Oh, but there is! Scarlet isn't anything like the awful thing it used to be. The really tiresome side of it is that it's so lengthy—six solid weeks. However, we can't help it. Thank Heaven Jack got us extra help!"

By the end of the week the school San was packed, and one dormitory in St. Hild's had been requisitioned. Matron had the rest of the house cleared out, and the girls were packed away in odd holes and corners. Twice a day temperatures were taken, and in three weeks at least half the school was down and most of the small fry living around in the chalets. But, thanks to the measures taken by the school, the disease was confined to the Görnetz Platz.

"And what about our exams?" croaked Josette Russell as, wrapped in a blanket, she was borne off to St. Hild's.

"Mercifully, you ought to be over this by half-term, and

you'll have the second half and all next term till June to prepare," Miss Ferrars told her unsympathetically. "Anyhow, Josette, if you aren't ready now you ought to be. Stop fussing!"

"I did hope I'd escape!" Josette wailed.

"Well, you haven't, but you're going to be a very light case."

"I feel rotten enough now," Josette informed her. "My throat is *sore*!"

"Then stop talking and give it a chance to rest!"

Matron had issued an edict that no one was to be allowed to feel sorry for herself, and anyone who tried to bid for pity was briskly treated.

"What's happening to the St. Mildred crowd, I wonder?" Mary-Lou asked of the thinned-out Sixth form common room during the last week of quarantine.

"I can tell you that," Hilary Bennet said. "So far, they haven't had a single case. If they keep all right, they're going down to Unter die Kiefern until the place is clear. What's more," she added, "any of us who escape are going down with them. There's glory for you, my sweetiepies!"

"How do you know?" Vi demanded.

"I was in the office helping Deney to sort the correspondence, and she told some parent or other over the phone. She knew I was there, so she obviously didn't mind my knowing, and she said nothing about keeping it to myself."

"Well, it's something to look forward to, anyhow," Mary-Lou allowed.

"Where is Unter die Kiefern?" Naomi asked. This past week or two had done something to turn her thoughts away from herself, and, as Vi had remarked only that morning, for her, she was becoming quite chatty.

"It's the shelf below this," Mary-Lou explained. "St. Mildred's used to be there. But it gets frightfully hot in summer, so they were moved up here, and the house was turned into a kind of hostel for people who came to see any of us or had friends or relatives along at the big San."

"It's where they had their first panto," Hilary said. "I say! I never thought of that before! What do you think will happen about this year's?"

"It's a fortnight past the date," Vi said. "I suppose they'll have to wait until all this mess is cleared up, and have it then."

"It's a good thing our Sale was moved to the summer term," Lesley Malcom remarked. "Someone at the door, Mary-Lou."

"Come in!" Mary-Lou called; and Len Maynard came in, followed by Con.

"Hello! What do you two want?" the Head Girl demanded.

"Deney's gone to bed with a smashing headache, and the second lot of mail has just arrived," Len began. "The Head wondered if some of you Seniors would go to the office and help sort it. Anyhow, she asked us to come and ask you."

Mary-Lou jumped up. "Of course we will! Come on, folks!"

Vi got up slowly. "I'll come with pleasure. But I wonder . . ."

She stopped there, and the others, including the two Maynards, stared at her.

"What are you getting at?" Hilary demanded.

"Well, the staff have gone free, so far," Vi said.

"Oh, my only aunt! Are you suggesting that some of *them* are coming down now?" Mary-Lou demanded.

"It's quite likely, isn't it?" Prunella Davies, who had sat silent so far, pointed out. "They've been in as much infection as we have, haven't they?"

"I never though of *them* getting it," Lesley observed. "But you're quite right, Prunella. Oh, my goodness! What's going to happen if many of them go down?"

"What happened last year when we had that 'flu epidemic," Mary-Lou said.

"It was the year before," Hilary corrected her. She projected a grin at Con Maynard, who was standing listening with brown eyes as wide as pennies. "What price Daniel in the lions' den, Con?"

Con, went scarlet. "No one will ever forget that. And it wouldn't have happened if I hadn't been thinking of something else."

"To wit: a poem," Mary-Lou said teasingly. "All right, Con. You aren't the only one to provide howlers in this school, though I'm bound to say that was one of the loveliest I ever heard." She gigled as she remembered it. "Meanwhile, ladies, may I remind you that the mail awaits our attention? Come on, whoever is coming, and let's get to work and stop nattering."

"All the same," Len said. "it's time that silly yarn was dropped. I daresay if I think round I can remember quite a few things other people have said older people than us, I mean."

After this, feeling that she had said enough, she gave Con a tug, and the pair slipped past Lesley at the door, and went scuttering off before anyone could call her to order.

"She's right," Mary-Lou said as the six or seven girls who were the sole representatives of the two Sixths at present, followed their juniors down the corridor, en route for the office. "Con's been teased enough about that old howler, and those three aren't really kids any longer now."

"What *did* she say?" Naomi asked curiously as she limped along beside Vi.

"Oh, the Head asked what happened when Daniel was in the lions' den and Con, who was in a dream as she frequently was in those days, said Daniel bit the lions," Vi replied with a giggle.

Naomi stared. Then, for the first time, her laugh rang out, startling the other girls considerably. It was such a very pretty laugh, bubbling up like a spring and rippling happily along. It was pure mirth and some of them laughed in sympathy. Mary-Lou jumped, and then glanced round sharply at her. If Naomi could laugh like that, why in the name of everything that was queer did she usually condescend to give only that sarcastic smile as a rule?

By this time they were at the office door, and saw the Head sitting at Miss Dene's desk, fishing out the great bundles of letters from the postbag. She looked up with a smile of welcome.

"What, all of you? Then this will be quickly done. Take charge here, Mary-Lou, and let me have all my own letters as quickly as you can. Typing is not an accomplishment of mine, so I shall have to answer what I can by hand."

Hilary came forward eagerly, "Miss Annersley, I can type—I taught myself on Daddy's old portable. Couldn't I do some of them for you?"

The Head had been going through the connecting door into the study. Now she stopped short, and looked at Hilary. "That's an idea, Hilary. Could you really manage, do you think? For, apart from what you can do for yourselves, I'm afraid you girls are going to be short on lessons for a while."

"Oh, are some of the staff down?" Mary-Lou asked anxiously.

"Yes; though I'd like you to keep it to yourselves for the moment. Miss Derwent certainly has it, and so has Miss Moore. Matron took them both over to San after Mittagessen. And I'm very much afraid that this headache of Miss Dene's is the forerunner of an attack, though her throat is still clear."

"Well, you'll let us help out, won't you?" Mary-Lou implored. "We VIa people have no exams to worry about, so we could help with the lower forms, couldn't we? And if Hilary can type, she can help in the office."

For the first time almost in her life, certainly since her accident, Naomi was moved to offer to help someone else in a difficulty. "I can type, too, Miss Annersley. If you have another typewriter, I could give Hilary a hand with some of the letters." Then she stopped and marvelled at herself.

Miss Annersley looked round at them all with shining eyes. "You dear girls! We'll be only too glad of any help you like to offer. It won't be for long—can't be! Your quarantine ends this week, and if you remain all right, we shall pack you off to Unter die Kiefern until we're declared free from infection. But if you *could* take hold for the next day or two until we can get things rearranged, it would be a tremendous help. I accept your offer with gratitude. You see, the only mistresses we can be fairly sure about are Miss Ferrars, Miss Wilmot and Miss Andrews. None of the others seem to have had it. Now Miss Derwent and Miss Moore have set the example, I'm just afraid that some of the others may follow."

"We'll help—we'll be glad to," Vi declared. Then she added diffidently, "That is, if we can. You won't ask us to take Va, for instance, will you?"

The Head laughed. "No; Va can look after themselves. But you could take the Lower Fourths for dictation in all three languages, and French grammar and a few things of that kind, couldn't you, Vi?" She turned to Naomi. "Naomi, if I agree to letting you help with the typing. I want your promise that you will stop if it makes your back ache, my dear. In fact, if any of you feel headachey or backachey, you are to report at once. Thank you very much, girls. This will solve quite a number of problems. Naturally, we can't import temporary staff at the moment."

She left them to it after that, and they sat round the table, sorting the letters and packages into forms, the staffroom, the domestic staff, and above all, the Head's share, which made up at least a third of it all.

"Poor Abbess, if she's got to look through all that lot!" Hilary said as she picked up the fat bundle. "What a blessing Daddy let me mess about with that aged affair of his when I wanted! I don't pretend to be very quick, but I can be accurate, which is something. What about you, Naomi?"

"Oh, I'm just moderate," Naomi replied. "But with two of us, we should manage quite a lot. Which is this packet for, Mary-Lou?"

"The two Upper Fourths," Mary-Lou said. "That's the lot done! Come on; we'll go and find out what our several fates are to be."

Thereafter, all the well members of the Sixths found themselves well and truly occupied. As Miss Annersley had feared, the mistresses began to fall before the foe, and by the end of the week seven of them were in San in addition to Rosalie Dene. She was the only one to cause any anxiety. She had not been too well before the epidemic began, and for a day or two they were very anxious about her. Then the obstinate temperature broke and danger was over, though she remained terribly weak for some time to come.

By this time all the Sixths had been marched off to Unter die Kiefern, where they joined the St. Mildred lectures and rejoiced in former friendships renewed with gusto among the girls who had gone on the previous September. This lasted for another three weeks or so, by which time most of the early patients were quite recovered and making up for lost time by devouring enormous meals and asking for more. Then, when only the mistresses who had gone down were left as inmates of the isolation rooms in San, Matron had a grand disinfecting of the entire school, followed by a thorough cleaning, and at last the girls came back.

"I suppose we may be thankful it's been no worse," Miss Annersley said wearily to Matron late that night. "St. Mildred's have escaped all through, thank goodness, and even Margot is convalescing most satisfactorily."

"*And* Naomi Elton has escaped," Matron added briskly. "I'm glad of that, I can tell you! What's more, she seems changed a little. She gave me quite a pleasant smile when I met her as that crowd went up to bed. Long may it last!"

"And Joey herself and Cecil have escaped, too," Kathy

Ferrars supplemented this. "I only wish Rosalie were stronger. She still looks awfully ill."

"She *has* been 'awfully ill', to quote you," Matron said. "However, it's only time and feeding up that are needed for her now. That temp took it out of her. I don't believe she has a rag she can wear with any decency! Her things just *flap* on her."

"We are going to have loud outcries about the way the girls have grown," Miss Annersley said, laughing. "Mdlle had everyone from the Fifths busy in needlework this afternoon, letting down hems to their fullest extent. And what Joey had to say about her twins when she first saw them was only beaten by Hilary's shrieks at her first glimpse of Marjory. All Felicity's frocks will have to be put aside for Cecil. They won't go near her now; and Joey had to hunt up some of the things Mike has outgrown for Felix."

"Well, at least it's ended now," Matron said with a sigh of relief.

Kathie Farrars echoed the sigh. "Thank goodness! I only hope we have no more awful trials for the rest of the term. I feel like something that's been put through the mangle a dozen times over!"

"Oh, so do I!" Miss Annersley assented.

Matron surveyed them both sharply. "You're tired out. Well, you can rest when half-term comes. Luckily, Easter's very early this year, so we can give a long half-term. As for you, Hilda Annersley, you are to go down to stay with Winifred Embury for the whole weekend, and she'll see you do nothing but rest. And now that we're really free from infection, we can get a temporary secretary to take the bulk of that work off your shoulders. Rosalie won't be fit for anything till next term, I'm afraid."

Matron got up. "It's late enough. Kathie, take yourself off to bed. Hilda, you can do the same thing. What's more, you can *stay* in it till I tell you to get up tomorrow. *You'll* be ill next, and we've had quite enough without that! Go on, both of you! I'm waiting!"

How the school would have chuckled if they could have seen not only Miss Ferrars, who was young enough not to count much, but the stately Head obeying Matron as meekly as the most junior girl of them all!

Chapter 8

HALF-TERM

MISS Dene was marched off to the south of France by her old friend, Evadne Lannis, who happened to be in Switzerland at the time. Evadne was the only child of an American millionaire. Expense meant nothing to her, and she insisted on bearing Rosalie Dene away to rest and recuperate in the best possible conditions.

Thursday saw the departure of nearly nine-tenths of the rest of the school to their homes or the homes of friends. In fact, when the Head had reckoned up the number of those for whom provision must be made, she found that there were only thirty-seven of them. Seven came from the two Sixths and Va and b accounted for eight more. The remainder were mainly younger girls.

Miss Burnett, the games mistress, instantly offered to take the entire twenty-two to Vevey where she had been proposing to sojourn herself. Her own special friend, Miss Armitage, who was responsible for all science below Vb, was going with her, so the Head had no scruples about accepting the offer.

None of Inter V had to be considered, and Mdlle offered to be responsible for the fifteen big girls. They were going to stay at a farmhouse not far from St. Moritz. Mdlle was an Alpiniste, an enthusiastic climber and outstandingly good at all winter sports. Kathy Ferrars, on hearing of their destination, eagerly begged leave to join them, and Nancy Wilmot, head of the maths, darkly hinted that no one was to be surprised if she turned up during the weekend. All the rest of the staff were off on a complete holiday—including the Head who was going to Lake Geneva where lived Mrs. Embury, very *nearly* an Old Girl, as she always vowed, and a firm friend of Miss Annersley's. Mrs. Embury had given all concerned her word of honour that the Head should spend the time in rest and recreation. Miss Wilson, her co-Head, would also be there, so Matron was hopeful that the weekend would prove a real holiday.

When the lists were put up, a good many people who were going home bewailed the fact that they must miss the Senior expedition.

"The Grisons!" Josette Russell exclaimed. "And I'm dying to go there! Oh, I do wish Mummy hadn't said I was to go home! How lucky some folk are!"

Lorraine Varley and Amandine Robinet, who had been expecting to go but, at the last moment, had been told they were going with Mr. and Mrs. Varley to Holland, agreed with her.

"Never mind; we'll tell you all about it when we meet again," Barbara Chester said soothingly. "Give me your address at the Hague—isn't that to be your headquarters?—and I might even rise to a picture postcard between you!"

They fell on her with cries of fury, but when Mr. Varley arrived to escort them to the Hague, they were ready for him. Both were very musical, and he had promised them two big concerts during the weekend.

Three other people were also deflected from the party, thanks to parents who had decided on the spur of the moment to come out to Switzerland and see for themselves that their daughters had taken no harm from the scarlet fever. So in the end, only ten girls were left to the tender mercies of Mdlle and Miss Ferrars. This party consisted of Mary-Lou and her "sister-by-marriage" as they called it, Verity Carey; Vi Lucy and Barbara Chester; Hilary Bennet and Prunella Davies and Naomi Elton, all from the two

Sixths; and three from Va, Monica Caird, Rosemary Lambe and Carol Younger who, despite a complete unlikeness of character, yet where bosom friends. Rosemary was an exceedingly pretty girl with hardly two ideas in her fluffy golden head; Monica was a sportswoman, pure and simple; Carol was a student, a girl who was never happier than when she had her teeth into a really stiff problem. What made these three so friendly was something that no one had ever been able to explain; but they were inseparables of the most marked type.

As there were so few of them they were to go by train from Chur. Dr. Graves, the owner of an outsize convertible had to go there on business connected with the Sanatorium, and he offered to take the entire party with him if they could crowd in.

The rest of the school had already departed when he drove up to be greeted with a resounding cheer from the twelve, who were waiting in the drive. Skis were strapped together and fixed to the roof, cases were piled up on the floor between the seats or under them and the excited girls packed in as best they could.

"This," the Head Girl remarked as she settled down in her seat, "is the goods! Are you all right, Hilary? It's more than a bit of a squash, isn't it?"

"I'm O.K.", Hilary said, laughing. "You all right, Barbara? Shove up a little, Carol. Vi has barely an inch to sit on."

"What a blessing none of us are fat!" Monica remarked as she, Rosemary and Carol all sat closer to give Vi a little more space. "Think what it would have been like with Hilda Jukes here!"

"In that case, someone—or two someones, even—would have had to ride on the roof on top of the skis," Barbara said with a chuckle.

Then they set off, along the Platz, to the head of the long, twisting road that ran direct to the plain from the shelf. Dr.

Graves put the car into bottom gear, jammed on his brakes and began to make the descent, slowly and cautiously.

Most of the girls paid no heed to it and went on chatting. But Mary-Lou, glancing across at Naomi, saw that her face was white as they negotiated the steep drop and bent across to speak to her.

"It's all right, Naomi," she said quietly. "I know the staff often go this way in the car, and I've done it myself once or twice. It's only a case of going slowly and carefully and having good brakes—and no one messes round with faulty brakes in this part of the world if they value their necks."

Naomi stiffened. "Oh, I'm not afraid," she said mendaciously. "I didn't expect anything quite so steep, though."

Prunella leapt into the breach. "I'm longing to see this farmhouse we're going to. Didn't Mrs. Maynard put us on to it? It'll be marvellous at that rate. And it will be fun, living with the people, won't it? By the way, does anyone know anything about St. Moritz? I like to know something about a place before I visit it."

"Apart from the fact that it's a world-famous spa and also a sports centre, I can't tell you a thing," Hilary said. "Thank goodness! Here we are at the end of that ghastly road!"

They had indeed reached the end of it, and now Dr. Graves swung out on to the magnificent autobahn, heading for the east past Interlaken and then on, along the south bank of Lake Brienz. Mary-Lou, still keeping watch on Naomi, saw the colour come back to her face, and was thankful.

Now there was nothing to prevent Dr. Graves from getting all he could out of the convertible, and the great motor-roads of Switzerland are kept in excellent fettle. They had set off early, and, in any case, this was not the height of the tourist season. They reached Chur in good time to have a meal there before they boarded the train to St. Moritz, which place they reached before darkness fell.

"This," said Mary-Lou with shocking disregard for school rules about the use of slang, "certainly is the job!"

They were standing outside the big farmhouse where Joey Maynard, who knew the owners very well, had arranged for them to stay during half term weekend. It was built of white stone with deeply pierced windows with oblique sides. Borders were painted down the edges of the walls, and between the windows were designs in gay colours that looked as fresh as if they had been done only the week before. The girls were startled when Herr Tratschin, the owner of the farm, assured them that the painting had been done in the previous spring and was due for renewal any time now. The big entrance door was finely arched at the top, and the arch bore another border to match those at the wall edges.

Miss Ferrars laughed. "Mary-Lou! And you are Head Girl! What appalling slang and what an example to the rest."

"Are we all here? No; I see Naomi isn't. And neither are Verity nor Barbara. What are they playing at? I thought we were to get off early so as to have plenty of time for exploring. Shall I go and hurry them up, Mdlle? Then we can get off," Hilary asked impatiently.

Mdlle nodded and she dashed back into the house, calling the three loiterers at the top of her voice. Verity appeared at once, full of apologies for being late.

"I've been talking to Frau Tratschin," she explained in her tiny, silvery voice.

Naomi came limping along after her; and Barbara was not far behind.

"And that's the last," Miss Ferrars said. "Get your skies on, all of you, and hurry up. I hope no one has forgotten her sticks?"

No one had. They hurriedly strapped on their skis, and then waited to hear what the next step was to be.

"We will visit the town first, I think," Mdlle said after a glance at her watch. "You will enjoy the shops and the lake—we are a little far from the lake here. Also, there is plenty to see that will interest you. Naomi, we have a toboggan for you, as we must not let you tire yourself. Who will tow Naomi?" She turned to the others while Naomi's lips went down in the familiar droop. She hated to have any notice drawn to her disabilities.

"I will!" Even Rosemary joined in the chorus, and Naomi suddenly flushed. She knew well enough that she was a favourite with no one. She had given none of them a chance to know her or like her. And yet, though she would never have owned it, the steady kindliness and consideration shown her by almost everyone was beginning to take effect on her.

"Prunella and Hilary to begin with, I think," Mdlle said after a moment. "It's not very far—about a couple of kilometres. Once we reach it, we will leave toboggan and skies at a shop on the outskirts where I am known and then we can all walk. Two others will draw Naomi home when we have had enough," she added with a trill of laughter. "See, Naomi! Here comes your carriage!"

A small boy appeared round the corner of the house, pulling after him a toboggan. Mdlle smiled at him, said, "Danke, Gaudenz!" and handed him a slab of chocolate in exchange for the ropes. He gave her a shy grin and an even shyer, "Danke, gnädige Fräulein!" before he went scampering back.

Meanwhile, the girls had crowded round the little toboggan, exclaiming in delight at its beauty. It was of wood and the sides and up-curving back were adorned with a delightful design of alpine flora with a perfectly carved chamois surmounting the top of the back. It was well-cushioned, too, and Vi expressed the feeling of everyone when she cried, "Oh, what a marvellous thing!"

Mdlle laughed. "Sit down, Naomi, and let us pack you in. That is right! And here is a rug in case you feel cold with sitting."

Hilary and Prunella took up the ropes, once Naomi was settled, and they sped off over the frozen snow which, today, was glittering under the bright sun in a way that made them thankful for their coloured glasses.

"We can have time to look round properly, can't we?" Barbara Chester asked coaxingly. Then, in tones of surprise, "Why! Isn't that the church spire over there? But it's *leaning!*"

"Yes," Mdlle told her tranquilly. "The leaning spire of St. Moritz is well known. And yes, Barbara; you may have plenty of time to see all there is to see. But not too much. Snow is forecast for later in the day, and I should prefer to have you all safely in the house before it comes. So do not loiter. And now, here is my shop. Stop, all, and unstrap your skies. Naomi, Miss Ferrars and I will help you to your feet. Wait a moment, ma petite! There! That is right!"

Vi had pulled off her skis and handed them to Mary-Lou. Now she came forward, crooking an elbow invitingly. "Will you have an arm, Madame? Pray do me the honour."

Naomi glanced up at her enchanting face and saw it alive with laughter. Something melted within her, and her own rare laughter answered as she slipped a hand through the arm, saying, "Thank you. I shall certainly feel safer."

The others hurriedly collected their skis and sticks and followed Mdlle to the shop where she addressed a few words to the girl in charge. Everything was handed over, and then they all set out in a body, chattering hard, to explore the little town.

They wandered around until it was nearly time for Mittagessen and Naomi was beginning to look very tired. She had walked more that morning than she had done for some years past. Mdlle had kept an eye on her and she decided that it was enough for one morning. Naomi could spend the afternoon lying down if she felt like it. And so might Verity Carey, who was also looking as if she had done enough. The rest were full of vim still, and cried out when the mistress told them that they must return. However, Mdlle, though she might slacken the reins considerably when she saw fit, always knew when to pull them in. They set off back to the shop where they retrieved their skis and the toboggan, and then, with Mary-Lou and Vi on the ropes and Verity between Monica and Hilary, they all whirled back to the farmhouse.

"I'm very much afraid we shall have snow," Verity said as they went. "The sun's vanished and those clouds look awfully heavy, Mdlle. Shall we get back before it comes, do you think?"

"But yes; certainly." Mdlle said. "I have been watching the sky, and I know we can manage it."

All the same, she gave the order to quicken pace, and they flew across the snow which now had lost all its glitter. Frau Tratschin was at the door, watching for them. When they came skimming up, she gave an exclamation of relief.

"I am glad to see you all safely here! The sky means mischief, beyond a doubt. Come in—come in, all! Mittagessen is ready and the soup is hot. Hasten, now. Ah! Here it comes!"

The last girl passed in, and she shut the door with a bang on the whirling snow that had just begun to fall with a force that showed it meant to keep on and there would be no further expeditions that day.

Chapter 9

MARY-LOU TAKES A CHANCE

"WHAT shall we do with ourselves?" Verity asked as they helped to clear the table after Mittagessen.

"Oh, we'll manage to amuse ourselves all right," her "sister-by-marriage" replied before she went off to the kitchen with a loaded tray. She was back a few minutes later, her hands equally full, but this time with a zither.

"Where on earth did you get that?" Miss Ferrars demanded.

"From Frau Tratschin. I saw it hanging on the wall when I took the tray out, and I asked her if she played it. She said it was her son's. Then she asked if any of us played it, and if we'd like to have it to amuse us. I told her I hadn't an idea about the playing, but I thought we'd rather love to borrow it. So she handed it over. *Does* anyone know how the thing works? What about you, Naomi?" She had seen a strange look on Naomi's face, and she knew that the girl loved music.

Naomi shook her head. "I've heard it played, of course; but I've never attempted to touch one. I couldn't do a thing with it."

"I can play a little," Mdlle said, with an amused smile. "I think, though, that you will enjoy yourselves more if you try to pick out tunes for yourselves. Did Frau Tratschin give you the plectron, Mary-Lou? For, if not, I fear you may have sore fingers if you try it. Some of the strings are of wire of various kinds."

Mary-Lou felt in the breast pocket of her blazer and

produced a small ring which, as Mdlle explained, you wore on the thumb of your right hand. A tiny quill attached, plucked the strings.

"How do you hold it?" Vi asked curiously.

"You place it on the table—so." Mdlle took the instrument from Mary-Lou, sat down at the table, and showed them the correct position. "The air is played with the thumb and the bass accompaniment is played with the other fingers of the right hand. The strings are divided into groups of five notes. To make others, you stop the strings with the fingers of the left hand. Keep the right wrist on the side of the zither parallel with these pins which are known as hitch pins, and the thumb over the finger-board."

As she talked, she plucked the strings, first softly and then with considerable force, and the girls all exclaimed at the sweetness of the notes.

"Yes; it is a very good zither. A large one, also, as it has forty-two strings. Now I shall leave you to amuse yourselves. I have letters to write and shall go to my room. Miss Ferrars, what will you do?"

Kathy Ferrars bounced off the stool on which she had been sitting. "I've letters to write myself. I owe at least three. After that, I shall indulge in a new novel I brought with me and be thoroughly lazy." She paused and glanced at Mdlle. She remembered that that lady had said Naomi ought to lie down that afternoon.

Mdlle took no notice. She had seen the colour come back to the girl's face after a delicious meal. Naomi was laughing and talking—not much, it is true, but more than she had ever done before. Not for worlds would Mdlle have put a stop to this approach to normal girlhood. She merely smiled at the girls, remarking that if they wanted her, they knew where to find her, and went off with her colleague.

Left alone, the girls began to experiment with the zither. It was not easy, and one by one they gave it up, even Vi, who, as a violinist, managed better than most. Verity, who had stayed in the background, came forward now.

"Let me try," she pleaded. "I'd like to try to make tunes on it. What a lovely rich sound it has!"

Mary-Lou pushed it across the table to her, pulling off the plectron with which she had been producing some odd sounds, and putting it into her hand. "There you are! Go ahead and see what you can make of it. It's plain that music is *not* my strong point. You go on with it, Verity."

Verity fitted on the plectron and touched a string. "I think I can see how to manage. Are you all quite sure you won't mind if I play round with it a little?"

No one made any objection. Verity carried her treasure off to one of the windows, where it fitted nicely on the broad sill, and proceeded to enjoy herself. The rest, chattering gaily, paid little heed to her. After years of boarding school they were quite able to shut their ears to any extraneous sounds. Only Naomi frowned as the zither player made false notes and harmonies now and then.

Mary-Lou glancing up on one of these occasions, saw it and guessed that Verity's stumbling efforts were setting her teeth on edge. She lifted her voice.

"Hi, Verity! Can't you take that thing off somewhere where we don't have to listen to you killing pigs or whatnot?"

Verity remained calm under this cheerful insult. "I want to ask Frau Tratschin about one or two things. I'll take it to the kitchen."

She picked it up and vanished into the kitchen, where Frau Tratschin, her domestic labours over for the moment, was sitting at her lace-pillow, making the bobbins fly as she twisted her threads, moved her pins and produced a cobwebby effect that made the would-be musician exclaim in delighted amazement before she settled down to her questions. The kindly farmer's wife was pleased to give any help she could, and Verity and she were soon going ahead.

Meanwhile, most of the others were seated round the

table, playing an exciting game of rummy. Mary-Lou had retired to a window-seat with a book, and Naomi was at the other with another book.

Presently the new girl glanced across at the tall prefect absorbed in her reading. She forgot her own, and stayed gazing at Mary-Lou with a very thoughtful expression on her face. Presently that young woman felt the gaze, and looked up with a smile. Something she saw in the other girl's eyes made her close the book, get up and come over to her.

"Bored, are you? What have you got there?" She glanced at the book. "Goodness, Naomi! I don't know if we're supposed to read that."

Naomi looked down at *Humphrey Clinker*. "Why not? Not that I'm exactly enamoured of it. What have you got?"

"A thriller. I rather love a really good whodunnit, don't you?"

"I can't say. I don't think I've ever read one. I say, Mary-Lou, could we go upstairs to a bedroom, do you think? I—I'd like to talk to you."

"O.K., where's your stick? Those rowdies," Mary-Lou cast a grin in the direction of the card-players whose shrieks certainly merited her epithet, "will never miss us. We'll go and have a good natter together."

However, when they were finally settled in the bedroom Naomi was sharing with three of the others, she speedily found that she had let herself in for a good deal more than she had bargained for.

The Head Girl insisted on Naomi lying down on her bed and being tucked up under a big rug, while she herself calmly robbed Prunella Davies's bed of another before sitting down on a chair close at hand. Naomi gave her another of those queerly thoughtful looks. Her back had been aching and it was bliss to lie down like this. But how did Mary-Lou know it? She had said nothing.

"How did you know?" she asked abruptly.

"Know what?" Mary-Lou demanded.

"Know about my back."

"Well, I thought you looked all in, and I know what it is to have an aching back," Mary-Lou explained. She paused and fished in her pockets, finally coming up with a slab of chocolate. "Have some choc? We may as well be comfy."

"How do you mean?" Naomi persisted as she accepted the chocolate.

"In what way? Oh, about the back! Well, you see, two years or so ago I was mixed up in a toogganing accident and dished my own back pretty badly. Oh, it's all right now, thank goodness; only aches when I'm really deadly tired. But for quite a time it was weak. In fact, if you really want to know, there *were* two or three days when no one knew whether I would ever walk again."

"How simply awful!" Naomi spoke with a fervour that sprang from her own experience. "How did it happen?"

"I told you—a toboggan accident. I bashed my head—I had a lump like a football on the back—and bruised my spine. That's when my hair was cut. It had been as straight as a yardstick before then. But they had to shave my head, and when my hair grew again, it grew *curls*! So, on the whole," Mary-Lou concluded with some complacency, "I reckoned I'd gained by it."

"Well, I didn't gain a thing by *my* accident," Naomi told her bitterly. "I only lost. Before it happened I was as straight as anyone. I was keen on dancing, and my people promised me I should have my chance to train as a ballet dancer."

Like a flash Mary-Lou's warm hand caught one of hers. "Oh, I'm so very sorry!" she cried. "That must have been dreadful for you!"

"Dreadful? You can't begin to know how dreadful. Because my parents died in the same fire. I lost my father and mother and my power to dance all at once. Do you wonder," Naomi wound up, still in that bitter tone, "that I don't believe in God? Or if He really is there, then He just doesn't care."

Mary-Lou remained very still for a minute or two. Somehow she felt that if she could only think of the right things to say and do, she might be able to put an end to this unhealthy way of thinking. How could anyone bearing the disabilities she did go through life without some help, and who could give it but God?

"Naomi, I didn't understand. But oh, don't either say or think such dreadful things. They simply aren't true."

"How do you know? *You* have got better. You can walk and run and dance as well as ever. I'm done for anything of that kind. I've been all over to all sorts of wonderful surgeons. They all say the same thing. The ligaments or something are shrivelled, and it's caused the shape I am now."

"Well, I don't know enough about that to argue with you; but the minute I can get hold of him I'm going to talk to Uncle Jack," Mary-Lou said firmly.

"Who is he?" Naomi asked languidly. She was tired physically by her morning's activities, and the sudden letting down of the barriers even by so little, had wearied her mentally.

"He's Dr. Maynard—Aunt Joey's husband. He's head of the San at the Platz, you know. He's brilliant, I've heard people say. And what's more, he manages to keep abreast of all the latest cures. Naomi, don't give up hope! They can do such marvellous things now with surgery, and every day, almost, they make new discoveries. Oh, I don't say you would be able to dance—"

"I couldn't anyhow. I'm too old to start now," Naomi said. "But never mind that. I've had all these years to make up my mind to it that that is *off*. But if it was possible for me to be straight again and walk about and move normally, oh, Mary-Lou, if it ever happened, I'd believe in God again and love Him!" Then her excitement died as suddenly as it had come, and she added wearily, "But I don't see how it could happen. It's just your thinking of it."

"But you could *hope* about it, couldn't you?" Mary-Lou pleaded. "And another thing, Naomi, why do you go round as if—as if you always had your arm up to protect your head against having your ears boxed? I mean that metaphorically, of course. You must have been with some really unpleasant people if you can imagine that's the sort of thing you'll get from us."

Naomi flushed. "I hate being pitied and looked at as if I were something out of a wild beast show! I loathe it when people *stare* at me and look sorry for me!"

"Oh, don't be so silly! No one is likely to do that to you if you'll only behave naturally. People," said Mary-Lou wisely, "are awfully given to taking you as you think of yourself. Of course, if that's your idea of yourself, you can't very well expect them to think differently."

Naomi's jaw dropped. Never had anyone talked to her like this before. She remained silent, and Mary-Lou, having said as much as she dared at one time, was silent, too. She glanced at the girl on the bed rather fearfully. Naomi was lying quite still and her eyes were closed. She got up to her feet cautiously, but at her movement, the eyes opened.

"I'm not asleep," Naomi said, "or not yet. All the same, I'd like to be alone for a while now. You've given me something to think about."

"O.K. I'll go down, then, and join the rummy gang," Mary-Lou agreed affably. "You do rather look as if a nap would do you good." As she turned to go, a hand came out from under the rugs and caught her wrist.

"I'll think it over. And Mary-Lou! I know you do truly believe in God and all that. But you haven't had to face what I have. Only," she added, "if there *should* ever be anything in what you said about modern surgery, and it really happens, then I *will* believe. I couldn't do anything else!"

"Right! That's a bargain!" Mary-Lou assented. "Now I'm going and you try to get a sleep. You'll feel a lot better after it."

And she left the room and raced off downstairs to join the rummy players. But she had certainly started something that afternoon, though neither she nor Naomi could possibly know how it would all end.

Chapter 10

AVALANCHE!

NEXT morning they woke up to find that the snow had died off during the night, and the day was sunny and still. Mdlle ordained that they should skate today. Naomi could not skate, of course, but a small high-backed sledge was procured. She was packed in, and the girls took it in turns to push her round the lake. When they finally left off to go and seek a sheltered nook where they could devour their sandwiches, cakes and hot coffee with which Frau Tratschin, warned beforehand by Mdlle, had provided them, everyone was flushed and laughing and eager to go at it again as soon as possible.

They had to leave the lake when the sun set, but Mdlle informed them that, as it was full moon, they should go for a moonlight ski after Abendessen. This was something quite new, and they enjoyed themselves enormously though they were all tired when they finally returned to the farm, where hot milk and buns awaited them before they went off to bed where even Naomi fell asleep as soon as her head touched the pillow.

The next day was Sunday, which meant church for all of them. Mdlle took the Catholic girls to High Mass, and Miss Ferrars went off with the rest to the Lutheran church since there was no English service for them to attend that day.

"Wish we'd gone with you," Mary-Lou grumbled later to Hilary. "I don't like the Lutheran service, and it was all in German, of course, and a fearfully long sermon into the bargain. I found it frightfully difficult to follow, and, to crown everything, I think the pastor must have either just *got* false teeth or else was trying out a new set that didn't really fit."

However, Mddle took them off on a good ski-run in the afternoon, so she forgot her discontent and in the evening, as the weather still continued fine, they went for a short run between Kaffee and Kuchen and Abendessen. Bedtime came early. As Mdlle pointed out, they had had a strenuous time, and on the morrow they were to go into the mountains for tobogganing.

Monday was a grey day and unseasonably warm. Mdlle looked uneasily at the sky, but the clouds were fairly high so she agreed to the tobogganing, though Herr Tratschin warned the girls not to shout too much when they were in the mountains.

"But why not?" Mary-Lou demanded.

"Because, meine Fräulein, it may be that with this fresh snow and then the warmer weather some of the cornices are loose and ready to fall—though I am sure it is safe where I am sending you," he added.

"Do you think he's said anything about it to Mdlle?" Hilary asked when he had gone.

"Oh, sure to. We're going where he advises. He wouldn't send us into danger, you know!" Mary-Lou sounded very certain.

"No; I suppose not. O.K. How do we divide up?" Hilary asked.

Mary-Lou eyed her warily. "I'm going to ask you people to let Naomi come with us if you don't mind. I've had a word with Verity, and she says she doesn't mind going with some of the others. You see, she's so helpless in some ways—Naomi, I mean—and I'd like to be sure she was with people who understand. You don't mind, do you?"

"I can think of other folk I'd rather have with us," Hilary said drily. "Still, I see your point."

At this point, Miss Ferrars arrived with Naomi, so the talk stopped. Mary-Lou gave her invitation, and Verity joined up with Barbara, Prunella and Vi, while the three inseperables made a dive for the first toboggan without any argument. The last toboggan was taken by the two mistresses. Finally, they all set off, Naomi travelling as usual on her toboggan.

They all went on skis. Herr Tratschin had told them there was a hut at the foot of the slope where they could leave all their gear, including their midday meal, for Mdlle had said they would spend the day tobogganing. This was their last full day, for though they were returning by train, they must leave shortly after midday in order to reach the school before Abendessen.

They went flying over the snow, laughing and talking as they went, and presently they were beginning to go up until at last they reached the small hut Herr Tratschin had mentioned. Beyond, the slope rose sharply for some distance before going in a gentle curve round the side.

"This is something like!" Mary-Lou proclaimed in her usual clarion tones.

"Hi! If you go on yelling like that, you'll bring the entire lot down on us!" Hilary cried, laughing.

Mary-Lou laughed. "Sorry! I didn't mean to yell. But it really is something! Our own isn't bad, but this must be four times the distance. What a gorgeous run down we shall have! Mdlle, how far up may we go?"

"I will come with you and show you," Mdlle replied.

"And Mary-Lou, do remember what Hilary says. Herr Tratschin assures me it is safe enough here; but you would not wish to involve us all in an avalanche?"

"I would not." Mary-Lou's voice had dropped. "I'll remember, Mdlle."

Mdlle started them off, warning each girl as she passed to remember not to shout, and presently the long steep slope was dotted with figures. Mary-Lou and Hilary led, still pulling Naomi on their toboggan. Vi and Co. followed, with

Verity as passenger. She was not very strong and apt to tire quickly. Monica, Carol and Rosemary came next, and the two mistresses last of all.

The road led up the straight slope, round a spur of the mountain, and on up to a shelf where stood another hut. They had it to themselves, and there was a silence up here that overawed even Mary-Lou the exuberant.

"The hut seems to be closed," she murmured softly to Mdlle. "Do you know what it is?"

"Me, I had no idea of it," she said. She wrinkled her brows thoughtfully. "No; I am sure—very sure—that Herr Tratschin never spoke of a second hut."

"Perhaps he forgot about it," Mary-Lou suggested. "It might be a herdsman's hut for the summer months when the cows are up, but closed during the winter, and so he never thought of it again."

"Yes; that might be," Mdlle agreed. She glanced round at the mountain slopes towering above them, white with their thick covering of snow. "Well, we must ask him when we return. Meantime, let us toboggan. And remember, all; no screaming! I see no cornice very near nor overhanging this part, but we have had new snow, and today is certainly warm. Who goes first?"

That set them off, and presently the four toboggans were flying down the long incline at ever-increasing speed. By the time they had done the run four or five times, everyone was glowing and flushed. Even Naomi had forgotten her woes and grievances. She was laughing softly and her eyes were shining with genuine pleasure. Mdlle saw it and nudged her colleague to draw her attention to it. *This* was not the Naomi they had all known so far.

By the time a halt was called for Mittagessen the sun was blazing down, so that more than one of the girls begged permission to discard some part of her clothing. It was forbidden, of course. No one wanted them to wind up the holiday with odd cases of pneumonia, and if the sun was hot at present, there was no saying how long he would continue.

They went to the lower hut to reclaim their knapsacks, and then moved away to a little grove of birches behind it, where they all squatted down on the toboggans, and enjoyed the delicious lunch Frau Tratschin had packed for them. But once their meal was over, they were all anxious to resume their tobogganing. Mdlle gave the word, and once more they climbed up the long slopes to the closed hut, where they stood talking in undertones and laughing softly.

Suddenly, without warning, the great stillness was filled with a terrible roaring which grew and grew until it seemed there was nothing left in the world but the thunderous noise. The blue sky overhead vanished. A cornice of fresh snow overhanging the straight part of the run had become loosened from its hold by the heat of the sun and came crashing down, tearing away from the mountain slopes great rocks and boulders, tree trunks and slabs of earth as it fell.

The girls screamed and made for the shelter of the hut. Mary-Lou beat on the door with fists and feet until the latch gave way beneath her assault, and they all practically fell into the place.

All? No; Naomi, lifted off her feet by the frantic rush of the others, fell headlong just outside. Mary-Lou, who had managed to keep her balance, saw her, even as Mdlle struggled madly to her own feet. Instantly, the prefect dashed out again, regardless of the rain of pebbles, earth and snow that was showering down, grasped the other girl under the arms, and dragged her into the hut in one lightning-like movement. Then the rest of the avalanche came down and the light was blotted out completely. When all was still again, they found that their route down was blocked by a huge mass of snow, rubble and pine trunks, though the hut, built under a bulge in the mountain-wall had escaped. Most of them were bruised and cut from the flying débris; and on the floor lay Naomi, still, white and senseless—to all appearance, dead.

Chapter 11

IN THE HUT

"MARY-LOU—are you awake?"

Mary-Lou, dozing fitfully on the floor of the herdsmen's hut, roused up, rolled over and stretched out a hand. Naomi, who had spoken, clutched it in a feverish grip. She had come round shortly before Mdlle had ordained that they must all lie down and try to sleep. She was very white, and there was a nasty gash from her ear to her chin, but that was swiftly remedied. Matron never allowed anyone to go off on an expedition without a first-aid kit, and Mdlle and Miss Ferrars had both been carrying theirs strapped to their backs when the disaster happened.

Most of the girls were too worn out by the time the moon rose, flooding into the hut doorway, which they had to leave open as a boulder, protruding into the one room, prevented them from shutting it, to be anything but sleepy. They had soon dropped off, much to the relief of the two mistresses. Only Mary-Lou, who had strained her back slightly in that wild effort to save Naomi, and Naomi herself whose shocked nerves would allow her no chance to rest, were awake now.

"You're all right, Naomi. We're safe enough here. Can't you sleep? Let's see if I can make you more comfy." Mary-Lou slipped an arm under the thin shoulders, raising Naomi a little and the younger girl suddenly clung to her.

"Mary-Lou, aren't you—afraid?"

Mary-Lou considered. "I can't say I'm exactly pleased with this set-up. Who would be? I'm frantically hungry, and goodness only knows when we shall get out of this. But as for afraid; no, I'm not exactly afraid."

"I am," Naomi said simply. "I'm *terribly* afraid."

"But why? They'll get to us in time—and not such a long time at that, either."

"How can you possibly know that?" Naomi demanded.

"Well, use your common sense! The Tratschins know exactly where we are. You can bet that when we never turned up by Abendessen, even if they hadn't heard of the avalanche before, they'd simply raise the neighbourhood to get at us. 'Tisn't as if we'd gone off into the blue and no one knew *where* to look for us, you know."

"I hadn't thought that out," Naomi confessed. "Yes; I think you're right there."

"I know I am," Mary-Lou said with a calm certainty that made Naomi gasp. "They'll get us out one way or another. But in the meantime, unless the herdsmen left a few tins or something up here, we're going to have to go on frightfully short rations for the time being. And I *am* very worried about what our own folk are going through. I should think they'll go frantic if we aren't yanked out pretty quickly."

"I never thought of their side of it," Naomi said. Then she shivered.

"Cold?" Mary-Lou asked. "Sorry I can't do any more about it. Get as close to me as you can and we'll keep each other warm."

"No; I'm not really cold. But I was thinking—oh, Mary-Lou! You know how—how I've thought and talked about things. Do—do you think God's punishing me this way?"

"Talk sense!" said Mary-Lou. "Honestly, Naomi, you simply *can't* talk rot like that! That would be punishing the rest of us as well, and that would be unfair. God's never unfair, let me tell you. Pull yourself together and for goodness sake stop talking such rot!"

"Are you sure?" Naomi cried. "Oh, Mary-Lou, are you quite *sure*?"

"'Sh! You'll wake the rest if you yell like that! Of course I'm sure—positive."

"And you do truly think that they'll get us out sooner or later?"

"Certainly they will! What *were* you imagining?" Mary-Lou gave a low chuckle. "Honestly, Naomi! You pipe down and try to go to sleep, and so will I. Stop thinking, anyhow, for your thoughts are simply crackers."

Naomi sighed and fell silent. Soon Mary-Lou went under a deep wave of sleep and Naomi lay quietly, turning over in her mind what the Head Girl had said to her during that eventful weekend, but she drowsed off finally. It was broad daylight before there was any further sound from the hut, barring the quiet breathing of the sleepers and an occasional mutter from Barbara, who was given to talking in her sleep. A ray of morning sunlight found its way through the space above the boulder and struck full across the eyes of Kathy Ferrars, who was lying against the opposite wall. She stirred sleepily, wondering what had become of the bedclothes. Then she opened her eyes, stared round wildly, and came to full consciousness.

Afterwards, Kathy said that she had never imagined herself in such a scene. The girls were lying closely huddled together on the floor. A hump near the boulder represented Mdlle, who had insisted on taking the outside place. Everyone was sleeping as if for a wager. She decided to make a start towards some sort of a meal. She herself was famishing, and she could guess what the girls would be like when they woke up.

Her first step was to collect her knapsack. She had retained it the day before because in it was their first-aid kit, but she knew that it also held a slab of chocolate and at least one orange. It was not much for twelve people, but it was better than nothing. First came the kit. Then the chocolate, two oranges, a bag which held a bun and another with three sandwiches which were dry and curling at the edges, but still edible.

"Well, that's a lot better than I expected," she muttered. "Some of the girls are safe to have oddments of chocolate, too. What's this—oh, glory! Biscuits! I forgot I'd shoved that packet in at the last moment. Wonder what Jeanne has?"

As if she had heard her own name, Mdlle stirred and then awoke. She sat up, stretching herself, and Kathy clambered across the legs of the girls, and reached her side with her treasure.

"Jeanne! Do you think I could possibly get up that rock and bring some snow in? Then, if we can only find something to burn, I've chocolate here, and we could melt the snow and give the girls a hot drink. And I've a few fragments of food as well. What have you got?"

Mdlle felt in her pockets and produced another slab of chocolate and two packets of almonds and raisins, which set her colleague to searching her own pockets from which she produced a third packet as well as her cigarette case and lighter.

"It'll be what you might call a mixed meal," she said with a low laugh, "but better than nothing. I suppose the men aren't likely to have left any tins of anything. Where should we look?"

Mdlle stood up and looked round. Her eye was caught by a kind of corner shelf in the far corner. "But I think over there would be the most likely place."

"It would be! I suppose the girls *have* only two legs each, but when I was coming to you just now, I wondered if some of them had developed an extra one overnight."

At this point Hilary suddenly sat up yawning. She looked round. "Lumme! Where have I got to?" she demanded loudly.

It acted like the rising bell at school. One by one the girls woke up and gave tongue. Finally Mary-Lou staggered to her feet, and gazed round on them.

"*Well!*" she observed in shocked tones. "A more ghastly collection of scarecrows I never beheld in my life!"

"You're none so beautiful yourself!" Vi retorted. "Your face is filthy and you've straws in your hair!"

"I'd like a wash," Verity remarked plaintively. "And I'd like a drink and something to eat! Oh, and I've got something to eat! I've just remembered! I've got a packet of figs in one of my pockets."

This set them all off. By the time the pockets were emptied a miscellaneous heap of chocolate, almonds and raisins, biscuits, figs and dates were in the middle of the floor. Then Miss Ferrars, who had been investigating, let out a veritable yell of triumph and emerged from the corner with a flat cake of stale black bread in either hand.

"There's something more there," Miss Ferrars cried, going back to rummage. She produced two more of the rocklike cakes and two tins of condensed milk.

"Oh, well, we shan't starve for the present, anyhow!" Monica said.

Verity had come to the boulder and was gazing up at it. "I'm the smallest of us. If some of you folk would give me a leg up, I believe I could crawl through that space and get some snow. If we buried the bread in it, it would soften by degrees, and then we could eat it."

"We'll do better than that," Mdlle said in her own tongue. She had been rummaging on her own account, and had discovered a faggot of resinous twigs and branches. "If we can find a can or a pan, we will build a fire. Miss Ferrars has her lighter, and we can mix the chocolate with snow, and that will give us a hot drink. Look round, all of you, and see if you can find something."

It was Naomi who spied, tucked up among the rafters, a large flat pan. Hilary made "a back", and Mary-Lou climbed up and managed to bring the pan down. Meanwhile, on the flat stones which clearly served the men for a hearth, Mdlle piled up twigs and branches, the lighter was put to work, and in three minutes a fine cloud of smoke poured out into the room, setting them all coughing and choking as the twigs caught and blazed up.

This lasted only a minute or so. There was a hole in the roof, and presently the smoke was pouring up through it. They had their fire!

The next thing was to get the snow. Mdlle was doubtful about letting Verity or anyone else venture out, but Verity insisted. She easily wriggled through the space, and presently she was looking through into the hut.

"It's all right, Mdlle. There's a kind of shelf in the rock here and I can stoop down and scoop up the snow, if you'll give me something to do it with."

This was a puzzle. The herdsmen had left no mugs or cans. Finally, Miss Ferrars turned out all the oddments from the first-aid box, and that was passed through the opening to Verity, who set to work at once.

It was a long slow job. The pan had been placed before the fire which was now dying down to a bed of glowing ash and wood, and they ran to and fro with the piled-up box and emptied it as quickly as they could. Verity's long curls lost the ribbon which kept them back from her face. She was scarlet, and before long her back was aching badly; but she stuck to it despite Mdlle's commands to give it up and come back.

"Oh, I must get some more, Mdlle. I'm sure there isn't enough to give us even half a cup each. When it melts it always goes less. And then it isn't even as if it were just snow. There's such a lot of mud and stuff mixed with it."

This was all true, but would have mattered nothing to Mdlle if she had only been in a position to enforce the order Verity so calmly and stubbornly refused to obey. She was a quiet, gentle girl as a rule, but, as everyone knew, she had a marked streak of obstinacy in her which, when touched, was apt to overlay her other qualities.

Mary-Lou put her oar in. "Verity Anne Carey! You do as you're told and come back at once! You're worrying everyone, and it's jolly unfair of you!"

Verity's face appeared in the gap. "How full is that pan thing?" she demanded.

"Er—well, quite full enough to give us each a little. You come back—*What's that*?" She broke off sharply, and Verity wriggled round to stare down into the valley.

The sound which had startled the pair of them was a long yodel. It was repeated, and then Verity gave vent to a positive howl.

"There are people down there! They've come to find us! Give me something to wave, someone—quick!"

"You be careful!" Mary-Lou warned her as she stripped off her scarf and pushed it through. "For mercy's sake don't fall off that perch of yours!"

"O.K. I'll be careful," Verity promised. She turned carefully so that she was facing down the slope. She could just glimpse the valley and the people looking like ants far below, but she could hear clearly the yodelling which was going on continually now as one person after another took it up.

Everyone in the hut could hear it now, and they left the fire and the pan where the snow was melting fast, and crowded round the foot of the rock at their side.

"Let's yodel back," Hilary cried. "If we all do it together, they'll hear us."

"Good idea!" Miss Ferrars exclaimed. "Take your time from me! One—two—three—*yodel*!"

The noise they made was enough to waken the dead. Verity, acting as look-out, reported results excitedly, clinging to her shelf with fingers and toes.

"They're moving about—they've heard—I don't think they can see us, but someone is waving something! They're coming—oh, I can't see now! But I'm *sure* they're coming to find us and rescue us! Shall I come in now? I can't help any more."

"But yes, my child; certainly come in, and at once!" Mdlle said firmly. "Stand back, girls! Be careful, Verity!"

Mary-Lou scrambled up the far side of the boulder and

thrust out her head to watch the progress of her "sister-by-marriage". It was not easy. The Head Girl watched her slow movements with fear and trembling. A great mass of soft snow mixed with rubble and earth was piled up just below, and if Verity fell, she ran a grave risk of being buried alive. She did slip once, and Mary Lou, making a mighty effort, got an arm through just in time to grip her wrist and save her from going altogether. To the two who knew what had happened, it seemed an eternity before Verity found her footing, though it was a bare twenty seconds. Then she was safe again, and a moment or two later she crawled through the narrow opening and descended headfirst on top of Monica, Hilary and Prunella, who were standing by ready to catch her.

Mdlle took tiny Verity in her arms. "Are you hurt, chérie?"

"No—except that Mary-Lou nearly wrenched my arm out of its socket when she grabbed me just now. But if she hadn't . . ." Verity shuddered.

"Forget it!" Miss Ferrars said quickly. "Two of you girls get that pan on the fire and bring it to the boil. The snow's pretty well melted now. Vi, sort out the chocolate and break it up. We'll have to drink out of my box and that means putting the chocolate into it and pouring the water in on top. Where are those barley sugars Naomi handed out? Here, Verity! Suck this. Anyone got a knife? You, Hilary? Then pierce holes in this tin of condensed milk."

Thanks to her wit, they were all soon at work, and Verity, who had been lowered to the hay, was recovering the colour which had left her face.

"My legs feel all gone," she complained. "And oh, how my back aches with stooping. I've never been half sorry enough for you, Mary-Lou—or you, Naomi. I shall know how to sympathise now when either of you has backache!"

"The pan's beginning to bubble," Vi said. "Get your scarves off, everyone. The rim will be blazing hot."

"Here, let me! I can lift it!" big Monica said imperiously, taking the scarves. She lifted the pan carefully, and set it down on the floor. "Now how do we manage?"

"Build up the fire first!" Barbara cried, bringing an armful of twigs and branches. "If they see the smoke, they can find us quicker."

"Good, Barbara!" Mdlle exclaimed. "As for how we are to manage, we must take out a boxful at a time, break up the chocolate into it and add the milk. We cannot pour from that big pan or we shall spill most of it. Do not fill the box, though. Miss Ferrars, will you take charge, please? Give Verity hers first."

Kathy Ferrars dipped the box in by its lid, skimming the top of the water to leave the mud behind as far as possible. Chocolate was broken into it, and then the condensed milk was added. It was very thick and poured slowly, but at last, each girl and both mistresses had had a hot drink of sorts. Then the food was shared out, and, once that had been eaten, there was no more to do but to sit and wait.

A long wait it was, too. It was halfway through the afternoon before the prisoners were relieved by Herr Tratschin's voice sounding through the smoke-vent in the roof.

"Hé, there! Is all well?"

Mdlle had been standing by the boulder, listening anxiously. Now she ran across the floor like one of the girls. "Herr Tratschin? Yes; we are all safe. Can you get us out soon?"

"We dare not try to free the doorway, for what has fallen is soft and lies deep—very deep. We must clear the roof and reach you that way. And to do that, men must be let down by rope. But have no fear. Soon we will have you out. First, though, put the fire out."

Greatly wondering what he meant, Mdlle summoned Miss Ferrars, and together they carefully raked out the embers of the fire. The girls stood waiting to trample out each little heap as it fell to the ground, and Hilary, by a sudden inspiration, poured the mud from the pan over everything when the hearthstone was bare.

Mdlle nodded approval as she stopped up to the vent and called, "It is done."

"Good—that is very good! Now I lower a parcel of food and another of coffee in flasks, very hot and strong. Watch for him!"

Two great bundles came slowly through and Mdlle caught first one and then the other, unfastened them and handed them over to her colleague.

"Now," ordered Herr Tratschin, "all go to the far side and stay there, for we come to pull the logs from the roof, and there are rocks tied on which may fall."

They all skipped across to the farther side as fast as they could, and then, while the two mistresses handed out coffee and great rolls sliced and filled with butter and meat, they heard the men beginning to work on the roof.

"This *is* an adventure!" Vi said as she finished her first roll and held out her hand for a second. "But I do hope the family don't know anything about it yet."

"Yes," Mary-Lou agreed, "but they'll also know that we've been found. I don't expect they'll have had very long to worry. Is there a spare roll? I've got a safe place for it if there is."

"It's getting dark," Rosemary said suddenly. "How will they see to work?"

"Oh, for that, they will have lights. They can take the batteries from cars and run the lights from them. I have heard of it being done in other rescues."

"Good!" Barbara said with emphasis. "I'm not grumbling, but I don't exactly want to spend another night here!" She paused to take a drink of the hot, sweet coffee before she continued, "Won't it be *paradisial* to go to bed between sheets? After a night on the floor, I can't imagine anything more heavenly."

At this point there came a splintering sound. A log in the roof shifted. There was a shout from the men working on it. Then a sudden gush of bitterly cold air poured into the hut as the log was slowly levered up and pushed aside. The girls cheered lustily, and Carol, who had a mouthful of roll at the time, choked and had to be patted on the back. But even she spluttered as soon as she could speak again, "Oh, thank goodness! They'll get us away tonight!"

They did; but it was dark and the skies were powdered with stars before Herr Tratschin was finally lowered into the hut. It was bitterly cold and everyone was shivering, but when they saw his broad, kindly face they all cheered loudly again. Their ordeal was ended, and soon they would be back at the farm.

"With hot baths, I hope," Mary-Lou said as she watched Herr Tratschin and another man who had joined him rope Naomi securely before they gave the signal, and she was drawn slowly up through the roof. "I'm filthier than I've ever been before, even in my wild youth! I'll be sorry for Frau Tratschin's sheets if we have to go to bed unbathed!"

One by one they went up on the ropes until they reached the broad ledge from which the men had been working. Great toboggans stood there, and they were packed in, and then a man bore each load away, pulling until he came to an opening between two great rocks, when he sat down, kicked off, and they went skimming over the snow which here was untouched by the avalanche, down—down—down, until they were flying across the plain to stop near a little encampment where each girl was seized on by a mistress from the school, hugged vehemently and then hurried away to where enormous sleighs, drawn by horses were waiting. By midnight, everyone was safe in bed. Matron ordained a full day's rest for everyone concerned, and further, kept Naomi, Verity, Barbara and Mary-Lou in bed until the end of the week, just to make sure. But after that, and when all parents had been heard from and knew that the girls were safe and sound, the school heaved a sigh of relief and returned to its normal activities.

"But I hope," Miss Annersley said when all the staff were at coffee on the Sunday night, "that that will prove the last of our trials for this term. If there is much more of this my hair will be white by Easter, and you had better book a place for me at the nearest mental hospital!"

Chapter 12

Lost Property

"WELL, it was all very exciting and might have been a lot worse, but I hope it's the last excitement we have to worry about until St. Mildred's panto," Mary-Lou remarked a week later when the two Sixths were enjoying life together in the common room.

"That won't be *our* excitement," Vi remarked as she handed round a box of fudge.

"No; that's so. Scarlet fever has done every last one of us out of taking part in it. This year we shall be merely audience for once."

"A welcome change," Prunella said with decision. "I've had all the thrills I want for one term, thank you!"

"I wonder what tale they've chosen?" Verity observed.

"Goodness knows! They never let us know until the last minute," Hilary reminded her.

However, they didn't have long to wait. On the Saturday morning a large notice appeared on the noticeboard in Hall.

"Grand Annual Pantomime!
PUSS IN BOOTS
To take place in St. Luke's Hall
on the afternoon of Tuesday, April 1st.
Volunteers to sell programmes and refreshments and
to act as usherettes will be welcome."

Beneath was a note in Miss Wilson's characteristic hand: "Members of VIa and b alone may apply."

"*Puss in Boots*! Well, that's a change, anyhow," Prunella commented when they had a spare moment together. "I wonder who will be 'Puss'?"

"It's a gorgeous part, if I remember the story right," Josette said.

"I bet your Sybil will be the 'Princess'," Barbara observed. "She's the St. Mildred Beauty Queen."

"I wish she could hear you!" Sybil's sister said feelingly. "She *would* tell you where you got off!"

"I should just think so!" Vi exclaimed. "You're right there, Josette! To hear her talk, sometimes, you'd think it was a positive crime to be pretty."

"Yes; I've noticed that," Hilary agreed. "I've always meant to ask what was at the bottom of it. Do you know, Jo?"

Josette shook her head. "Haven't the foggiest. I only know the quickest way to make her absolutely raging is to comment on her looks. She's always been like that, so far as I can remember."

"You're her sister; you ought to know," Hilary agreed. "A kink in her character, I expect. Oh, well, that's better than if she was all upstage about her beauty—for she *is* really lovely, you know. You and young Ailie aren't a patch on her, Josette, and you're neither of you exactly plain."

Before Josette could think of a sufficiently biting reply, the bell rang and they had to hurry off to classes again, so the subject was dropped.

During the evening preparation period, Mary-Lou, who had been having a special history coaching arrived in the prefects' room to demand with some indignation if anyone had seen her fountain pen or biro.

"I had to take notes in pencil and the point was blunt, and goodness knows if I can read half that I got down!" she complained bitterly.

No one knew anything about either. Doris Hill suggested

that she must have left them in either the library or the geography room.

"I didn't," Mary-Lou said. "I've been there to see, and they're nowhere about. Miss Moore was in geography, and she said they hadn't been brought to her and she'd seen nothing of them. I can't imagine myself being such a goop as to leave them lying around there, anyhow. I *don't* scatter my belongings broadcast!"

This was true, but, as Lesley Malcolm pointed out, the best of us may forget at times. "You'd better ask Josette," she added. "She's library pree. She's down in Lower IVb tonight, in case you don't know."

"I'll go; but I'm positive I left them both in my case after that lecture we had on Shelley from the Head," Mary-Lou replied, leaving the room to seek Josette and ask her if she knew anything about the missing articles.

"I haven't seen them myself," Josette said, thankfully giving up work on a very sticky piece of geometry. "No one has brought them to me, either. But it isn't like you to leave things around, Mary-Lou. What have you been doing? And that reminds me. Have you looked in Lost Propery?"

"I have not. In fact I'd forgotten about it, it's so long since I had anything there," Mary-Lou responded. "However, I can't find them anywhere else, and no one seems to have seen anything of them, so I'd better go and look, I suppose, though it's a last hope, I may tell you. Thanks a lot, Josette. Sorry to have interrupted you."

"Oh don't mind me. I was only too thankful for a break!" Josette retorted. "I've got the nastiest piece of geometry I've had all this term."

Mary-Lou laughed and went off to demand the key of Lost Property from Vi, who, as Second Prefect, always had charge of it.

"Lost Property? You *must* be desperate if you're reduced to hunting there!" Vi said, getting up from the table in the prefects' room. "OK. I'll go and fetch it. It's in my bureau—

for safety's sake. You trot along to the cupboard and wait for me. I shan't be more than a minute or two."

Mary-Lou went along to stand opposite the cupboard dedicated to Lost Property, while Vi ran off to her cubicle to get the key. She came down to find her friend awaiting her with a good deal of impatience.

"What an age you've been! Remember, I've had coaching since prep began, and so far I've scarcely done a thing!"

"Sorry, but I couldn't find it at first. It had shifted itself somehow to the very back of the drawer, and I had to fish under everything before I found it," Vi explained as she inserted the key and turned it.

The door did not wait to be pulled open. It simply *burst* open and at once an avalanche of mixed belongings cascaded from the shelves. Blazers, berets, gloves, books, pencil cases, pens, pencils and erasers tumbled out, not to mention a workbasket, the lid of which had fallen open so that it discharged its contents everywhere. Reels of cotton went rolling gaily down the corridor, followed by a thimble. Skeins of darning-wool and silk fell in every direction and packets of needles and pins, a pair of scissors and a bag of toffees showered over the rest. Mary-Lou had to chase one enterprising reel to the far end of the corridor before she caught up with it.

"What on earth . . ." she began as she came back. Then she interrupted herself. "Heavens! Here's that snap-album Lesley Bethune was bemoaning all yesterday! How on earth did it get here?"

"And here are Naomi's beloved Patience cards," Vi added, picking up the little case. The next moment, she dropped it to swoop down on a small brooch. "My tennis badge! How on earth did it get here? I haven't been wearing it lately."

"This," said Mary-Lou, the light of battle in her eyes, "is someone's idea of a joke. This blazer is Prunella's—here's the name tape. And this is Hilda's scarf. Oh, and my old purse that I keep stamps in!"

"But who under the sun would be such a complete idiot?" Vi demanded with some point as she stirred up the mess on the floor. "Gracious! Here's Lesley Malcolm's protractor and Hilary's gym shoes." She stood up and surveyed the pile with blazing eyes. Then she swung round on the Head Girl. "You're right, Mary-Lou! Someone has had the unbounded *sauce* to interfere with our things—for quite half the stuff here belongs to one or other of the Sixths. What are you going to do about it?"

Mary-Lou had listened to her in silence, and a grimmer expression spread over her face than most people had ever seen there before. "Do about it? When we've found out who is reponsible for this latest piece of idiocy, I propose to make whoever it is sorry that she—or they—was ever born! There's a limit to the practical jokes that can be played in this establishment, and they've gone well beyond it this time. I'll go and fetch one of the packing trays and we'd better clear all this lot up."

"Right! You scram and I'll do what I can—though, honestly," Vi added, "I just don't know where to begin, there's such a hotch-potch here!"

Mary-Lou giggled and fled, and Vi, squatting on the floor, began to sort things out. Certainly, as she reflected, whoever had been responsible seemed to have gone through all the rooms with vim. In fact, as she shrewdly suspected, this affair was the work of quite a number of people. One or even two girls could hardly have been responsible for such a collection!

Mary-Lou returned a few minutes later with one of the light wicker trays they used for unpacking, to find Vi surveying the heap of belongings thoughtfully. "I say, Mary-Lou! Has it ever struck you that whoever did this must have been at my drawers?"

"*What*? What on earth do you mean?"

"What I say. Think a sec. Where do I keep the key? In my hanky-box under the hankies. At least, it's always in that drawer. I won't vouch for it's always being in the box."

Mary-Lou's lips tightened into a straight line. "*That* sort of thing must stop pronto! They know, down to the newest Junior, that you don't go meddling with other folks' drawers. But that would account for the ages you took to find the thing. Probably whoever did it just shoved the key back anyhow when they'd finished with it. For you know, Vi, this isn't the work of *one* person. It's a lot too—too comprehensive for that!"

"I'd got as far as that myself," Vi assented, and turned back to her sorting. She brandished a bunch of pens, pencils and biros. "Better look through these and see if yours are here. Who do you think is responsible?"

"I don't know, but I'm jolly well going to make it my business to find out."

"*Poor* kids! I wouldn't be in their shoes for all the tea in China! That's fairly sorted out now, I think. Let's take this lot to our own room. Then we'd better get down to work."

The pair quickly filled the tray with the various heaps, and then bore it off to the prefects' room. They had expected to find one or two, at least, of their confrères there, but it was empty. They set the tray down, and then Mary-Lou glanced at her watch. The yelp she let out startled Vi, who asked anxiously what was wrong *now*?

"It's half-past eighteen and we ought to be down in the library for extra French! Come on! Look as apologetic as you can! We don't want to have to explain too much to Mdlle until we've gone into conference about this."

Mercifully for them Mdlle herself had been detained, and by the time she arrived in the library with apologies for her tardy arrival, the pair were in their places and looking, as Hilary said later, as if butter wouldn't melt in their mouths! After the lecture, the prefects gathered up their possessions and trooped off upstairs to their room to go on with their work, all unwitting of the fact that so far as lessons were concerned, little work would be done by them *that* evening.

Chapter 13

PREFECTS IN COUNCIL

"—AND all I've got to say is that, if I've got to remember all those writers of the Revolutionary period and their . . . My sainted aunt Sempronia! *What's all this?*"

Hilary, talking as she went, flung open the door of the prefects' room, and stopped dead, staring with eyes that looked ready to drop out of her head at the piled-up tray Mary-Lou and Vi had planted on the table.

At her words, the pair responsible grinned at each other. The rest pressed forward to see what on earth had happened to cause such amazement.

"What—on—earth——" Lesley Bethune began, but was interrupted by Prunella, who leapt forward with a cry of, "My blazer! How on earth did it get here? I left it on my peg. Who's been doing what to make it look as if I'd gone to bed for a week in it?"

Hilda Jukes followed her. "And my scarf!"

Hilary swung round on Mary-Lou and Vi. "You two! This is your doing. Oh, not the collection, idiots! But you two brought it here! What's the meaning of it?"

Mary-Lou slid round the excited throng and took her place at the head of the table. "Keep calm—keep calm—all of you! As for what's been going on and who's been doing what, will all of you please take a dekko at this lot and bag anything of yours among them. Here's your snap-album for one, Lesley. And your gym shoes are there, Hilary."

The prefects goggled at the miscellaneous heaps in silence. Then Hilary picked up her gym shoes and that broke the spell. They surged forward and for a moment or two cries and exclamations sounded as they found belongings that some of them had never even missed. Finally, Hilary, still staring as if she could not believe her senses, demanded, "What does it mean, anyhow? Where did you get this lot?"

"From Lost Property," Mary-Lou said blandly.

"But," Lesley Bethune cried loudly, "how on earth did it all get there? The only thing *I've* put there this week was Richenda Fry's umbrella, which I found sculling about loose in their Splashery instead of being hung on her peg."

"And I haven't had a thing," Doris Hill added. "Besides, if you come to that, will you explain how my geom. instruments came there? To my certain knowledge I put them away properly yesterday and I haven't had them out since."

Prunella, having pulled on her blazer, turned to the Head Girl. "What's the meaning of it, Mary-Lou?"

"Best sit down," Mary-Lou said, pulling out a chair and setting the example. "Now then, all of you, lend me your ears. And keep any comments until I've finished. Someone—or several someones, for I don't for a moment think that *one* girl is responsible for the size of this lot—has thought it funny to go round gathering up things regardless. Then, if you please, someone must have gone to Vi's cubey and helped herself to Lost Property key and shoved the whole lot in."

Mary-Lou's voice was very quiet, but her eyes glinted like pieces of steel, and the listening prefects realised that she was furiously angry. If it came to that, they were angry themselves. Many of the things they had rescued could only have been taken from their desks or pegs or Splashery lockers, and that was a piece of impudence that had not happened before.

Hilary spoke first. "Do you really mean that they had the *cheek* to go to Vi's drawers and help themselves! Who would do such a thing? I can quite well see that some mindless wenches might think it funny to shove the things into Lost

Property if the door were open already—and," she added in parenthesis, "I'd like to know how they ever managed to get it shut again on that lot!—but surely no one would do a thing like that?"

"Obviously they did it, since the thing was done," Vi said. She, too, was plainly very angry. Her deep, violet-blue eyes were flashing in a way few people had ever seen them flash, and her pretty mouth was a straight line. She had had time to realise the cool impudence of the business, and though, like Mary-Lou, she was quiet outwardly, inwardly she was raging.

There was a silence. Then Hilda Jukes, a big, good-natured girl whom no one had ever seen out of temper before throughout her whole school career, spoke with an edge to her voice that gave them all a fresh shock.

"This is beyond a joke! I hope when you find out who did it, you'll make them smart for it, Mary-Lou. We'll all back you up, whatever you suggest! We can't have that sort of thing going on. It's downright cheek and none too honest, either."

"Don't you worry! When we've discovered who it is we'll give them a lesson they'll remember to their last day!" Mary-Lou retorted. "Look here! It's getting on for Abendessen. Make sure you've got all your own things, and then we'll dispose of this lot. Prefects' meeting after Abendessen, all of you!"

Once more the prefects turned their attention to the heaps of oddments. Two or three things such as fountain pens and biros had been overlooked and were now claimed.

Mary-Lou, rather calmer now, took charge. "Well, if you're all sure you've got everything that's yours, I vote we shove the rest into the bottom of the cupboard. Give me a hand, someone. Open the doors, will you, Vi?"

Vi opened the double doors at the bottom of the huge cupboard in which the prefects kept their private belongings, and Mary-Lou and Hilary lifted the tray and pushed it gently in on the floor, where it just fitted in.

During Abendessen, the prefects, though they talked lightly among themselves, were mainly occupied in regarding the younger girls carefully. Remembering her own impish day, Mary-Lou had an idea that the perpetrators would probably be keeping an eye on on the prefects to see if they could find out whether or not the grandees of the school knew about it yet.

"Thank goodness for that, anyhow!" Hilary, who sat next to her, muttered.

Mary-Lou started. "Thank goodness for what?"

"I was watching the IVa folk to see if any of them looked self-conscious or were extra giggly, and I can't see that they're any worse than usual. Heather Warner and Connie Winter have been tittering, but that's nothing fresh for them. No; IVa are out of it all right."

"I was at the same game myself," Mary-Lou said when she had finished her soup. "I've absolved both Upper Fourths. But I'm by no means so sure of Lower. Ailie Russell has been squinting across at us whenever she thought we weren't looking, and so has Janice Chester. Those two are demons, and they never bother to think, but do whatever mad idea enters their silly heads on the instant."

"Gosh! If young Ailie is in it won't Madame be mad if she ever hears of it!" murmured Hilary, referring to Lady Russell who had established the school when it was in Tirol. She was far too busy these days. Her three girls, Sybil, now at St. Mildred's, and Josette and Ailie had naturally become pupils at the first possible moment. If Ailie really had any hand in the stealing of Vi's key, and her mother ever heard of it, she certainly would be furious.

Doris Hill, sitting at Mary-Lou's other hand, had overheard their talk. She leaned across the table to Hilary. "If it's that crowd, it's simply an extra bad attack of insanity," she said in low tones. "We can deal with that all right!"

Mary-Lou was looking relieved. "So long as it isn't any of the Senior Middles! But you're right, of course, Doris. With that crew, it's merely spring madness. Bless their little hearts! They're for it, all right! We'll see to it that whatever else they may do they'll never play that joke again—or not in this place!" Her eyes went across to the table where the members of Lower IVa were sitting, and Ailie Russell, stealing a furtive look across at *her* at the same moment, caught the look and turned scarlet.

"What's wrong with you?" demanded one of her two boon companions, Janice Chester.

"That Mary-Lou, drat her!" Ailie muttered under her breath. "I say, Jan, I rather think they know. She was staring over here looking like—like the Judgment Day!"

After that the pair kept their eyes on their own table, but Mary-Lou had seen Ailie's look though she had not seen the colour sweep over the small face under its fair curls, and she was almost sure in her own mind now that Lower IV knew all about the affair. She promptly dismissed the whole thing from her mind and began to chat in her ordinary manner. Those members of VIb who were not prefects, but sat at the same table had been feeling the constraint and wondered what was at the bottom of it. Now, thanks to Mary-Lou's sudden return to insouciance, it vanished, and everyone breathed more freely.

Prayers came immediately after Abendessen, and after Prayers, though the Juniors went off to bed, the rest had a free period when they might amuse themselves as they chose so long as they were quiet. On this evening the three Fifths and two Upper Fourths remained in Hall for dancing, Mddle Lenoir, the junior music mistress having consented to play for them. The two Lower Fourths retired to their common room, and Mary-Lou, looking rather like a cat who has stolen the cream, so bland was her expression, invited what was ieft of VIb to the prefects' room, where the story was unfolded to them and they were invited to hunt for their own possessions on the wicker tray.

"Who's responsible for all this 'ere?" Virginia Adams asked flippantly.

"We can't be sure, but we rather suspect the Lower Fourths," the Head Girl said. "Naomi, your Patience cards are there, for I saw them. Have you found them?"

Naomi nodded. "They were right on top. What are you going to do about it?"

"Hold a meeting and discuss it first. One thing I can promise you people. When we've done with whoever it is we won't hear a peep out of them for a long time to come. It was cheek of the worst to touch any of our things, especially as they must have taken things that were in their proper places all right. Don't you worry. They'll be told exactly where they get off, I promise you!"

Clare Kennedy looked up suddenly. "You know, Mary-Lou, I rather think this is an effort to get back on us because we have been so strict about untidiness."

"Do you really think so?" Mary-Lou asked.

Jessica Wayne assented to this. "If you ask me, they're lumping the whole of us Sixths together. I know I ticked Janice Chester off good and hard for leaving her shoes lying in the middle of the Splashery floor, and she had the cheek to say, 'You're not a pree, so it's none of your business!' I nearly ate her without salt," she added reflectively.

Hilary rose from her seat. "I know we aren't having a regular prees' meeting at this moment, but I should like to put a suggestion to all prees, just the same."

"What is it?" The question came from seven people at once.

"That we co-opt the rest of Lower Sixth for this affair. Look!" she went on eagerly. "It's nearly the end of this term. There's one more to go, and then where shall *we* all be? Most of us at St. Mildred's, I know; but the others are leaving school altogether. So how about starting the non-prefects in

VIb by bringing them in on this? It ought to be a help to them when they have to step into our shoes, you know. And they can probably help us by making suggestions about how to deal with those young demons."

Mary-Lou pursed up her mouth. "Can we do it without going to the Abbess first, do you think?"

"I think we can," Vi put in. "Oh, I expect we'll have to let her know all about it later—off the record, of course."

"OK then. Seeing you're all here, find chairs and sit round the table and let's get to business. You folk will have to get seats from other rooms. I don't think we've anything like enough to seat all of you."

There was a bustle, and, ten minutes later, they were all crowded round the table with the non-prefects from VIb looking extra portentous at this unexpected responsibility that had been thrust on them.

"Well," Mary-Lou said, rising when they were all ready, "there's no need to explain why we're having this meeting. You all know the reason, so I think we'd better set to work at once and discover how we can best deal with it. The meeting is open for discussion." Then she sat down and looked round them expectantly.

Prunella got up at once—with some difficulty, they were sitting so close together. "I don't think we need bother about either of the Upper IV forms," she said. "I've had an eye on them, and I honestly don't think they know a thing about it."

"I think you're right there," Mary-Lou agreed. "It's the Lowers we have to consider—especially that gang that Ailie Russell leads."

"If Ailie and Judy are in it, Janice certainly will be," Barbara said gloomily. "Those three always hunt together."

"What a little ass she is!" her cousin Vi remarked frankly. "Didn't Uncle Peter say that if she got into any more major rows here he'd take her away and send her back to Carnbach for another year?"

"He did—and I shouldn't be sorry, either!" Barbara said fervently. "Mummy would be furious with her if that happened, and so would Beth. Bethy always says she had a fairly blameless record at school, and I haven't done anything very bad. If young Jan spoils our record, she'll get it in the neck on all sides. And the worst of it is Daddy seems to think I ought to keep more of an eye on her! As if *I* could stop her behaving like an imp of darkness!"

"Order—order!" Mary-Lou cried. "Just confine yourselves to the business in hand, please."

Hilary stood up. "I should like to propose, Madam Chairman, that we call a meeting of those two forms and ask them who was responsible for the latest."

"I'll second that!" Lesley Malcolm cried.

"There's one blessing!" Hilda Jukes said. "They won't try to lie about it. They're imps of the first water, but they *are* honest."

"How are you going to deal with them when you've found out who it is?" Naomi asked suddenly.

Mary-Lou turned to her quickly. "I don't think any of us have got that far. Have you any ideas, Naomi? If so, for goodness sake trot them out! Lines won't meet the case, nor black marks, either. And I don't want to fine them if it can be helped. Besides," she added frankly, "I'd rather like to make the punishment fit the crime if we possibly can."

Naomi flushed. "I've got an idea, but it mightn't work."

"Tell us what it is," Vi urged. "Quite likely it's just the thing. Go ahead, Naomi! We're all waiting."

Naomi went pinker than ever. "I'll tell you; but if you think it's mad, mind you say so. I shan't mind. Only what Mary-Lou said about making the punishment fit the crime—well, I rather think it *might*."

"Oh, go on!" Clare implored. "You're working us all up by this mystery. What *is* your idea?"

Naomi spoke then for a space of five minutes. When she stopped, everyone else clapped loud and long.

"It's a honey!" Hilary exclaimed. "As you say, it does, exactly, fit the crime, and they'll simply loathe doing it. Besides, everyone concerned will tell them their exact opinion of them—including our noble selves. And that reminds me. We all claimed our own things, didn't we? We'll have to put them back again."

"What? But I can't do without my pen or my biro!" Mary-Lou cried.

"Well put one back, then. But they've got to have something for each of us or we shan't get *our* chance. Believe me, I'm looking forward to it. Just let me once get my claws into those little whatnots and they'll be sorry they ever were born!"

In the end it was decided that every single member of the two Sixths must put something on the tray. When that was done, the bell rang for bed, and they hurriedly set the room to rights before they all trooped off to the dormitories.

Naomi, limping along, was overtaken by Clare and Jessica Wayne.

"You really are a genius, Naomi!" Jessica declared. "I'll bet anything you like that once this business is over that gang will be as meek as Moses for the rest of the term!"

Naomi blushed and then laughed. "I hope so, I'm sure. But there's no genius about it, Jessica. I only thought what I should most hate myself if I were in their shoes and that came like a flash."

They had reached the dormitory then, so she said good-night as Clare and Jessica were in another. But as she slowly undressed and got ready for bed, she realised that she was beginning to feel one with the others—something she had not done for a good many years now. Mary-Lou's straight talk had started her off on a new path. This business of the Juniors looked like being a long step forward.

"I was mad about my cards," she thought when she was finally in bed, "but now I'm not so sure I don't feel like blessing those imps. And—and I'll do as Mary-Lou wants.

I'll ask Dr. Maynard if he thinks anything can be done about me. And—and . . . ."

But here she suddenly stopped thinking, and acted. Very solemnly she prayed with all her heart that this new happiness which seemed to be coming to her might help her for the future to be like other girls in some things if not all.

Chapter 14

NEMESIS ARRIVES

"MAY you have the two Lower Fourths for inquisition immediately after Kaffee und Kuchen this afternoon?" Miss Annersley sat up in her big armchair and eyed her Head Girl with interest. "What have those young monkeys been doing now?"

"I'd rather not say, if you don't mind, please," Mary-Lou replied, standing very tall and upright in her winter evening frock of deep blue velveteen.

"And why not, pray?" But there was an amused look in the keen blue-grey eyes surveying the girl.

"Because it's something we feel it might be better to handle ourselves. You see," Mary-Lou continued with the stunning frankness they had all come to expect from her, but which still could take away the breath of the person treated to it, "if we hand it over to you, you'll feel bound to take notice of it, and—well—well—the St. Mildred pantomime is awfully close at hand."

"I see." Miss Annersley smiled. "Are you sure it's something you can deal with yourselves quite adequately?"

"Oh, *yes*!" Mary-Lou replied with such fervour that the Head broke into a peal of laughter. "I promise you they'll think a hundred times before they embark on such doings again."

Miss Annersley recovered herself. "That sounds portentous! Very well, Mary-Lou. I'll be quite pleased to be saved from pronouncing any very heavy judgments at this late date. You may have them. By the way, it's nothing really *bad*?"

Mary-Lou grinned. "Not bad—merely mischief and unheard-of cheek!"

"Then in that case, by all means settle it yourselves. But don't forget I shall expect to hear the whole story when it's all over—off the record, of course."

Mary-Lou chuckled. "Oh, you shall—you certainly shall! It would be much too good to keep from you in those conditions. Anyhow, Auntie Joey is to hear of it. She hasn't been feeling awfully well this last week or two, Len tells me, and she loves to hear any *startling* school news. I'm going to tea with her on Sunday, you remember, and I hope to give her the whole yarn then. I know perfectly well that she'll spill the beans to you sooner or later—er—I mean tell you." She amended her sentence in some confusion. "But it *will* be off the record, won't it? I mean, we don't want to mess up their reports."

"Off the record," the Head promised solemnly, her eyes dancing. "And while I think of it, be a little more careful of your language, please. You can't very well pull up the younger girls for slang if you are perpetually using it yourself."

"No; it would be a case of Satan rebuking Satan, I supose," Mary-Lou said cheerfully. "I'll be careful—we all are in public. Thank you, Miss Annersley. I'd better go now. The gong will sound for Kaffee und Kuchen in three minutes, and I'm on urn duty this afternoon."

"Off you go, then. Come along here after the Middles have gone to bed—all of you, I mean—and let me know the latest. I'll have coffee and biscuits."

"Oh, thank you; that will be gorgeous. I'll tell the rest." Mary-Lou turned to leave the room, but before she had reached the door she was called back.

"Oh—one moment, Mary-Lou! While you're about it, you might improve the occasion with a few remarks on general tidiness. Quite half Vb turned up at my lesson this morning minus either writing materials or textbooks. If it wasn't one thing, it was another. I'm not going to pass that sort of thing, and it might come better from you prefects than me. See to it, please."

Mary-Lou reddened, rather to the Head's surprise. "I'll see to it," she promised hurriedly before she bobbed her curtsey and made good her escape.

"Whew! That was a near touch!" she thought as she hurried along to the main building where the Speisesaal was. "Hope I didn't give anything away by going red in that idiotic way. The Abbess is always so appallingly on the spot!"

She entered the Speisesaal where Clare, Verity and Hilary were already busy at the big urns, filling the long rows of cups with steaming coffee. She nodded to them as she entered, and went to take her place at the remaining one.

"The Head has agreed?" Verity asked eagerly.

"Oh, yes; but we knew she would. She's always reasonable. The only thing is, she insists on hearing all about it off the record. We're all to go and have coffee and biscuits with her after the Middles' bedtime. But she did give me rather a jolt as I was coming out. She asked me to say something about tidiness. Half Vb had to turn up at her lesson minus their belongings. I couldn't explain then, of course, so it looked like being rather awkward."

"What did you do?" Hilary demanded.

"Told her I'd see to it, and *ran*. There goes the gong! This subject must now drop!" And she turned her back on the others, and applied herself to filling the empty cups at top speed.

Unaware of the excitement that awaited them, the school filed in, marched up to their appointed urns to take their cups, and went to their places at table. The prefects finished their job, carried off their own cups, and sat down to enjoy rolls and butter, fancy bread-twists and buns.

"What exactly did the Head say?" Vi asked when the meal was well begun and everyone else was far too busy to pay much heed to the prefects.

"Oh, asked if I was sure we could deal adequately with the situation. I said we could, and she said she wasn't sorry as she didn't want to have to administer any heavy justice at this late date."

"Trust her!" Vi said in a tone full of affection. "There isn't much that she misses, is there? Well, you did say we must tell Auntie Joey the whole yarn when we went to tea with her on Sunday, and if she knows, it won't be long before the Abbess and Bill know, so I suppose they may as well hear it firsthand from us."

"When are you going to warn the little wretches?" Doris asked.

"As soon as this is over. I don't want to spoil their meal. They'll need all the support they can get from it!" Mary-Lou chuckled.

"I'm sorry for them from the bottom of my heart," Clare observed, looking her saintliest. "Mind you rub it well in! We don't want any more bothers of this kind next term. I don't suppose they'll feel like anything but behaving themselves for the rest of *this*, once they've finished."

"Don't worry! I'll see to that, all right!" Mary-Lou said grimly.

The meal was not quite ended when she sipped the last of her coffee, put down her cup, and rose to clap her hands for attention. The buzz of chatter and laughter died down at once, and everyone turned to look at the prefects' table, most of them with surprise.

"All girls from Lower IVa and b will remain behind after the tables are cleared," the Head Girl said, her clear, bell-like voice carrying to every corner of the room. "The rest of you, when you are finished, please hurry with the clearing and leave the room at once. That is all." She sat down again and shot a smile round the table, receiving answering smiles from everyone.

The greater part of the school remained silent for a moment or two from sheer surprise. Then the clatter began again. Only at the tables where the two Lower Fourths were congregated was there a marked lack of noise. One or two of the girls wondered aloud what Mary-Lou wanted with them; but several people looked suddenly blue and there were appetites to seek amongst them. In fact, it was noted then, and remarked on later, that Ailie Russell and her two satellites stopped eating, and Ailie would even have left half her bun on her plate if the Senior in charge had not reminded her of it.

"Eat your bun, Ailie," Rosamund Lilley said firmly. "And what have you people been doing now, I should like to know?"

She got no reply; she had hardly expected one, and had turned at once to continue with the light gossip she had been exchanging with her friend, Jo Scott. But Ailie looked like a thundercloud as she choked down her remnant of unwanted bun.

Judy Willoughby, seated next to her, nudged her. "Ailie! Do you think—"

"Oh, shut *up*! But I'd like to know how they got on to us. Who's squeaked?"

"No one has," said Janice Chester, a leggy eleven-year-old with straight black hair dropping in pigtails over either shoulder. "I *warned* you Mary-Lou would be on to us at once, and you said she wouldn't. Well, I was right!"

Ailie flushed angrily. "You always are, aren't you, Miss Knowall? I notice your ideas didn't keep you out of the fun, all the same."

Janice looked both hurt and surprised. "What did you expect? You two were in it, and when you *would* go on, I couldn't very well stand out against you all by myself, could I? We're *pals*!"

"Oh, well," Judy put in with some idea of smoothing things over, "it was a good joke on them, anyhow! I'll bet Vi got a shock when she opened Lost Property door!" She suddenly giggled. "The whole lot must have collapsed on her at once. It was all we could do to keep it in while we locked the door. I only wish I had been there to see it!"

Ailie's face lightened as she thought of that picture. "It must have been awfully funny," she admitted; and swallowed the last bite of bun.

All the same, they were not really sorry when Kaffee und Kuchen came to an end, and the rest, scurrying under the stern eyes of both Sixths, cleared the tables and then fled to make the most of the interval between the meal and preparation.

The two Lower Fourths had obediently gone back to their tables and sat down again. When the last of the other girls had left the Speisesaal, carefully closing the door behind her, Mary-Lou moved to the high table where the staff usually sat. They all eyed her apprehensively, even those whose consciences were fairly clear at the moment. *What* was going to happen?

She stood looking at them in silence with a pitying smile on her lips. The horrid pause lasted fully two minutes, by which time Ailie, at least, was on the verge of bursting into a wild yell. Then the Head Girl spoke.

"Which of you," she asked sweetly, "was responsible for cramming everything into Lost Property?"

Silence! Then Ailie gave a gulp that was little short of a whoop, and scrambled to her feet. At once her two main supporters got to theirs. From round the two tables sundry other people rose here and there until seven Junior Middles were finally standing, all with a hangdog expression which made Mary-Lou and some of the others bite their lips.

The Head Girl waited until it was clear that no one else was going to join the throng. Then she turned a piercing look on Ailie, whom she shrewdly guessed to have been the ring leader. "Is this all, Aline?" she asked.

The use of her full Christian name floored Ailie completely. "I—I think so!" she gasped.

"Don't you *know*?" Mary-Lou demanded.

"I—yes; it is," Ailie muttered.

Judy, not quite so upset, lifted up her voice. "I'm not *quite* sure that Janice ought to stand up, Mary-Lou," she said. "She didn't want us to do it one bit, and did all she knew to stop us. She said . . . ."

At this point the Head Girl looked straight at her with steely eyes, and she found herself finishing with an incoherent mutter, so none of the Sixth ever knew what it was that Janice had said. Mary-Lou continued to look until the young lady's head drooped and her long lashes swept her crimson cheeks. As for Janice, she opened her mouth to speak, and then thought better of it and closed it again.

Mary-Lou continued with her gaze for a full thirty seconds. Then she transferred it to the sitting girls. "In that case, as you folk have nothing to do with all this, you may go. Go quietly, please. Josette, you might see them through the corridors, if you will. You, too, Barbara. They are to go to their common room and stay there until the bell rings for prep. You two had better remain with them, I think, until whoever is in charge comes along. Do you mind?"

Thankful to be out of it, the two elder sisters got up and went to usher the major part of the two forms to their common room. As she went past the Lower IVa table, Josette deliberately turned on her small sister a look that almost literally froze that young woman. Barbara simply stalked past Janice without looking at her, and Janice was nearly reduced to tears. Mary-Lou waited until the party had gone. Then she turned her attention to the seven culprits.

"Come and stand up here—before the table," she said. "At once, please!"

There was the crack of a whip in her last words which made the seven hurriedly shuffle out of their places and come to stand in a straight line before the high table. Not one lifted her eyes, and when they got there they twisted their fingers madly together, shuffled their feet, and Janice, who was addicted in moments of stress to standing on one leg and rubbing the instep of the other foot up and down it, nearly overbalanced in her agitation. A more guilty-looking set of girls it would have been hard to find.

Mary-Lou did not spare them. "Well?" she said sharply. "What have you to say for yourselves?"

No one spoke, not even Judy the audacious. As that young person said later, it mightn't have been so bad if it had been only Mary-Lou or even just the prefects. But to have the whole of both Sixths sitting there, staring at them as if they were toads or slugs or adders simply didn't give you a chance to think of a thing you could say!

Hilary took a hand now. "You set of *crawling* insects!" she said—and the sinners cringed before her wrath—"how dared you do such a thing?"

"Yes," Vi cried. "And how dared you go to my drawers and rifle them for the key? Of all the disgusting, dishonourable, dishonest things to do! Janice, I'm ashamed to think you are my cousin!"

At this diatribe, Janice found her voice—the only one to do it just then, for the rest merely tried to make themselves as small as possible and wished the floor would open and swallow them up.

"We didn't, Vi! We *never* did!" she cried indignantly. "We wouldn't do such a horrid thing!"

"Indeed? I am glad to know that even *you* seem to have your limits," Vi told her with such an edge to her voice, that her small cousin only just escaped bursting into tears on the spot.

Mary-Lou had been looking at them with an expression of mild curiosity that hurt when any of them ventured to glance up and see it. "Then how *did* you get the cupboard open?" she inquired. "I'm sorry to seem so unbelieving, but if you didn't go to Vi's drawers and help yourselves to her key, how did you manage? I'm only asking for information," she added kindly.

They could have done without her kindness. Every word she said brought home to them the enormity of their conduct and they didn't dare to think what might follow when sentence was pronounced. Janice gulped loudly, and Ailie only kept the tears back by blinking hard, gripping her fingers together until they hurt, and swallowing.

The information came from another member of the party, Tessa de Bersac, a French girl, and daughter of one of Joey Maynard's closest friends, once Simone Lecoutier of earlier annals of the school. In her agitation she forgot that it was an "English" day, and spoke in French. Mary-Lou cut her short.

"Repeat what you said in English, Tessa," Mary-Lou said severely.

Thus urged, Tessa stammered, "Mais—I only said—I said—th-that we were *not* dishonourable and—and we d-did not t-touch Vi's d-d-drawers." After which she burst into tears and wept loudly.

"Stop that!" Mary-Lou said very quietly, but with something in her tone that made the emotional Tessa gulp loudly and, producing a handkerchief that had seen distinctly better days, mop her eyes fiercely.

The bell rang for preparation, but no one took any notice of it. The Middles were far too overcome to heed anything but their own particular trouble, and the prefects were determined to finish up this business before they dismissed the seven.

Mary-Lou was silent while it was ringing. When it was dumb and the sounds of hurrying footsteps had died away, she returned to the charge once more.

"If you did *not* steal Vi's key," she said—and oh, how the

polite scepticism in her voice hurt!—"may I ask how you managed to get the door open?"

Ailie pulled herself together. "The—the key of the cupboard in our form room fits," she muttered, not daring to meet the Head Girl's eyes.

Mary-Lou gasped. This was something of which she had *not* thought. However, she recovered herself instantly. "I see. In that case, I must ask Matron to have the lock of your cupboard changed at once. We can scarcely trust you again."

The seven were all darkly crimson, but none of them ventured to say anything. She allowed her final remark to sink in. Then, after a quick look round her colleagues, she pronounced sentence.

"You are silly, empty-headed little girls. When you planned your great joke, you didn't even stop to think that if you got a Head's Report for this affair, it would mean that you would miss the pantomime."

She stopped there as seven separate gasps of horror answered this. They had *not* thought of it. In fact, they had forgotten all about the pantomime. Surely, this was not to be their fate?

"It would serve you all right if we *did* give you Reports, especially as you had the impudence to go to other people's desks and lockers and pegs and help yourselves from them!" Hilary interjected. "How Tessa can say that you are not dishonourable is more than I can say!"

They flinched before her righteous anger. One or two were clearly on the verge of tears and Mary-Lou decided that she might as well finish it up.

"We are not giving you Head's Reports," she said curtly. "Instead, we have decided that the best thing to do will be to see that you undo, as far as possible, the annoyance and inconvenience you have caused other people. First, your pocket money for the rest of the term will be confiscated to pay for the fines other people would have had to pay if all this had not been found out so soon."

"B-but . . . b-but . . ." stammered Judy, the only one of the seven with enough self-possession left to make any sort of reply to this horrid judgment.

'Be quiet, please. You have nothing to do but listen to what we have decided," Mary-Lou said severely. "I have not finished yet. Besides losing your pocket money, you will take all the things to which you helped yourselves and you will return them to their owners, apologising to each girl at the same time. I don't know just how you will explain yourselves," she added sweetly. "That is for you to consider. But that is what you will do. Furthermore, as soon as your prep is over, you will begin at once. Every single article has to be returned to its rightful owner before you go to bed tonight. If it makes you late, you can explain to Matron just *why* you are late. That is all."

She sat down and the appalled septette began slowly to realise the full awfulness of their punishment. Meanwhile, Vi and Doris had left the room quitely. They returned at this moment with the wicker tray piled high with all the oddments the giddy crew had thought it such fun to put into Lost Property. They could see no fun in it now.

Something snapped in Ailie at the sight. "We won't do it!" she exclaimed. "You've no right to try and make us—"

"We have *every* right," Lesley Bethune interrupted her. "Anyhow, it's that or a Head's Report."

"And be quick and make up your minds which it's to be," Prunella added. "*We* have work to do if *you* haven't. You've wasted quite enough of our time as it is with your silly ongoings!"

There would be no choice, of course, in spite of Ailie's outburst. Not one of them would willingly have missed the pantomime, not to mention all the other dreadful penalties attached to a Report. The seven began to weep like waterspouts. Not that it got them anything but an admonition to stop at once and go and make the best use they could of what was left of their prep time.

"We'll carry this thing to Lower IVa for you," Mary-Lou said. "As soon as the bell goes for the end of prep, you may begin at once to sort it out and return the things. One of us will come and oversee the sorting for you. And remember! you are to apologise fully and properly to every one you have victimised."

Judy mopped her eyes and raised a timid hand. "Please, Mary-Lou, what does 'victimise' mean?" she asked.

Mary-Lou nearly choked with sudden laughter. She had forgotten Judy's passion for new words. However, she made a wild clutch at her vanishing gravity and replied stonily, "'made a victim of'. Now go and wash your faces and then straight to prep. You've less than half-an-hour left," she added.

They fled in short order. But the less said about their work that evening the better. Every single one of them found herself with at least one returned lesson next day and most of them with the lot. Apart from that, Janice and Ailie had to face the wrath of elder sisters who did not spare their tongues when they got them alone. All the same, every single article had been returned to its owner by bedtime, though the work kept them going until the bell rang and, in fact, three of them would have been in trouble with Matron for coming upstairs late if that lady had not been on the telephone for ten minutes after they were due in their cubicles. They had to make the apologies and quite a number of people told them exactly what they thought of them before they let them go. However, the nastiest part of their punishment was over when the last handkerchief had been claimed. After that, it seemed to matter very little that they must be penniless for the last fortnight or more of term. But it is on record that never again did the seven play such a joke. The results of the first had been too awful!

Chapter 15

The Unexpected

"WELL," Joey Maynard said as she sat down in the most comfortable chair in Miss Annersley's pretty drawing-room, "I only hope that's going to be the last."

"The last of what?" Miss Wilson queried, bringing her a cup of coffee.

"The last of our trials, of course. Goodness knows, this term has been chock-a-block with them. I don't know about you folk, but I'm at the stage where I'd like to lie back and take life easily for the next few weeks. What with scarlet fever and avalanches—"

"There was only *one* of that!" Nancy Wilmot pointed out.

"One too many, if you ask me. And don't interrupt. It's most horribly rude!"

"Poor old Joey!" Nancy said, laughing. "It *has* taken you badly! Never mind, though. I don't see what can go wrong in the last week or two of this term which, I don't mind owning, has been more than the outside of enough! About everything that could go wrong has done it. But there's only the St. Mildred's pantomime left, and that, thank goodness, is not our affair."

"No; but it's ours," Miss Wilson reminded her.

"True for you. By the way, are you going to let us into the secret of how you are going to manage when you have to provide the entire cast?"

"Not I! You may wait for the night. It will," Miss Wilson said very primly, "be a good exercise in patience for all of you."

"Isn't she maddening?" Joey murmured. "I vote we change the subject. What's the news of Rosalie? She hasn't done much about letter-writing since she went."

"Oh, she's completely cured now. I had a letter from Evvy yesterday," Peggy Burnett said. "Rosalie has regained all her old colour and weight and is eating well and sleeping well, and looks a different creature from the washed-out object she took away with her. They're coming back for the panto, they hope."

Nancy Wilmot looked up from her knitting. "I had a letter, too, and if you ask me, I should say something's been happening. Evvy was—well—*mysterious*."

"In what way?" Joey sat up and looked interested.

"I couldn't tell you. It was more what she said than what she didn't."

Joey chuckled. "If Evvy's taken to being mysterious, wild horses won't drag any sense out of her. I know that much."

The pantomime was always a matinee for the sake of those folk who might not be out-of-doors, once night had fallen. St. Luke's Hall stood at the gates of the great Sanatorium of which Jack Maynard was head, and quite a number of people from the villages round made the trip to enjoy the girls' production. All the Seniors had volunteered to act as usherettes, sell programmes and see to the refreshments they always had during the intervals. Apart from them, of the school proper, only members of the orchestra were taking part this year, thanks to the scarlet fever outbreak. St. Mildred's had had to revise all their plans in a hurry and handle everything else for themselves. They had gone about with pleased smirks for the past three weeks, and, which maddened the rest more than anything else, there was no getting any information out of the orchestra. As a result, the school at large was on tiptoe with expectation, and when, at last, they set off they were all wild with excitement.

Arrived at the hall, those helping in the front of the house departed to get their orders and the rest filed into their places, pulled off berets and coats and waited impatiently for their programmes. They were wildly curious by this time to know how St. Mildred's had contrived to manage without their help. A concerted groan arose when they found that the cunning "Millies" had merely listed the names of the characters without saying who was playing what.

"Cheatery!" cried Hilary, surveying the list with disgust.

"I wonder just who they've roped in to help?" Mary-Lou said thoughtfully.

"I don't see who they *could* get," Vi chimed in. "Well, we'll just have to hold our horses till the curtain goes up, I suppose." Then Joey came sailing down the aisle with her small Cecil in her arms and the twins trotting gaily in front of her. The girls gave it up, and turned to welcome her joyfully.

"Where are you sitting, Auntie Jo?" Josette demanded.

"Cecil and I are going to sit at the back with the staff just in case she demands to be taken out," Joey explained. "I'm leaving the twins in front of you folk, and you can keep an eye on them among you." She turned to the pair. "In you go, in front of Josette and—Naomi, isn't it? It's not like me not to know the new girls, Naomi, but this has been such a term, there hasn't been a single chance for you to come over to Freudesheim. However, we can alter that next term. Now, twins, listen to me a moment. Felix, you are *not* to talk while the play is going on. Save up your remarks for the intervals, please. Felicity, if you want to go out, wait till then, also, and then ask Josette to take you."

The milk-fair twins nodded solemnly, and promised that they would be good.

"Can I have my sweeties, please?" Felix demanded.

"Here you are." Joey put a bag into his fat hands, and gave one to Felicity. "Marshmallows for my girl and toffees for you, Felix." She turned to the girls. "Please, all of you, don't offer them any of yours. They have enough, and I don't want to spend the night attending to bilious babes! They may each have an ice in the first interval, but that's all. See to it,

Josette, will you?" She cast a somewhat harassed look at her twins, and then retired with Cecil to seek her own seat beside the Head.

"Give me Cecil," that lady said. "How she is growing! Quite a big girl for two! And Con's miniature!"

"Yes, isn't she?" Joey agreed, handing her over and sitting down. "Con's fearfully proud of that. She and Cecil are the only really dark members of my family so far. Now let me see this programme we've heard so much about." She laughed as she opened it, and looked mischievous. "The girls haven't a clue, you know! I heard them when I parked the twins just now."

Miss Annersley laughed, too. "Don't I know it! They're all bursting to know what it means and no one would give them a hint."

She got no further, for at that moment, a slim, very elegant young woman came down the side aisle to stop and gaze round, and then pause beside Joey with the remark, "Hi, Joey! I guess you didn't think we'd make it, but here we are—or here I am! Rosalie's 'way off talking to half a dozen folk, so I said I'd come and find our seats. Bill sent me the tickets in case we could do it."

"Where *are* you sitting? Row and number?"

Evadne glanced at the counterfoils in her hand, and looked at the rows. "Here, just on the other side of the aisle. Goody! I hoped it would be near you."

Joey laughed. "Trust Bill!—Hilda! See who's turned up! Evvy, no less—and she says Rosalie's here, too. And Evvy, Carla's behind—look! A real gathering of the clans, isn't it? Carla, you remember Evvy Lannis, of course!"

"But how could I forget?" Carla asked. "At least I could never forget the band she and Corney Flower got up. Oh, Joey, *do* you remember the concert they gave us?"

"Do I not! I laughed till I was nearly sick!" Joey gave a deep chuckle at the memory. "And they had the nerve to call on me for a solo! I suppose, Evvy, you are aware that if it hadn't been for where it was I'd have broken your necks?"

Evadne smiled complacently. "But you couldn't. We were safe enough, and we knew it. Say, Joey, I've something to show you and some news for you."

"Oh? What is it? Nice news, I hope. We've had all the horrors we want for one term."

"Very nice, thank you." Evadne looked round but no one was bothering with them at the moment. The Head was standing up to make sure that her flock were all safe, and Carla had turned to reply to a remark made to her by her next-door neighbour. Miss Lannis gave a gulp, and then thrust her left hand into Joey's lap. "Joey—look!"

Joey glanced up at her face. It wore an expression of modest pride mingled with shyness in a way that Joey, in all the years she had known Evadne, had never before seen on her face. Then she looked down at the slim hand with the diamonds flashing on the fourth finger.

"Evvy! You're engaged! Oh, I'm so glad, so very glad! Who is he? When did it happen? Tell me everything at once!"

Evadne withdrew her hand and sat down in her seat, and a little party of somewhat indignant people swept past them to find seats near the front.

"I was blocking the gangway. I knew you'd be glad, Joey."

Another bunch went past, and then Joey reiterated her demand to be told who the gentleman was. "Who is it, Evvy? You'll be Mrs—?"

"Not 'Mrs' anything!" Evadne retorted, her own woman again, now that Joey knew. "Believe it or not, Joey, I'm going to be a *Lady*!"

"If you're not already a lady," Joey said scathingly, "I'm afraid there's not much hope for you at this late date." Then her tone changed. "Lady—who?"

"He's Sir Edgar Watson and I'll be Lady Watson. He farms. And say, Joey! I'll be a stepmother! He's a widower—his first wife died seven years ago—and I'm stepping right into a ready-made family."

For a minute Joey stared at her, literally too stunned to speak. Then her golden laughter rang out. "Oh, Evvy! Not really? Well, I hope you'll be a kind stepmother to your stepchildren—or is it only one?"

"It's three—a boy and two girls. I've known him quite a while, you know—three years. We've been good friends for more than a year now, but things were only settled properly last week. And what do you mean—be a kind stepmother! I love the children dearly already. Ned—he's Edgar, after his father—is a fine boy—just twelve. And Thea and Marcia are sugarpies, both of them."

"When's the wedding to be?" Joey demanded, then added in a different tone, "Hallo! Here comes the orchestra. We'll have to pipe down now, but the first minute there is, I must hear every last detail." Then she chuckled softly while the orchestra took its places.

"What's the joke?" Evadne asked suspiciously.

"None! I was only thinking—what a thrill the school will get when they hear the very latest! Here comes Plato to conduct so we *must* dry up! But just you wait! I'm hearing everything or *else*. . . ."

With this ferocious threat, she turned to the stage as the houselights died and the footlights sprang up. The orchestra swept into a gay overture, based on the tunes of old nursery rhymes, and Evadne had to sit back and wait for the interval before they could continue their conversation.

Chapter 16

"PUSS-IN-BOOTS"

THE overture ended and when Mr. Denny had bowed in return for the storm of applause that greeted the final chord, he swung round, tapped his desk with his baton and the orchestra swept into a jolly tune which the school, at least, had no difficulty in recognising as the old Morris dance tune, *Country Gardens*. The curtain swung back to show "The Village Green" with quite a throng of people on the stage, dancing the gay old dance and singing—with some help from the wings:

"Come, come to dancing, turning and prancing!
Come to our May Day with song and shout!
Laughter is ringing, all voices singing!
Join, join our courtiers in merry rout!
Here is our May Queen,
Fair by the day seen.
But by moonlight still fairer to see.
When night is falling and owls are calling
None in the land can be fairer than she!"

"I only wish I could hear the Abbess on the subject of *that* doggerel!" Mary-Lou whispered to Vi with a low chuckle. "Who on earth was responsible for it?"

"Betsy—she told me so last Sunday," Vi murmured back. "I must say it *is* rather ghastly. Writing verse isn't one of Betsy's gifts!"

"You," said Mary-Lou with emphasis, "are telling me! I'm surprised at her!"

Then the dance came to an end. The villagers whirled away from the centre of the stage to fall into picturesque groups at either side of the flower-decked chair on which sat Felicity King, a very pretty girl and prettier than ever in her May Queen's attire. Behind her stood a tall youth in baggy breeches and smock frock.

When the music died away, Felicity rose and thanked the villagers for their homage in a speech as flowery as her seat. The villagers cheered and then, from the wings, came a queer figure in Georgian attire of black, a barrister's wig a size too large, judging by his antics with it, on his head. Perched on top of the wig, was a tricorne hat and between the two, *The Lawyer* was so hot and bothered, it was a miracle that he remembered his lines.

At sight of him, however, there came a great round of clapping from the girls, for in him they recognised an old friend, Nancy Canton, who had left school the same term as it left at St. Briavel's and whom few of them had heard much of since. Above the storm of applause, Maeve Bettany's voice rose in a shriek of, "Nancy—Nancy Canton! Oh, scrummy!" which, as her own gang did not fail to tell her later, was most undignified in a girl from Va who had every reason to suppose that the next year would find her in VIb and, in all probability, a prefect!

Poor Nancy stopped dead in her progress and turned richly purple under her make-up. Then she clutched at her self-control, while the staff, scattered about among the school, hurriedly "shushed" the people nearest. The noise died down and the pantomime continued.

The tall youth came to meet this gentleman, bowing to him and saying, "Good morrow, Master Graball. I take it you are come to tell us what was my poor father's wishes with regard to his property. Pray seat yourself on this log and I will hasten to summon my brothers."

"Do so!" said the lawyer in an unexpectedly deep bass voice—Nancy was on the verge of wild giggles—as he scanned the property-log carefully with the aid of an enormous pair of spectacles he suddenly produced from a tail pocket and balanced on his nose, almost to the upsetting of his head-gear.

The school began to titter and the titter rose to shrieks of laughter as he picked up the tails and dusted the log with them before seating himself. "Pray return yourself if you are, as I think, one of the sons of my late lamented friend, Matthew the Miller. I recognise his nose in your face."

Fresh laughter from the audience while the young man bowed, replying, "I am Richard, his second son, commonly known as Dickon."

"Ah, quite so! Then there should be . . ." *The Lawyer* opened the enormous portfolio he carried under his arm, sorted out two or three sheets of paper of equal size and continued, "your elder brother Simon and the younger, John."

Dickon bowed again and darted off, while *The Lawyer* hotched about uncomfortably on his log in a way that caused Miss Wilson to mutter to Mlle de Lachenais sitting at her right hand, "If Nancy squirms about much more, she'll have that unfortunate log in smithereens!"

However, *Dickon* arrived before that happened, followed by *Simon* and *John*. There were no surprises here. *John* was played by tall Blossom Willoughby who made a delightful Principal Boy with her curly bob of brown hair surmounted by a green cap of the Robin Hood variety, and her lengthy legs clad beneath her green tunic in tan-coloured tights. *Simon* was Ailsa Thompson and she made a delightful contrast to the two younger brothers, for she wore a wig of straggly black locks and beard to match, and was attired in a loose garment of the dressing-gown variety in purple. Her normally pleasant face had, by means of greasepaint and lining-pencil been turned into a sour, pinched-looking one and altogether, she was a most unpleasant-looking customer!

The three young men stood before *The Lawyer* who now produced from his case a document adorned with ribbons and enormous seals as he announced, "I have here your late lamented father's will."

Murmurs rose from the crowd—"Now we'll know all about it!—who's got what, I wonder?—Let's hope it doesn't all come to Simon!—Simon's a sour, mean, nasty creature—John would be the man for my money, etc."

"Well?" *Simon* grated out in a falsetto squeak. "How do things stand, eh? The mill is mine, I take it? I am the eldest son."

The Lawyer gave him a severe look. "Not so fast—not so fast, if you please!" He wrestled again with his spectacles, spread out the sheet of paper and proceeded to announce: "As you surmise, Master Simon, the mill is yours, together with the house and the land whereon both stand. Master Richard, yours is the ass, Milleton, together with his cart and all his harness, feedbags and the whip. Master John, to you, your late father leaves his black cat. Further, he bequeathes jointly to you all the following advice—or perhaps I should say one part is joined. The other is one piece of advice for each.

At this point, the spectacles tumbled off his nose and in bending to scoop them up, he lost his hat. This was an entirely unrehearsed effect and nearly brought the house down. At last he was ready and proceeded to read very impressively: "Lastly, I would wish my three said sons remember that all that glitters is not gold, and that even the finest diamond has to be cut and polished before it can sparkle; wherefore, I bid my son Simon not to be oppressive and money-grubbing; my son Richard to remember that there are more kinds of asses than one and that most of them move faster for a carrot than a whip; my son John to recall the old saying that even a cat may look at a king and why not a princess while he is about it?"

Having read aloud this remarkable Will, *Master Graball* proceeded to remove his glasses before he rolled up the document and held out his hand to *Simon*, demanding, "Six-and-eightpence, if you please!"

Simon grumbled loudly while he fished in each one of eight pockets and finally handed *The Lawyer* a handful of small coins. *Master Graball* carefully counted them over before he dropped them into a pocket, bowed to the brothers, the Court of the *May Queen* and, for good measure, the audience, and then turned round and began to march off. *Simon* rushed after him and caught his arm.

"Hey! Wait a bit! You haven't got my brothers' fees!"

Master Graball released himself with some dignity. "Only the chief legatee pays a fee," he said. "Good morrow to you all!" and left the stage amid loud clapping from the audience, though Vi did murmur that fairytale law seemed rather more than a little cock-eyed!

Simon raved helplessly, claiming two-and-three from each of his brothers as their share of the fee. The villagers all cried shame on him, and the *May Queen* rising from her throne announced that this ended it. Both *Simon* and *Richard* had been courting her but before she would marry such a miser as *Simon*, she would rather beg. She turned to *Dickon*, holding out her hands.

"I'll come with you and Milleton and the cart, Dickon," she said. "And when, between us, you've become a wealthy merchant, we may send our corn to Simon to be ground. Come! Let us go and seek the priest and be wed at once."

With a cry of "A wedding—a wedding!" The Villagers surrounded them and danced round them, singing to the tune of *Haste to the Wedding* another doggerel produced by Betsy Lucy, and the curtain fell on them finally forming a procession with *Dickon* and *John* leading the *May Queen*, followed by the rest while *Simon* stamped about furiously.

The next scene showed "The Mill Kitchen". Enter on the scene *Simon*, still in a towering rage. He kicked a stool out of his way and then tried to kick *The Cat* which slithered out from under him so that he staggered and nearly went headlong, just as *Dickon* and *John* entered, the former somewhat surprisingly leading *The Ass* which wagged its ears alternately, opened its mouth and gave vent to a portentous noise which bore small resemblance to a bray. Then it kicked out neatly with its right back hoof, catching *Simon* with rather more force than was intended so that the "*Ow*! he produced was very realistic. *The Ass* turned its head to look at him with such a wicked air that the audience was convulsed. *Richard* tugged it to the left and *Simon* recovering from the shock rounded on his brothers who were not backward in answering him, so that no one was surprised when he finally ordered them out of the house at once.

"Take your traps and your wretched beasts and GO!" he roared.

"What—*now*?" *Richard* asked with such incredulity in his voice that the audience giggled again. Then he added, "But we haven't had our supper."

"And you'll want it so far as I'm concerned!" *Simon* bellowed. "I've had enough of you! This place is mine and I won't have you in it! And where's the two-and-threepence you each owe me? Hand it out and be quick about it!"

Richard winked and *The Ass* followed suit. "And you've just given us the key of the open road!" its master said. "Oh, no, my fine brother! You can save it out of the supper we haven't had. You've got the mill and the house and a roof over your head and Jack and I must fish for ourselves and I've my wife to find for, too. You can count my share your wedding gift to us—a cheap one enough. Come on, Jacky! Collect your puss and we'll be off! Margery and I are for the city. We can hope to turn a penny there by using Milleton and the cart as carriers. What about you?"

"I'm for the forest," *John* replied. "At least Puss can catch rabbits and birds so we shan't starve there. You go and become a wealthy merchant. As for me—"

"As for you, to judge by what our father said, you stand a good chance of wedding a princess. Come on, Milleton! No carrots for you till you've helped to earn them. Farewell, Brother Simon. We won't forget you. When I'm a rich man maybe I'll invite you to dinner each Sunday, just to make sure you get *one* decent meal in the week."

"And I'll think about having you for a whole day on the Wednesdays," John said impressively. He turned to *The Cat* which came sidling up to him with a ridiculous effect and rubbed its head on his arm. "Good old Puss! You shall catch rabbits and I'll fish for fish for you and we'll do somehow—until that princess comes along, you know."

They made their exit, *Simon* flying after them, bawling, "Hey! I'm coming, too, to see you take naught that's mine!"

"A Wood" was the setting for the next scene, and St. Mildred's had managed well. The log from the first scene was there, and some enormous scarlet toadstools faced it with a great frog squatting on one of them. The frog, incidentally, was papier mâché and the cause of much trouble among the handcraft experts, but he looked very fine now he was done. Music stole out softly and on to the stage tripped a bevy of *Fairies*. It should have been a ballet, but most of the ballet dancers belonged to the school proper, so St. Mildred's had wisely left it to graceful movements and an airy weaving in and out and it was quite as effective as the frog and very pretty. Finally, they fell back to the sides of the stage to reveal a throne—the May Queen's throne, but now veiled in strips of many-coloured art muslin—on which sat the *Fairy Queen*—another Old Girl, Peggy Bettany, who had been in her time a most popular Head Girl. At sight of her, the combined school lost its head and yelled, "*Peggy*!" in concert.

Peggy blushed furiously. Then she rose with great dignity and sang in a charming mezzo-soprano a welcome to the fairy hall. As she finished, *Puss*, who all this time had been lying behind the log, sprang up, ran forward and knelt at her feet.

"A boon, oh, Queen—a boon!" he cried.

"Say on," *The Queen* replied in a voice nearly as silvery as Verity's.

"Grant to me the power to help my master in all things!"

"It is granted if you will pay for it," *The Queen* replied.

"I will pay. He has been good to me—to all. What is the payment?"

"Over yonder in the next country lives a wicked ogre who has vowed that he will wed the daughter of the king and so become ruler of the land. If you and your master can slay him and save the princess from so dreadful a fate, I will give you the powers you seek."

"Mistress, 'tis done!" *Puss* cried. "Give me the words of power and grant to me the gift of speaking in his own tongue that I may advise him."

The Queen raised her hand. Music stole out and the entire chorus sang softly a verse which, as it was made up of the names of all the herbs St. Mildred's could remember or find, sounded like so much gibberish to the audience. Suddenly, the stage was blacked out and when the lights came back, it was to a moonlight effect. The throne had vanished, and curled up beneath the toadstools was *John*, apparently sound asleep. *The Cat* came bounding on and proceeded to rouse him by taking its tail and brushing his face with the end until he sat up, yawning and stretching.

"Hello, Cat!" he said as he got to his feet. "Where have you been?"

"To visit a friend of mine—and yours," *Puss* replied.

John jumped and set the toadstools rocking, whereupon a voice from the wings was distinctly heard by the front rows of the audience to exclaim, "Oh, bother Blossom! I *warned* her not to stand too near!"

"But—but you can talk! *John* exclaimed.

"Certainly, if I wish to do so," *Puss* replied haughtily.

"Then why did you never do it before? Though on the whole, I'm thankful you didn't. That beautiful elder brother of mine would certainly never have let me have you if he had heard you. He would have kicked me out into the world alone and sold you to some circus for every penny he could squeeze out of the proprietor."

"Have no fear!" *Puss* replied. "He would never have heard me. I have not forgotten how he tried to kick me and grudged me even a spoonful of milk when he saw you give it to me from your own mug. Master, you have been good to me ever since you rescued me from the millpool where Simon threw me when I was a kitten. Now it is my turn. Only promise me to do exactly as I say and I will promise you great happiness and fortune."

"I don't see how you can manage that. We shan't make much of a fortune, even if we sell every rabbit you catch. As for happiness; wealth doesn't mean that always."

Puss squatted down before him. "Tell me, Master, what makes happiness?"

The orchestra was quick on its cue. It broke into a lilting air and *John* sang a charming song with which Betsy Lucy had had nothing to do, in which he declared that happiness lay in love and love only.

When he had finished, *Puss* said, "I can promise you love as well as wealth. Only promise to do as I ask."

"Very well. I promise. What is your first wish, Puss?"

"Go into the town at the further end of this wood and buy me a pair of boots."

"*Boots?*" *John* goggled at him. "Oh, very well. Anything else? I have precious little money, you know, and we've got to find food and a bed yet."

"Bring me the boots and a large bag with a draw-string and leave the rest to me," *Puss* returned.

"You're the boss," *John* responded slangily. "I shan't be long."

He made his exit and then *The Ass* rather unexpectedly turned up and the pair proceeded to perform a burlesque of the Fan Gavotte which nearly brought the house down. Then

The Ass clattered off as *John* arrived with a pair of top-boots in one hand and an enormous sack in the other. He handed them to *Puss* who sat on the log, tugged on the boots and then, throwing the sack over his shoulder, walked off calling, "Wait here, Master. I shall be back ere long."

John turned to stare after him, scratching his head in a bewildered fashion before he sat on the log with great caution and proceeded to warble a ballad about a fair maiden behind a hedge who met a poor shepherd. They fell in love, but, it seemed in vain until her swain flung off his disguise and stood revealed as the lord of the manor. By the time it was finished, *Puss* came bounding in to throw a small jingling bag at his master's feet.

"Lo, Master," he said, "I caught six hares in my sack and took them to the palace in the next country where the head cook bought them for five crowns. Now we shall fare well. Furthermore, the next I catch shall be a gift to the king himself from the Marquis of Carrabas."

"From who?" *John* demanded.

"From you, Master. That is your title. Ere long, you shall own a castle and broad lands and have many servants and labourers to till your lands. But do as I say and all will be yours—even the love you so greatly desire. But we must not tarry here. By dawn tomorrow, we must have entered the next country where all awaits you. Come, let us set forth. When we are there, we have to kill an ogre, you and I."

"Kill a what?" *John* gasped.

"An ogre, Master, that means to marry the king's only daughter, a damsel as fair as the day and as good as she is beautiful. Would you not dare everything to save such a lady from so fearful a fate?"

"Aye, indeed. Lead on, Puss! As for the ogre, I'll do my best or die in the attempt!"

"No need of that, Master. And when he is dead, all that is now his will be yours and you will free the land from his wicked sway and," *Puss* wound up with startling effect, "all will be gas and gaiters!"

The pair turned and as they did so, the curtains fell and the first act was over!

Chapter 17

The End Of The Pantomime

As the house lights sprang up, those of the Seniors responsible for the refreshments left their seats and scurried off to the side-rooms, where trays of tea, coffee, tubs of ices and sweets and chocolate awaited them. They distributed their wares quickly and efficiently and had time to have a hot drink themselves before they collected the cups.

They had just finished when the house lights went down and the footlights blazed again. The orchestra had come in and were taking their places, and a moment later a stately minuet rang out, and the curtains went up on the court of *King Amyas of Catmalania* to show court ladies and gentlemen dancing the minuet. *The King* sat on his throne, looking very stately in white Georgian suit and crimson mantle, but even his wig and the magnificent crown pressed down on it could not disguise Clem Barras, a much-loved Old Girl whose schooldays had ended only two years before. When his Majesty rose as the dance ended and the dancers swung across the stage to the sides with much billowing of panniers and coat-tails, the school broke into tumultuous clapping.

Warned by what had happened to Peggy, Clem lost not a whit of her self-possession. She stood waiting until the clapping died down, then took a cautious step forward, and announced: "My people! I take this opportunity to make it known that I have decided it is high time we were relieved of the presence of the wicked ogre who has taken up his abode in the borders of our land and is robbing us of our people to make them into mutton pies. It is our design to offer lands, wealth and the hand of our daughter, our only child and heiress, to him who shall slay this monster and so free the land from him."

At this point every light in the place winked violently and went out—even the guidelights at the back and sides of the auditorium. There was a loud gasp from the audience, and a voice rose in a howl—a voice that Joey recognised with an awful qualm. Felix was startled and frightened, and when that happened, he yelled. What was worse, his twin always copied him. Sure enough, a second howl rose as a voice from the stage exclaimed, "Please keep your seats! It's all right!"

Close on the heels of this came another voice. "Twins! Shut up at once! It's only the light failed for a moment. Oh, somebody, smother them—quick!" Despite her anxiety, Joey chuckled. She recognised Maeve's voice.

Evidently someone did do something about it, for the howls died down fairly quickly, and at that moment the lights blazed forth again. The actors had been well-drilled and not one of them had moved, though the shock of the sudden darkness had caused *The King* to jerk so violently that his crown was cocked over his left ear. He calmly put up a hand and straightened it, and he went on with his speech.

He called on *The Princess* to ratify his statement, and she came forward. Sybil Russell was a lovely girl, and she looked even lovelier than usual in her court dress. She spoke the few lines given her in a very sweet, clear voice that reached to the back of the hall. When she sat down again, the doors at the side were flung open, and a tall footman announced in tones that were nearly suffocated with laughter, "An emissary from the Marquis of Carabas with a gift for your Majesty."

The girls recognised yet another of the Bettanys—Bride—and there had to be a brief pause to allow the girls to express their delight at seeing her again. Then *Puss* bustled in with an invitation to *His Majesty* and *Her Royal Highness* to take dinner next day with the most noble, the Marquis of Carrabas.

The King read it aloud to the assembled company, and then turned to *Puss*. "The Marquis, your master, is indeed generous. He has loaded us with gifts of fresh game, delicious wild fruits, and such flowers as we have not known before. Upon my word, Sir Puss—"

Out went the lights, and *The King* was left to continue his speech in the darkness, which he did with great firmness, thus saving a second outbreak of woe from the twins. The rest of the cast followed his example, giving, as Joey remarked over Cecil's head to Evadne, the effect of a radio programme. By the time they came on again, the scene had changed to an attic where *John*, judging by his speech, was spending his days with much boredom, though he still retained his trust in *Puss*. Enter to him his *Landlady* to demand the rent—which he had not got. She held forth with much vigour on the iniquity of lodgers who expected to be housed and fed, never to speak of keeping a great, nasty cat, and all for nothing! *John* replied to her with much dignity that she would have her money all in good time, but that was no use. She wanted it then, and she hustled in her husband—an enormously tubby man—to back her up.

The three went at it hammer and tongs, and the audience were in fits of laughter, especially as they all talked at cross-purposes and interrupted each other regardless. It ended when *Puss* stalked in and proceeded to empty a bag of tin money all over the stage and bid the couple take their rent and go. Both crawled about on all fours, after the coins, while *Puss* and *John* watched, making remarks and pointing out gleaming silvery circlets they had missed. One had rolled into a corner, and the old man with an entirely unrehearsed effect, gasped, "If I stand on my head, I'll get it!" and promptly elevated his heels, stunning his fellow actors into startled silence before he completed a neat somersault and turned right side up again.

At this point, several people wept gently, and Mary-Lou uttered a strangled whoop as *Puss*, in very shaky tones, spoke his lines. As for *The Landlady*, she remained sitting on the floor, gaping at her agile spouse until *John*, who had edged nearer, poked her with his foot when she remembered her speech and gave it—very flatly.

There came a roar of cheering and laughter when the curtains fell. And that is to be taken literally. For some reason they stuck halfway. The two people responsible tugged violently, and the wire-rope snapped with a loud twang! The curtains collapsed, completely obliterating *Puss*, who squawked loudly. And that was where the lights, having kept everyone on tenderhooks for the whole of the latter part of the performance, expired finally. There had been a failure at the power station, and the entire district was blacked out.

There was nothing to be done but to end the show. The orchestra stood, and, with a good many false notes since they were playing in the light of two torches someone had produced, played the National Anthem, and the pantomime was over.

"And to think they still have full daylight in the valley!" Mary-Lou groaned as she helped to organise the return of the school in the various cars that had been put at their service. "Oh, I know it's not pitch dark up here yet, but it's dusk. Are we to see the Old Girls, does anyone know?"

No one did; but it gradually leaked out that those ladies were staying up at the Platz until the next day when they expected to leave by the same train as the school.

"If it's running!" Hilary said forebodingly.

"What do you mean—if it's running?" Vi demanded as the prefects, having obtained leave to walk back, since every vehicle was packed, set off.

"Well, what about the railway? It goes by electricity, doesn't it? If it's off, too, will you tell me how we're going to get down tomorrow? We can't walk all that way *and* carry our cases!"

The entire body stood stockstill at this awful thought. They had forgotten about the railway. And the road was still closed to wheeled traffic, so that was no help, either.

Clare moaned loudly. "There's been a hoodoo on this term! I'm convinced of it! Never, since I've been at school, have there been so many awful happenings!"

"And what about our people?" Josette cried. "They'll be expecting us at home the day after tomorrow. If we can't get down tomorrow we shan't be at home till the end of the week!"

Mary-Lou called them to order. "If it comes to *that*, the Abbess will let them know somehow—if it means sending people down to cable from Interlaken. Meanwhile, may I remind you that Kaffee und Kuchen will be waiting, and there won't be a prefect in the place? Come on! Besides," she added plaintively, "I'm hungry!"

"She's right," Hilary Bennet said. "Come on, folks! Best foot forward! Tonight, we have Spot Supper, remember, and even if we don't go home tomorrow, we'll certainly get off next day, and all will be well."

But when they reached the school, they found that Fate had reserved the worst blow of all till then. Naomi had been packed off in a motor-cycle combination belonging to one of the young doctors, for she was very tired. Just at the bend in the road before the school, he had skidded and she had been flung out against a big boulder. The Maynards' car had been just behind, mercifully, and Jack Maynard, driving, had braked instantly, nearly entering a skid himself, and leapt out. The doctor himself was shaken and bruised, but Naomi was concussed and they were afraid of internal injury. Dr. Maynard had lifted Naomi into his car, and gone, hell-for-leather, back along the road to the Sanatorium. Now, permission or no permission, Naomi already lay on the table in the operating theatre where the doctors were at work on her, performing a long and difficult major operation, since, if it was not done at once, she must die.

Chapter 18

HAPPY ENDING

"IS there any news yet? Have any of you heard?" Verity Carey, bringing a message from the Head to the prefects, asked anxiously.

"Not a thing," Hilary replied. "Perhaps there's news now, though, and that's why the Head's sent for us."

It was nearly nineteen o'clock, and the Seniors, at any rate, all knew what news might come from the great Sanatorium. It was no part of the Chalet School training to shield the elder girls from all sorrow. The great aim was to turn them into strong, helpful, reliable women. When Joey had brought the first news the Head had said instantly that Naomi's own clan must hear.

The prefects left their room in a body. They had kept together most of the time since the news had come, feeling comfort from each other. The Head was in her drawing room, and when they arrived, she lifted a strained face which made Mary-Lou run forward to kneel beside her. "Miss Annersley! It wasn't *your* fault!" she cried. "I know you've got the responsibility, but please, *please* don't look like that! Naomi is stronger than she was when she first came, and—and we've all been praying that she may come through. And even—even if she—she doesn't, she'll have gone to join her father and mother, so it will be all right for her!"

The Head put her gently to one side. "Thank you, Mary-Lou. I know all that, child; but, as you say, the responsibility is mine in the end. Find seats, all of you. I want to speak to you about Spot Supper."

"Oh, we can't possibly have it now!" Vi burst out. "Not all that row and singing when—when—"

"But that is just what you must do," Miss Annersley said gravely. "Oh, not the speeches! I agree that that would be asking too much of us just now. But the meal is ready and must be eaten. And we can't think of ourselves only. There are the younger girls. They know that Naomi has met with an accident, but we haven't told them the worst as we have you Seniors. We must have our singing and carry on as nearly as we can for their sakes."

The prefects looked at each other. How could they do it?

Miss Annersley leaned back in her chair, her eyes going from one grave young face to another. "I know it seems impossible," she said quietly. "All the same, I want you to do your best. Furthermore, it is what Naomi herself would wish, I know. She wouldn't want the last day of term spoiled for the younger girls for her sake. Naomi is stronger in very many more ways than in health, you know. She has been learning to think for others, and she would be very sorry to think that the little girls were deprived of their usual fun because she was hurt. I know it seems a lot to ask of you, but in the years to come, you may have to face trials as bad or even worse than this." Then she added what proved the turning-point for the most doubtful of them. "I am prepared to do my part. Will you do yours?"

One by one, after a little pause, they agreed to do their best. She nodded.

"I thought you would. Thank you, girls. Then the gong will sound shortly, and though I think we'll omit the usual procession, we'll go to Abendessen and not hurt Karen's feelings by rejecting the feast she has planned for us."

"Is there any news, Miss Annersley?" Hilda Jukes asked.

"Not yet. But if Naomi comes through it they hope that much of her lameness will be relieved and she will be stronger than she has been since the accident. It will be a long convalescence for her, but if she pulls through, it will be to a much fuller life than she has known for more than six years."

"Does her aunt know?" Mary-Lou asked.

"I cabled her at once, but I don't think she will have got it yet."

"Then—then is she alone?"

"No. Joey Maynard has gone to be with her."

Lesley Bethune gave a sigh of relief. "Oh, I'm so glad! Mrs. Maynard can be just like one of us, but—"

Prunella took the words out of her mouth. "I know. When she likes she can be nothing but a *mother*. She was that to me, years ago, and I'll never forget it. Even if her aunt can't come Naomi will have all the mothering anyone could want."

"Quite all right, Prunella. Now, will you all go and get ready for Abendessen? Some of you look wild and all of you could do with a wash. You'll feel better for it." The Head rose to her feet, and they knew it was dismissal. They filed quietly out of the room and went to obey her. But when she was alone for a moment with Hilary and Vi, Mary-Lou said thoughtfully, "Did you notice the Head's hair? *I* did. The lamplight caught it, and there were white hairs in it. I've never noticed them before."

"We've got to back her to the limit," Vi said with conviction. "Come on! I mean to eat my share. We can't give her a single worry more, and, you know, she *will* worry if she thinks we're grizzling or being miserable."

"It's a bargain!" Hilary said. "I'll do likewise."

"And so will I!" Mary-Lou turned. "Time we were turfing out the kids from their common rooms. Let's get cracking!"

So Spot Supper was held, though without the noise that usually accompanied it. The only speech made was the Head's. When the meal was ended, she stood up, and the girls turned to the high table at once, eager to know if news had come from the Sanatorium. She guessed it and shook her head.

"No, girls. I have no news for you yet, and do not expect to have any for at least another hour. You shall know as soon as it comes. Meanwhile, we will have a sing-song for an hour, and after that, Prayers and then bed. As you can see for yourselves, the electricity is still off. It is unlikely that you can get off early in the morning as we all expected; but I have contacted the authorities, and they say they hope to have the railway running again some time tomorrow. Postcards have been sent to all your people to tell them what has happened, so they won't worry about you. Now I want you to go to Hall where we will have a sing-song until Prayers. Stand! Turn! Forward—*march*!"

As one girl the school marched out. Most of the staff went with them, but two or three of the younger mistresses remained behind to clear the tables, and the Head went to the study to ring up the Sanatorium and ask if there was any news. There was none, and she had to join the school with an anxious heart.

Sing-song was quieter than usual. With one accord they let the usual shouting songs like "Fhairshon" and "October" alone. But they had "Drink to me only" and "Golden Slumbers", "Cherry Ripe" and "The Lark in the Morn", and a good many others of the same kind. When the hour ended, they had Prayers and many were the silent prayers that went up for Naomi just as she was laid in the high white bed, safely through the operation itself, though no one could yet say how she would stand up to the shock.

Jack Maynard himself rang up the school when it was all over, and gave the news to a Head surrounded by her full staff.

"She's come through so far, but it's going to be touch and go with her. I'm staying here all night, and so is Joey in case she rouses. At present, she's still under the anaesthetic. There's one thing, Hilda. If she does come through she'll be almost normal. But you won't get her back for a long time. It's going to mean a long convalescence. She isn't Mary-Lou, you know! And we had to do a lot—three ribs badly broken and a piece of bone to remove from the skull, besides minor injuries. But at least she's past the first stage. Now I must go. Joey will stay for the present, but I hope to get her home tomorrow. It'll mean drugs for the first day or two, so it'll make no difference to Naomi then. Goodnight."

So the Head was able to go round the dormitories and tell all those awake that the operation had been successful. It satisfied most of the girls, who promptly thought that Naomi would soon be better. But Vi was a doctor's niece and Lesley Bethune and Josette Russell doctors' daughters. They knew that it was still not certain. So did Mary-Lou when Miss Annersley appeared in the little room which was hers by virtue of being Head Girl. She was in bed but not asleep, and she sat up at once when the light of the big torch glowed through the opening door.

"I'm awake, Miss Annersley. Is there—is there any news?" she asked.

"Yes, and it's good news. Naomi has come safely through the operation."

Mary-Lou nodded. "How is she after it?"

"No one can say yet. It's too soon. But at least she is through."

"Well," said Mary-Lou with the stunning assurance that was a characteristic of hers, "that means that she's still in grave danger, doesn't it? I mean, I've heard Uncle Jack and Uncle Jem talking, and you've got to face the shock of it all."

"Yes; there is that," the Head assented, wishing inwardly that the two doctors had held their tongues before a quick girl like Mary-Lou. "But the news is good so far, Mary-Lou. Be thankful for that, and lie down and go to sleep."

Mary-Lou nodded again. "I will if I can—go to sleep, I mean. Oh, I hope she'll come through! Miss Annersley!"

"Yes?" the Head said, wondering what was coming next.

"She may need blood transfusions. If she does, and if mine's all right, may I be the one to give it to her?"

Miss Annersley gasped. "No; you may *not*!" she said firmly when she got her breath back. "For one thing, you're too young. For another, they have all the plasma they want at the San. Now stop talking, and go to sleep. I hope and I believe that the news in the morning will be better. But we must wait for that."

"OK." Mary-Lou snuggled down. "But you'll let us know as soon as there is any, won't you?"

"As soon as I know myself. I'm going. Goodnight, Mary-Lou. God bless you, child." Miss Annersley got herself out of the room—the last of all she had to visit—but when she finally reached the study again, she flung herself into the nearest chair and went off into such a peal of laughter as made the startled staff seriously wonder if she had become hysterical from the strain.

She pushed them away as they thronged round her, and, still laughing, repeated Mary-Lou's amazing offer to them. They heard her, thunderstruck. Then little Miss Andrews began to giggle, and before long they were all laughing.

"But oh, how like Mary-Lou!" Mdlle exclaimed, mopping her eyes. "She is always ready, n'est-ce pas?"

"Rather too ready this time, if you ask me!" Nancy Wilmot rejoined. "But you've said it, Jeanne—it is, just exactly, Mary-Lou; I can say no more!"

"Well, I certainly never expected to end this day with a burst of laughter," Miss Annersley said as she stood up. "I fancy there is coffee for us in the drawing room. Shall we go and see? And then, I think we had better go to bed. It has been a long day for us all, and these last hours have been terrible. Please God, the worst is over now. Somehow, I feel that Naomi will pull through."

Next morning, Jack Maynard rang up the school at seven o'clock to say that, although no one could speak with any certainty as yet, so far Naomi was holding her own.

Shortly after came the news that the railway would be open again by sixteen o'clock that afternoon, so the girls would be able to leave that day after all. Announcing this after Prayers, the Head told them that they would spend the morning in going for walks. Mittagessen would be at thirteen o'clock, and Dr. Jack had promised to ring up at fifteen so that they should hear the very latest news before they went home. Then she shooed them all off to get ready for their walk, and told them to take biscuits with them as they were to be out most of the morning. Leaving at so late an hour would mean the night train to Paris, and she meant them to sleep through as much of the journey as possible.

The prefects held a consultation as soon as Mittagesen was over—a somewhat scrappy Mittagessen, since no one had expected the school to be still at the Görnetz Platz by that time—and when, at fifteen o'clock the bell rang to summon them to Hall, they had a plan prepared.

Miss Annersley held Prayers first. Then the door opened, when the Catholic contingent had returned to Hall and Joey Maynard mounted the dais. She looked very tired, but there was triumph in her face as she came forward to the reading desk.

"Girls!" she said, "the good news holds! Naomi is still making progress, even though it is almost infinitesimal. But the doctors all agree that her hold on life is stronger than it was last night. She is still in danger—don't think *that* is over yet. It won't be for some days. Dr. Jack told me to tell you that if this goes on,—by the time you come back for the summer term she will be well enough to have visits from you all. And another thing! During last night's operation they were able to put right something that has been wrong ever since her first accident. When she is able to move about again, her lameness will be much better and she will be much straighter."

She was about to step back, but Mary-Lou jumped to her feet and checked her with a ringing call of, "Auntie Joey!"

Joey stopped and looked at her. "Well, what now?"

"Just this. We all want to know how Naomi goes on, of course, but no one could write to even all us Seniors—too much work, altogether. So we prefects have made a collection—I'll give it to you in a minute—and would you please send a notice each week, to one of the big dailies, just to tell us how she is?"

Joey forgot that she was Mrs. Maynard. "Gosh!" she exclaimed. "What *will* you folk think of next?" Then she grinned. "Not that it isn't a good idea. Hand the cash over, and I'll be personally responsible for it. I'll put it in *The Times* and head it 'Naomi'. Look down the Personal column and you'll soon find it."

Joey kept her word, and twice each week during the holidays notices appeared which told them that all was going well and Naomi, having started to cling to life, was gripping it with a tenacious hold. On the Monday of the second week, when Mary-Lou and Verity were staying at the Lucys' with Vi, she read the last one aloud at the breakfast table.

"Naomi recovering steadily. All well."

"Good!" said Mrs. Lucy with a smile at the joyful faces.

Mary-Lou removed the paper from Vi's grasp and read it to herself. She looked up. "Well, no one could say last term was peaceful in the slightest degree. In fact, I never remember a term so full of the most ghastly trials before. But this makes up for a lot. And the greatest beauty of it all is that, thanks to the accident, Naomi will be more or less all right and that's something that might never have happened otherwise. Good for the Chalet School!"

Theodora of the Chalet School

To June
who gave me my elder god-daughter

First published in a single volume in hardback in 1959 by
W & R Chambers Ltd
First published in paperback in 1984 in Armada

Chapter 1

Expelled Three Times!

"This really is one of the most extraordinary epistles I've ever been fated to read! I wouldn't have believed it of any parent, not even Professor Fry in his worst paddy!" Rosalie Dene, secretary of the Chalet School, broke the silence of the peaceful afternoon. She was sitting in the salon of Joey Maynard's home Freudesheim, while Joey herself was trying to correct the proofs of her latest book.

"Heaven grant me patience! Why, oh why, did I take pity on your lonesome state and invite you to spend the day with me and bring your work so that you could get on with it?" Joey uttered a sepulchral groan which made her indignant friend giggle in spite of herself. "Now stop tittering in that inane way and go ahead and tell me the worst."

"I'll read it to you and you can hear for yourself, and then you won't be surprised at anything I might do or say," Rosalie retorted. "Quite apart from the cool assurance of the lady, I can't imagine any decent parent behaving like this. Keep cool, for pity's sake, and I'll start it at once."

"I should hope so!" Joey spoke severely as she settled herself to listen. "Go ahead and spare me all comments until you've done."

"The comments are much more likely to come from you—I know you, Joey!" And Rosalie read aloud:

"Dear Madam,

"My daughter Theodora has left her present school and I have been advised to write to ask if you have a vacancy for her at the Chalet School this coming term.

"Theodora is fourteen and will be fifteen at the end of October. I believe she is up to the usual standard of work for her age except in French where she seems to be well beyond most of the girls at her latest school. At the same time I feel that I must warn you that this is her third school and that, from this and her first school, I have been requested to remove her. From the second one, she was publicly expelled. In each case, it has been for bad behaviour and insubordination and in no case have I felt I could blame the school.

"Unfortunately, though far from attractive in looks, Theodora seems to possess a fascination for a certain type of girl. Her last headmistress assured me that she is a born leader. She always leads in the wrong direction. She has never been out of trouble at her latest school and what makes things even worse is the fact that she seems to feel no regret or remorse for the disgrace and worry she has brought on me. Indeed, I can only feel that she is completely hardened."

"At fourteen?" Joey interrupted. "Much more likely that the poor kid has gone from one row to another and is miserable and too proud to let anyone know it. I'll bet this wretched woman has shown her not the slightest pity or sympathy, nor made the least effort to try to understand her. Good gracious me! If it had been my own Margot, do you think I'd have let it go on without at least trying to get to the bottom of it? What does she think she's a mother for, anyhow?"

Rosalie was silent. Then she said, "There's quite a lot more of it. Shall I read on?"

"I don't want to hear it, thank you. I don't want to be sick! I'd like to get hold of that idiot of a woman and try to hammer some sense into her head. Give me the gist of it and let it go at that. I've had enough of the original!"

"Well, it seems that her final effort was to join up with three other young demons and the four of them were caught smoking out of a bathroom window."

"Oh, no! But how unoriginal! Couldn't she do any better than that?" Joey's face was alight with laughter.

"It was the climax of a term in which she seems to have excelled herself. She played the fool all round, if this letter is to be believed; and her followers copied her, with the result that discipline in her form went to the winds. Anyhow, according to Mrs.—Mrs. Grantley," Rosalie hastily refreshed her memory, "she was told that in no circumstances could the school receive Theodora back for the coming term. The Head also suggested that it might be an idea to engage a governess and see if concentrated personal attention would work a reform. However, that had been tried before and was just a waste of time. Then someone seems to have put her on to us, though she doesn't say who, and instanced two or three cases of difficult girls with whom we have worked miracles. Therefore, she is offering her demon to us. And," Rosalie concluded, "considering the character she gives the girl, I must say it strikes me as cheek of the sublimest kind."

"Tell me this. Was this child ever expelled for dishonesty or—or nastiness?" queried Joey.

"Her mother doesn't mention it, and she's written three pages describing her brighter devilments. There's no mention of dishonesty or cheating or anything like that, and the letter her last Head sent doesn't mention it either. She simply says that she cannot have thirty other girls upset by Theodora's wildness and rebellious example!"

"Then that's all right! In that case, I'd advise Hilda to give the poor kid a chance with us. There are some things we couldn't pass over, but original sin of that kind isn't one of them. If it were," Joey concluded with a broad grin, "there are quite a number of girls in the school who would be fired regardless—not omitting my own Margot."

Rosalie laughed. She looked considerably happier now that she had laid the problem before her friend. "Oh, Margot has reformed—to a certain extent," she added cautiously. "She certainly doesn't listen to her devil nearly as much."

"I know, and thank Heaven for it! I don't mind admitting to you that I've had spasms of being quite hopeless about her. I've always said she got a bigger share of natural wickedness than all the rest put together."

"You laid good foundations," Rosalie said thoughtfully. "It's helped many a time. But to get back to Theodora. Hilda is safe to ask what I think about taking her, you know. Especially as she seems to get an influence on other girls."

"If Hilda asks me, I shall advise her to give the girl a trial. Otherwise, it's going to be a case of giving a dog a bad name and hanging him. That is the sort of thing that hardens a child of fourteen, and if you ask me, it is largely at the bottom of this trouble. Her mother seems to have decided that the child is a bad lot and let it go at that. If you're given a reputation, you generally try to live up to it, don't you? That's what young Theodora has done."

She stopped short there and ruminated for a minute or so. Then she looked up. "I've got an idea! Has it ever struck you what a ghastly name Theodora is? Enough to make any girl hit the ceiling."

"It's rather late in the day to think of that," Rosalie reminded her.

"We can't very well rechristen her I admit. But surely we needn't use it all? Isn't there a possible 'short' we could use? Let's see—Theo—Dora—oh, no, I think not! 'Theo' isn't so bad. Or what about 'Ted'? That's pounds better! I wouldn't call a dog I like 'Theodora', but 'Ted' has a tang to it. That's it! You listen to me, Rosalie. Hilda, if I know her, will tell the kid that this is a new beginning—if she comes, that is—and so far as we are concerned, she's coming with a clean slate. Make it a clean slate all round. Start her off with a new name. It's my belief it'll have a real psychological effect on her. Theodora was the Bad Girl of the School! Ted has a chance to make good. I believe she'd play up to it."

"I wonder?" Rosalie spoke thoughtfully. "It might do the trick. Perhaps if she realise that everyone here is out to help her to get off on the right foot, it may make a difference. And if, as a beginning, we call her something quite fresh, well, that should be a help, too."

"I'm certain it will be. But I wonder who on earth it was

who put Mrs. Grantley on to us? She certainly seems to have known something of our history."

"It might be a former mistress," Rosalie pointed out. "Are you giving me tea, Joey? Because if so, look at the time! Hilda was coming up by the 16.15 train, so she should be here any moment now. I'll just clear this lot away and then ring up the school and leave word for Hilda to come over here. You go and see about tea. Hilda will be tired after a day of interviewing parents in Interlaken. It'll do her all the good in the world to be here having tea without perpetual interruptions from the phone."

"Good idea!" Joey got up and began to gather up her proofs. "You hop off while I go and put the kettle on."

They parted to their several jobs and the result was that as Miss Annersley, Head of the Chalet School, opened the side door she was met by one of the maids with the information that Mme Maynard had rung up to say she wished to see her as soon as she arrived. Miss Annersley was hot and tired and sticky and her first impulse was to go to the study and ring Joey to tell her that she wasn't moving until she had a wash and something to eat and drink. However, she thought better of it. She handed her shopping-bag to Miggi and went round the house, across the garden, and through the gate set in the hedge that divided the grounds of Freudesheim from those of the school. Here, she was met by two excited creatures so charmed with their own cleverness that they both talked at once, and it was not until they were sitting down to tea in Joey's pretty salon that she was able to disentangle the threads of their story. But when she had finally got it all clear, she agreed heartily with all they had to say. Theodora was to be welcomed at the Chalet School and told that the school proposed—unless she objected strongly to the idea—that henceforth she was to be Ted, and make a completely fresh beginning in her school life. The past was to be forgotten and no one was ever to learn about those three awful expulsions.

Chapter 2

THEODORA

JOEY Maynard slipped through the gate in the hedge and made her way to the school along the narrow path flanked on either side by flowering bushes. She ignored the turning which led to the front of the house, and continued on her way towards the back where had been built a small but pleasant annexe where Miss Annersley had her own rooms.

Joey kept both eyes and ears open. This was the first day of term, and the big coaches which brought the girls up from the valley were due any time now. She had no wish to be mixed up with a crowd of girls all milling around and all highly excited. She walked into Miss Annersley's pretty salon by way of the open French window and looked around. The room was empty, and a glance at the cuckoo clock hanging on the wall told her that everyone would be in the entrance hall by this time, awaiting the arrival of the school. She left the room to walk through a maze of corridors to the wide entrance hall. Here, she found that she was right. The Head, surrounded by such of the staff as were not on escort duty, stood in the doorway. Behind them, filling the hall and even mounted on the lower stairs of the great staircase which swept down to the centre of the hall were those girls who had arrived earlier—including her own triplet daughters. The Head suddenly caught sight of her and came swiftly to her friend and ex-pupil.

"Joey! This is an unexpected honour! You don't generally appear among us as early in the term as this!"

"And I shouldn't have done it this time," Joey said with an infectious grin, "only Margot, having forgotten to pack her hankies, likewise forgot to bring them with her. I came to hand them over, having visions of her awful fate if Matey discovered tomorrow that she'd left the lot behind her. Besides," she added in a confidential undertone, "I've had a letter."

With one ear alert for sounds from outside, the Head said, "A letter?"

Joey nodded. "As you remark. Further, I deem it my duty to meet young Ted Grantley the first moment she sets foot in this establishment."

"Why?" the Head demanded. Then, "Oh, I see! The letter was about her."

"Go up top! It was. I'm coming over later to read it to you—and I mean the lot of you. There isn't time now. Those coaches will be along before you can say 'Knife!' Meanwhile, may I have a word with my child?"

"You may; and I hope you'll rub it well in that carelessness of that kind won't get her anywhere. Margot never troubles to think."

"OK, schoolma'am! I'll tick her off. And may I bag your study for ten minutes or so? I want Len to bring Ted to me at the first possible moment."

"What are you up to?" Miss Annersley demanded suspiciously.

"Please, teacher, I only want to give the poor kid a really hearty welcome to this place. You don't mind, do you?"

Her friend glanced at her keenly. "Don't you trust us, Joey?"

"I do; but I also want to make sure that she also feels she has a warm welcome to Freudesheim. With your kind permission I'll hand over her belongings to that sinful child of mine and tell Len what I want. Then I'll depart. I don't want to be rushed by a wildly excited mob of girls just at this moment."

"Neither do I want it for you. Very well; Len may bring Ted to you as soon as I've done with them. Go to the study and keep quiet, Joey." Then she added, "You are very free with your Teds. How do you know she will like it?"

"I'll soon bring her round to my way of thinking, if she doesn't. I shouldn't think myself that that would be necessary. Is that a motor horn I hear?"

Miss Annersley gave an exclamation. "It is! I must go!" and she hurried to the door again, to be ready to welcome the school back for a new term.

Joey turned to the stairs where her daughters were jigging wildly, and held out her parcel to Margot much in the manner of an emissary of the Borgias handing over a cup of cold poison.

"Margot Maynard! You're the most heedless monkey I ever knew!"

Margot went pink to the roots of her red-gold curls. "My hankies! I forgot them. Did you come just to bring them? You *are* a pet of a mother!"

"That's all very well, but what would you have said to Matey in the morning if she wanted to know where your clean hanky was? It would have served you right if I'd left you to it. I will do another time, let me warn you. It's high time you could look after your own things. You aren't a baby now!"

"I'm sorry," Margot murmured.

"Well, don't do it again or I'll leave it to her to sort you!"

"*And* she would," put in Len, the eldest of the long Maynard family, as she hung over the bannisters, her long curly tail of chestnut hair tumbling over her shoulder. Joey reached and gave it a friendly tug.

"I thought I'd save her this once. But it's the last time for any of you, so remember that! I'm not going to run after you and fetch and carry for you any more. You three will be fifteen in November, and must be responsible for your own possessions and your own doings."

"Well, you've saved me this time, anyhow," Margot said with a chuckle. "You really are a poppet!"

"She always is," said brown-eyed Con, who had shuffled along the stair to join the party. "Are you staying to welcome the others, Mamma?"

"I am not! And by that same token I hear a horn at the

gate." She laughed up at them. "Off you go and be ready to take your places. Just a moment, Len. I want a word with you!"

The other two raced off, and Len stood with eyes like English wood violets fixed on her mother's face. "Anything wrong?"

"Nothing, thank you. I'm going along to Auntie Hilda's private study. You have one new girl this term, and I want to see her as soon as possible. You can't miss her as she's the only one. As soon as Auntie Hilda dismisses you, fetch her along to me, will you? Or," with belated caution, "you'd better take her to the Splashery first. But bring her after she's ready."

Len nodded. "Right you are! What's her name, by the way? I can't very well go up to a stranger and say 'Hi, you!' She mightn't like it!"

"Her full name is Theodora Grantley. I'm hoping she'll let us cut her down to 'Ted', though."

"I should about think she would! What a simply ghastly name! OK; I'll see to it for you." Len hung over the bannisters and kissed her mother before leaping down the three stairs above which she had been perched, and going to join the throng.

Joey laughed softly, and then went off to the study to await the arrival of Theodora.

Meanwhile, her daughters had joined the mobs of girls who were leaving the coaches and joining on to one or the other of the long lines stretching across the drive. Small girls came to the front, big ones stood in the back lines. The triplets joined on to one made up of girls of their own age or a little older, giving subdued squeals of welcome to friends as they arrived. The escort mistresses had left their parties and gone to join their confrères in the doorway, and the settling of the girls was left to the prefects.

These were headed by a tall handsome girl of nearly eighteen, whose thick golden-brown curls framed an oval face that was full of character. The sensitive mouth was offset by a determined chin and steady blue eyes, and at a word from her even the twelve- and thirteen-year-olds, who had been scrambling and pushing, got into line smartly and became quiet and correct at once. This was Mary-Lou Trelawney, the Head Girl of the school, who was beloved by most people, even those who were given to grumbling that it was all very well, but Mary-Lou was a lot too much on the spot when she wasn't wanted! She had the reputation of being very just, willing to listen to both sides of a question and understanding to an amazing degree for her age. Her own kind frequently accused her of getting away with things that none of them could have done, but they always backed her up loyally.

When members of Vb arrived, the triplets were kept busy answering questions and asking others in their turn, until the last of the Juniors had been pulled into line with her form. Only Len, with her mother's charge in mind, kept scanning the faces of the girls as they marched to their places. With only one new girl to worry about, it ought to be easy enough to pick her out.

"I wonder why she's coming this term?" the eldest of the Maynards mused as she watched. "New girls in the summer term are rather a rarity with us. Quite right, too! The poor things must be all at sea if they come for the last term of the year!

At long last she saw the new girl being brought along by Miss Wilmot, the senior maths mistress, herself an Old Girl of the school. Miss Wilmot pushed Theodora Grantley gently into place beside Jennifer Hughes, the form prefect of Inter V, and then strolled up to the house.

All the time the Head was welcoming them to the new term, Len was looking curiously at the back of the new girl. She hadn't been in time to see her face. Judging by her back view she was thin enough to be called scraggy. She was on the short side, being at least half a head less than Jennifer and a head shorter than leggy Len herself. She wore the beret in which they all travelled, and from beneath it escaped a thick bunch of black hair, straight and lank, which just reached to her shoulders.

"I wonder what her face is like?" Len pondered. "And why hasn't someone done something about her hair? Matey will have something to say about it, that's certain!" Then she stopped wondering about Theodora, for the Head, having finished her remarks, changed the tone of her voice.

"And now, girls," she said, "I know you are all very anxious for the latest news of Naomi Elton. You will be delighted to hear that Naomi is well out of danger now, and though it will be a long time—more than a year, I'm afraid—before she will be on her feet again, she will be able to walk in time, and even to run and enter on most of the less strenuous activities of you folk. Now that is all for the moment. When I dismiss you, go straight to the Splasheries and change, and then to the common rooms and wait for the gong. Abendessen is due in fifteen minutes' time, so you mustn't delay over your tidying. School—turn! Forward—march!"

As one girl the school turned smartly to the left, and, led by the Second form, marched off round the house to the side-door, where they made for the various Splasheries, as cloakrooms were always called at the school. Len, watching her opportunity, dashed after Inter V, and came up with Jennifer and the new girl just as the former was preparing to hunt for Theodora's peg and locker.

"Hello, Jen!" she said. "You go and fix up. I'll see to Theodora for you."

Jennifer, who was looking worried, smiled at her. "Oh, thanks a million!" she said fervently. "You can't move in this place when everybody's here and I haven't the foggiest notion where Theodora ought to be."

"I'll soon find out," Len said. "Come on, Theodora! This way! I expect you're down here somewhere. I'm Len Maynard, by the way."

Theodora followed her meekly to the far end of the cloakroom, where a label under a new peg proclaimed that it was hers. While she hung up coat and beret, Len found her shoe-locker, and, when she had changed into house-shoes, towed her off to the toilet basins at the other end, and waited while her charge washed hands and face and ran a comb through the untidy locks without, incidentally, making much better of them. The hair was so extraordinarily thick, quite apart from the fact that its natural tendency seemed to be to stick out in all directions, that she looked positively over-weighted with hair. She had a long, rather narrow face, at present marked by a look of mulish sulkiness. Her wide mouth turned down at the corners, and the eyes, black and big, with lashes as thick as her hair but with an upward tilt to them that helped to redeem her face, held a queer look of unhappiness which made the eldest Maynard feel sorry for her. What on earth was wrong with her? Then Len spoke. "Ready? OK. Come along with me and I'll show you where to go."

Theodora followed her into the passage without demur; but when they were going along a side corridor, she asked, "Why are you running me round? I thought that mistress told Jennifer to look after me."

"I expect she did; but you saw what it's like." Len giggled. "Everyone goes completely haywire at first. Besides, my mother wants to see you, and she's in the Head's private study. Come on! Through this door!"

"Why should I have to see your mother?" Theodora demanded.

"Search me! I rather think she knows some of your people at home. Anyhow, she told me to fetch you to her as soon as I could."

Theodora had gone darkly red at Len's explanation. "Which of my people does she know?"

"She didn't tell me—only that I was to fetch you. Don't be scared! She's quite a poppet, if I do say it!"

Theodora said nothing. She followed Len into a sunny room where her cicerone paused to close the door before she said triumphantly, "Here she is, Mamma! Theodora, this is my mother."

Theodora looked, her mind in a complete whirl. What she had expected, it is hard to say. Certainly not what she got. A tall woman with laughing black eyes turned from the window where she had been standing, and held out both hands.

"Welcome to the Chalet School!" she said—and Theodora thought she had never heard a lovelier voice, not even the Head's.

"Shall I leave Theodora with you and come back for her later?" Len asked.

Mrs. Maynard laughed at her. "Theodora?" She turned to the stunned owner of the name, and asked plaintively, "*Must* we?"

"Must you what?" Theodora gasped.

"Make it the whole thing? Mayn't we make it 'Ted'?" Then, as Theodora stood staring dumbly at her, she added, while her eyes danced, "Of course, if you've any special objection to that we could always make it 'Theo'." She sat down, pulling Theodora to a seat by her side on the broad windowsill. "You'll have to make up your mind to it, my lamb! 'Ted' or 'Theo' but *not* 'Theodora'! All right, Len; you may leave her and come back in ten minutes."

Len nodded and skipped off, and Joey, still holding one of the thin hands, continued, "Come along! Make up your mind which it's to be, for call any girl Theodora whenever I speak to her, I will *not*! And I warn you, the school sees a lot of me in one way or another—as a general rule, that is. Which is it to be?" Then, as Ted still remained dumb, she abandoned her whirlwind tactics, and said gently, "Don't you understand? You've come here to make a new start. We're washing all the past out. It's done and gone. We can't do anything about that. But you can do quite a lot with this fresh chance. As a beginning, we thought you'd like to forget all about Theodora and all the horrible trouble she has been in and see if Ted—or Theo, if you prefer it—couldn't make us glad she had come. Don't you like the idea?"

Theodora came to her senses at last. "Do you mean," she said slowly, "that it doesn't matter that I've been chucked out of three other schools already?"

Joey shook her black head with its deep fringe and great flat plaits over either ear. "Not unless you force it on our notice. It depends on you. Once a thing's paid for, it's paid for. Whatever you may have done in the past has been paid for. It's no affair of ours, and we aren't interested in it. What we are interested in is what you do here. You've a chance to make good—turn into a different person. What about it—Ted?"

With a sudden smile that wiped all the sullenness from her face and explained to Joey her mother's statement that the girl was attractive to her own kind, she replied, "I'll be Ted! And," she paused and then went on with a rush—"and I'll try to make good. It's the first really decent chance I've had since they fired me from the Beehive when I was just a kid of nine. If I'm really to have it, I'll take it—and that's a promise."

Joey nodded. "Good for you! I hope you will. But don't forget it means climbing back, and that's never an easy thing to do. But you stick to it and you'll find it isn't as bad as it may seem. And another thing. I shan't be here quite as much as usual this term—I'm going to be very busy. But if things really seem to be getting you down, go to Miss Annersley and ask leave to come and talk it over with me. We'll soon be able to set things right again. Is that a promise, too?"

"Oh, it *is*!" Theodora's face lighted up, and Joey decided that when she had grown to her features, she might easily turn out a handsome creature. Only something must be done about her hair. However, Matey could safely be trusted to deal with that.

She bent to kiss the girl. "Good! And now, there's Len, and you must go. Good-bye! Good hunting!"

Chapter 3

EXPLAINING THEODORA

THE Chalet School staff who had been on the go all day, heaved a collective sigh of relief when the bell sounded for the Senior bedtime at half-past nine. Their duties for the day were over and they might rest and relax. The first full week of school was ended and they had got into the full swing of things.

"Come on, Kathie!" Nancy Wilmot, head of maths, said to her great friend and coadjutor, Miss Ferrars. "Let's go along to the common room and see if there are any refreshments going. I heard Jeanne de Lachennais murmuring sweet nothings about coffee and biscuits when she went off a few minutes ago. I could just do with a cup of Jeanne's coffee!"

"Oh, so could I!" Kathie Ferrars agreed with fervour as she followed her senior upstairs and through the door into the part of the school dedicated to the staff. "It's weird, but I honestly think the first ten days of term are more tiring than all the rest put together. Everything seems on top of one, and then there's the worry of escort duty. I never draw a really free breath until I've seen my own party safely in line, listening to the Head's welcome."

By this time they had reached the door of the staff common room. Nancy opened the door and they both strolled in.

"At last!" exclaimed an unexpected voice. "You two are the very last. Even Matey got here five minutes ago. What have you been doing all this time?"

"Joey!" Miss Wilmot exclaimed, crossing the room to pull up a chair and sit down beside her. "What, in the name of wonder are you doing here at this hour?"

"I've come to read a letter to you," Joey said. "Hello, Kathie. You look like something the cat's brought in. What on earth have you been doing?"

"Oh, this and that. I'll be all right after a cup of Jeanne's coffee and a nice quiet night in my little bed."

"Here's the coffee," Rosalie Dene said, bringing a cup in each hand. "Find a seat, Kathie, and let's get down to this letter Joey's being so mysterious about. It must be frightfully important for she's refused to say a word about it until we were all here."

"Well, so it *is* important," Joey said as she sipped her coffee. "I had it on the first day of term, but there hasn't been a moment since it came."

The Head, who had been talking to one or two of the rest, looked at her with a smile.

"I seem to remember you murmuring something to me about a letter I must see," she said. "Is that it, Joey? Am I to have it now?"

"You may have it if you want as soon as I've read it aloud to the assembled company. I rather think it'll make you open your eyes. Anyhow, everyone who was with us during the first years in Tirol! This will interest you."

Rosalie Dene laughed. "Will it? Why, Joey?"

"You'll see in a minute. Remember our staff then? We had Mdlle Lepâttre and Bill and Hilda; my sister-in-law, Mollie Maynard and the two Dennys." Joey stopped on an upward note and those people who had been there, and were present now, stared at her. She grinned and went on: "Mdlle left us for Paradise years ago. Bill and Hilda and the Dennys are still with us. Mollie, as you all know, is married and living in New Zealand. Can you think of anyone else?"

"Carty!" Rosalie cried. "Joey Maynard! Do you mean to say you've got in touch again with Carty at long last? You do?" as Joey nodded. "But this is news. No one knew where she was when we were compiling the albums of Old Girls and Staff last summer, so we had to leave her out pro tem. Let me have the address and I'll see to it now."

"Will do, later on," said Joey. "Meanwhile, more coffee, please, Jeanne, and when I've drunk it, you may all lend me your ears and I'll read you what she says. I think that you'll be interested, even the folk who have never heard of Carty before."

"Why?" Nancy Wilmot demanded.

"Because her main reason for writing to me is our latest effort."

"Our latest effort? What on earth do you mean?" Kathie Ferrars asked.

"Young Ted," Joey returned with a smirk which made her friends feel like shaking her. "She's told me the whole yarn. It's thanks to her that we have Ted now. However, you'll know all about it when you hear her letter."

Miss Annersley had been lounging comfortably in her big armchair. Now she sat up. "Kindly finish that coffee and read the letter to us at once or give it to me and I'll read it."

Joey chuckled. "In my own time. I decline to be robbed of my full enjoyment of the nectar Jeanne calls coffee for anyone!"

However she condescended to empty the cup and then settle down to reading. Everyone was waiting. To most of them, the name of Carty was something they had heard only a minute ago; but Ted Grantley was a very present problem which must be faced now. They were glad to know anything that would help solve it.

"Carty—otherwise Miss Carthew—is back in England," Joey said, shuffling her sheets into order. "Mrs. Grantley is a cousin of hers. I can only add that Carty seems to have the lowest opinion of her. You'll see when you hear what she says." She ceased teasing and plunged straight into the letter then.

"My Dear Joey,

"Now turn to the back page and see who is writing to you! I only wish I could be with you to see your reactions! Yes, it's 'Carty'!

"I really do feel ashamed of myself for not getting down to it sooner, but life has been very crowded of late and I was never a good correspondent. But I've never forgotten my happy time at the Chalet School nor any of you people who were there when I was. I've always meant to pick up the threads, but somehow, I've never got round to it. When you have a lusty family of four, it takes you all your time to keep up with them and the past simply gets shoved into the past.

"First of all then, I am a widow. My husband died nearly eighteen months ago from heart trouble. I was ill for some weeks after he had gone. He had been ill for two years and I'd done most of the nursing myself, so I was just worn out. As soon as I could pull myself together, I decided to come home. Early this year, we arrived at Southampton and made tracks for King's Caple, my old home in Dorset, where a cousin of mine lives and had found a house for us. I can't say we've ever been dear friends. In fact, not to put too fine a point on it, I've never had much use for Myra Grantley. As a schoolgirl, she was an empty-headed little ninny. Pretty enough if you like them fluffy-headed and with blue eyes like a doll's. I don't! She was the child of elderly parents and grew up the most spoilt little wretch I've ever laid eyes on!

"When she was eighteen, she married a man considerably older than herself who adored her at the time. Later, when the glamour had worn off, I rather think that died, too. At any rate, he carried on the spoiling process. Myra has a temper, one of the whiney-piney whimpering kind and she's a nagger into the bargain. It was probably the thing that most made for peace. They had three boys—she was only nineteen when Gerald was born and the twins came two years later. There was plenty of money and Myra had nurses for the boys and only saw them when she wanted to show off with them—uncharitable me!—which was quite often. Then, when the twins were fifteen, she had another baby—a little girl. She was *furious*!

"To begin with, she didn't want any more. If she did, she wanted another handsome boy. What she got was a queer little dark thing, the image of her father who was no beauty, though he had a good face—strong and kind. By that time, too, money was getting tight. The boys were at public school and costing heavily. Theodore lost a good deal during the war with foreign investments. The cost of living was rising sky-high and you know what help was like. No nurses now to take all the worrying part of the baby off her hands. She had to tackle that job herself, with help from a young girl who didn't know much more than she did.

"Myra has never had much more use for me than I for her, but this was when she began writing to me long letters of bitter complaint. I suppose it made an outlet for her, for I couldn't do anything about it, being in Cape Town at the time. But I can tell you, I felt horribly sorry for both Theodore and Theodora—she was named after him.

"Along with his name and looks, she also inherited his brains and that has made matters a hundred times worse, for she very soon jumped to it that her mother had precious little use for her. She clung to her father who adored her, for the boys were away most of the year, of course, and anyhow, were so much older they must have felt like uncles, rather than brothers!

"Then Theodore died quite suddenly of coronary thrombosis when Theodora was just five. His will was an even worse shock than his death for Myra. He left the boys' shares to them outright as soon as they came of age. Myra got everything else upon trust for Theodora except a certain sum which was set aside for her education and so on. By that time, he knew his Myra too well to leave things in her hands and he appointed trustees for that and the rest of the estate—*not* Myra at all! I had another raging epistle or two about that.

"I think that clears the board. You've got the position — Myra with little or no love for her daughter and the disposition of funds taken right out of her hands. And a good thing, too, or goodness knows what sort of an education the child would have got!

"When she was six, Theodora was packed off to boarding-school. Myra chose it and it was about as bad as it could be. The Head seems to have had no idea of keeping order. The children did more or less as they liked and Theodora found a good many things to do that wouldn't occur to the average child. I told you she had brains! When she had been there a year, her mother was requested to remove her. More wails to Cape Town!

"The next effort was even worse—a *very* select school where the girls learnt ballet, riding, French conversation —she's scored there. She speaks French like a native! —art embroidery and I'm not sure that painting on china wasn't included! Myra's choice again. The trustees hadn't got wise to her then. She lasted there for three years. When she was ten, she topped up a series of wild pranks by giving a bareback display on one occasion when they were out for their usual tame canter along the roads. She really seems to have created a thorough sensation and the Head, terrified lest such a performance should affect her school, expelled her publicly.

"A private governess followed and lasted six months. Apart from the fact that Theodora seems to have gone all out to force the poor soul to resign, Myra found that she must forego several of her little pet luxuries if she was to keep her. That wasn't to be thought of for a moment, so she left and, for the rest of the year, Theodora seems to have played around, wasting her time and being nagged at perpetually by her mother.

"This was where the trustees stepped in and insisted that she must go to school. This time, it was their choice —quite a decent place and it might have done the trick, but one of the staff from her last school had arrived there the term before. She lost no time in broadcasting Theodora's doings. Even so, the Head seems to have done her best but by this time I think the poor child felt it was a case of giving a dog a bad name and hanging him. She has a queer fascination for her own kind and she was leader in one mad trick after another. The climax came when three of them were caught smoking out of a bathroom window at midnight.

"The other two, having more or less of characters, got off with a few of the more unpleasant penalties; but Theodora, having already been well warned that one more major row would mean that the school would not keep her, was sent home in disgrace.

"This was where I came in. I had been in England a while and I had seen how things were going. I was determined that the child shouldn't be ruined if I could help it, so I made inquiries, discovered that the Chalet School was still in existence both here and in Switzerland and that you, now a married lady, were living nearby. I rode roughshod over Myra, who was alternately weeping over her own woes and raging at her child.

"I got the name of the chief trustee and went to interview him. I kept on until he agreed to insist that Theodora should go to the Chalet School and to the Swiss branch where Myra isn't likely to see much of her. Then I went home and wiped up the floor with Myra in my best style. She hadn't a leg to stand on and she knew it.

"I had intended to write to Hilda Annersley who, I have been told, is Head now, but I've had no time, for Myra needs an awful lot of keeping up to things. However, I worked it in the end by producing a West Indies cruise which, as I pointed out, she could perfectly well manage if Theodora was out of the way. That did the trick.

"I have a feeling that going to the Chalet School will either make or mar Theodora permanently. Please let it make her. I don't know what Myra may have said in her letter to the school, but she isn't a *bad* girl. She's honest and truthful and she is, thank goodness, free from silliness and the kind of unpleasantness that to me constitutes a really bad girl. She is daring, mischievous and impudent and she has a gift little short of genius for thinking up things no one in their sane senses would ever dream of forbidding and doing them! Myra's continual nagging has made her defiant, but I don't altogether blame her for it. In short, she is thoroughly naughty but she is not bad! I honestly think that if only you and the school can get hold of her she has a chance of becoming something even Myra, may in time, be proud of!"

"The rest," said Joey, shuffling the pages together, "is asking endless questions about my own doings and the school. I must make time somehow to scrawl a line to her tomorrow. But I thought you'd all better hear the vital part, for then you'll be able to understand and help the poor kid."

Miss Annersley nodded. "I'll write to her myself if you'll give me the address, and let her know that whatever happens, unless we find the girl absolutely impossible, we shall keep her. And I have a feeling that we shall do just that."

"Good!" Joey stood up and picked up the light wrap she had tossed down when she first came in. "Well, folks, it's getting late, and time I was back in my own little shanty, never to mention bed. Think it over, all of you, and make up your minds to develop endless patience and kindness and let young Ted have what looks to me like the first really decent chance she's ever had." She went to the door, opened it, and with her hand on the knob, turned, her wickedest look on her face. "Oh, and if she shows any further inclination to smoke, send her straight over to me. *I'll* larn her!" With which she slid out, shutting the door firmly behind her and they heard her going quickly along the passage.

Chapter 4

TED SETTLES IN

WHEN Ted Grantley's entrance papers had come up for discussion, there had been some furious arguments among the staff concerned as to which form she should enter. It was finally agreed that she should start in Inter V for at any rate the first half of the term, with special coaching in maths and Latin and especially German.

Ted herself, on her arrival at the school, had been in a curious frame of mind, especially after her interview with Joey Maynard. Part of her wanted to play up to that lady's firmly expressed conviction that she could not only make a new start, but could make it a good one. Part of her thought, "Oh, what's the use? Sooner or later something will go wrong and then it'll be just the same old story over again and I'll be hoofed out of a fourth school! Who cares, anyhow?"

The first two or three days while she was feeling her feet, she had little time to dwell on this. For one thing, so much at the Chalet School was entirely different from anything she had known previously. By the time she was safely in her pretty cubicle in Tulip Dormitory, she was usually so tired with all the new experiences that she could think of nothing but getting to bed and going to sleep. She had no chance of lying awake, thinking up hair-raising exploits wherewith to dazzle her little playmates. During the day, of course, she had so much to do there was no time then either.

French days were no trouble to her. Her second school had certainly done so much for her. She could chatter in French almost as easily as she did in English. German, however, was another question. She had had about a term of it with her governess and never touched it since. As a result, on Mondays and Thursdays, which were German days, she had to be either silent or put up with being corrected by anyone who overheard her, and found that even her form-mates were prepared to see to it with enthusiasm. Being as imitative as a monkey she found that while her vocabulary was, to say the least of it, scanty, she was picking up an accent that satisfied most people. But it certainly filled up her days to the limit. Ted actually got through the first ten days or so of term without one major row and that was a record for her!

The second Sunday of term broke with a cloudless sky, though below the Görnetz Platz, the gulf was filled with a thin white mist which, as Pen Grant informed her, was a sure sign of a hot day. She had already discovered that Sundays at the Chalet School were almost as full as week-days, though in a different way.

Morning service was at ten o'clock and as Frühstück, as she found breakfast was called here, was at nine o'clock, it took them all their time to have it, make their beds, and walk to one or other of the two chapels the Platz boasted, in time for it.

"We ought to have our own chapels next term," Pen said as she passed the rolls to the new girl. "They've got on with them quite a good deal now. We're building them to celebrate our coming-of-age—last year, that was."

"Is the school as old as that?" Ted exclaimed.

"Oh, yes; didn't you know? And the year after the year after next, we'll have the Silver Jubilee. That," Pen said with an elderly sigh, "will be my last year here. I'll be nearly eighteen then."

Ted said nothing. She was wondering if the Silver Jubilee would find her still there or not. She had nearly lost hope that any school would keep her long. However, that was no business of Pen's.

She enjoyed the service to which she presently went. Vater Franz kept in mind the extreme youth of a number of his congregation and Ted found to her amazement that she was really listening to a sermon for once.

"What comes next?" she asked Len Maynard who happened to be partnering her.

"Ramble, most likely, seeing what a gorgeous day it is," Len replied.

"Is that what you call a walk here?" Ted asked doubtfully.

"We do not. I *said* ramble and I *meant* ramble. Wait till we get back and you'll see," Len told her with a gurgle.

Ted felt rather stunned. "Do you really mean," she said slowly, "that we'll go rambling about just as we like? Not a prim and proper croc at all?"

"Oh, we have to croc as long as we're on the Platz," Len explained. "Once we're well away, though, we break ranks. We'll have a mistress or two and probably a couple of prefects. We take Mittagessen with us and picnic somewhere."

Ted found that as soon as they reached the school, the first thing everyone did was to crowd into Hall to inspect the big noticeboard to find out what their next activity was to be. She had only half-believed Len's statements, so she was duly thrilled when she saw that rambles were, indeed, the order of the day. Len had brought her in with a hand tucked through her arm and when that young person saw the board, she uttered a squeal of delight.

"Rambles it is! And we've got Ferry, Mary-Lou and Vi Lucy! You Inter V people are joining up with us. Get cracking, Ted! You've got to change into uniform and put on walking-shoes and then be down to grab your parcel. Don't forget your rucksack, by the way, and if you want to take snaps, tuck your camera in it."

Ted took to her heels and went up the stairs like a runaway colt. She deserved to be caught, since that sort of behaviour was against the rules, but everyone was busy, so she got away with it for once. She dived into her cubicle where she changed into her clean uniform, found her camera, actually remembered an extra clean handkerchief, and then scurried off downstairs to change into stout walking-shoes in the Splashery and don rucksack and big shady hat before following the others out to the path where some of the maids were standing before a trestle table loaded with packages and thermos flasks which they were told to tuck into their bags. Then the prefects who were all on duty, moved them on to join their own rambles.

Len was partnering Rosamund Lilley, a great friend of hers, and Miss Ferrars nodded to them to lead on and they set off at a smart pace down the highroad towards the big Sanatorium.

"Which way are we going?" Pen, who had taken charge of Ted out of kindness, asked anxiously as they passed the mistresses.

"To the station," Miss Ferrars said briskly. "We're going by train to the Rösleinalp. From there, we walk up the path to Mahlhausen where we'll have our picnic and you can explore. Keep together, girls! Don't loiter and don't race ahead."

Mary-Lou and Vi Lucy, who were great allies, had gone to the back of the long procession to act as whippers-in. The mistresses had hurried on to the head and, thanks to the steady pace that was set them, they reached the tiny station—merely a roofed-in shed—in plenty of time to watch for the train coming up the far track.

Ted stared down the long, shining tracks and watched the queer little train of glassed-in cars—three of them—being hauled up by an equally queer little electric engine which formed the front of the first car. Down there, it looked very tiny and she was startled to see that it was really quite a good size when at last it drew up before the Görnetz Platz shed. Not that she had much time to consider it, for the moment the doors slid apart, Len and Rosamund climbed up the steps into the first carriage and the rest followed. There were a double row of seats down each side and as there were only three other passengers who stared as the girls came marching in, they all found seats. The doors slid together again and the brave little train went on gliding up the steep slope.

Ted had never experienced anything quite like that smooth, steady upward movement—not even in a lift. Just before they reached Unterhofen, the downward train slid past them and then they continued on up, stopping at two or three tiny stations on the way.

As they neared the end of their journey, Miss Ferrars spoke. "Listen, girls! We are nearly at the Rösleinalp. Let me remind you all to make sure you've left nothing behind. You've seen for yourselves what a short time they stay at each place and there can be no question of holding up the train because half-a-dozen of you have forgotten and left your rucksacks or your hankies or anything else. Remember that the trains work as a pair and what affects one affects the other. So whatever you leave will have to stay left and go sailing up to Mahlhausen without you." She raised her voice "Anna and Zita, you're nearest the doors. Be ready to jump out the minute they open and the rest of you follow as fast as you can."

As she finished, the train glided up to the usual shed and the doors parted. Duly warned, the girls were on their feet and in the least possible space of time, they were out and standing on the rough short turf, sweet with thyme and other herbage, while the train slid off at the given moment. Mary-Lou and Vi knew what to do and they swiftly marshalled the crowd into something like order and then marched it off to some bushes where Miss Ferrars and the other mistresses came to join them and everyone was silent while she gave them their final instructions.

Chapter 5

A First Climb

"All present and correct?" Miss Ferrars queried when they were all standing in silence. "Everyone got everything? Good! Now listen, please, for I'm not going to repeat anything twice. First of all, remember that if the prefects tell you to do anything or not do anything, they are to be obeyed. No arguing and no coaxing!"

She fixed one or two people with a stern eye and there were smothered giggles and a few blushes from sinners in that direction. "Secondly, anyone who doesn't behave herself today, won't come on the next ramble. Understood?"

They said it was and she nodded and went on.

"Now listen carefully. We turn left from these bushes and the path lies about twenty yards ahead. You may break ranks, of course, but don't go racing ahead. No one will get any chance to loiter behind. We shall have our usual sheepdogs. You may not be less than four together. You are forbidden to try to climb to the top of the railway bank. We don't want to have to go back and explain that we're sorry but we've left two or three of our number behind us, frizzling on the live rails!"

Shouts of laughter greeted this sally and she let them enjoy their laugh for a minute before she held up her hand for silence again.

"I'm saying nothing about the rock side. Anyone who thinks she can climb that is welcome to try! Finally, don't all yell at the tops of your voices at once. I doubt if we shall meet any people, but there may be one or two and there are always the cars going up and down. Remember that you are in uniform and everyone around here knows that uniform. Please don't get us a name for rowdiness.

When we reach Mahlhausen, we'll have our picnic first and then, after I've shown you your limits, you may go off exploring. In the meantime, let me remind you that if you hear me whistle the recall you're to come at once. Don't forget that we must catch the sixteen o'clock train down and it won't wait for us if we're not on the spot when it arrives. Last of all, don't forget that no one may go wandering off by herself. Now make up your groups and let's be off. Time is flying!"

The girls broke up into small clumps at once and Vi Lucy set off with the first batch, with Con Maynard on one side of her and a French girl and Ricki Fry, a great friend of Con's, on the other. Immediately behind them came Margot Maynard; her boon companion, Emerence Hope; Heather Clayton; who had once been a demon for mischief, but was toning down, now that she had reached the mature age of fifteen; and Charmian Spencer, another of the same class.

Miss Ferrars, after a quick consultation with Mary-Lou, set off with a crowd of all the worst imps of Inter V and Miss Bertram went with her, leaving Miss Derwent with a bunch of Vb and two or three from Inter V. Mary-Lou was left to take charge of the rest, including Pen and Ted herself. However, Len Maynard and Rosamund Lilley were among them and those two young people had a well-trained sense of responsibility, considering they were both so young. Len, as the eldest of nine, came by it naturally. Rosamund, the family baby, had developed it during her years at the school.

Mary-Lou looked over her party with calm assurance and summoned Ted and Pen to keep her company. The rest, she sent ahead, with Len and Rosamund as leaders.

"We three will be whippers-in," she told her chosen companions with a grin. "It won't be needed so much today. There's only the one path and it's a lot too narrow for anyone to go straying off; but it's always as well to make sure that no one has a chance to dillydally. There they go and it's our turn. En avant, mes amies!" And she marched them off to where the path running alongside the tracks, went up the mountains.

When they were going well, she smiled at Ted who had remained silent, though Pen had chattered easily enough. "Ever done any climbing before, Ted?"

Ted shook her head as she returned the smile. "Never been near any mountains. We live in Dorset, but I've been at school since I was a kid and mostly in flattish country. Of course, there are some good cliffs in Dorset, but I've never had any chance to play round them. We live about twenty-five miles from the coast."

Mary-Lou laughed. "I've seen the Dorset cliffs. I shouldn't think climbing about them would be exactly a piece of cake. Anyhow, it was mountaineering I meant, and really, going up a path like this." She gestured ahead to the path which wound up the mountain slope with many twists and turns, all of them steep enough to test the girls' power of endurance as fully as need be.

"No," Ted replied. "Anyhow, at my last school, if we did do anything you could call a ramble, it was over the Downs—the school was in Sussex—and there's nothing to call a real climb there. Do we often do this sort of thing?"

"When it's possible—this term, of course, the early part of next, and sometimes the last few days of the Easter term."

Ted stared round. The path was a kind of miniature canyon, with a high grassy bank on the left-hand side and a sheer wall of limestone rock on the other. The rock tended to slope over the path and she could easily understand why Miss Ferrars had given that casual permission to anyone who liked to try to climb it. Only a fly, she decided, could hope to negotiate that. Then she gave it up and attended to the path which was not only steep, but rough, with snags to be avoided and, here and there, outcroppings of the rock that must be scrambled over.

From above, they could hear the voices of the others and at first, Ted chattered quite as gaily, finding Mary-Lou something of a change from other prefects she had known. That young woman was hail-fellow-well-met with most folk and Ted was no exception to the rule. But before long, she found that she had not much breath left for talking. It was taking all she knew to keep up with the rest. Besides that, her legs were beginning to ache with the unaccustomed strain on her muscles. Not that she said anything. She was much too proud for that; but before they had been going very long, she found herself wishing that someone else would ask for a breather.

Oddly enough, no one had explained to her that the usual manner of walking was apt to be very tiring on mountain slopes. Mary-Lou, knowing that Pen was doing "sheepdog" as the girls called it, had taken it for granted that she had told the new girl how to manage. She was busy just then, in keeping her eyes and ears open for any possible tricks, for half her group had gone round the curve and were out of sight and they contained Francie Wilford and Carmela Walther who still had a good deal of sinful reputation to live down, though both had improved considerably since being put up to Vb. By the time they were a third of the way up, Ted was beginning to wonder however she was to drag one foot after the other. She even began to think that she must sink her pride and beg for a few minutes' respite.

It did not come to that, however. Finally satisfied that Miss Ferrars' remarks had gone home, Mary-Lou gave her attention to her companions. A glance at the new girl convinced her that unless she did something about it, Ted would be a very lame duck by the time they reached Mahlhausen.

"Scoot on and tell that crowd to put a slight brake on it, Pen," she said. "Tell them from me that if they steam ahead like that, they'll end up by barging into the back of Miss Derwent's little lot and I don't suppose she'll be too pleased."

Pen was off, but Mary-Lou shouted after her to tell the others to wait for her and Ted at the halfway shelf. Then she turned to Ted who was thankfully leaning up against the rock wall and trying to get her breath.

"Hot, isn't it?" she said genially. "Let's have a minute's squat against the bank, shall we? Come on!" And she hauled Ted over to the bank and sat her down on a narrow ridge just above the ground. Then she leaned up against it herself, pulled out her handkerchief and mopped her face.

"Ouf! It's a scorcher today! Hang on a sec while I rummage in my rucksack. I think I remembered to put in my eau-de-cologne ice." She swung the bag down, fumbled for a moment or two and brought out the tube with a whoop. "Here we are! Rub that over your wrists and face. It'll cool you down a little."

Ted took it gratefully and found it most refreshing. When she had finished, Mary-Lou used it herself. Then she put it away, shouldered the rucksack once more and took the new girl's hands to heave her to her feet. "Sorry I can't give you longer, but you tend to stiffen up if you lounge around after a stiffish bit of walking like this. *Hup* you come!"

Up Ted came, but even the brief pause had helped her to second wind. "I suppose it's like messing around after the first good game of hockey of the season," she said.

"Exactly. Or a really stiff set of tennis. You play hockey, then? Well, it's no use telling Hilary that, though it would have rejoiced her heart earlier on. Next term she'll be a Millie and the school hockey won't concern her, except that the school and the Millies meet in the inter-house matches."

Ted stared. "I don't know what you mean," she said bluntly.

Mary-Lou chuckled. "Hasn't anyone told you yet that the finishing branch is dedicated to St. Mildred? We always call them Millies. I'll be one myself, next term, worse luck!" she added ruefully.

"Oh?" Ted was not very sure what to say. Luckily, Mary-Lou did not wait for a reply. She was anxious to help the new girl, having taken rather a fancy to her.

"She's got a lot in her," she thought as she glanced down from the height of her own five feet nine inches at the pointed face, at present rather tired, but vivid enough for all that.

"Here's something else for you," she said as she pulled Ted's arm through hers in a chummy way. "That is that on a walk like this, you've got to bend your knees very slightly at each step. It saves your shin muscles enormously. Didn't anyone explain that to you? No? Careless apes! Well, you try it, and you'll soon see that you can get over the ground more easily."

Ted meekly obeyed her and discovered after the first awkwardness of it that what the Head Girl said was true. It did help to relieve the strain on her muscles and, once she had got into it, the aching ceased to worry her quite so much.

"Take the longest breaths you can and breathe through your nose," Mary-Lou instructed her. "It all helps, you'll find."

Up and up they went, higher and higher, now shielded from the direct rays of the sun for a short space; then, at a turn in the path, coming out into the full blaze. Ted grew hotter and hotter and her thick black hair flopped about her till, for two pins, she would have grabbed the first knife handy and shorn it all to the nape of her neck. Even Mary-Lou, eyeing it with secret horror, could think of nothing to do about it just then. But at last they reached the halfway place where the rest were waiting for them and Ted was glad to see that she was not the only one to feel parboiled. At least half of them were ripely scarlet and even active Len, whose long legs seemed to eat up the distance, was mopping her face freely.

Mary-Lou and Ted were greeted with shouts and the others clustered round the Head Girl to know if they might go on. Only Len detached herself from them and came to grab Ted and pull her to the gap in the bank, saying, "Look, Ted!"

Ted looked and gasped audibly. It was a very clear day and for miles and miles she saw through the break, across the rude fence put there to guard it, mountains rising over mountains, heaving great shoulders against the blue sky. She caught the dazzle of sunlight on ice on one or two of the highest and saw the white peaks of others and cried out with delight. She was looking at her first snow-capped mountains, and that ice could be nothing but glaciers!

"There! Did you ever see anything to beat that?" Len demanded impressively.

Mary-Lou overheard. "You sound as if you'd done it all yourself," she grinned.

Len grinned back. "Isn't it miraculous? Like it, Ted?"

"Well," Mary-Lou elected to chip in here, "we'd better get cracking again. I'm beginning to feel hollow, not to mention the fact that if we don't do something about it, Ferry will be coming to see if I've pushed a few of you over to get rid of you. Get down to it, folks!"

She shooed them on and Ted was startled to see how instantly she was obeyed. She was accustomed to the prefect system, of course, but even at her last school, she could just imagine what grumbling and arguing there would have been among the younger girls at being moved on so summarily. She glanced up at Mary-Lou who was too busy looking after the others to notice. She swung along beside the new girl with an easy, graceful movement and if her manner was masterful, it was also very friendly. At the same time Ted realised that she could be a stern disciplinarian when she chose. Something about the blue eyes warned her that on occasion they could glint like steel and the smiling lips could set in hard straight lines.

At this point, Mary-Lou spoke. "You're coming on much better now. You're getting nicely into the swing of it. Legs aching very badly?"

"Just a bit," Ted owned—and wondered at herself for owning it. Normally, she was far too proud to admit that she was up against anything. Then she added, "All the same, it's worth it. That view of Len's was the cat's bath-mat!"

Mary-Lou broke into a peal of ringing laughter. "What a ghastly description! But I see what you mean. All the same, my love, I'd advise you to sort out your adjectives. Speaking decent English is a biggish part of our training here. And while I think of it, avoid 'marvellous' as you would the plague! The Head's dead nuts against it. That's why Len and Co. call things miraculous and magnificent or almost anything else. I believe they had a good wigging on the subject from the Head last term. You may as well start off well, you know."

"Yes, I see. Thanks a lot," Ted said in her meekest voice. Inwardly she was wondering at herself; also at Mary-Lou. The Head Girl at her last school had been a very apart person and so had the rest of the prefects. Certainly, they had never mingled with their juniors in quite the way that the grandees of the Chalet School seemed to do; and that without prejudicing their dignity one iota.

"Where is the nearest glacier to here?" she asked a minute or two later.

"Up there," Mary-Lou said, waving her hand upwards and to the right.

"Up there? Do you mean on this mountain?" Ted demanded.

"What else? Not that you'll get a sniff at it today. Too far off and anyhow it's right round at the other side. The station for that is Wahlstein which is the end of the railway at that side. All our crowd have seen it and I don't know that I'm anxious to see it again." She shivered a little.

"Why?" Ted smelt a story at once, but Mary-Lou only shook her head and laughed.

"That's another story. If you really want to know anything about it, ask Mdlle de Lachennais. She's climbed all round these parts."

"Mdlle has?" Ted couldn't believe her ears.

"Why not? She's a member of the French Alpinist Club and jolly good."

This left Ted without any breath for comment. What on earth sort of school was this when one of the mistresses was a member of the Alpinist Club? As she toiled upwards by Mary-Lou's side it struck her forcibly that when her cousin had told her that she was having a complete break with her old life, she had spoken no more than the truth.

"I'll bet Mother knew nothing about all this or she'd have put a spoke in my coming somehow," she thought with sudden bitterness. Then she had to give up thinking for she found that, steep as their road up had been, they had reached an even steeper slope and for the next fifteen minutes or so she was fully occupied with dragging herself up. The perspiration was pouring down her crimson face when she ventured at last to hint to Mary-Lou that it would be easier if she might carry her blazer.

"Not unless you want to risk pneumonia! And whether you like to risk it or not, I'm not having any! I can just imagine Matey on the subject and I'd rather be excused, thank you. It's best to keep in her good books —if you possibly can," she added as an afterthought. "Be warned, Ted! Keep the right side of Matey. You'll be awfully sorry for yourself if you don't."

So far, Ted had not fallen foul of Matey, but she had heard her remarks to Heather Clayton only the night before when Heather had dropped her tube of toothpaste in the corridor and stamped on it, bursting it and spreading the paste in every direction. She decided to take Mary-Lou's advice.

Just when it seemed as if she couldn't drag herself another pace forward, the voices which had been coming faintly to them, suddenly sounded close at hand as they turned a sharp curve. Mary-Lou hauled her up the last few feet of the way and she found herself standing on a grassy shelf, panting for breath, hotter than she had ever been in all her life and yet with an exultant feeling. She had done it! Then Miss Ferrars joined them, just as Mary-Lou said, "Well done, Ted! Jolly good for a first climb!"

"What on earth have you two been doing?" Miss Ferrars began. Then she caught sight of Ted's scarlet face. "Ted! My dear girl, you look as if you had been well and truly boiled! Come out of the breeze and sit over here behind these bushes and cool off or you may catch a chill. Make room beside you for Ted, Len, and let her cool off slowly. No, keep your blazer on for the present, Ted. You may take if off when you've really cooled down, but not before."

Len and Rosamund obligingly made room for her and Ted dropped down beside them thankfully. It was a relief to stretch her aching legs on the short, sweet turf, smelling of thyme and other aromatic herbs, and get out of the blazing sunshine. She pulled off her hat, lay flat on her back and fanned herself for a minute or two. Then the packed rucksack digging into her back made her sit up with an "*Ow*!"

"Take it off, you goop!" Len said, bending to help her. "You've done jolly well, Ted. It's a pretty stiff climb up, even if it was as safe as houses. Shall I take out your eats? Ferry was just saying before you and Mary-Lou arrived that we had best have our picnic now and then we'll have more time for a really good roust about on the shelf."

Ted rolled over on her side and watched as Len unpacked the parcels. By that time, she was beginning to cool down a little and she was able to sit up and take an interest in the spread the kitchen had provided. There were sandwiches of cheese and redcurrant jelly; a meat pie with the meat embedded in a rich jelly; a little polythene case held salad, almost as crisp and cold as when it had been taken out of the refrigerator; another was filled with something sweet and cold and fluffy; finally, there was a bag containing a big double handful of ripe golden gooseberries. At one side was a small thermos flask of Karen's delicious lemonade which was made with real lemons and sugar and agreeably acid to the taste.

Len and Rosamund had the same and when everything was unpacked, they bent their heads to say their Grace and then fell to with sharpened appetites.

It was very pleasant up there, with the soft breeze blowing and little but the sound of their own tongues to break the stillness. It must be owned that they made quite enough noise among them, even though they remembered Miss Ferrar's warning and talked and laughed quietly. When the last crumb had vanished and the flasks were empty, everyone sighed contentedly. They packed away the papers, cases and bags into their rucksacks and then one or two jumped to their feet.

Miss Ferrars rose to hers, too. "No, you don't!" she said emphatically. "You may rest for half-an-hour before you do another thing. Sit down again, girls, and keep quiet until I give the word!"

They dropped instantly, though Heather asked, "Can we talk, please?"

"Judging by what I know of you all, you certainly can! So far as I am concerned, you equally may. Really, Heather!"

Heather went red. The Head was dead against the loose use of "can" for "may" and the girls were well drilled into it. However, Miss Ferrars only laughed at her, so she curled up and lay silent until she had recovered her normal colour which did not take long. Heather was rarely badly upset. For the next half-hour, they all sprawled, or curled up as suited them best and though there was an undercurrent of chatter, it was a very quiet one. Quite a number of them just lay there, enjoying the peace, the champagne-like air and their well-deserved rest.

All the same, when the mistresses gave the signal by jumping up, no one was behindhand in copying them. Miss Ferrars blew a blast on her whistle and when they were all standing silent, she gave them their instructions.

"You may go where you like about the shelf so long as you keep away from the edge. Keep your hats on. The sun is terrific and I'm sure none of you want a go of sunstroke. Now that's all for the moment. Don't forget to come the moment you hear the whistle."

She sat down again beside Miss Bertram and Miss Andrews and the girls, set free of the place, began to make up their parties before they set off to explore.

Chapter 6

An Unexpected Event

While the others were joining forces in groups, Ted stood a little to one side. She was very unsure of herself, and had no idea what she ought to do. She was in Pen's charge, but Pen was one of a chummery of five who did everything together and no matter how polite they were, she always had the feeling that they merely tolerated her because the Head had handed her over to Pen. On the other hand, she knew that Len and Rosamund were close friends and she felt that if she tagged on to them, she would be just as unwelcome.

She had got this far when Len put an end to it by holding out her hand. "Come on, Ted! You come with Ros and me. We're going up into the pines and through them to the far end of the shelf and then round by the edge. That'll give you a chance to get really cool, for we aren't going to hurry ourselves."

Pretty Rosamund Lilley joined in the invitation. "Yes, you come with us, Ted. Pen's gang always like to go off by themselves and you'll have more fun with us."

"Are you really sure?" Ted asked doubtfully, half ashamed of her own eagerness to close with the offer, but anxious, all the same, to take it.

"Shouldn't ask you if we weren't!" quoth Len. She laughed at Pen who came up to extend a half-reluctant invitation to the new girl to come with them. "Too late Pennywise! Ted's coming with us. You buzz off and leave us three to go our own way. Come on, you two! I've been up here before and I can show you everything." Len slipped one hand through an arm of Rosamund, and the other through one of Ted's. "We'll do a saunter across to the pines. It'll be cool there."

"Coveys of flies, though," Rosamund said, laughing, as they swung off across the shelf. "They seem to swarm under the pines. However, this weather, you get them wherever you go."

As they went, the other two chattered gaily. Ted was too busy pondering on Len's unexpected friendliness. She knew well enough that in most schools, you kept to the people in your own form. Why, then, should Len—and Rosamund, too, for that matter—be so chummy? She was not to know that Len Maynard was her mother's own girl when it came to helping other folk. When she had been at the Chalet School, Joey Bettany, as she then was, had earned for herself the reputation of being a champion butter-in. Len gave every sign of following in her mother's footsteps in this as well as in a good many other ways. She felt dimly that all was not right with this new girl. Why, for instance, did she always seem to be on the lookout for trouble? And what was wrong with her home? Without meaning it, Ted had let slip one or two remarks that had given Len to think furiously. She had been forbidden to tell the others what had happened at her other schools. She herself was not exactly anxious for any of them to know that she had had to leave for bad behaviour, but she had a careless tongue and more than once she had nearly let the secret out.

Now, as she strolled to the back of the shelf with Len's arm through hers and both Len and Rosamund talking hard, she thought to herself that while the Chalet School had been really decent, so far, she had not expected anything quite so friendly as soon as this. She hardly knew either of the girls so it could have nothing to do with the undoubted fascination she could use on her fellows when she chose.

As they reached the beginning of the tall pines which grew in a belt all along the back of the shelf, she kept stealing glances at Len. How pretty she was with her chestnut hair tied back off her delicate, mobile face in a long, curly tail! She had a perfect complexion, too; and as if that was not enough, her eyes like English wood violets were fringed with long black lashes and her eyebrows were slender arches. Remembering the heavy black lines that nearly met over her nose, Ted heaved a deep sigh. If she had looked like that, her mother might have managed to be fond of her. But she didn't and her mother wasn't—Ted was under no delusions there!—and, so far as she could see there was nothing to be done about it.

"What's the why of that?" Len demanded. "You nearly blew Ros and me right through the pines, sighing like that. Anything wrong?"

Ted came back to Mahlhausen and forced a laugh. "Nothing! It's so gorgeous up here and the air's so marvellous! I feel as fit as a fiddle again and as if I could walk miles and miles."

"Don't worry! We shall have the mile and a half from the station when we go back," Rosamund pointed out. "Anyhow, unless you propose to go round in circles I'm afraid it can't be done. Didn't you say the shelf comes to a sudden stop over there, Len?" She gesticulated with her free hand.

"It does," Len agreed. "You can see for yourselves where that huge sort of cliff stands out. It goes sheer down and though I believe you can get over it, we aren't doing any more climbing than we've done already. You can go on up at the other side, of course; the path continues up; but it's rather tricky, I've heard Mamma say. Here we are at the trees, thank goodness! Isn't it lovely and cool? I'm taking off my hat. Ferry wouldn't mind here." And she removed her big, shady hat and slung it on one arm by the elastic.

The other two followed suit. They had dropped arms now and were loitering through the ranks of black-trunked pines and Ted put her troubles behind her. They had plenty to do to keep off the flies. Ted used her hat as a fan until Rosamund pointed out that she wasn't doing the brim any good.

"Matey'll have a lot to say if you take it back with a battered brim," she pointed out.

"I've heard Papa say that walnuts are among the few trees where you aren't pestered with insects," Len chimed in, slapping vigorously at her tormentors. She suddenly giggled. "What we really want is a few cigarettes. He always smokes his pipe when we go through the forest in summer. That keeps them off. They loathe tobacco—or it may be the smoke. I wouldn't know."

"Have you ever smoked?" Ted asked curiously.

"No fear! Mamma said if any of us started that game before we were seventeen at least, she'd give us a punishment we'd never forget. She didn't say what it was, but from the way she said it, I should say it was something too nasty for words! What about you, Ros? Ever done it?"

"Mum would have my blood if I did," Rosamund said simply. "My elder sisters both do and she knows, of course; but they don't do it at home."

Len turned to Ted. "Ros is an aunt! D'you think she looks like one!"

"Well, so am I," Ted replied, "though as I've never seen my nephews and niece, I never think about them very much. They live in Canada, you see. My eldest brother is fruit-farming out in British Columbia, so it's rather far for a week's trip either home or there."

It was the first time she had been so expansive, and Rosamund took instant advantage of it. "Your brother must be years older than you?"

"So he is—eighteen years older. And the twins are fifteen. I was an afterthought."

Rosamund laughed. "I'm rather like that myself. Charmian, the sister next to me, is six years older than I am."

"If you're going to swank about things like that," Len said, elevating her pretty nose, "let me remind you that we three are nearly thirteen years older than Cecil. And when the new baby arrives—only we're all dying for twins again—we'll be almost fifteen years older."

Ted stared at her. "More babies? But I thought there were nine of you already?"

"So there are, but Mamma and Papa say: 'The more the merrier' and Mamma says it's far easier to run a family if there are plenty of you. We're hoping it'll be twins because they'll be company for Cecil when they grow and she'll be only two years and a bit older. Mike, my third brother, was three years younger than Charles and three years older than Felix and Felicity and he was the outside of enough last year and the year before. Now, of course, he's at prep school with the other two."

Ted suddenly looked wistful. "I only wish I had a brother or sister my own age. With the boys so much older, I've always been alone."

"But not when you're at school," Len pointed out briskly.

As no one had ever encouraged Ted to pity herself, she was brought up short and Rosamund, noticing her blush, changed the subject to the two highlights of that term — the sale of work in aid of the free beds in the children's ward at the great Sanatorium at the far end of the Görnetz Platz, and the school sports. Ted forgot her own griefs and listened with deepening wonder.

"What sort of thing will we do for the sale this year?" she asked.

"Goodness knows! We'll have to be thinking about ideas for it, Ros. You know how they like to have ideas from each form. Let's get down to it early and have a chance of putting in something they're likely to use," Len proposed.

"OK, but not now. It's much too hot!" Rosamund said, using her hat as a fan.

Their description of the sports made Ted gasp aloud. She was accustomed to school sports. At her last school, they had been taken in grim earnest. People entered for any events trained for them most professionally. They practised hard in their free time. Diet was watched with anxious care and when the day came and the winners of the various heats met in the finals, it was a darkly businesslike affair, quite unlike the lighthearted events Len and Rosamund related.

"Remember last year's blindfold race?" Len asked with a shriek of laughter, "and how you and Mary-Lou would insist on walking into each other's arms? And Gwen Jones marched straight into the umpire's ladder where Burnie was perched and sent it flying and Burnie landed in a thorn bush?"

The pair yelled with laughter in which Ted joined.

"And Hilary Bennet ran across the court and plonked herself down on Dr. Jack's knee!" Rosamund bubbled with a fresh peal.

"And then she grabbed Mamma's hat and pulled all her hair down!" Len wound up.

"I think the funniest of all was the final of the tug-o'-war," Rosamund said, mopping her eyes. "The rope snapped—remember?—and every last one landed on top of Hilda and Blossom! How they all yelled!"

"What gorgeous fun your sports seem to be!" Ted said.

"Don't say 'your' like that!" Len scolded her. "Say 'our'. You're one of us now. Oh, and Ted, do go in for the blindfold race this year. Ros and I mean to."

"We could practise together in our spare time," Rosamund added.

The expression in the new girl's eyes as she said this, baffled them completely. It was a mixture of surprise, doubt and gratitude and they had said nothing, so far as they knew, to call it there. But the fact was that this was the first time that Ted had met with such open-hearted friendship. At her other schools, her own kind had admired her daring and resourcefulness when it came to thinking up and doing wicked deeds; but she had never once had a genuine friend. Len's inherited trick of greeting her with almost open arms and Rosamund's quieter kindliness nearly stunned her. As for her fellow conspirators at her last school, they had mostly contrived to slide out of the scrapes they had shared with her, leaving her to bear most of the blame. She had felt no affection for them. But here were two girls who knew nothing about her, and yet who seemed ready to be real friends withhher.

"I wish I was in your form!" she said on a sudden impulse.

"Can't you make it?" Len asked. "What's stopping you? Not brains, I'll bet."

"Oh, I don't know. My maths, for one thing, I should think. And then I didn't know the first word of German.

When you've got to do lessons in a language you just don't know for two days every week, it's a bit of a snag."

"But that'll come all right," Rosamund assured her. "I didn't know a word myself when I first came, but I soon began to pick things up. What's wrong with your maths, Ted?"

"Oh, I never loved them and then we always ragged in maths at my last school."

"Well, don't try that game on here," Rosamund warned her. "Willie's a pet, but try to rag in her lessons and she leaves you wondering how much is left of you!"

"I can imagine it!" Ted murmured.

"Let's sit down. We've oceans of time," Len said with a glance at her watch. "Go on about your work, Ted. Is there anything else? For if it's just maths and German, we can soon get you on in those."

"My Latin's not up to it. I've only learnt two years and—well—we rather ragged in Latin class as well as maths."

"You seem to have done an awful lot of ragging!" Len said severely. "Didn't you get into ghastly rows with the Head?"

Ted had no more to say, but her cheeks were scarlet.

"Leave it," Rosamund ordered. "Ted, I'm sure you can manage to pull up in both Latin and German. I overheard someone say that your French is miraculous and you're Mdlle's blue-eyed boy in those classes. You ought to be able to manage other languages quite as well. As for maths, well, you won't get any chance of ragging with Willie. I should say you'll soon find yourself going ahead there, too."

"I'll give you a tip," Len observed. "Learn ten new words of Latin and German every day. It's vocab that so often holds you up, but if you do that, you can't help getting on. Ros and I could hear you say them at odd times."

"But you're in Vb and I'm only Inter V," Ted pointed out.

"I know you are, but you don't have to stay there, you goop! If you do a spot of extra hard work in lessons and prep and we two give you a hand now and then, you ought to go shooting ahead in no time. If you're really good, you'll be shoved up all right. I don't see why you shouldn't manage it by half-term, say. I never heard that any of the rest of Inter V were geniuses!" Len finished with a giggle.

"You try that," Rosamund chimed in. "We'll help you out. I was helped like anything when I first came and needed it. You see, Ted, I'd never been at a school like this before and lots of things I just didn't know. But everyone rallied round and I found I was able to keep my end up and when Len and the rest went up this year, I did, too. I hadn't expected it and it took the whole year and a term for me to make up what I didn't know. But this year, it's been different. I can manage quite comfortably. So will you because you've done some Latin and geometry and I hadn't." She glanced across at Len who gave a slight nod. "Have a go, Ted—do! We'd like to have you in Vb with us."

Ted was silent. She knew all about her own powers of attraction, but she could never have imagined that they would affect girls like Len Maynard and Rosamund Lilley. Hitherto, it had always been the worst and wildest spirits who had followed her. The other two were silent as well. Neither could have said just why they felt they wanted Ted with them, but they knew that they did.

"I somehow know that it would be the best thing for her," Len thought. "Why? I don't know. Could I go to Auntie Hilda and ask her—out of school, of course. No, p'raps not. She might think it cheek. I'll have to get Mamma on the job. Now when can I see her? For the sooner it's done the better."

Ted spoke at last. "I honestly don't see why you should, but I can see you really mean it, so I'll have a go. Whether I'll make it or not is another thing."

"Good! Then we'd better be getting on or we shan't do all I planned," Len said, jumping up. "Give me a brush down, one of you. I'll do as much for you."

They brushed the pine needles off each other and then sauntered along again. They reached the end of the pines where they paused to pull on their hats for the sun was showing what he could do when he tried. Then they looked round. They were facing the great spur Len had pointed out, and a small hut which seemed to nestle under it. Huddled outside the door was a small girl of eight or nine who was sobbing bitterly.

It was not in Len to see such woe and not do her best to give comfort. She rushed forward, dropped down beside the child, put an arm round her and said in her pretty German, "Oh, don't cry like that! Tell us what's wrong and we'll help you. Here! Take my handkerchief and dry your eyes and tell us all about it."

The other two had come up by this time and were squatting down beside the pair. The child was sobbing out a long story in what sounded to Ted and Rosamund like gibberish, but Len managed to get the drift of it and cuddled the small girl, speaking words that literally cooed with sympathy.

"Her mother's ill and her father sent her out of the house and she's not feeling awfully fit herself," she explained to the other two at last. She took one of the grimy hands in her own and gave a cry. "I should jolly well think she isn't! She's burning hot! One of you knock and see if she can't go in and go to bed. I'm sure she's feverish! She keeps on shivering and yet she's so hot!"

"I'll go!" Ted straightened up, marched to the door and gave it a hearty thump. It flew open, showing a tall, brawny man who looked at her blankly. From behind him came a low, rapid muttering and Ted could make out a badly tumbled bed at the back of the room. It contained a woman, whose long hair tossed as she flung about from side to side.

Suddenly a man's voice sounded behind her. "Len—Rosamund! What on earth are you doing here? Come away from that child at once—at once I say!"

There was an imperative note in his voice that admitted of no disobedience. Ted, turning, saw Len and Rosamund getting up. And then he saw her.

"Come here, you!" he said; and Ted shot back to join the others.

Len looked up at him with fearless eyes. "Uncle Phil! I'm most awfully glad to see you! This kid says her mother's ill and I think she's ill herself—"

"Thank you," he broke in. "You need tell me nothing. Who brought you three up here and how long have you been hanging about the child?"

"Miss Ferrars did," Rosamund said, seeing that Len remained silent. "We're on a ramble. Len and Ted and I—that's Ted who was at the door—came through the pines and we found the kiddy crying her eyes out, so we thought we ought to see what we could do to help."

"I see." His lips closed in a firm line. Len looked at him anxiously. "Uncle Phil, is it something infectious?" Then, as he nodded, "Oh, my goodness! What will Matey say?"

He gave her an exasperated look. "So that's all you can think of? Let me tell you, young woman, you won't see Matey or anyone else in the school for the next eighteen days—none of you! You're going straight down with me to San and you're going into isolation. Now keep away from everyone else. Don't let them come near you. Do you understand?"

Scared, they agreed that they did and he picked up the child who was sobbing wearily, and went into the hut. He emerged a little later, carrying a steaming pan in which lay a syringe.

"Now then!" he said, when he reached them, "up with your sleeves!" He set his case on the ground, opened it and proceeded to lift the syringe from the boiling water, fill it and then inject them all before he opened his lips again.

"Thank heaven I guessed what was wrong up here and came prepared! Now listen to me. You are to stay here until I come for you. A stretcher is coming up for Frau Wilhelm and we'll have to put Margrit on it as well. When that's gone down and not before, I'll come for you and take you down with me. Rosamund, where is Miss Ferrars?"

"We left her and the other mistresses sitting up by the path under the bushes," Rosamund said in subdued tones.

"Right! She must take all the rest down at once before the stretcher comes. I'll get into touch with Matey as soon as I've seen that off and she can send what you're likely to need for the next fortnight or so—"

"Will you let Papa know or Mamma?" Len broke in anxiously.

"I'll let them know. Stay here as I told you and don't dare to let anyone come within fifty yards of you!"

With this, he was off, racing at top speed over the rough grass. Ten minutes after he had vanished round the curve of the shelf, they heard the blast of the whistle coming faintly from the other end. They knew, then, that it was unlikely that any of the other girls would appear and all relaxed.

"What do you think it is?" Ted asked nervously.

"I don't know—something deadly infectious, anyhow," Rosamund replied soberly.

But by bedtime that night, everyone was aware that the trio had been in close contact with a smallpox case. Dr. Graves had whisked them off to Isolation, and there they must remain until he could be sure that the vaccination he had so promptly administered had taken effect.

Chapter 7

LEN TAKES A HAND

THANKS to Dr. Graves' prompt measures and to the efforts of all the authorities at San, there was no smallpox epidemic. The unhappy pair who had first become ill remained the only ones. Not even the three who had been in such close contact caught it, though Rosamund's vaccination certainly took with astonishing virulence and for two or three days she was very miserable. Her arm swelled to monumental proportions, her temperature went up with it, and Isolation Sister was sufficiently anxious to put her in a private ward by herself, leaving the other two to entertain each other as best they might.

Joey Maynard drove nearly everyone frantic with her unceasing pleadings to be allowed to go and see to the girls. Finally, Jack Maynard put his foot down firmly and she calmed down—the more easily because by that time, four days had passed and if Rosamund was really ill with the vaccination, neither of the others was a penny the worse. As a slight consolation, she was allowed to go and stand under the windows of the ward where they were and relieve her mind to them.

Len and Ted stood silently at the open window, listening to her diatribe. It lasted quite a while, for when Joey had really got going, she found plenty to say. When she paused for breath, Len was quick to seize her chance.

"But, Mamma," she protested, "I couldn't do anything else and we didn't know it was smallpox or anything else infectious. The poor kid was just breaking her heart. You'd have done it yourself if you'd been there and you know it!"

This was so true that Joey was left without a word to say

more. She gave it up, laughed, chattered with them on various ordinary subjects and went home at last, her mind set at ease, much to the relief of everyone concerned.

In any case, Mme Courvoisier, she who had been Biddy o'Ryan, provided the school and all her friends with a fresh topic for conversation by presenting them with a son and daughter.

That was the day that Len and Ted, both bored to tears by being kept in close confinement with very little to do, asked Soeur Marie-Anne if she would beg the school to send them some old textbooks that didn't matter so that they might do a few lessons by way of amusement.

The nun looked at them and laughed. "I agree that it would be well if we found a little work for you, *mes petites*. I see no reason why you should waste so much time while you are here. Once, I meant to teach, and I will give you lessons in mathematics and also request you to write essays for me. For six hours each day you will work. Perhaps that will keep you out of mischief." Her soft black Provençal eyes danced merrily under her big horned coif. "No need to ask the school for books. I have plenty. See you, clear those two small tables. I will bring paper and pencils and you may set to work at once. Three hours every morning and two hours every afternoon after the siesta. Each evening, you will sew for an hour. We have plenty of mending to occupy you so long."

"Oh, my only aunt!" Len said dismally. No more than her mother did she love her needle, though Joey saw to it that all her daughters were good needlewomen.

Soeur Marie-Anne was as good as her word. She brought books and writing materials and that very morning the pair found themselves set down to arithmetic and algebra, Latin grammar and Swiss history; and when the afternoon came, they each had a French essay to write and more Latin and a French poem to prepare.

"We will have a little school," she said cheerfully, "and when cette pauvre Rosémonde is better, she shall join you."

So it began and by the next day, Len was bubbling over

with a new idea. As she and Ted were dressing that morning, she expounded it to the dismayed Ted.

"Ted, I've had an idea. We're going to talk nothing but German during lesson hours."

"But why ever? I scarcely know a word of it!" Ted objected.

"That's why, dunderhead! Don't you see? It's a jolly good chance for you to learn to talk and when we get back to school, you'll find things a lot easier on German days."

Ted saw. "So it will! What a smashing idea!"

"Well, don't say 'smashing' or you'll get yourself fined at school," Len warned her. "No one minds *some* slang, but things like that are definitely forbidden. Anyhow, there are heaps of other words that'll do just as well."

"Oh, lor'! Well, I'll do my best to remember and saints can't do more!"

Len had yet another idea when Soeur Marie-Anne, having set them to work and gone off to her own duties, proved to have judged them to be at the same standard. It was work that Vb had done the previous term, but two or three of the algebra problems were beyond Ted. Len instantly proposed that she should show the other girl how to do them and, indeed, help her out with anything beyond her.

Ted closed with the offer at once. She was naturally a clever girl, but she had wasted so much time before, that she was behind Len in a good many ways. What Joey had said at the beginning of term about starting with a fresh sheet had gripped her and she was anxious to make up for lost time. Len took her firmly in hand and by the time their quarantine was up, thanks to this and to the fact that Ted had set her mind firmly on her work during lesson hours, she had come on amazingly. Her maths were advanced and, as Len also took her Latin in hand, that, too, was greatly improved. German, she simply had to pick up when she spent six hours of every day speaking nothing else. Len was a stern tutor and when Rosamund was able to join them, she entered into the scheme with acclamations. Between the pair of them, Ted found that she must either try to speak German or else go dumb for they became instantly deaf to anything else. When Soeur Marie-Anne discovered what they were after, she backed Len up and spoke in German herself. What was more, she changed the lay-sister who had been looking after their needs to a very new German who spoke little but her own tongue. It was a great help.

Apart from the German, Ted found that she was really understanding maths as she had not done before. Len had a genuine gift for teaching and she exercised it to the full for her new friend—for friends the three girls were soon to become. These days together helped them to know each other as little else would have done. Certainly they grew close much faster than they could have done at school.

"You *can* teach!" Ted said gratefully once when Len had explained a sticky theorem in geometry to her. "I really do get this now."

"Oh, I mean to teach when I'm grown up," Len said airily. "I'm going to Oxford to get my degree and then I expect to teach in English schools for a year or so before I come back to teach at the school."

"But why not come straight back to teach? I'm sure they'd have you."

Len grinned. "No fear! I'm waiting until everyone at school with me has left. They'd know a lot too much about me otherwise!"

Len changed the subject. "What are you going to do?"

"Haven't thought much about it so far. Not teach, anyhow! And I don't think I'd much like being a nurse. I'd always be afraid of doing something wrong."

"Ros is going to be a gardener. What about that for an idea?"

Ted shook her head. "Too slow! I like to be on the go all the time."

They had to leave it at that, but Len and Rosamund between them were putting new ideas into Ted every day. She found, much to her surprise, that she had simply next to no time to spend planning evil deeds.

What was more, she didn't even want to plan them. Life was much too full at present for that sort of thing!

It was at this time that Ted's long-sleeping conscience began to wake up. Hitherto, it had never bothered her much; but now that things seemed to be going better for her than ever before, it began to whisper. Len and Rosamund had taken her into their friendship most wholeheartedly and she felt that come what might, these two would always stand by her.

"*They* wouldn't come in on the fun and then slide out and leave me to hold the baby," she thought one night when the bright full moon, shining across her face, had roused her. "If they were in any of it, they'd be in the lot. I couldn't be pig enough to do things that would get the lot of us into trouble. Not when they've been so all round decent to me! But can I go on working and all that and chuck thinking up mad things altogether?"

The question worried her badly for the next night or two. She was only human and it was most unlikely that she could turn right round and become a new person in so short a time. "I suppose," she thought on the last night of quarantine when, unable to sleep, she perched on the broad windowsill beside her bed, "I'll just have to try not to think of mad things. It won't be easy and I'll find it dull at first, at any rate, but I don't see what else I can do. Only I hope to goodness no one ever puts up a dare to me. I've never yet passed up a dare and I don't think I could do it."

The door opened softly. It was midnight and Soeur Marie-Anne, coming to seek her rest, had glanced up and seen Ted silhouetted against the open window. She had come to find out what was wrong. As it was a light night with the moon little past the full, she carried no torch and Ted, buried in her perplexities, had no idea she was there until a hand was laid gently on her shoulder.

"Hush! You must not wake the others!" the Sister said in low, firm tones. "Why are you not in your bed, *ma fille*?" Her fingers touched hand and cheek, but Ted was quite cool. She was not ill, though the eyes she lifted to Soeur Marie-Anne's face were troubled enough.

"I was thinking—and I couldn't sleep," she said in an undertone.

Soeur Marie-Anne looked at her thoughtfully. "We cannot talk here. Put on your slippers and come with me. Tell me what is troubling you and if I can help you, I will."

She took Ted into the vacant ward next door and sat down on the first bed, pulling the girl down beside her. "Now *petite*, tell me what is the matter."

Ted went crimson. "I—I—it's a bit hard to explain," she stammered.

"Do I not know it? But confession is good for us all. When we have humbled ourselves to own our sins, the devil is put to flight. Tell me what troubles you that you cannot sleep."

Thus urged, Ted did what she had thought she could never do—tell the story of her misdeeds to someone else. Soeur Marie-Anne listened in silence. When at last the halting confession was over, she waited a moment.

"Are you sorry for all this?" she asked at last.

Ted thought. "I—I don't know. I—I don't think so," she owned honestly. "Only Len and Ros have been so decent to me and they're the kind that stand by you. I couldn't get them into rows, but I don't see how I'm to help doing mad things—especially if anyone dares me."

"By yourself—no, my child. But you need not try to do it by yourself. God will always give you strength to fight if you ask Him. Ask, and you will see that it is so—if you ask truly wishing it." Then, as Ted remained silent, she added, "Come, *petite*, give me your promise that when you leave us to go out into the world again you will try it. You will find that what I am saying is true and then you will wish to do it."

"All right, I promise," Ted said slowly.

The Vincentian looked down at her, pity in her eyes. "Poor little soul!" she thought. "But she has a chance now, with our good school and her two good friends. Holy Mary, watch over her and keep her safe!"

Chapter 8

Insects—and a Shock for Ted

Quarantine ended at last. Dr. Graves kept them there for three weeks, observing that where smallpox was concerned, he preferred to be safe rather than sorry. On the Sunday morning exactly three weeks to the day when the trouble had all begun, they packed their cases. They said goodbye and thanks to Soeur Marie-Anne who kissed them and blessed them. Then Dr. Jack arrived with the family runabout, bundled them in and drove them straight back to school.

It was late May by this time and the sun was blazing down as he had blazed on that momentous Sunday. Dr. Jack decanted them at the gate and left them to go and report themselves while he went on to Freudesheim. This was his free weekend and he proposed to spend it peacefully.

The three picked up their cases and walked demurely round the building to the side entrance. They went to their Splashery where they hung up their big hats and changed into garden sandals before they went off to find someone to whom they might report.

Most people were at one or other of the church services, for Jack had come for them at ten; but after some searching, they found Miss Dene who was on duty with those people who were literally under the weather. This often happened during the very hot weather and as Rosalie herself had attended the early morning service, she had volunteered to take charge though it was a free Sunday for her. The entire party was in the rock garden which, at this hour, was well shaded from the worst efforts of the sun. The girls were resting quietly in deck chairs, reading or chatting. Rosalie herself was busy with her private correspondence. When she saw the girls at the top of the steps, she waved to them and waited until they reached her.

"So here you are at last!" she said, smiling as she looked them over. "You don't look a penny the worse for your three weeks, not even you, Rosamund. I only hope you mean to settle down to work now. You must have missed a good deal."

The three of them looked at each other and grinned, but said nothing. What had happened was a matter for themselves and they were not going to take even Miss Dene into their confidence. Let her get the shock of the results along with everyone else!

"What should we do?" Len asked. "Unpack our cases and settle in first?"

"Yes; I think that would be best. Then find yourselves books and come out here until the rest come back. No ramble today, by the way. The radio promises us something outstanding in the way of heat so we're going to take life very quietly. Now go and unpack — and don't forget your hats when you come back. We don't want you to risk sunstroke on top of your latest!"

They joined in her laughter and then moved off keeping carefully in the shade. The sun was much too hot to be comfortable.

All three were not only members of Ste. Thérèse de Lisieux House, but also of the same dormitory where Rosamund was a dormitory prefect. Unpacking was a very easy matter and then, after hunting out books from the library shelves in the common room, they went out to the rock garden where the others presently found them when they returned from church.

There was a rapturous meeting between Len and her triplets and even Ted was greeted joyously by Pen and Co. News of all kinds had to be exchanged, including the names of the Courvoisier twins which the three ex-prisoners had not, so far, heard.

"The girl is to be Marie-Thérèse and the boy, Patrick Joseph," Margot Maynard announced. "Mamma says they're to be Marie and Pat for everyday use."

The rest of the Sunday was very quiet. All meals were carried out into the garden and it was strictly enjoined on the girls that they must not run about.

The Head had given permission for all Catholics to attend Vespers and the usual May procession at the little chapel beyond the school. Quite a number of the other girls had also begged leave to go. So long as they had written permission from their parents to do so, it was all right. On this evening, all the prefects and most of the rest of VIb turned out and so did a fair number of the Fifths. Several of the mistresses also attended. The Head herself was not of the party, but Rosalie Dene went and so did Kathy Ferrars, Nancy Wilmot, Rosalind Moore and Peggy Burnett. The escort mistresses were Mdlle de Lachennais, Mdlle Lenoir who took most of the junior piano, and Frau Mieders, the domestic science mistress. All in all, quite a large body from the school filed into the seats generally reserved for them.

The chapel had been built in a curve of the mountain wall. On the brightest day it was dark and shadowy and cool—which, it is to be feared, is one reason why some of the girls joined the long lines. The lights were switched on before the school arrived and the doors had been set wide for even here it was hot for once. On this evening, the procession had drawn a larger congregation than usual and before the procession began the chapel was quite full.

Small girls in white frocks and flowing veils came first, scattering flowers. Then came the statue of the Blessed Virgin, borne high on the shoulders of four brawny mountaineers, followed by the altar servers and the priest. They circled the little church going round all the aisles before leaving it, passing round outside while the congregation sang hymns. Then they re-entered the church and Vespers began.

Most of them knew the service and they joined in devoutly. The last blessing was given and the priest, preceded by the procession, the candle-bearers and with two acolytes holding the edges of his cope, passed into the sacristy. The six great candles were still blazing steadily and that was a pity, but the altar boys had had no time to come round with the extinguishers.

The girls had dropped on their knees for the final prayer when there came the sound of a deep humming. The next moment, a swarm of great insects swept into the church, making blindly for the lights. The noise as many of them struck hard, horny heads against the electric light bulbs or the walls of the church was amazing. A number flew straight into the candles, others tangled themselves in the headgear of the women and the beards of the elder men, not to speak of the hair of all. Some of the women screamed and one highly nervous visitor fainted. Several folk went into hysterics. And all the time, the cockchafers, as they turned out to be, buzzed and bumbled helplessly round the interior of the chapel, banging themselves anywhere and everywhere.

Apart from Meg Whyte and Christine Vincent who were terrified, the prefects kept their heads and so did most of the rest of the Seniors. They began to bundle the terrified Juniors out of their seats with stern reminders as to where they were and orders to stop that noise at once! They got the sobbing children out into the open air and set to work to free them from their unwanted attendants. The Middles followed suit and by the time Vater Moritz had got all the lights put out while Dr. Courvoisier, assisted by the mistresses, worked to restore some kind of order, the little edifice was emptied.

It had been a really alarming affair. Con Maynard, in whose black curls no fewer than three of the things had been entangled, was white and shaking and even Rosamund, who had succeeded in freeing herself from the only one which had clung to her, looked pale when they reached the daylight. However, most of them pulled themselves together and they were marched back to school where retailing accounts of the incident to the others helped to calm them down considerably, especially when a good many of them found they were objects of envy.

The sequel came later and gave Ted a shock she did not forget for a long time.

When Matron heard what had happened, she promptly issued orders that everyone who had been to Vespers was to come to her room before going to bed for a dose of her own calming medicine. Bed came early on Sunday nights in any case, so any doctoring stopped there. As quite half the school had been present, Matron had her work cut out to attend to them all, so it escaped her notice that while even Rosamund looked like her normal self, Con Maynard was certainly whiter than usual and there were faint shadows under her eyes. She was by far the most highly-strung of Joey's children and it would have taken more than the very mild dose Matron issued to steady her down properly.

Like everyone else, Ted fell asleep quickly as soon as she was in bed. It must have been two o'clock in the morning when she suddenly woke up. She sat up in bed, wide awake on the instant. She had no idea what had roused her, but she felt that all was not well. Then she heard the handle of the dormitory door being quietly turned and wondered who it was.

The hinges squeaked slightly as the door swung open. No one else seemed to have wakened, though she could hear an occasional muttering from Natalie Mercier's cubicle next door. That wasn't what had wakened her. The very first evening, Len had told her that Natalie talked in her sleep and it had never roused her before. Then she heard the pat-pat of bare feet coming slowly up the dormitory. At that hour and in the pale light of the waning moon, it was more than creepy. Ted felt the short hair on the nape of her neck stirring as she listened. Nearer and nearer they came until they reached her cubicle. Then they stopped dead.

If she could have moved, Ted would have shot under the sheet which was all the covering she had, but she was rigid with terror and could no more have moved than she could have flown. Worse was to follow. By the dim light, she saw long, slender fingers parting her curtains and then a figure came through and stood still with the curtains dropped behind it.

That was bad enough, but it was the aspect of the figure which alarmed poor Ted more than anything. In fact, she was too far gone for a second or two even to recognise it. It stood there in a loose white robe, black curls tumbling about its face and shoulders and with its eyes set in a wide, unseeing gaze. Scared nearly out of her senses, Ted glared back. Then there came a blessed break. Natalie began to mutter again and the sound broke the trance of horror that had frozen Ted. She realised that the invader was Con Maynard. What was more, Con was merely walking in her sleep.

"Well, that's something I can tackle, thank goodness!" she said aloud to herself as she tossed back the sheet and got out of bed. "I'd better fetch Ros—or no; she was pretty well shocked herself. Len's the best."

Deliberately breaking rules, she slid through the side curtains into Natalie's abode. It was silly, but she felt that she simply couldn't go past that terrifying figure, even though she knew it was Con. Moving as silently as she could, she slid out into the aisle and began to slip down the dormitory to Len's cubicle at the far end near the door. She was quickly there and woke Len as noiselessly as possible.

"H-sh!" she muttered. "Don't make a sound you can help. Con's walking in her sleep. She came into my cubey and I left her there."

Len sat up, wide awake at once. "Oh, *drat* her!" she exclaimed in an undertone. "OK, Ted. I'll cope; I've done it before. She doesn't often do it now unless she's been all revved up. I might have guessed it would happen after tonight. Come on! We'll get her back to her own cubey and then I'll fetch Matey while you stay with her."

Ted had no wish to stay with anyone who looked as uncanny as Con had done, but she decided that the less talking there was, the better. Len pulled on her slippers and kimono and they tiptoed along to Ted's little abode. It was very dark now, for the moon had gone behind a cloud, but they dared not risk switching on the light and neither had a torch. They reached the cubicle, Len pulled the curtains aside and they looked in. There was no Con to be seen! Apart from the furniture and Ted's clothes, it was empty so far as they could see.

"Oh, heavens!" Len said, still speaking almost inaudibly. "She must have gone in to someone else while you were waking me! Come on! We've got to find her before she scares someone out of their senses. It's a mercy your head's screwed on all right! The last thing you do is to scare a sleepwalker awake."

They peered through the curtains of each cubicle in turn, but no Con was to be seen.

"She must have gone out," Len groaned. "Look, Ted; go and put on your kimono and slippers and we'll go and dig Matey out and let her cope. It's beyond us now."

"OK," Ted said, going slowly to her cubicle for it was still very dark and she had no wish to trip over something and waken the rest. She found her kimono where she had tossed it down before getting into bed that night and shrugged herself into it. Then she stooped down to fish for her slippers under the bed. The next moment, she uttered a queer sound, half gasp, half gulp. Len was beside her friend in a flash.

"What is it?" she demanded, her voice uncautiously loud.

Ted held up her hand. "Shut up!" she hissed. "I've found Con!"

"*What*? But where?"

At that moment, the moon sailed out from behind the cloud and her light, streaming in at the uncurtained window gave the answer. Lying comfortably curled up in Ted's bed was the missing Con, sound asleep. For a full ten seconds they stared at her. Then Ted pulled Len out of the cubicle and back to the door.

"What do we do now?" she demanded. "She must have got in when I was coming to you. Ought I to go to hers for the rest of the night—or what?"

Len was spared the problem. Matron, who seemed to have a sixth sense where the girls were concerned, was with them before they even knew she was coming. Both gave vent to smothered howls of surprise.

"What are you two doing out here?" she asked

peremptorily. "What is wrong?" There was suspicion in the glance she cast at Ted, but Len gave her no chance.

"Oh, Matey! Thank goodness you're here!" she cried. "Con's been walking in her sleep again. She went into Ted's cubey and woke her up and Ted came to fetch me and when we got back, she had got into Ted's bed and she's there this minute—fast asleep."

It was a much edited version of the story, but as Len said later, it was as well to give Matey the gist then and add the frills later. It was enough for Matron, at any rate. Con had treated them to more than one sensation by her sleepwalking tendency. Mentally, she apologised to Ted for that moment's suspicion, even as she went to the cubicle where she found Con as they had said.

The pair had followed her. As she stood looking down, Ted said in a low voice, "What ought we to do? Should I just go and find her cubey and sleep there for the rest of the night?"

Certainly not! Do you know where it is? Then," as Ted shook her head, "how do you propose to find it at this hour? I'll wake Con—she's sleeping normally now—and take her back and you can get into your own bed as fast as you like. You, too, Len!"

Matron might talk, but waking Con proved an impossibility unless she wanted to rouse the rest of the dormitory. That young woman was sunk fathoms deep in sleep and all Matron's gentle shaking never reached her. In the end, the stalwart Miss Wilmot had to be summoned and between them, she and Matron carried Con back to her ownbed while the other two meekly got into theirs and lay down.

Both had been certain that it was impossible to go to sleep again after such an excitement, but when Matron, having made certain that Con was sleeping soundly, came to them with beakers of hot milk to soothe them, she found them as fast asleep as Con. She left the milk beside them in case they wakened later, but when the rising bell woke them next morning, the milk was still there with a good thick skin on top.

Chapter 9

ANOTHER SHOCK FOR TED

"TED—Ted Grantley! You're to go to the Head in the study at half-past ten this morning!"

Ted looked up from her task of sorting out the books and other oddments she would need for the first half of Saturday morning with a startled face. "Whatever for?"

Primrose Trevoase giggled. "She didn't confide in me. All she said was, 'Please tell Ted Grantley that I wish to see her in the study at half-past ten'. You'll find out when you get there, I expect."

Ted looked anxious. "I can't think of a thing I've done to deserve such a summons to the mat."

"It may not be that," Primrose said, checking her giggles. "You haven't been to have tea with Mrs. Maynard yet. She always has the new girls during the first three weeks or so of term. Quarantine has held you up, of course, but it's quite likely she wants you tomorrow and that's what the Head wants you for."

Ted shook her shaggy head. "It can't be that. Len told me that her mother was taking things quietly this term and there wouldn't be any Freudesheim parties."

"Then I can't think. You'll just have to wait till you see her."

"I wonder if I can guess." Pen Grant shut the lid of her desk down and sat on it. "You've simply shot ahead since you came back from Isolation. How you've done it, I wouldn't know, but I'll bet when we hear the form lists on Monday, you'll be well up the form. You've had A for every single French lesson and you've never fallen below B in anything. And why did you tell us you didn't know the first word of German?" she added in injured tones.

"Because it was true. I didn't—not even 'ja' and 'nein'!"

"Rot! You were gabbing away all Thursday. Don't tell me you've learnt it to that extent in the short time you've had at school, for I don't believe anyone could!"

"But," said Ted, her eyes dancing with mischief, "that's just exactly what I have done—cross my heart!"

"Then all I can say is you're the world's wonder!"

Ted relented. "I learnt most of it in Isolation, if you really want to know. The lay-sister who looked after us was German and couldn't speak a word of anything else and Soeur Marie-Anne said we must talk to her in her own language. Len helped out enormously and so did Ros, once she was well again. We talked German the best part of the day and I simply couldn't help myself. It was ghastly the first few days, of course. French is easy, but German's the limit with its predicates at the end of the sentences. But I just had to stick to it and then it got easier and easier and I'm glad of it now. At least I can understand what's said to me on German days and I can even talk after a fashion and it seems weird, but it gets easier and easier all the time."

"Sez you!" Pen retorted, risking a fine, since this piece of slang was strictly forbidden. She escaped her deserts as there was no one older than Primrose to hear her and for that young lady to pull her up for slang would have been a case of the pot calling the kettle black with a vengeance! How Inter V would have enjoyed themselves reminding her that people that live in glass houses shouldn't throw stones! Primrose let it alone.

"Mind you go the minute the bell rings," she said, taking her departure just as the said bell summoned them all to Prayers which, on Saturdays, were followed by mending, finishing odds and ends of prep left over from Friday and writing their home letters.

Ted had no mending as it happened. With a complacent grin at those near enough to see—which made some of them yearn to hit her!—she proceeded to set to work on her algebra and when that was done, to scribble her duty letter home. Then, everything done, she ignored her library book and took out her Latin grammar and proceeded to make hay while the sun shone.

Since she found herself making such strides with Len's help, she had started a new ambition—to get up to Vb in the shortest space of time possible. As she had excellent brains, a good memory and was working honestly for the first time in her life, she felt she had a chance of doing it if only she could keep on. As she struggled with construction rules, she wondered if, just possibly, the Head had noticed how she was improving and was sending for her to say that if she went on as she was doing, she would go up with the rest of the form next term. If it were that—! Ted hugged herself at the bare thought. Then she set it aside and plunged even deeper into her Latin. So hard did she concentrate that she never heard the bell for Break and Pen had to rouse her with a nudge.

"Wake up, Ted! The bell's gone and you're to go to the Abbess. I'll clear your desk for you or you'll be late. Half a sec!" as Ted jumped up. "You can't go to her looking like that!" with a meaning glance at Ted's thick untidy hair which looked like a hurrah's nest at the moment. When she was concentrating, she had a bad habit of running her fingers through it

"Oh, bother! I'd forgotten about my hair! It's the bane of my life! OK, I'll tidy before I go. Thanks a lot for clearing up for me, Pen!" And Ted shot off to the Splashery to do what she could about it.

It was not much. It grew in an untidy way with a swirl from the crown of her head. After Christmas, her mother had taken a sudden whim and ordered her to grow it. At the moment, it just reached beyond her shoulders and as it was abnormally thick, it was impossible to plait it. Its springiness put paid to any hair ribbon or slide and she generally wore it with clips at each side which were supposed to keep it off her face and which never did for more than half-an-hour at a time. As a result it was forever in her eyes or her mouth and Matron had already ventilated her opinion of it to her.

"Wish I could shave it all off and wear a wig!" she grumbled to herself as she clipped back the side pieces. "There! It's as decent as it ever is."

She looked at herself in the mirror and made a face at her reflection. Then she set off for the study where she tapped at the door, wondering just why the head wanted her. She didn't think it was for any sin, for her conscience was clear. Life had been much too full for her to have time to get into mischief.

Miss Annersley was seated at her desk, sipping coffee and trying to clear up some of the piles of correspondence while she waited for her newest pupil. Ted entered and bobbed the curtsy demanded of all the girls coming for interview with the Head.

Miss Annersley laid down her pen and gave the girl a genial smile. "Come along, Ted! Have you had your elevenses yet?"

"Not yet; I thought I had to come at once," Ted explained. "I only stopped to tidy my hair."

Miss Annersley regarded the mop thoughtfully but said no more.

"I see," she said. "Pull up that chair beside me and sit down. I'll try not to keep you long."

Ted obeyed. Then she fixed her dark, intelligent eyes on Miss Annersley's fine face and waited.

"When you first came," the Head said, "we thought it best to try you in Inter V as it seemed probable that you would find the work of Vb too much for you and we didn't want you either to feel that you must work yourself into a series of headaches, or become discouraged and sit back saying, "I can't!" But all this week, so I'm told, you've been surprising everyone who teaches you by the improved quality of your work. Now can you explain this?"

"We—we did lessons in Isolation," Ted said, stammering a little. "It was so awfully deadly having nothing much to do. And then Soeur Marie-Anne told us she had been going to teach before she became a nun and she would help us if we liked. I mean she set us work to do and corrected it. And when I couldn't get things, like some of the maths, Len showed me how. Rosamund showed me, too, and—and I got really interested. And—and it was quite true when I said I didn't know a word of German when I came. I honestly didn't, Miss Annersley. Only Len said we would talk it all our lesson time, and that was six hours every day but Sundays. And the lay-sister who looked after us was German, too. Then, you know, Len seemed to know just what I found hardest and she helped me—and—and that's all."

"Not quite, I think. Len may have helped you—she means to teach when she has finished at university and we all think she has a real gift for it—but all the help in the world couldn't have got you where you are now if you hadn't done your share and worked hard. And what I want to know, Ted, is this. Is this just a flash in the pan, the result of your being bored in Isolation? Or do you mean to go on as you've begun and work steadily all the time?"

Ted gasped. "I—why—I mean to go on working. I never have before," she added with innate honesty, "but now I've really got down to it, it's rather—well, fun."

"Yes, if you've never really enjoyed work before, I can imagine you would feel that way," the Head agreed.

"It's such a decent feeling when you've got your teeth into a really sticky problem and can worry it out for yourself," Ted said, startling herself by this confidence.

"I know. I'm glad you've discovered it for yourself. Well, now, Ted, I have a story to tell you and an offer to make to you." Miss Annersley glanced at the clock. "First, though, I think you had better have your lemonade and biscuits in here. Touch the bell, will you, dear?"

Ted was presently sitting with her glass of lemonade and biscuits, listening with all her ears.

"You do know, don't you, that many of the girls are here because they have a relation at the Sanatorium? Last week we were asked to take a girl of your age who has only an aunt in all the world. The aunt has been ill and is coming to the San for treatment. Renée could be a boarder at her convent school in Brussels, but both she and her aunt would much rather she was close at hand in case of need. That being so, we have accepted her, and she must certainly go to Inter V. They have sent me examples of her work from the school and she couldn't touch Vb work. But, and it's a big but, Inter V has twenty-six girls already and we never like more than twenty-five in a form. If we move you up to Vb which has only twenty- four at present, it would have its full complement and would leave Inter V with just one girl too many which won't matter for one term."

"I see." Ted spoke because the Head had paused and was looking at her. "But, Miss Annersley, aren't there lots of girls who've been in Inter V all the year and who could be moved up even better than me?"

"'Than *I*', please, Ted! It could be done, of course; but it will be easier to move you, a new girl, than one of those who has been in the form the whole year. Any girl we move up would certainly miss her chance of one of the school prizes because in set books, such as literature and French and Latin for instance, she would be at a great disadvantage. If you go it will make no difference to you as you won't hope for form, exam or subject prizes when you have only just come. If you make good there, you will stay there and work with those who come up for the new year; but it might mean that you would be lower in form over the whole term than if we let you stay down. Now is that going to dishearten you and make you feel it isn't worth while to do your best?"

"No," Ted said instantly. "I'm sure it won't."

"Then would you like to try it? Of course, if we find that the work is too much for you, we must bring you down again. Health comes before even lessons every time in this school! But to judge by what I hear from the staff, I think you can do it. I don't really know you yet, Ted. Thanks to Len's butting in, there has been no chance. But I think you're a very clever girl who can do really well if only you will put your back into it. I'm hoping you will and so prove to us that we are right in putting you up. And now I want to speak about something else. My dear girl, is it really needful for you to go round looking as if you had been dragged through a hedge backwards?"

Ted reddened. She had had to listen to strictures on her personal appearance all her life, but no one had ever spoken quite like this. From sheer amazement she said, "It's my hair! I just can't help it. Oh, Miss Annersley, can't I have it all cut off? It's the bane of my life!"

Miss Annersley gasped and then went off into a peal of laughter. "Oh, my dear girl, what a question to ask! Most certainly you mayn't! Your mother would be very angry with us if we took the law into our own hands in that fashion." She stood up and came to inspect the untidy mop more closely. "Yes, I see what you mean. Hair like yours can be a terrible nuisance. We must think it over and see what we can do to help you. I wonder if it would be any use to tie a snood round it to keep all those long ends out of your eyes? We must certainly do something or we shall have you developing a squint! Suppose we try now. Wait a moment!"

Flashing another smile at the stunned Ted, she left the room to return with a length of crimson ribbon and a brush and comb.

"Now let's see what I can do for you! Sit up and I'll play hairdresser."

Ted sat bolt upright, wondering if she were dreaming with her eyes open, The Head brushed and combed the thick hair until it gleamed and was perfectly smooth. She took it all back from Ted's face, securing the ribbon at the back with a firm knot. The two clips were fastened to hold the band in place and the hair very slightly loosened in front. Then she stood back and inspected her work with an approving nod.

"Yes, that's much better. The band won't slip; I'll guarantee my knots! How does it feel—comfortable?"

"I feel *cleaner*"!Ted said dazedly.

Miss Annersley's lovely laugh rang out. "The result of having all that mop out of your eyes and mouth! Matron must take you when she next goes to our hairdresser and get him to thin it thoroughly. When the really hot weather comes, you will find it painfully heating if we leave it. There goes the bell for the end of Break. Take your glass to the kitchen as you go. Oh! Before I forget! On Monday you will be excused the morning walk and may spend the time changing over to Vb. Don't forget to take your set books to the stock room. I'll let Miss Dene know before then and she will have the new ones ready for you."

"Yes, Miss Annersley." Ted halted there; then she asked half-shyly, "May I tell the others?"

"Yes, but I rather think you'll find that some of them, at any rate, more than suspect already. By the way, you'd better ask one of Vb to stay from the walk on Monday and help you get settled. Let me know who it is before bed-time tomorrow and I'll excuse her. Now you must run and I must see what I can do with these letters."

Ted went to the door bearing her glass. She managed a bob before she went out, but then she cast rules to the winds and went scuttering down the corridors first to hand in her glass at the kitchen and then to go flying out to the garden in search of Len and Rosamund. She wanted them to be the first to hear her great news.

As she went, new thoughts came to her. She had been inclined to be quaky when she went to the study, but it had been all right—more than all right! And what a peach of a Head Miss Annersley was! Fancy taking all that trouble over her hair!

"I'll jolly well prove to her that I'm grateful," Ted vowed inwardly as she came in sight of the tennis courts. "And that's another reason for keeping out of rows and doing my best. Oh, surely I can make good this time when I've had such a tremendous shove off on the right road!"

Then she had reached the courts and Len and Rosamund were charging down on her, wild with curiosity to know why the Head had wanted her. However, her changed appearance was the first thing to catch their eyes and with one voice they exclaimed, "Ted! What have you been doing to yourself? You look different!"

"Not me—the Head," Ted said, laughing from sheer happiness. "And I'm to go to your hairdresser with Matey and have chunks cut out of my hair because when it's really hot, it will be far too much for me! And what I want to know," she laughed again, "is what do you call this weather if not really hot?"

Chapter 10

Margot

Len and Rosamund were delighted when they heard Ted's news, though both declared that they weren't surprised.

"We really did do something when we were in Isolation," Len remarked with a smirk of satisfaction. "It was jolly well worth it after all."

"And you know, Ted," Rosamund added rather more quietly, "you really have brains. You'll soon find your feet in Vb and then you'll go ahead."

Ted grinned. "Well, thanks a lot, both of you. I know I owe it to you two and especially Len. You won't mind my saying that, Ros, will you?"

"Why should I?" Rosamund demanded. "After all, I only helped with the German. Len gave you a lift in half-a-dozen things, didn't she? And if you're in the same form as us, we can both go on giving you tips when you need them."

"How frightfully decent of you!" Then she added in rather different tones, "But there's one thing that's bothering me a little."

"What's that?" Len asked.

"Well, what about the rest of Inter V? Quite a lot of them are jolly good and better than me in maths and so on. Won't they be rather mad that it's me that's been put up?"

As she made her highly ungrammatical statement, she watched their faces keenly. The Head had reminded her that there was the question of prizes to be considered, but grown-ups might overlook something that girls would feel.

"No fear!" Len said. "This is prize-giving term and anyone put up would lose her chance of anything like form or exam prize. If that's all that's wrong, you can take that worried look off your face. Most likely they'll be only too thankful that it's you who's been sent up and not them."

Ted's face cleared. "The Head did say something like that, but I wondered."

"Don't worry!" Rosamund said laughing. "No one likes to lose the chance of prizes by being put up in the last term of the year. I shouldn't myself. They're much more likely to be thankful it's you, as Len said."

"When are you coming to us?" Len asked. "I mean do you shift up today or do you wait till Monday?"

"Monday morning. I'm to miss the walk and move my things then and change my set books and things like that. The Head said I could ask someone to help me—"

"You'd better do it, Len," Rosamund said quickly. "I asked Joan Baker to be my partner on Monday and you know how touchy she can be."

Len nodded, a rather more serious look on her face. She had suddenly thought of someone else who was touchy. All the same—then she set it aside. "Will you have me, Ted? I'd love to help."

"If it won't upset your plans," Ted said quickly.

"Hadn't made any as it happens. That's settled, then. I say! There's the bell for walk! Are you coming with us or with Inter V?"

"The Head didn't say, only that I was to change my books on Monday. Which ought I to do, d'you think?"

Len looked at Rosamund. "What do you say, Ros? It's a bit of a puzzle." Rosamund knitted her brows. "It certainly is. You wouldn't like to go back to the study and ask, would you, Ted?"

Before Ted could reply, a fresh voice sounded behind them. "Now then, you three, why aren't you getting ready for the walk?"

They swung round to meet the severely judicial gaze of the Head Girl.

"Oh, Mary-Lou! Just the person to know!" Len cried. "Look! Ted's coming up to Vb on Monday, but the Head didn't say a thing about which form she was to be with over the weekend. What do *you* think?"

"The Head said nothing about it?" Mary-Lou addressed Ted directly.

Ted shook her head. "She never mentioned it."

"I expect she had so many other things to think about, she forgot," said Mary-Lou, her eyes on Ted's transformed head. "Congratulations on your promotion, by the way! I think the best thing will be for me to go and ask her while you three change your sandals and get your hats. I'll tell you what she says as soon as I know myself. Now, scram!"

"Oh, thanks a lot, Mary-Lou!" Len exclaimed. "Come on, folks! We'll have to fly, whatever Ted has to do, or we'll be late."

Mary-Lou had vanished already and the three raced to the Splashery where they found quite half the girls there. They were leaving quickly, however, to join up with the lines waiting for instructions, so it was easy for once to get into the Splashery and find their pegs and lockers. They changed into the stout sandals they wore for walks and put on the big hats so necessary against the blazing sun of Middle Europe at that time of year.

Pen was still there and as they came in, her eyes fell on Ted and the new coiffure. She gave an exclamation at the sight.

"Goodness, Ted! How different you look with your hair taken back like that! It does suit you. Honestly, you look quite pretty. Whose idea was it—Matey's?"

Ted had gone crimson at the compliment. "Ass!" She muttered gruffly. " No, it was the Head's. She says I've too much and I'm to go down with Matey some time and get it thinned. This is just for the time being. Shan't I be glad, though, to be rid of some of it, anyhow!"

Len giggled. "You ought to have your head shaved and then the hair might grow in curly like Mary-Lou's did,"

Ted paused, her hat in her hands. "What *are* you talking about?"

"Mary-Lou's hair. It used to be as straight as yours. Then she had a most ghastly accident and they had to shave her head. When the hair grew again, it came in all curls like it is now and she's kept it short ever since. Not," Len continued as she went over to the mirror and set her hat on her own curly head, "that she didn't rage when she first found out what they'd done to her. But when she found she'd got curls out of it, she piped down. I'll tell you the whole yarn some time. Meanwhile, we'd better get cracking. Mary-Lou's a poppet, but when she gives an order, you obey it if you know what's good for you!"

Even with her more or less brief experience of the school itself, Ted had learned that it was usually better to fall into the clutches of the staff than those of the prefects. She pulled on her hat with due care for her snood and followed Len out of the Splashery whence both Rosamund and Pen had vanished a minute before. As she passed the mirror, she took a quick glance at herself and nearly gasped aloud at what she saw. Not only had taking her hair right off her face improved its shape and taken away the wedgelike effect, but she had lost the yellowish tinge she had always had. Her cheeks were pink and since she had had little reason for scowling this past five weeks or so, the lines were fading from between her eyebrows.

"Oh gosh!" she thought. "What's happened to me?"

Mary-Lou was waiting at the door for them. "It's OK, Ted. The Head says you may as well begin as you are to go on and go with Vb today. They're round at the front. Scoot and join them, you two. I'm coming in a moment—I'm on escort duty with your lot today."

"Oh good!" Len said instantly.

Mary-Lou laughed. "Glad you're so pleased. Ted, you had a partner for the Inter V walk, hadn't you? You'd better break it gently to her that she can't have you. Don't stay nattering with her. Just break the news and then go on to Vb."

"Partner with me!" Len shrieked after Ted as she ran off. Then, to Rosamund, "You don't mind, do you, Ros? Just for the first walk as a Vb-ite!"

Rosamund laughed. "It wouldn't matter if I did. I don't, as it happens. Ricki Fry was partnering Joanna Kiefen, but poor Joanna has raging neuralgia and Matey's sent her to San for the day, so Ricki would have had to tag on to someone else, but now we can partner each other."

"Did I hear you say Joanna had neuralgia?" Len asked. "Sure you don't mean toothache?"

"Well, Ricki told me it was neuralgia," Rosamund said doubtfully.

"Huh!" Len grunted, feeling with her tongue for a tooth of which she was nervous. "Let's hope it is only that! Matey will hold a tooth inspection if she thinks it's a tooth. I don't mind Herr von Francius as a man, but as a dentist I loathe him!"

"Funk!" Rosamund laughed, even as Ted came flying back to join them.

"They're all stunned with surprise!" she announced gaily. "It's quite OK though. Pen and I were going together, but she's taking Lisa Sybel who had no one. She wants to hear the whole yarn, though, when we get back. I had to tell her Mary-Lou said I wasn't to stay nattering about it."

"Good!" Len said. "Ros is taking Ricki Fry because her proper partner's got neuralgia, worse luck!"

"Hard luck for her." Ted said as they went to take their places.

"If it only ends at that! If it turns out to be toothache, though, Matey will hold a tooth inspection and anyone who needs it will go down with her to Berne next day. Well, in that case, you'd go to the hairdresser. Hope *your* teeth are all right?"

"They ought to be," Ted said ruefully. "Cousin May took me to her dentist the week before school began and did I have a doing!"

"We missed these hols. Our crowd were all in France, staying with Tante Simone and she thought we'd been before we went there so she said nothing about it nor did we. Matey's safe to find something that needs doing if she has an inspection." Len's voice was equally rueful. "Oh, well, it can't happen before Tuesday. I'll forget about it and enjoy today. Better straighten our lines. I can see Mary-Lou and Josette tooling along. Mary-Lou's bad enough, but Josette's our cousin and she seems to think she ought to come down most heavily on us because we're relations!"

"Are you? I didn't know that," Ted said as they straightened their lines.

"We are. Mamma and Auntie Madge are sisters and Auntie Madge is Lady Russell who started the school, so that makes us cousins. I say, Margot, you and Emmy had better get decently into line. You know what Josette can be like!"

Margot, who was partnered by her boon companion, Emerence Hope, nudged Emerence further into the line and turned to stare at Ted. "Are you coming with us? But why? You're Inter V."

"She was. From now on, she's Vb," Len returned with a glance along the line as Mary-Lou, accompanied by their cousin Josette and Jessica Wayne of VIb came round the end of the hedge.

By that time, the line was as straight as could be expected and everyone was looking as good as in her lay.

Mary-Lou projected a grin at Josette. "Too good to be true!" she observed. "Pity it never lasts! OK, you people. We're only waiting for Hilary and then we can get off. Where's Con Maynard?"

"I'm here," said a meek voice immediately behind Len and Ted.

"Matey says you haven't been for your tonic and you have to go to her for it as soon as we get back. Why didn't you go, you young goop? She'll have something to say when she does see you."

"It wasn't my fault," Con protested indignantly. "Herr Helfen turned up to give Joanna Kiefen an extra violin lesson and as she's in San, he sent for me just as I was going to Matey and he kept me till the last minute."

"And you thought you could skip that tonic and forgot to go," Mary-Lou added acutely. "I know you, Con!"

Con's round pink cheeks were scarlet. The tonic she had been ordered after her sleepwalking exploits not only tasted vile but lingered. She had not been sorry that Herr Helfen's summons had come when it did. But trust Matey never to let you slip! She knew better than to say anything, however, and Mary-Lou, with an annoying grin, passed on to the head of the line.

At that moment, Inter V under the escort of Vi Lucy, Lesley Bethune and Barbara Chester marched swiftly past. Every head was turned as the girls of her ex-form looked at Ted and she was hot with blushes by the time the last of them had gone.

"Rubbernecks!" Len said, loudly enough to be heard by most of them. "Don't you worry, Ted. I'll bet they're envying you, even though they wouldn't thank anyone for bunging them up this term!"

"Your language!" Mary-Lou said in pained tones. "Honestly, Len, if you go on using such expressions, you'll find yourself penniless in short order."

"Here's Hilary at last!" exclaimed Josette, breaking in on them. "She's been long enough! What on earth have you been doing, Hilary? We're the last to go."

Hilary Bennet had come tearing up. "Sorry, everyone!" she jerked breathlessly. "I was with Burnie, discussing the tennis six and I simply couldn't get away!"

"Oh, well, better late than never," Mary-Lou said easily. "Ready, everyone? Lead on, then, Marie and Wanda!"

The leaders, two Swiss girls who had been chattering together in German, set off and the rest marched briskly after them. Jessica and Josette took their places about the middle of the line and Mary-Lou and Hilary brought up the rear.

"Where are we going?" Len demanded of Josette who was near them.

"Down to the meadow and across and up the path to the herdsmen's shelf. Along there as far as the stream and down that path and round back to school by the road," Josette replied amiably. She was a tall, pretty girl—very pretty with her wavy black hair, blue eyes and pink-and-white complexion. She was also exceedingly clever; by far the cleverest of the Russell girls, for Sybil, now at St. Mildred's, was only average and Ailie, the youngest, was a tow-headed irresponsible who scrambled through her lessons as easily as she could manage.

"Oh, good!" Margot cried. "I love that walk and it's such fun seeing the cows and hearing their different bells ringing as they graze."

Emerence made a face. "I like the walk all right, but I don't like the cows!"

"Do cows wear bells in Switzerland?" Ted asked amazed.

"Of course they do! Didn't you know that?" Margot asked scornfully.

"Seeing this is Ted's first visit to Switzerland and any-how, she's spent most of the time in Isolation, it's hardly surprising she didn't," Len put in quickly.

Margot glanced round at her sister. "She could have read about it in books." Then she turned back to embark on a gossip with Emerence and took no further notice of the pair behind them. Con and her partner, Jo Scott, were discussing the question of how soon the school would begin to go down to Lake Thun for swimming and boating and Len, talking over her shoulder, joined in and dragged Ted into the chatter.

They marched across the rough pasture to where the mountain began to rise with a belt of pines growing up the slopes. There, they might break ranks and they climbed the wide path in twos and threes, all talking hard, since Saturday was very much a go-as-you-please day, once it came to break. The four Sixth form girls kept behind the rest, ready to act as whippers-in if anyone strayed too far from the path, and talked tennis with vim and point. Len and Ted, Con and Jo kept together and, for once in a way, Margot declined to go off alone with Emerence and tag-ged on to their group.

She was, in many ways, the most difficult of the Maynard children. As a tiny, she had had a violent temper and it had taken great firmness and careful training to teach her to control it. She was also an imp of mischief and had involved herself and her friends in a good many alarms. She had been struggling to overcome this tendency for the past year or two and was certainly much better. Brilliantly clever when she chose, she hated working steadily. As she said, she liked "to go bust" and then rest on her oars for a while. It had taken the whole of her nearly nine years at school to persuade her that until she stopped being satisfied with this sort of thing, she could never hope to be with her sisters in form. In fact, she had only accomplished it lately.

Two years in Canada with her Aunt Madge had given her a certain amount of surface sophistication and so far, she had been content to make her closest friend of Emerence Hope, one of the naughtiest girls in the annals of a school which had never lacked its full share of sinners. No one had quite liked it, but there was nothing to be done about it. As the Head had said, you couldn't interfere with their friendships.

Len and Con were not nearly so complex. Len was a clever, hard-working girl. Her position as eldest of the family had developed her sense of responsibility. For a good many years she had been content with being friendly with most folk. Then she had formed friendships with Prunella Davies and, later, with Rosamund Lilley. Prunella was much older and a prefect now, so the friendship was not as close as it might have been; and Rosamund, youngest of a family of six, was a quiet character. The pair had had a chummery of contented peace, for they thought alike in many ways and neither was over-demonstrative.

Margot had been none too pleased about it, for she liked being the centre of attraction wherever she was and was inclined to be jealous of her eldest sister's affections. When Len have become friendly with Prunella, Margot had watched it gloomily, but said nothing. She liked it even less when her sister had added Rosamund Lilley to her closest circle. Now she was far from pleased that it looked as if her eldest sister was going to find yet another pal in the new girl.

Len, with her mother's trick of "getting into the skins" of other folk, saw the signs and felt alarmed. She had liked Ted from the first and during the weeks of quarantine, they had got to know each other much better than if they had only met during school hours. She felt, though she could never have said why, that the new girl was on her guard at present. If Margot started any spats, there would be trouble.

She thought hard as they climbed up the path. "What on earth shall I do? I like Ted and I hope we're going to be real friends like Mamma and the aunts. I'd like us and Ros and Jo all to be pals like that. But if Margot's going to get her monkey up, it's going to make things jolly difficult all round. And I've a feeling that Ted might go off if there were any fusses. I wish Margot wouldn't mind so much when I have a chum! She'd make row enough if any of us started in about her palling with Emmy!"

Chapter 11

MARY-LOU BUTTS IN

"LEN, will you partner me for the walk tomorrow morning?"

"Sorry. I'm afraid I can't!"

"Why ever not?"

"Because *Auntie Hilda*"—Len laid heavy stress on the name—"has told me that I'm to miss the walk for once and help Ted Grantley move all her books and things from Inter V to Vb. I'll fix up with you for Tuesday, if you like."

"I'm booked with Francie Wilford for Tuesday. Can't someone else take on Ted Grantley?" Margot's blue eyes suddenly flamed with a light her sister knew and dreaded. "Plenty of other folk to hold her hand! I want you tomorrow."

"You know as well as I do that when Auntie Hilda gives an order you've nothing to do but obey it. I'm awfully sorry, Margot, but I can't manage it. Can't you get Francie to swop days with someone else for once? I'm booked up every day this week except Tuesday, as it happens."

"No, I can't," Margot replied shortly. "It's the one day Francie has free this week. I kept Monday especially for you and I think you might arrange it somehow. You could if you tried. Ask Auntie Hilda—"

"I can see myself!" Len spoke with conviction. "How much d'you think would be left of me after I'd tried that on? It's no use, Margot. I'd have come if it had been anything else—or pretty well anything else," she added cautiously. "If you haven't a partner, what about Con? You aren't booked, are you, Con?" She turned to the third triplet who had been sprawled full length on the rug they were sharing, buried fathoms deep in a book, and paying no attention to her sisters' talk.

At the sound of her own name, she lifted her dark eyes from the page and asked vaguely, "Did you want anything?"

"I only asked if you could partner Margot tomorrow morning on the walk. I can't. Auntie Hilda snaffled me to help Ted Grantley change forms and said we were to miss the walk tomorrow and get it done then before school begins."

"I'm not booked so far," Con said, closing her book and giving her mind to the matter. "Betty Landon and I were booked and then her folk arrived yesterday and took her off till Monday morning, so she's out. That'll be all right, Margot."

But if Len and Con thought that settled the matter, Margot soon showed them it had done nothing of the kind. She flushed to the roots of her hair and said, "I can fix up my own walk partners, thank you! I'm afraid Con won't do. Anyhow, if I can't have you, there's no need for you to try hunting up someone for me. I'll see to it myself, thank you!" She got up as she spoke and picked up her book. With a final glare at Len, she stalked off, her back very straight and her head high in the air.

Con stared after her with dismay on her face. "Oh, goodness! Why on earth should she make so much fuss because you can't partner her in the morning? She knows quite well you can't go to Auntie Hilda about it. In school, she's the Head and finish! What's it all in aid of? That's what I want to know!"

Len sat up, curling her long legs under her. "I'm awfully afraid that devil of hers is talking to her and she's listening. But what can I do?"

"Gone off pop over it, hasn't she?" Con was wide awake for once. She rolled over on to her face, laying her book aside, and propped her pointed chin in her hands. "It's awkward, isn't it? What are you doing about it?"

"I don't see what I can do. I was an ass, of course, to propose anyone else for her partner when I'd told her I couldn't manage it myself. I might have known she'd blow up about it!" Len spoke gloomily.

Con shook her head. "You're wrong there. It's ages since Margot went pop over things. I don't see how you could foresee that she'd do it at just this time."

Len stared at her. "Come to that, if Margot really wants me so badly, why can't she put Francie off for once? Francie wouldn't mind."

"I can guess," Con suddenly looked very wise as she sat up, crossed her ankles and gripped one with either hand.

Len looked at her. Suddenly she coloured. "Do you mean—? Well, yes, I expect you're right. Oh, what a mess-up! If it's that way, we may look out for squalls. I haven't forgotten what she was like when Ros and I first became chummy."

"She still doesn't like Ros awfully much," Con said, pushing back her heavy fringe from her hot face.

"I know it! Oh, Con, I hope to goodness you're wrong!"

"Why are you so revved up about it?" Con asked curiously.

"Well—I may be all wrong, of course—but I have an idea that just before she came here, Ted wasn't having a very good time and she's still sore about it in spots. She's got a temper and if Margot starts in on her—"

"Hair and skulls will fly!" Con said pensively. "No, we certainly don't want that to happen. Besides, if it's really Margot's devil that's got hold of her again, she may say or do anything. We'll just have to do something about it — though I can't see what!" she finished, looking harassed.

"What's the trouble, you two? You look as if you had the cares of the nation on your shoulders!" Mary-Lou had been passing and noticed the worried faces of the pair. It was not in her to let it go, and she had crossed the grass and was standing, looking down at them with dancing blue eyes. She dropped down beside them and mopped her face. "What a scorcher of a day! Much too hot for any enormous problems! Tell me what's wrong."

As neither answered her at once, she spoke again. "Anything I can do for you?"

"I don't see how you can," Len said slowly while Con looked at the Head Girl with hope coming to her eyes.

"You never know! Where's your third, by the way. I thought you three were together?"

"So we were. Margot went off a few minutes ago," Con told her.

Mary-Lou shot a quick glance at her. So Margot was partly the cause—or even wholly? She must go carefully. The triplets were very loyal to each other, even though they might have quite fierce spats among themselves at times. But she was a keen-eyed young woman and during the past week, she had noticcd one or two things. She began to feel her way carefully.

"Where's Ted Grantley?" she asked.

"Sharing the hammock over there with Ros," Len said, nodding towards one of the standing-hammocks which had been set under a cluster of silver birches. "She was all in, not being accustomed to heat of this kind. Ros had bagged the hammock, anyhow, so she asked Ted to share it with her as she thought it might be cooler than anywhere else."

"Are Ted and Rosamund getting friendly, then?" Mary-Lou asked. "I'm glad to hear that. Ros has always rather stood alone, except for you, of course, and I've been sorry for her. One of the best parts of school is the pals you make there. I ought to know! Look at our Gang! We've rather broken up nowadays, but we're still matey."

"Like Mamma and the aunts," Con said. "They've been a quartet ever since the word 'Go' and though they can't often meet, they're still pals. But Mary-Lou," she fixed her eyes on Mary-Lou's, "everyone isn't like that. I don't think I am. Do you think there's anything wrong with me?" She looked anxious as she waited for the Head Girl's verdict.

"Good gracious, no!" Mary-Lou cried. "But I'll tell you what I think about it. In one way, you three were rather handicapped at first for that sort of thing. When I first met you, you always stuck together like clams—or do I mean barnacles?"

"But how could that handicap us?" Len demanded, knitting her brows.

"Easily! It meant that all your early years you were enough for each other. Then Margot went to Canada with Auntie Madge and that made a break. In fact, it shook you apart."

Con nodded. "That's true, of course. Margot was there a whole year before the rest of us went. When we got there, we found she'd got mixed up with other people and somehow it's never been quite the same since.

"Well, you two still had each other in England, but Margot was alone and had to stand on her own feet without you to back her up. It was bound to make a big difference in her."

"We didn't think of that—then," Len said abruptly. "It's only this last year that I've understood why she seemed so—changed and not quite one of us in some ways."

Con continued in her rather sleepy, placid way. "You see, Mary-Lou, it made Margot sort of looser in our bunch. And when she got so chummy with Emmy Hope, she stood more away from us than ever. The thing is that now Len is making friends—she's got Prunella, though she's more or less in the background, now she's a pree, and then Ros. And now," she smiled at her triplet, "I rather think there's going to be Ted. So you see, it's only me that's standing out from things like that."

Mary-Lou gasped. "Heavens! I'd no idea you dug down like that!" She gave Con a curious look. "Of course, at fourteen and a half, it's what you ought to be doing. As for the pals question, I'll tell you what I think. You've had what the other two haven't had—your story-book people. I rather think that's what's helped to keep you from wanting ordinary friends. But if you can see it for yourself, then you must be waking up to the need for human friends as well. We all ought to have them, you know. We need them or we don't grow properly."

Len, who had been sprawling, sat up. "Then you do think it's right for us to go out to other people?"

"Of course! That's one reason why we're put into the world. No one can live entirely by herself."

Mary-Lou hesitated a moment. Then she asked bluntly, "Is Margot objecting to you having friends? I can see that she might, of course."

"I don't think she quite likes it," Len said carefully.

Con broke in. "Margot's my triplet and I love her and Len almost more than anyone else in the world. We *belong!* But I've got to say it, for Len won't. Margot is jealous. She doesn't like us to like other people. She has Emmy for herself, but she doesn't like it if Len has someone and I don't think she plays fair."

Len darted a look of reproach at her triplet. She had done her best to keep this failing of Margot's out of it. Con paid no attention. She was sitting with great dark eyes fixed on the Head Girl's face, waiting for a comment.

"Poor Margot!" Mary-Lou said gravely. "She's going to make herself very miserable unless she takes hold of herself. Besides, she's got it all wrong. You can't keep anyone entirely to yourself. You've got to share them. Being jealous and possessive isn't really loving people. What's more, it's downright selfish. In the end, you lose your friends by it."

"But what can we do?" burst out Len.

"First, remember that you are triplets and let Margot see that you feel it and know it for a strong bond between you. Secondly, have your special friends, whatever she may say or do. You musn't give in about that. You needn't be always pushing them down her throat but make her understand that you claim the same right to pals as she has. Finally, if things get really bad, ask if you can go to Aunt Joey—oh, but you musn't! Not yet, anyhow. Well, come to me if you like and I'll do my best. Saints can't do more!"

She jumped up and went off and the two left behind looked at each other. They were aware of snags of which Mary-Lou knew nothing.

"I wish she'd talk to Margot!" Con sighed at last.

"It might be better if she could talk to Ted," Len said slowly. "However, we can't exactly ask her to do that. We'll just have to wait. Let's hope the devil leaves Margot alone when she's had time to think it over."

But there didn't seem to be much reason for the hope. Margot had all too clearly been in one of her worst moods when she had marched off and her sisters shivered when they thought what that might mean presently.

Chapter 12

Margot's Devil Takes Charge

Margot was in her worst mood when she left her sisters so abruptly. It was a long time since she had felt like this, though it had happened often in her early days. She had always been selfish and egotistical, ready to claim the best for herself and unable to see why she shouldn't have it, even if it meant other people having to do without.

Two years in Canada where children are much more independent and grow up earlier than English children had given her surface grown-upness. Underneath, however, lay a childish determination to get her own way and a total inability to see why she should ever give way to others. All this had come up to the top this afternoon and she was seething as she stalked off.

Very early in life, she had produced "my devil" on whom she blamed all her lapses with a matter-of-factness that sometimes had its funny side. The family had had to accept him and his "whisperings" to which she listened far too often, though recently he had not come up at all. But her smooth selfishness was something that she had so far failed to recognise for yet another of his temptings and it was as bad as ever.

It would have been a relief to her to be able to let go and fling herself down kicking and screaming with rage, but at fourteen and a half, such conduct would be undignified and Margot had a strong sense of dignity. If she stayed, she felt sure she couldn't help breaking out.

The only safety lay in flight and solitude. She chose the one place where she thought she would be alone—the garden at Freudesheim. Jack had had a gate set in the hedge dividing their own grounds from the school's and

Margot had a hidey hole not too far from it which so far no one else knew about. It meant breaking rules for they were not supposed to leave the school premises, but it was better to break a rule than go up in smoke as she might do at any minute.

She slipped through the gateway and made her way along a narrow path to a tangle of bushes. She wriggled through into the centre and gave herself up to the fight with her temper. It ended in a burst of tears, but they didn't last long. When she had mopped her eyes for the last time, the devil had been put into his proper place for the present and she felt better. She rolled over on to her back and lay staring up dreamily at the glimpses of blue sky through the branches.

In their spare time, Joey and Jack had turned what had been a huge cabbage patch into a rose garden. Jack had had it dug out to a depth of about six feet and then the pair of them had turned it into a rose paradise through the years they had been there. It was a favoured stamping-ground with Joey and her friends for, thanks to its being sunk, it was comparatively cool in hot weather and was sheltered from the wind as well.

On this fateful afternoon, Rosalie Dene had come here to rest and relax with her old friend.

Margot, turning drowsy in the heart of her bushes nearby, was aroused by their voices and nearly squeaked with horror! She knew what would happen if they caught her there! She was just preparing to crawl out as noiselessly as she could, when Joey's voice came clearly to her and the sentence she overheard checked her at once.

"I'm so glad Ted is settling down so well, poor lamb! After being expelled three times you might have expected fireworks. As it is, she seems to have really turned over a new leaf! I'm so very glad!"

Her mother's statement made Margot forget she was eavesdropping. Ted Grantley had been expelled from *three* schools! This was something she must find out about! Her jealousy of the friendship between Ted and Len flooding her anew, Margot forgot that she was doing something that not only her family but the whole school would condemn; forgot everything, in fact, except that here seemed to be something she could use against the girl who was stealing some of her sister's affection from her.

But the school bell rang for Kaffee and Kuchen before wicked Margot heard any more. She dared not be any later than she could help. She squirmed her way out of the bushes as quietly as she could and even so had a nasty shock when she heard her mother remark, "Is there a cat or a dog or something in the garden? I'm sure I heard something in the bushes."

Margot slid down to the path and scuttled along it on tiptoe. Not until she was safely in the school grounds again did she dare to draw a full breath. However, for once Nemesis did not fall on her—then. It was a pity. Things might have been different all round if she had been caught just then. As it was, she was able to join Vb and when Len saw her next, it was with a big basket of bread twists in her hands. She grinned at her sister when they met and, apart from being rather quieter than usual, both Len and Con were thankful to see that she seemed to have recovered herself.

Margot contrived to keep away from the other pair for the remainder of the evening. They knew nothing of her doings as she was well aware, but something made it impossible for her to be with them and chatter as usual. Besides, she was rather afraid of Len. That young woman had an uncanny gift for almost reading the thoughts of both herself and Con. Margot wanted no one to know the thoughts she was having at present and certainly not either of her sisters!

Chapter 13

"I'M FINDING SOMETHING TO DO ABOUT IT!"

HILARY Bennet stalked indignantly into the Prefects' room, tossed down her racquet and net of balls on the nearest chair and then threw herself down on the broad windowsill of the casement window near which Mary-Lou was sitting. She had been reading a book on ancient Egypt with deep interest, but at the obvious indignation of her chum she laid it down and looked up at Hilary with a lazy smile.

"Well, what's the matter with you, may I ask?"

"You may! What's more, I'll tell you. There are times and seasons when I wish I had a good springy cane and the right to use it!"

"You do seem to feel bad. What's the why of all this? Have a choc, by the way? It may," Mary-Lou added with a grin, "help to sweeten you a little."

Hilary helped herself. "Thanks! I certainly need something! As for the why of it all, it strikes me that the one way to reform Margot Maynard *is* with a cane."

"She's fourteen—nearly fifteen. You can't very well use a cane on a girl of that age," Mary-Lou pointed out.

"Then more's the pity! That's all I've got to say. Someone will have to do something to bring that young demon to her senses—and pretty soon, too, or it'll be too late."

"What's she been doing?"

"Nothing—and I mean exactly that. Nothing at all — except to cheek me till I nearly boxed her ears on the spot."

Mary-Lou's eyebrows went up into her curls. "You do seem to be revved up!"

"You'd be revved up, as you call it, if you'd been in my place! Listen to this! This last period, I had some of that crowd for extra coaching. As you know, those three are all pretty good, but Margot is the one that shines. She has a very pretty style; she can place her balls with quite a good deal of cunning; she's getting quite a nasty, twisty service; she's always on the spot and it's the rarest thing in the world for her to poach. I don't say she's headed for Wimbledon or anything like that, but she's good. When she's older and has the strength and staying power, she'll be very good."

"Well?" Mary-Lou queried as Hilary stopped short. "What about it?"

"It isn't well—it's about as ill as it can be this week. Today, she went from bad to worse and played so abominably that I saw red. She might never have had a racquet in her hand before. She foot-faulted, she poached, when she did succeed in getting anything over the net, nine times out of ten it was right out of court and she'd skyed it like a junior. When I ticked Margot off—and she deserved every word I said to her!—she turned round and cheeked me all ends up. I sent her off the court and told her that so far as extra coaching was concerned she could stay off until she had made up her mind to beg my pardon for being so impudent and to play properly as well."

"In fact, a good time was had by all! Well, it's no more than she deserved. Are you reporting her to Burnie? You'll have to, won't you, if you refuse to let her have extra coaching? Burnie would want to know why."

"I told her to report herself—and I only hope Burnie eats her up, the little tick!"

Mary-Lou thought of something. "Did you see Len or Con playing? Were they all right? I mean," as Hilary stared at her, "I suppose nothing's gone wrong at Freudesheim?"

"Not so far as I know. Len and Con were at the practice boards and I noticed Con's backhand is coming on. They seemed all right so far as I could judge. No; I don't think you can explain Margot that way, Mary-Lou."

"Then," said Mary-Lou with deep conviction, "it's her devil come back. Unless she was feeling poorly."

"Nothing poorly about her. All I know is that she played like a Third former or worse, took not the slightest notice of a thing I said and when I did call her to order was downright rude to me. I'm having nothing more to do with her until she sees fit to come and apologise!"

Mary-Lou fetched a sigh from the soles of her sandals. "Oh, *drat* the young pest! I really thought she was more or less reformed these days. What does she mean by it?"

"Ask me another! I suppose the reformation was never much more than skin-deep and now it's worn off." Hilary eyed her friend with interest. "You seem a trifle upset yourself. Why?"

"Because Aunt Joey's been none too well these past few days. She was frightfully worried over the smallpox scare and the heat's been literally tropical lately. If Margot gets into any major rows, she's bound to hear of it and that'll mean more worry for her and it's bad for her just now."

"I wonder Margot didn't think of all that before she started this latest attack of devilitis."

"Didn't think of it, I suppose. She's only fourteen, after all. You don't think awfully deeply at that age—I know, I didn't."

"But Mary-Lou, she's not so very far from fifteen. And apart from that, I'd have said Margot was the most grown-up of that combination."

"So she is—on the surface. Beneath, there's a lot of the spoilt kid left in her. She *was* spoilt, you know, when she was tiny. She was so ghastly frail and Aunt Joey always said that she meant her to have a happy life if it was to be a short one. I don't mean she wasn't kept in order; but she was the centre of attraction and I expect she's assumed that she always will be."

"And how on earth can you know that?" Hilary demanded. "You couldn't have been more than a kid yourself in those days. You're only—how much?—not four years older than the Trips."

Mary-Lou laughed. "Oh, I didn't know anything about

it then, though I realised at a very early date that Margot wanted to be head and chief everywhere. It's what I've heard Mother and the aunts say since I grew up. Besides, it's never been easy for Margot to be really good. She was always the naughty one. And for all her would-be sophistication, she's a good ten years younger than Len in a good many ways. Even Con looks at things from a more grown-up angle than she does."

Hilary considered this. "I see what you mean. Yes; I think you're right there. Of course, Len is the eldest. That would make a difference, I imagine. Being a one-and-only myself, I can't speak from experience."

"I think you're right. Even when she was quite a tiny, I remeber Len being all responsible. The amazing thing to me nowadays is the amount of quiet influence Con seems to have with that lot."

"Con?" Hilary exclaimed. "But she's just a kid!"

"No; not now. I think the fact is that she's such a quiet creature, apart from her poetry, that one tends to ignore her. I have an idea that she does a lot of her growing-up—the mental side, anyhow—inside her and then something happens to show you and you're left gasping at the change, She isn't a leader like Len—or Margot, either, for that matter; but she really has influence among that crowd and whether they know it or not, they think a lot of what she says."

"Then I wish she'd turn a little of it on to that sister of hers!" Hilary said crossly. "If Margot goes on as she's doing, there's going to be a major row—I can tell you that much. You don't suddenly go out of your way to cheek a prefect. Something has to have been boiling up before you get to that pitch. "And there's another thing I haven't liked about her lately. She seems to be making a dead set at that new kid, Ted Grantley. I've overheard her more than once saying things. There's nothing wrong with what she says; it's the way she says it. I've seen Ted flush up and look miserable when Margot's been at her. And for the life of me, I can't see why. Ted's a nice enough youngster."

"You can't see why? Are you blind?"

"Not that I know of. What are you getting at?"

"Do you mean to say that you don't see that Margot is as jealous as sin about both Len and Con? She can't bear them to have any close friends—"

"*What?* But why on earth shouldn't they? Besides, Margot's as thick as thieves with Emmy Hope. If she has Emmy, what earthly reason has she for resenting it when the other two have friends?"

"I know; but I'm certain that's what's at the bottom of all this latest fuss—not excepting the affair with you this afternoon."

"Then she's a silly little ass—and a selfish little wretch into the bargain. I haven't an atom of sympathy with her!" Hilary said bluntly. She was devoid of that sort of thing herself and she simply could not understand it. Mary-Lou was not given to it, either, but, to quote Joey Maynard, she could see much further through a brick wall than most folk. She gave her friend a curious look before she added to her first remarks: "Sure you aren't imagining a lot, Mary-Lou? Surely no one could be so eaten up with herself as all that?"

"That's Margot, I'm afraid," Mary-Lou replied gravely. Even when she was an infant, Margot was like that. The reason it hasn't bobbed up of late years is, I suppose, because there's never been anything much to bring it up." "The thing I'm afraid of," she continued, "is that Margot will try to break up that combination so far as Len is concerned. In that case, my lamb, look out for squalls! Len has a temper, though we've never seen much of it. If Margot tries that on, she'll set Len against her and it'll take a lot to put that right."

"I say!" Hilary whistled. "We look like having a peach of a time, don't we?"

"If it came to that, we do," Mary-Lou agreed. "But I won't let it. Oh, I don't say we mustn't keep an eye on them; but I don't mean to leave it until it comes to us having to interfere if they scrap. I'm finding something to do about it."

Hilary grinned. "Trust you! The world's worst butter-in—that's what you are. OK; I'll back you up as far as in me lies." Then she added in a different tone, "I say! What's happening? It sounds as if a tornado or two had got loose on the stairs."

Even as she spoke, the door burst open and the rest of the prefects came pouring in to announce that Miss Dene was putting up the notice about the half-term arrangements that evening. The members of Vb were forgotten by even Mary-Lou as the grandees of the school speculated excitedly about what might have fallen to their lot.

Chapter 14

Con Blows Up

"Oh, goody, goody, *goody*! We're booked for Zermatt! And with Mdlle de Lachennais and Ferry! Whoever was decent enough to arrange anything so—so miraculous?" Len Maynard danced a jig of pure joy and the girls standing near laughed.

She stood in the centre of a group composed of herself, Con, Margot, Rosamund, Ted, Emerence and a shy French girl, Odette Mercier. Con was by way of being friendly with her, mainly because she felt sorry for her, and brought her with the others as much as she could. Odette had made very few friends, even after two terms.

"It'll be utterly magnificent!" Con agreed rapturously. "I've been yearning to visit Zermatt, but somehow all our trips have been in other directions."

"I wonder if they'll let us do a spot of climbing?" Len said wistfully. "I'm dying to have a shot and I've heard there are three or four quite easy climbs round there. Mdlle's a member of the Alpine Club and Aunt Rosalie says Ferry is really awfully good, considering she hadn't done any when she first came. Wouldn't it be smashing if they would take us up two or three?"

Emerence wrinkled up her pretty nose. "Rather you than I! It's not my idea of a holiday! I like to rest and take things easy. I don't mind strolling round the place, but I should hate having to struggle and climb up mountains."

"No one ever called you lazy, did they?" Len retorted scathingly. "Come off it, Emmy! It would be huge fun and I'm longing to have a go. The only thing is I'm afraid they'll say there are too many of us to risk it."

Rosamund laughed. "Twenty-six of us? Well, rather! Oh, I don't say they mightn't agree to take those of us who want to try it for one easy climb, but that'll be the limit."

"There's the bell for Abendessen!" Emerence exclaimed. "Come on! If we're late they'll say things about Seniors setting a good example!" She slipped her hand through Margot's arm and gave her a little tug. "Come on, Margot! What's wrong with you, by the way? You're awfully quiet. Don't you want to go to Zermatt?"

Margot freed herself with some dignity. "Don't drag like that, Emmy! It's too hot! Of course I want to go to Zermatt. It's one of the places we've never seen and I want to see it."

Emerence stared at her, but said nothing. They went with the others who were all talking as long as they were outside. Once they entered, that had to cease, but when they were all seated at table, they made up for lost time. The Head had taken pity on their excitement and though Wednesday was an "English" day, had given leave for them to use any language they liked during the meal, so long as they did not make too much noise.

"Must let them blow off steam a little," she murmured to Mdlle, sitting next to her when she sat down again. "Otherwise, they'll all burst with excitement."

"Oh, thrilled to the last degree!" Nancy Wilmot, who had overheard, chimed in. "I foresee you having to use the bell perpetually. Listen to them!"

The noise was rising and though the Head laughed, she replied, "I'd better warn them. We don't want any passers-by to get the idea that we allow our girls to behave like inmates of the monkey-house at the zoo on occasion!" before she rang the bell and when silence had fallen, gave her warning.

It helped to calm them down a little and the noise was, for the most part, no greater than usual.

"And just as well," Matey said when someone pointed this out. "They were beginning to clack like a lot of windmills. Odd how shrill girls get when they're all talking against each other!"

Miss Wilmot waited until everyone was busy again. Then she looked at Mdlle de Lachennais on the opposite side of the table. "Jeanne, what about inviting me to join your party? The bottom's fallen out of my plans."

"Then come with us by all means. We are delighted to have you."

"Especially," put in Kathie Ferrars from her seat beside Nancy, "as we shall have some of the stormiest petrels in the school with us. Margot and Emerence, not to mention Heather Clayton, Francie Wilford and Carmela Walther can do with all the eyes on them that we can manage. So welcome to our midst!"

"In that case, may I beg a place, too?" This was little Miss Andrews, one of the Junior mistresses. "I didn't expect to be free so I've made no plans and I've never visited Zermatt, so it would be new ground to me. I'll undertake to help look after your stormy petrels."

"What about it, Rosalie?" Nancy turned to Rosalie Dene on the other side. "Will it upset any arrangements you've made?"

"As it happens, not at all. In fact it keeps them as they were."

"What do you mean?" Miss Derwent asked with interest.

"We had a letter this morning from Mrs. Baker. Joan has to go home. Her eldest sister was to have been married at the end of August, but the bridegroom, who is on leave from his bank in Winnipeg, has been recalled unexpectedly—sickness seems to have decimated the rest of the staff—so the wedding has been pushed on to Wednesday of next week. Joan is chief bridesmaid, so she's going on Monday and won't be back till the week after."

"And," added the Head who had been listening to this, "Paul Scott rang up just before the gong went to ask if Jo might go home and take some friends with her. I said it was all right and Jo is taking Eve and Primrose with her."

"Then in that case, Sharlie, there'll be heaps of room for both you and Nancy," Kathie Ferrars said happily.

So it was settled and the talk drifted to other subjects.

Meanwhile the girls, having taken the Head's warning to heart, were discussing as quietly as in them lay the various expeditions arranged for half-term. They were all excited with their prospects, but they knew that what Miss Annersley said, she meant, so they kept their voices down and anyone who showed signs of forgetting was instantly shushed by everyone else. Only Margot remained quiet and had little to say for herself. Not even Emerence paid much heed to it; but Len noticed it and she glanced more than once at her sister with an apprehensive look.

"I wish I knew what's best to do," she thought as she tackled her sweet of iced custard and wild strawberries. "If I have it out with her now, Margot will blow up and that won't help anyone. If I let it go on, there's always the risk that she may do it at Zermatt. It's bound to come sooner or later. Oh dear! I wish to goodness she hadn't a devil! Or at any rate that she didn't listen to him as she does every now and then. She can be such a dear and he makes her such an utter pest! Once she gets going, she never stops till she's got rid of it all and she really doesn't seem to care what she says or does then."

It was still unsolved when they went to Prayers and though poor Len prayed hard to be shown what she ought to do, she had had no inspiration by the time they were dismissed to make the most of the time till bedtime. Nor could she do anything more about it then. Her cousin, Josette Russell, had invited her to make up a set with their cousin Maeve and Josette's great friend, Clare Kennedy. Josette was a prefect and, cousin or not, it was an honour to have such an invitation. Len did not see how she could possibly back out now, but she went to change her shoes and find her tennis racquet with a worried frown on her face. Mercifully, it was a hard-fought set and Len simply had to concentrate on her game and leave Margot and her doings on one side just then.

While Len was playing hard, Margot, forbidden the courts out of school-hours until she chose to apologise to Hilary for her rudeness that afternoon, picked up her library book and sauntered off to the rock garden in a very bad mood. She was well aware that those girls who had been present at the scene were condemning her. At the Chalet School, the prefects were regarded as the Head's representatives among the girls and impudence to them was impudence to her. There would be no out-of-hours tennis for her until she had made the apology Hilary had demanded and she loved tennis. She knew very well that she was a highly promising player and it was one of the few things she always worked at steadily, so the punishment hit her where she felt it most. Worse than that, she had to report herself to Miss Burnett before bedtime or else face a Head's Report. That would mean no trip for her and then her parents would know of it and want to know why. Besides, she wanted to see Zermatt as much as anyone else; but just at present, she was ready for neither apology nor report.

"I suppose I'll have to go to Burnie some time," she thought as she reached the top of the steps leading down to the rock garden. "I can't do it this minute, though. I saw her going off with Mary-Lou and her gang and they all had their racquets. I can't go barging into a set just to report myself. Burnie would be madder than she will be anyhow. I'll wait a little. As for Hilary, she can whistle for an apology from me! I couldn't care less!"

Seeing the mood she was in, it was unlucky that she should run into Con at the top of the steps. No one had ever with any truth accused Con of being tactful. What she thought, that she said, frequently with startling results. Margot would have avoided her if she could. She didn't want to talk to anyone.

"Margot! Oh, *luck!* Are you doing anything in particular? If not, then do come and make up a set with Ted and Ricki and me!" Con said eagerly. "We've bagged a court."

So far, only Hilary and the other three girls knew what had happened that afternoon. The others had said nothing about it and the notice about half-term had put it right out of their heads. Neither Len nor Con knew anything about it.

"I'm going to read," Margot said sulkily.

Con looked at her. The mulish expression on her sister's face warned her that there was trouble in the offing. Being Con, she did her best to avert it. Also, being Con, she did it about as tactlessly as possible.

"I say! What's wrong with you?" she asked.

"Nothing's wrong with me! I don't want to play—that's all!"

Con slipped an arm through Margot's. "But it isn't all! You can't get away with that sort of thing with me. We're triplets! I always know when there's something wrong with you or Len." She was at her most coaxing. "Tell me what's the matter with you, Margot. Perhaps I could help."

"Well, you couldn't!" Margot returned, wrenching her arm away. "Let me alone!"

Con was a sunny-tempered young thing as a rule, but she had her limits and Margot's tone and action had been little short of insulting. Con let go of her hold and drew away. "Oh, very well, if that's what you want. Sorry I asked you."

"Well, I do want it! For piy's sake mind your own business and I'll mind mine!"

"Certainly—if you're feeling as badly as all that."

"What do you mean?" Margot snarled.

"Well, you don't seem awfully inclined to be friendly to anyone at present. Never mind! I can ask Odette to make a fourth. And if she doesn't want to play, she'll say so pleasantly and not growl at me as you've done!" Con turned to go on, but Margot caught her arm and swung her back, none too gently, either.

"Are you going to be at it, too?" she demanded furiously.

Con stood stock-still. Sheer amazement wiped the anger from her face. "Be at what? What do you mean? What's come over you, Margot?"

This was where Margot suddenly let go of all but the last shreds of her self-control. "You know well enough what I mean! You're going off with that ghastly French kid and Ricki Fry, just as Len has taken to going off with Ros

Lilley and now that beastly Ted Grantley girl!" she stormed. "You neither of you care whether I'm left alone or not! I think it's rotten of you both!"

Con's own temper began to slip badly. "And what about all the times you've gone off with Emmy Hope and left us alone?"

"That's a different thing!"

"Oh, is it? It's OK for you to have a special pal, but it isn't for Len and me! We're to hang round and make do with what scraps of your time you like to spare us!" For once in her life, Con was fully roused. "Of all the selfish things I think that's the worst I ever heard! What's more, I, for one, won't put up with it! I'm going to have all the friends I want, whether you like it or not, and it doesn't matter what you say or do. I'm not giving them up just to suit you! So now you know."

Margot was staggered. She had had spats with her sisters over and over again, but neither of them had ever spoken so plainly to her before and it added fuel to the flames. For a moment, she was speechless with surprise. Then the thought of all her fancied wrongs overwhelmed her.

"You needn't talk of selfishness to me!" she shouted—and it was as well that side of the building happened to be deserted just then!—stamping her foot violently. "You're selfish enough yourself! Anyhow, I'm not going to have it! I won't have it, I tell you! And I'm not going to have Len making a pal of that horrid Ted Grantley—a girl who's been expelled from three other schools already!"

It was Con's turn to be breathless. "Oh, don't talk such rot!" she said when she could speak again. "You must be going crackers!"

"'Tisn't rot! It's true! Mom said it! So now!"

"Mamma told you *that!* I don't believe a word of it!" retorted forthright Con. "Even if it was true and she knew about it, she'd never say anything to any of us and you know it! You're making it up! And don't call her 'Mom', either! You know how she hates it. She told us ages ago that we weren't to use it and you're doing it behind her back which is deceitful!"

"I'll call her what I jolly well like! Who're you to stop me?"

Con passed this over. Her anger was dying a little as she considered Margot's amazing statement and when she replied, it was more quietly. "Look here, Mamma would never tell us anything like that. How did you get to know it? You'd better tell me," she added. "I mean to know."

Margot knew from experience that when Con dug her toes in, she was immovable. "I—I overheard her and Aunt Rosalie talking about it," she muttered.

"You—heard—Mamma—talking to Aunt Rosalie—about a thing like that! But how could you?" Con literally squeaked on the last words in her surprise.

A modicum of sense told Margot that she had better soft-pedal this at once. The bother was that she couldn't see how. As usual, when she lost her temper, she had let out something she had never meant to mention.

"Never you mind," she said sullenly. "I heard them and it's true! If you don't believe me, go and ask her yourself!"

"Have a little sense! I wouldn't dream of it! Mamma would want to know where you'd been to overhear her and wherever it was you oughtened to have been there. I jolly well know that!"

"I didn't mean Mom, you idiot! I meant that wretched Ted! Go on—ask her!"

Con stared at her sister with eyes full of horror. "You must be clean off your head—bats—crackers! If you did hear her, then you were eavesdropping. I knew you could be nasty when you liked, but I didn't know you were dishonourable!"

What might have happened, it is hard to say. Con's pretty voice had taken on a cutting tone that no one had ever heard there before. It made Margot flinch and then hate herself for flinching. That stirred up her rage even more and her face was crimson, her eyes full of blue fire as she forced herself to meet the contempt in Con's brown eyes. But, at that moment, there came the sound of voices and then some of the mistresses came in sight, bearing books and needlework and clearly making for the rock garden themselves.

Con moved to one side to let them pass and Margot, still managing to retain enough sense to know that she must not give rein to the fury possessing her, hastily turned away from the steps, dropping her long lashes as she did so. The mistresses thanked them and went on, laughing and chatting among themselves, though Miss Ferrars glanced at the pair with some curiosity as she went past. Obviously, they were quarrelling about something, but you couldn't go butting in on the girls over everything and they wouldn't thank you for it if you did. Kathie Ferrars was near enough to her own schooldays to know that. She said nothing but she put it away at the back of her mind for later consideration.

In the meantime, Margot had followed Con round the end of the hedge. She did not quite know what else to do. Con stalked ahead until they were well out of earshot of the rock garden. Then she stopped and turned. Margot stopped, too, and looked at her. Con spoke very quietly and with tremendous dignity.

"I'm not going on with this. I'm too ashamed of what you've done. I think you've behaved abominably, but it's your affair. You can jolly well square it with your own conscience. But understand once and for all that I'm having all the friends I want and so is Len. If you try to make any mischief between her and Ted, I shall know who's doing it and I shall do something about it. Now you know what to expect. But if you care at all for Mamma, you'll stop all this. It would worry her badly and Papa told us she wasn't well and mustn't be worried."

Having said her say to a silent Margot, Con turned on her heel and departed. But with that last speech, something else had gone—her childishness. The Con who came into Vb next morning was indefinably older and very much a Fifth form girl. They all felt it, though no one could explain it.

As for Margot, when her sister left her, she was in a state midway between another outburst of fury and even wilder tears. A saving remembrance of the fact that she still had to seek out Miss Burnett and report herself kept her from either. She sought refuge in the kitchen garden where she wrestled with herself until she felt able to seek out the games mistress for, little as she liked reporting herself, she disliked the idea of a Head's Report even more. Con's final remarks had given her the strength to pull herself together enough for that. At bottom, Margot loved her mother dearly. The pity of it was that she still loved herself better.

Chapter 15

MARY-LOU BEGINS HER CAMPAIGN

MARGOT got off much more lightly than she deserved. When she finally sought the games mistress, that lady was in a hurry. She listened to the culprit's halting confession with a resigned look on her face. When it had ended, she merely glared at the sinner until the fair face was a dark crimson.

"I'm ashamed of you!" she said crisply. "Answer me! Whom does Hilary represent?"

"The Head," Margot mumbled very unwillingly.

"Would you speak to the Head in that style?"

"No" Margot did not add that she would never dare. Miss Annersley was gentle and long-suffering, but she had her limits and everyone knew it. Margot thought of what would have happened if she had been as impudent to her as she had been to Hilary and found herself feeling shivery inside at the bare thought.

"Quite so! Well, tomorrow, you may beg Hilary's pardon—and do it properly, please. When you've done it, you may come here and tell me. If I am not satisfied, you will do it all over again—in my presence. Lose two conduct marks for rudeness. Don't forget to give them in at the end of the week. Now you may go. Good night!"

This spiked Margot's guns very neatly. She dared not disobey the games mistress and everyone knew that Peggy Burnett was a woman of her word. There was nothing for it but to make that apology and make it in proper form. She did and Hilary, judging that she had had enough, accepted it, pronounced forgiveness and let it go at that. Margot departed, once more seething; but she firmly determined not to miss the Zermatt trip, so she had no option.

She kept herself very much to herself for the next two or three days and Hilary, marking her subdued demeanour, decided that Miss Burnett had given her a good dressing-down and it had done the trick. The form, however, were well aware that Con and Margot were at odds though not even Betty Landon, who had won fame as the most inquisitive girl the school had ever housed, dared ask either of them what was wrong. Con was on her dignity—very much so!—and something in her manner checked even Betty's curiosity. She was icily polite to her younger sister and avoided her as far as possible. Len did ask when they were alone, but she got no satisfaction.

"Has Margot said anything to you?" Con asked gravely. Len shook her head. "She hasn't said a thing to me. In fact, now I come to think of it, she's giving me the go-by as hard as she could. Her devil again, I suppose! Are you going to tell me anything, Con?"

"Not if Margot hasn't. Sorry, Len, but I can't. It wouldn't be fair."

Len gave her a shrewd look. "It's that way, is it? OK. If you can't you can't." She let the subject drop, much to Con's relief. All the same, the eldest of the three kept a close watch on her bad triplet.

On the Saturday of that week Mary-Lou, who had also been keeping an eye on Vb whenever she could, and had drawn her own conclusions from what she saw, contrived to catch their form mistress after Frühstück. Miss Ferrars had lingered behind to scold a Junior for bad behaviour at table. Odile Badrutt was finally sent off, feeling very sorry that she had ever tried to kick her opposite under the table, and Miss Ferrars was about to turn and go to the entrance hall when she became aware of the Head Girl.

Mary-Lou came forward quickly. "May I speak to you for a moment, please?"

Little Miss Ferrars looked up with a laugh at the handsome girl who towered above her. "You're doing it already, aren't you? What's wrong, Mary-Lou?"

"I'd like a word in private if you can spare me a minute or two, please."

"Come along to Vb, then. We shall be private there for the next twenty minutes or so. It'll take the girls all that time to finish their cubicles." And she turned and led the way to her form room. Arrived there, she shut the door, went to lean against the edge of her table and lifted querying eyebrows at the Head Girl.

"This do?" she asked, smiling. "Then go ahead! I'm all ears!"

To her amazement, Mary-Lou went violently red. "I—I'd like to say first that this isn't meant for cheek," she began abruptly.

Kathie Ferrars nodded, the smile leaving her face. "All right; I understand."

"Well, it's just—I know your party is going to be short of four people as Joan is going home and Jo Scott is taking Eve and Primrose to their place with her. What I want to ask is—er—" Mary-Lou stopped short. She took a deep breath and then blurted it out. "May I come with your party?"

Kathie Ferrars gasped. "Come with us? But why? You Sixth form people are going to the Ticino, aren't you? I've heard you say you would like to see it, so why are you throwing it up like this?"

Mary-Lou reddened again. "It's awfully difficult to explain without seeming rude or—or conceited and interfering, but—" her voice trailed off.

"How is it difficult?" Then as Mary-Lou remained silent, she laid a hand on the girl's arm. "I think you can trust me to understand. Is it something private? Or is it anything you can tell me off the record?"

"It's—so difficult," Mary-Lou repeated. "If I tell you the whole thing, it practically amounts to telling tales and I've always loathed that. If I don't, well it may look to you like outrageous impudence—which I don't mean—or interference in the staff and I don't mean that, either."

"I—see." Miss Ferrars thought hard for a minute or two. During her first half-term at the Chalet School, she certainly had misunderstood Mary-Lou. That was all over now and, out of school, she and the girl were good friends.

"Why didn't you go to Mdlle?" she asked. "She is head of our party."

"She went too quickly for me," Mary-Lou replied promptly. She blushed again as she added, "That isn't meant for rudeness. I was only going to ask her because I know, as you say, that she's the head. Then I saw you ticking off Odile, so I decided to put it to you. I'll go to Mdlle if you'd rather."

"I think we had both better be in on this," Miss Ferrars said slowly. "Will you leave it to me to arrange, Mary-Lou? I'll see Mdlle and let you know when we can talk with you. But I think you'll have to make up your mind to tell us more than this."

"I was afraid of that." Mary-Lou heaved a sigh. "Thank you, Miss Ferrars. I'll leave it to you. But I hope you'll both agree to my coming. The Head won't mind, I know."

"I don't suppose she will. Are you going to explain to her yourself?"

"Not if I can help it—or not at present. But she'll trust me!" Mary-Lou spoke with confidence.

"Well, I'll see Mdlle and tell you when to come later on. Meantime, you'd best go and see to your room or you'll be late for the walk."

Mary-Lou accepted the dismissal with a word of thanks. She was still worried but she felt relieved that Miss Ferrars had understood so far. On her way up to the tiny room she occupied by virtue of her position as Head Girl, she met Con, looking very serious. At the same moment, Margot appeared from the opposite direction. She gave her sister a quick glance and then turned away with a toss of her red-gold head. Con apparently took no notice. They passed each other without a word and that little episode decided Mary-Lou. Something must be done before the trouble between the pair and the trouble over Ted flared out in the open. Even if it meant explaining in detail to Mdlle and Miss Ferrars, she must go through with it now.

"But I'd like to take that devil of Margot's and bundle him headfirst back where he comes from!" she thought as she entered her room and began to make her bed.

Halfway through the working part of the morning, Mdlle came to the library where Mary-Lou and three other prefects were working hard on essays. She checked them when they would have stood up.

"But no, *mes chères*: I do not stay. Mary-Lou, I wish to speak to you later. Will you come to me in the rock garden at Break, please. Bring your lemonade and biscuits with you, for we shall not have much time otherwise."

"Yes, Mdlle," Mary-Lou replied demurely; and Mdlle, after flashing a smile round the four, left the room again.

"What have you been up to, Mary-Lou?" Vi Lucy demanded severely when they were alone again. "I'm surprised at you—and you the Head Girl!"

"Nothing that I know of," Mary-Lou replied, picking up her pen. "Pipe down, Vi, do! I'm only halfway through this essay and this is my last chance at it. It has to be handed in on Monday."

When the bell rang for Break, she threw down her pen with a sigh of relief and gathered up the sheets filled with her characterful handwriting.

"See you all some time!" she said as she gathered her books together. With that, she was gone before the others could collect their wits to attack her again on the subject of Mdlle's summons. By the time they had arrived in the Speisesaal, she had seized her lemonade and biscuits and was headed for the rock garden where she found Mdlle busy with Lower III's needlework. She looked up smiling as the girl came down the steps to her and waved her to a nearby chair.

"Seat yourself, *chérie*. Miss Ferrars will be here in one little moment with elevenses for her and for me. Meantime, begin on your own."

Mary-Lou sat down and sipped at her lemonade. Nothing more was said until Miss Ferrars appeared with a tray holding the glasses of lemonade and biscuits for themselves. Mary-Lou jumped up to carry it for her while Mdlle cleared her sewing off the rustic table at which she had been sitting to make way for the tray.

When both mistresses had begun to sip their lemonade, Mdlle turned to Mary-Lou. "And now, my child, I wish to hear this little history of yours. Miss Ferrars has told me that you desire to accompany us to Zermatt. But why?"

"Mdlle, please don't think me rude," Mary-Lou said, "but—this is right off the record, isn't it?"

"But that is of course. We are not in school now, so pray continue."

Mary-Lou finished her lemonade and set the glass on the tray. "It's this way. There's something wrong between the Maynards, and Ted Grantley is mixed up in it. So," she added, "are Rosamund Lilley and I think Odette Mercier. I have an idea what it is and I want to put a stop to it if I can."

"But how do you think that coming with us to Zermatt will help you to put a stop to it, as you say?" Mdlle asked.

"I think things are coming to a head. If they are—but I only say 'if'—there's going to be a frantic row—er—" as she suddenly remembered to whom she was speaking, "I mean great trouble. If that happens, it will mean that the girl who begins it will be sent back to school. I don't want Aunt Joey to get wind—I mean hear—of it, it might upset her again and she's all right this last day or two, Uncle Jack says."

Kathie Ferrars nodded. "I agree with you there. And, like you, I can guess what's happening. You think that Margot is jealous because the other two are making outside friends. But surely she's old enough to know that it not only was likely to happen but that it ought to happen."

"Miss Ferrars, I honestly think that right down inside Margot isn't a lot older than ten, say; or twelve, perhaps. The other two are."

"But there," said Mdlle in French and with great emphasis, "you have laid your finger on the right place. I have seen that Margot has been very unhappy for some weeks now. I think you are right, Mary-Lou, though indeed, you are young to see it."

Mary-Lou reddened. "Well, to tell you the truth, it isn't all guessing. Len and Con have talked to me. At least, Con did most of the talking. You know what she's like. She sits back and lets other folk do it and then all of a sudden she pitches in and tells you things no one else would dream of saying. She let cats out of bags all right last Sunday! And then, if you please, they wanted my advice!"

"And what did you say?" Mdlle asked with real curiosity.

"Oh, told them to hang on to their tripletship and try to make Margot see that it was a tremendous tie, but to have all the friends they wanted just the same. I didn't know what else I could say."

"It was wise advice so far as Margot is concerned. But I do not see how Ted Grantley comes into it," Mdlle said.

"Yes; I'd like to know that, too. Len and Ted are very friendly. I've seen that since Ted came up to Vb," Kathie Ferrars remarked.

"I don't know for certain, but I rather think Margot has got hold of something against Ted—something that happened at Ted's last school. What I'm afraid of is that she means to use it to try and break up the friendship. I don't listen to other people's talk, but it can't always be avoided. The other morning I went into their Splashery to inspect and those two were behind the peg-stand at the far end and couldn't have known I was there and I overheard Margot saying something about 'your last school' to Ted. What's more, the voice she said it in was as nasty as I ever heard. I said, 'Who is here at this hour?' and they came out at once and—well—I didn't like the looks of either of them. Margot seemed triumphant about something and Ted looked —browbeaten!"

The two mistresses looked at each other. Mary-Lou was gazing across the garden so did not see Miss Ferrars raise her brows nor Mdlle's answering tiny nod.

"Mary-Lou," Mdlle said, "I will tell you something that we—by which I mean the mistresses—all know. If Margot has heard of it, then it is indeed time that one did something for she must not use it to harm Ted. Listen, Mary-Lou. We will trust you; but pray do not repeat this to anyone. Ted left her last school because the Principal refused to permit her to return."

Mary-Lou literally goggled at her. "But what had she done?" she demanded.

"One had found her smoking in the salle-de-bain with other girls after Lights Out."

"Smoking?" Mary-Lou's eyes were blue saucers. "But good Heavens! That's not a—an expellable crime! Do you mean to say they refused to take the lot back?"

Miss Ferrars took up the story. "This, it seems was only the climax to a series of things of that kind. She was never out of mischief and she seems to have led a certain bunch of her own kind by the nose. Anyhow, her conduct reports were so bad that it looks as if the Head had had no option. Ted had been warned that one more major row would mean exactly what she got and she chanced it."

"Silly little ass!" Mary-Lou commented. "All the same, Mdlle," she turned to the elder woman, "do you happen to remember Emerence Hope's first term with us?"

"But indeed I do! What a terrible child she was!"

"Exactly! But there was no question of sending her away. Everyone stuck it out and now Emmy's no worse than most folk. Well, I'm thankful it isn't anything really bad. I should have been horribly disappointed if it had been for I didn't think Ted was the kind of girl to go in for helping herself to other people's things or cheating or—or things like that. She may be a young ninny, but I'm positive she's honest and honourable."

"Oh no," Miss Ferrars replied swiftly. "So far as we've been able to gather, there hasn't been a thing like that. It was the usual sort of wickedness only rather more of it than one usually gets. For instance," her eyes began to dance, "on one occasion she treated them to a bareback riding display during the riding lesson."

Mary-Lou broke into peals of laughter. "What a nerve! Well, so far as we're concerned I can't say I've seen much tendency to that sort of thing since she's been here. Of course, she wasn't in school for three weeks, but she's been quite all right since. But if that's all it was, can you tell me why she's begun to look so hangdog lately? If she thinks that the other girls will boycott her for that sort of thing, she hasn't thought much. It's far more likely to appeal madly to most of the wilder kind like Emmy or young Prudence."

"The trouble is," Miss Ferrars said, "that that was the third school which had refused to have her back and her mother seems to have treated her like a criminal over it. Ted came here with an awful reputation and feeling that she could never make good. She seems to have cheered up a little, but I have noticed that these last few days she's been going about looking hangdog as you say." Then she added after a pause, "If Margot is holding it against her, then it's little short of blackmail and I'm horrified."

"Do you, then, hope to arrange for this?" Mdlle asked curiously.

Mary-Lou nodded. "I hope so. If I can only get hold of Margot and make her understand that if you don't share, you end by losing, I think she'll take a grip on herself and then things will improve. I may come, then? Thanks, more than I can say." She got up, picking up the tray to bear it back to the kitchen. Standing with it in her hands, she looked straight at the two mistresses. "I'd just like to say this before I go. I'm certain Margot has no idea what it really is that she's trying to do. She's decent at bottom, you know. If she can be got to see it before there's a terrific bust-up all round, it'll save everyone a lot."

She departed after that and the two friends she left looked at each other. "It might be impudence in some girls," Mdlle murmured in her own language, "but this is just Mary-Lou!"

"I hope she'll do something," Kathie said. "I don't want Ted to be upset now!"

Chapter 16

ZERMATT

FOR the remainder of the time until half-term, Mary-Lou kept an eye on the triplets, Ted and Rosamund as far as she was able, which was mainly out of school hours. She did not think that Margot would dare to play any pranks during lessons. As a result, Miss Margot found it a difficult matter to get Ted alone and by the time the Thursday came along, the latter had lost much of her hangdog look and was doing well in her new form. It never dawned on the Head Girl that Ricki Fry might come in for some attention from the naughty triplet and Margot, finding her way blocked where Ted was concerned, did her best to break up any private confabs between Ricki and Con.

It was little she could accomplish there. For one thing, Ricki was an older girl than Ted and for another, Con had already had her eyes opened to what was happening. She kept them open for once in her life. Those few weeks did her all the good in the world for though she still revelled in her fantasy people, she learned then to make them keep their proper place. As a result, she improved in her work and began to move steadily up in marks.

"Not a very good report on work, Margot," Miss Ferrars said when she gave that young person her half-term report. "In a form of twenty-six, you have come twentieth and it's not good enough. You have plenty of brains if you choose to apply them. You choose next half-term and see if you can't come nearer Len and Con."

Margot said nothing, but her mouth dropped sulkily. Her form mistress passed on to Emerence with a word or two of praise for that young woman who had contrived to attain to twelfth and beamed as if life held nothing better for her for the moment.

This was in the morning. Mittagessen took place at twelve and after that, they all streamed off in various directions, some by means of the big coaches the school mostly used for getting about the country. Vb, however, had to go down by train to Interlaken where they caught the coach to Thun and boarded the train which would take them by way of Kandersteg, Brig and Visp to Zermatt.

It had been a very hot day—so hot, that the Head had ended lessons at ten-thirty that morning. The girls packed themselves into the carriages of the train going to Thun with more than a little grumbling about the heat, but once they rolled out of the station they met the breeze off the lake and the grumbling died down. Len had pulled Ted and Rosamund into one compartment with her. Con and Ricki had followed and Margot had instantly hauled Emerence along to join them. Mary-Lou saw it all and after a quick word to Mdlle, made her appearance among them.

"Room for a little one?" she inquired, beaming genially on them.

"Heaps!" Len replied. "Shove up a bit, Ted. Have this seat, Mary-Lou."

Mary-Lou sank down, pulled off her hat and fanned herself vigorously with it. "Ouf! This heat is really something! I'm melting at the moment!"

"Won't it be cooler at Zermatt?" Rosamund asked.

"I'm hoping so. If not, you'll probably have to leave me there as a large spot of grease in the main street! Thank goodness I'm coming with you and not going to the Ticino! I've been there before in the summer and I found it the outside of enough."

Thanks to Mary-Lou's presence, the girls chatted amicably enough throughout the long journey until the little train drew up in Zermatt station. The mistresses were out first and stood waiting until their flock were all clustered together. Then Mdlle took charge.

"Into line, *mes filles*!" she said firmly. "You will have time for wandering after we have reached our pension. Betty and Priscilla, lead, if you please. Follow Miss Ferrars and Miss Wilmot. They know the way."

They marched off briskly, casting curious glances round as they went. The evening sun was shining now, and Zermatt was very gay with the jingle-jangle of the horse-bells and the houses, all typically Valaisian, with bronzed guides hanging about the one street with the station and the main hotels at one end, then shops, smaller hotels and pensions, until at last it petered out into dark brown chalets running down to the bridge that crosses the River Visp to the green pastures where sheep and the soft-eyed cows grazed placidly.

They had taken barely three steps when a sudden joyful outcry from Len halted the line. "Look—*look*! The Matterhorn!"

They all looked and there was a concerted gasp as the loveliness of the great gleaming peak, lined by a thousand deep blue and purple shadows in the evening sunlight, broke on them.

Emerence spoke first. "*Oh*! I heard it was lovely, but I'd no idea it was *so* lovely! I—I think it even beats our Jungfrau!"

"Don't call her 'it'!" Mary-Lou said reprovingly. "Mountains are mainly feminine—like ships."

The rest took note. Mdlle let them gaze their fill. Then she moved them on again.

"You are hungry and, I am sure, fatigued," she said in her prettily accented English. "Come! We will seek our pension and wash faces and hands and make neat our hair. Then when we have had our meal, we will come out again and you may promenade as you will for an hour."

Mdlle was a delightful person when she chose, but her discipline was firm. With a last glance, they set off again and in five minutes had reached the quiet pension where they were to stay for the weekend. The hostess greeted them warmly, showed them to their rooms —three long narrow ones with beds set against one wall and a chair between each bed and the next. Rows of pegs were ready to hang frocks and coats on and there was a big armoire, black with age and gleaming with hard rubbing where the rest of their belongings might go. That was all, except that every room had electric light, of course.

"It looks," said Len with a giggle as she established her claim to one of the beds, "exactly like the dormitories you read about in old-fashioned school-stories."

"Are Mdlle and the rest in one of these?" Ricki asked in awed tones.

"Ask me another! I couldn't tell you!" Len had untwisted her heavy pigtail and was brushing it out before one of the windows. "Come and plait my wig, will you, Ted?"

At last they were all ready and trooped off downstairs, headed by Emerence and Margot. Abendessen was ready, with the Valaisian dish of raclette to give them a good start off. They were thrilled by it. One of the large local cheeses had been put to melt before the electric heater and it was brought to table hot and soft. From this, everyone scraped off fragments which they ate with floury potatoes cooked in their jackets and gherkins.

"I only hope," said Miss Ferrars as she looked thoughtfully round the table after the cheese had been removed to give place to dishes of strawberries, served with cream whipped to a thick foam, "that none of you will have nightmares after this!"

Abendessen over, they raced upstairs to the bathroom to wash their fingers free from stickiness and then, having been duly warned that they must keep to Zermatt for this evening, were sent out to wander about as they chose.

Len tucked a hand into the arms of Ted and Rosamund, and turned them towards the more rural end of the street. "I want to see the Visp up here," she announced. "Come on, folks! Let's go along here and take a dekko at it. Coming, Con? Coming, Margot?"

Margot, on the verge of refusing, changed her mind. It had struck her that if she was with them, she could keep an eye on Len and her doings. Con agreed easily and the party sauntered off down the street, admiring everything they saw. At first, they passed shops, small hotels and pensions. Then these gradually became chalets until they petered out not far from an entrancing fountain with marmots in bronze frolicking round it. From there, they strolled down to the bridge over the young Visp and stood on it, gazing down at the grey waters, tossing and swirling in their headlong rush to the valley to join the Rhône on its way to the Mediterranean.

"Why's it so grey?" Emerence asked presently.

"Because it comes from a glacier," Len explained. "Mamma says that all glacier-born rivers are like that at first. They lose it as they hurtle down, though. I suppose their colour changes with the rock and so on of their beds." She turned for a satisfying look at the Matterhorn and the village beneath it. Lights were twinkling from some of the windows and she marshalled the rest to turn back.

"It's going to be dark pretty soon now. We'd better be going back. Oh, aren't those chalets lovely? They remind me of Sion—remember, Ricki?"

Ricki gave a chuckle. "Do I not! I don't think I ever enjoyed a trip more than that one."

"It seems awfully odd to hear of a place called Sion in Switzerland," Ted remarked. "It always makes me think of Jerusalem!"

"Oh, heaps of places called Sion all over the world," Margot said airily. "I believe there are two or three in the USA, for instance. You never expected to see anything like that when you were at your last school, did you, Ted? What a good thing for you that you—er—left and came here?"

Ted flushed at the note in her voice, but before she could reply to her tormentor, Con had broken in. Speaking in the chilly voice she had used for the past few days to Margot, she said, "If you come to that, neither did we at one time."

It was Margot's turn to colour. She shot Con a most unsisterly glance. Con paid no heed to it, but Len saw it and gave the pair a startled look. So far, Con had said nothing about what had happened on that fatal Sunday and the eldest of the family knew nothing about it. But the little episode which had just occurred had told Len a good deal and she guessed at more. That Margot was jealous, she knew. Now she realised that she must be on the look-out or her younger sister would try to break up her friendships.

"And that, I won't allow for a moment!" Len thought. "What's more, the parents would back me up. But I hope it won't ever come to such a pitch that either of them has to know. That really would put the tin hat on everything!"

Chapter 17

A Pig!

On the Friday, they all went up to the Gornergrat by the funicular, and in the evening they went for a stroll in the meadows. Miss Wilmot was sauntering along with the triplets and their special friends surrounding her. They had left the village by way of the bridge over the Visp and were walking across a meadow where the ground sloped upwards. Beyond it was a farm, and, though they were not to know till later, a Scots family were staying there en pension. The McCleod family consisted of father, mother, young uncle and a small boy of five named Ian, who had an unbridled passion for babies of all kinds but human. This evening he met one of the young sons of their hosts, bearing a bucket of buttermilk to the family sow, who had just produced a family of eleven piglets. Nothing would serve him but that he must come, too. When they reached the pigpen, he was enthralled by the pink babies who snuffled and snorted with shrill little squeals as they nuzzled their mother. Ian grabbed the nearest baby and clutched it lovingly to him, talking to it affectionately.

Unfortunately, the pigling was terrified and he squealed his terrors abroad. Mamma heaved herself to her feet, grunting furiously, and lumbered towards Ian, who fled from the pigpen, still clutching his prey and made off, followed by the pig who was now raging.

He made for the open gate from the farmyard, his short legs going at full speed. Down the meadow up which Nancy Wilmot and her flock were strolling, he went. Behind him came the pig and she was followed by the farmer's son; Mr. McCleod, who had come round the corner in time to see what was happening; and Herr

Schultz, righteously angry at the thought of what all this might mean to a sow with babies to feed.

It took the Chalet School party not two minutes to grasp what was happening. With a shout, Nancy straddled the pathway to try to check young Ian's headlong flight while the girls scattered to try and turn the sow.

How it actually happened, no one could ever quite determine. Somehow, the terrified Ian and his squealing burden were diverted and the triplets caught and held him while Ted snatched the piglet from him, crying, "We'll give it back to her!"

The sow was so blind with rage that she simply hurtled ahead. Her head and forequarters passed under Miss Wilmot's legs, then as she pushed, she brought that lady down on her back and went rushing on. Instinctively, Miss Wilmot clamped the fat flanks with her knees, so she, too, went on, perforce, riding the pig hindside foremost! The unexpected weight—Miss Wilmot stood five feet ten and was plump to put it mildly, brought up the enraged animal before she reached the torrent where she might have come to a sudden and tragic end. She rolled over, tossing the mistress to the ground, and discovered that she had no more breath to run. Indeed, the farmer, rushing up first of the crew after Ian, was alarmed about her. Pigs are not built for racing.

By this time, Mr. McCleod had reached the party, snatched his son from the arms of Margot and Len, and taking him under his left arm, was proceeding to teach him a lesson. A more awful noise was never heard. The pig was grunting and gasping; Herr Schultz, shaken out of his usual monumental calm was letting off a series of exclamations in dialect; Ian was screaming for a good reason—his father had decided to give him a lesson he would never forget —and what with the piglet squealing, and the girls shrieking with laughter, the din must have been unique for Zermatt.

Mary-Lou heard it as she reached the bridge and her long legs made short work of the distance as she came up breathlessly to help Miss Wilmot rise and ask anxiously if she were hurt.

By this time, Herr Schultz had decided that his sow was not so much the worse. He put a brawny foot under her at a nicely-judged place, and got the lady to her trotters. Ted at once ran up and handed over her noisy burden to its owner. His son was busy fastening a cord to one of her legs, but he finished, handed the other end to his father and took the terrified baby with the remark that he would carry it back to its brothers and sisters.

Mr. McCleod had set his sobbing son down by this time, but still held on to him. "And what did ye think ye were doing, ye wee gomeril?" he demanded.

"I wanted to love it," the "wee gomeril" sobbed. "It was so wee and pink and long-nebbit! I thought maybe I might take it to bed with me!"

That really did top it! Even his father had to forget his annoyance and for the next minute or two, they all rocked with laughter. The rest coming up could get no sense out of any of them, but caught the infection and just what the worthy burghers of Zermatt may have thought who saw the scene will never be known.

Eventually, they managed to pull themselves together. Madam Pig was persuaded to walk up to her pen where her family were waiting for her. Ian was marched off, still weeping, to be put to bed on dry bread and milk, and the mistresses gathered their flock together and bore them off to their pension.

That night, Margot woke up to hear a queer sound from Ted Grantley's bed and when she went to demand what Ted thought she was doing, found that young woman under the sheets, giggling madly. She had dreamed the whole thing over again, wakened herself by laughing and was unable to stop.

Margot dealt with it promptly. She fetched a glass of water from a shelf where carafe and glass stood, and lowered it over Ted threateningly. "One more sound out of you and I'll chuck the lot over your head!" she proclaimed—as far as one can proclaim in a whisper.

Ted made a herculean effort and at last stopped, but her eyes were swimming in tears and she was fighting for breath. "S-sorry!" she gasped. "B-but it w-was so f-funny!"

"Yes, and if you bring Mdlle or Willy or anyone else here, it'll be funnier still!" Margot warned her. "Here! Drink this and don't be such as ass!"

Ted sat up and sipped and felt better. Margot took the glass when she had finished and put it back. But before she returned to her own bed, she bent over Ted to mutter, "Now you just shut up and to to sleep!"

Oddly enough, her devil sulked after this, but her guardian angel smiled. There was still a chance!

Chapter 18

MARGOT'S CLOCK

"OH, Margot! Con and I want to go to buy our gifts for the parents and we want to go now. Will you come with us? You're joining in, of course?" Len looked eagerly at her sister.

Margot frowned. "Oh, Len, I can't! I've promised Emmy I'll go with her to buy hers. Can't you wait till later on?"

"How can we?" Con asked reasonably. "It's now or never. We leave as soon as Mittagessen is over so if we don't go now, there won't be time.

The half-term was almost at an end. Whether it was due to the awe the amazing mountain panoramas had inspired in her or whether it was all the laughter they had shared over the episode of "Wee Ian" and the piglet, everything had gone smoothly. Margot had let Ted alone. Indeed, she had been almost friendly with her. Ted, basking in the peace, seemed happier than ever and was so fully occupied with all the new sights and sounds, that she had no time for anything else. The rest enjoyed themselves to the top of their bent.

Mary-Lou, who had been keeping a firm, if surreptitious eye on the triplets and their friends, felt that she might relax her efforts for a couple of hours and had gone off with Miss Ferrars and Miss Andrews for a last short scramble. She was friendly with both out of school hours and though she would be a "Millie" next term, there would be only one year of that. Then would come the university and thereafter her training as an archeologist and after that, as she had observed, she might be anywhere!

Mdlle had given the girls leave to spend what time was left to them before Mittagessen in buying such souvenirs and gifts as they wished. She had warned them once again that Zermatt was an expensive place, reminded them of the school's Sale, not so far away now, and then sent them off.

Most had gone already when Len put her request to Margot. Ted and Rosamund had joined forces and departed together, leaving Len and Con to collect their third. This had been Rosamund's idea.

"The Maynards are sure to want to buy something for their mother and it'll be easier for them if they go together. Shall you and I go on our own?" she proposed. "I asked Ricki Fry, but she's joining up with Betty and Alicia."

Ted was quite agreeable. "OK—though I haven't much to buy. It's no use getting anything for my mother. She's touring the West Indies and I haven't a clue where she is at the moment, so I couldn't send anything. But I want to get something for my cousin May. I can't afford much, but I'd like to get her some little thing. If it hadn't been for her I probably shouldn't have come here."

"Well, I haven't a lot to spend, either," Rosamund replied. "But I want a wooden bear for my niece and something for Mother. Postcards must do for the rest."

They went off after informing Len what they were doing and it had seemed to that astute young person that here was a chance to get Margot to themselves again and show her, as Mary-Lou had advised, that their tripletship was still the biggest thing in life to them. Unfortunately, Margot had plans of her own.

When they heard her reply, Len and Con looked at each other with dismay.

"Aren't you coming in with us?" Len queried. "We could get each of them something decentish then and that's better than two or three little oddments."

"Oh, I'll share all right," Margot returned. "But if you want me to come with you to help choose, you'll have to wait until Emmy's finished."

"But why shouldn't we all go together?" Con asked. "Then you could help Emmy and after that she could come with us while we chose for the parents."

Margot shook her head. "No; I promised Emmy we'd go together. But if you like to hang about until we get back, I'll come then."

The fact of the matter was that, to her at any rate, the most important part of Emerence's shopping was to be a present to herself.

On the Sunday morning, when they had been sauntering about the village, Margot and Emerence had gazed into the window of a jeweller's shop. There they had seen a gem of a clock and Margot had fallen in love with it. She had voiced her admiration aloud without, it must be said, ever thinking of having it herself. Emerence, who always had far more pocket-money than the school authorities thought at all good for her, had instantly proposed giving it to her.

"Emmy, you can't possibly!" Margot had exclaimed. "Besides, I couldn't let you. It must cost the earth! All that beautiful enamelling and the face has that rim of rhinestones round it! Do talk sense!"

"They're not proper stones—only chips," Emerence pointed out. "Besides, I've piles of money. Dad sent me a smashing big cheque for half-term, so I've any amount. Besides, I want to give you something decent, Margot — honestly I do!"

What she could not yet tell Margot was that this was to be her last term at the school. She was well past seventeen, though she was in the same form as girls of fourteen and fifteen. There was little hope that she would ever go much higher up the school than she already was and her parents had decided against giving her the usual finishing year at St. Mildred's. Mr. and Mrs. Hope proposed to visit the USA in the autumn and wanted their girl with them, and altogether it had seemed an excellent plan to them. Her father had told Emerence that she was to say nothing about the latest plans until much later in the term. Mr. Hope was a casual parent in many ways, but once he gave an order like that, he expected to be obeyed and his daughter knew it. She could not even tell her *alter ego* until he gave leave. But when she saw the size of the cheque he had sent her, she had made up her mind at once that Margot was to have a goodbye gift worth having.

Margot knew perfectly well what both father and mother would say about such a present, but when Emerence insisted, she had been unable to hold out. She wanted that clock more than anything she had seen before. She gave in. But it would never do for Len and Con to be with them. They would raise an instant outcry. It had been quite a jolt to her when Len had come to ask her to join them.

She proceeded to ram her opinion home. "Emmy doesn't want anyone but me with her. I don't suppose we'll be so very long. You two hang about and I'll join you as soon as she's finished," she said.

Con opened her lips to say something, but Len guessed what was likely to come and was too quick for her. "Very well. We'll go and be looking at things in the windows and get some idea of what we're likely to be able to afford," she said. "We're giving fifteen francs each. Will you do the same?"

Margot nodded. "Oh, yes; I can do that all right." She suddenly sighed. "I wish we were rich—like Emmy, for instance!"

"Well, we're not, nor likely to be," Con said with some tartness.

"Here's Emmy! I must go! See you shortly!" Margot raced off, thankful to get away without further trouble.

The pair vanished out of hearing before Con let loose. "Did you hear that?" she demanded of Len.

"I did—I did! But for pity's sake don't go barging in! I know all you're thinking—that Margot goes her own way and doesn't mind about us. But don't say it here and now, Con. We've got through the week end decently and let's finish it decently! Anyhow, she doesn't really mean it nastily, though I know it looks like it."

Meantime Margot, swinging along beside Emerence, was in high feather. They made for the jeweller's where they paused before the window a moment. The clock was still there and they stood admiring it.

It was a most expensive trifle, as Margot's own sense told her. Her parents would certainly have a good deal to say when they got to hear of it, but she told herself that she would get round them somehow. The thing that mattered was that she really did want it badly and Emmy was giving it to her.

As if she guessed what her friend was thinking, Emerence turned to enter the shop, saying, "Come on! If you're sure you really like it, we'll get it. I want to give you something you really want."

"I'd love it more than anything I can think of!" Then Margot's conscience roused a little and she added, "But it'll be frightfully expensive. Are you *sure* you can afford it, Emmy?"

Emerence grinned. "Of course I'm sure! Dad sent me a really noble sum this time and I've got the lot with me."

By this time, they were in the shop and an assistant was coming to ask how he could help them. Three minutes later and the clock in all its beauty was before them on the counter. Margot looked at it with longing eyes—and fell. It was easy enough to suppress the feeble protests of her conscience and the upshot was that they left the shop with the carefully packed parcel in Emerence's big handbag beside the sadly depleted purse of its owner.

"We'll keep it a secret to ourselves," Margot said as they left the shop. I don't want to share it with anyone else at present. Oh, it is dear of you to give me such a lovely thing! I'll keep it all my life!"

Emerence had been rather surprised at her first remark. Then the idea of a secret for just the two of them settled her. She was deeply fond of Margot and the younger girl had far too much influence over her to be good for either of them. She fell in with the idea and even offered to take charge of the clock until they reached school, as her bag was so much larger than Margot's.

Margot consented easily. To tell the truth she had begun to wonder how she was to get it back to school without either of her sisters finding out. She knew that it wasn't going to be easy to hide it, but she ought to be able to slip home during the next day or two and then she could tuck it away in her own bedroom.

They walked down the street and came up with Len and Con flattening their noses against the window of a shop that sold wood-carvings, peasant ware and other bric-à-brac. Both turned as Margot touched Len on the arm with an airy, "Well, here we are, you see! We haven't kept you long!"

"No; you've been awfully quick," Len agreed amiably. "I suppose, though, you knew exactly what you meant to get, Emmy. Margot, do you think Mamma would like those book-ends with the St. Bernard dogs?"

"Love them, I should think," Margot said, glancing at the book-ends.

"Then what do you say, Con?" Len turned to her other sister. "Shall we fix on those? We can get Papa one of those letter-openers. He says he can always do with another because most of his are always missing."

"Well, if we buy the book-ends, we certainly can't manage a pipe-rack as well," Con said. "OK. If you two are agreed, so am I. We'd better go and get them."

They trooped into the shop where they found Ted and Rosamund waiting while the pretty girl attending to them packed up the model chalet finally chosen for Rosamund's niece, and the similar one Ted had bought for her cousin May, the former Miss Carthew.

"Come and help us choose a letter-opener for Papa while you wait," Len promptly invited them. "We're getting book-ends for Mamma."

When that was settled, Margot, carrying matters with a high hand, swept off Emerence for "just one last stroll round". The rest had to wait until the parcels were packed. When their business was ended, they, too, trotted off to take a final look at the Visp tearing and brawling its way under the bridge and down the mountain slope to join the Rhone in the valley far below.

As it happened, this was the way Margot and Emerence had gone and once they were free of the crowds and standing a little way up the bank of the river, Margot begged for another peep at her new treasure. She had opened it and was standing, gloating, over it when the others arrived and, seeing them, turned to join them.

"Oh, Emmy, it's simply beautiful!" she was saying as they came up. "It's quite the nicest present I've ever had and I can't thank you enough for it!"

Then the rest were on them before she had time to think and she was standing there with the clock sparkling in the sunlight. Len and Con took one look at it. Len was stunned into silence, but Con, for once, was not. Tactless as usual, she gave her sister a horrified look, even as Emerence caught the clock from Margot and hurriedly bundled it into her bag.

"Oh, Margot!" she exclaimed. "You can't possibly let Emmy give you a thing like that!"

Chapter 19

Mary-Lou Butts In Again

That did it!

Never in all her life had Margot been so angry as she was at that moment. For once, she went white instead of red and her eyes gleamed like pieces of chilled steel. For a second, she was silent, literally unable to speak. At last: "Perhaps you'll try to mind your own business!" she said in as insolent a tone as she could produce.

"But it is my business!" Con assured her. "You're my sister."

"It's not! It's my business—mine and Emmy's! It's nothing to do with you, whatever you may think. Nor you, either, Len!" she added, swinging round on Len. "No, Emmy!" as that young person tried to intervene. "You leave this to me. It's time these two realised that if I am the youngest, they aren't my keepers. Do you hear, you two? You're to let me alone!"

Len eyed her steadily. "How can we when we know that you're doing something both Father and Mother would hate—"

"The one thing that surprises me," Margot said in low, venomous tones, "is that they're letting you pal up with a girl who had been expelled from three different schools! That's right, isn't it, Ted?" with a malicious smile at Ted.

Ted went white, but she held up her head as she replied sturdily, "Expelled from only one to be strictly accurate. The other two just asked my mother not to send me back. And how," she went on, carrying the war into the enemy's country, "did you ever get to know of it? Miss Annersley said no one was to know except just the people she told and she forbade me to mention it. So how do *you* know?"

"Yes—how?" Len cried, suddenly waking up to this aspect of it.

Margot reddened. In her fury, she had been careless and now she did not know how to turn the questioning aside. All she could do was to retort, "Never you mind!"

Con slowly turned and eyed her triplet from head to foot. She said nothing, however. She knew that it was her fault that this had ever started. If she had held her tongue until they were safely back at school, Margot would have kept her temper.

"Oh, dear!" she thought dismally. "I do wish I could learn when to speak and when not! Mamma's always said that if I didn't look out I'd end by hurting someone badly and now I've done it—and Margot, of all people!" Len's mind was on Ted. She turned to her. "Tell me this, Ted, since cats seem to be popping out of bags in all directions. Why were you expelled or whatever it was?"

"For thinking of mad things to do—and doing them," Ted said, looking straight at her. "The last lot was for smoking at midnight out of a bathroom window, but I only topped up with that. There'd been plenty of that sort of thing before. The Head had warned me what would happen if I got into one more really bad row and I more or less asked for it, I suppose."

"Oh, yes; you would say that, of course!" Margot sneered. She was possessed to hurt someone just then, so furious was she. "You never cheated at lessons—nor told lies—nor stole—"

"Pipe down!" Rosamund said, suddenly waking up. She turned and slipped a hand through Ted's arm.

Ted smiled at her gratefully. Then she swung round on her accuser. "Do use your common sense! Is it likely that Miss Annersley would have agreed to have me here if it had been that sort of thing?"

Margot stared at her. Then she suddenly sprang forward and boxed Ted's ears. "How dare you speak to me like that?" she shrilled, while the rest, suddenly galvanished into action, crowded round her, trying to hush her. "How dare you? I hate you, do you hear? You shan't steal my sister from me! I'll get rid of you somehow—"

"Will you, indeed?" A fresh voice broke in on Margot's diatribe and the horrified party turned to face Mary-Lou—and Mary-Lou was looking quite as angry as Margot. She had just been in time to hear Ted's speech and Margot's outrageous reply and it did not take her a moment to realise what was happening.

Margot, at the moment, was almost beside herself and not even the sight of the Head Girl looking, as Len said later, like an avenging Fury, could curb her.

"Keep out of this!" she shouted at Mary-Lou "It's none of your—"

Smack! Len did not intend to slap her sister, but she was in a hurry to stop any further enormities from her and when she removed her hand in a hurry, the marks of her fingers flamed on Margot's face. At least it had one good effect. The younger girl had been on the verge of hysterics and the sting of the blow brought her to her senses in a hurry. She said not another word, but she stood still, a blackly sullen expression on her face.

Mary-Lou slowly looked each one of them up and down. Emerence, the innocent cause of the immediate upheaval was crimson and nearly crying. Len and Con were red, too. Rosamund still held Ted's arm and Ted herself stood with her head held high, though she was rather white.

Mary-Lou spoke and her voice was as icy as the Matterhorn glacier itself. "You will all come back to the pension at once. No one will say a word of all this to anyone else—anyone at all! When we are back at school I'll see you all and deal with it. Until then, you are to be absolutely silent about it." She stopped a moment. Then her voice rang out like the crack of a whip. "Is that clearly understood?"

With Mary-Lou looking and speaking like that, they could do nothing but murmur, "Yes" and she set out at once. "Rosamund and Ted, lead the way," she said curtly. "Con, you take Emerence. Len, come with Margot and me."

She marched them back to the pension where most of the others had already arrived. With an eye to keeping them as much as possible from the others, she ordered them straight upstairs to tidy themselves for the meal, taking Margot with her. What was more, she kept the girl with her. Mdlle and Miss Wilmot were too busy to do more than note that there seemed to be some trouble with the Maynard crowd. Only Kathy Ferrars saw clearly that matters had come to a head.

As a result, she saw to it that the six were put into a separate compartment with Mary-Lou in charge so that if any of the other girls noticed anything, they were unable to ask questions for the present. Naturally, all of them had seen that there was something wrong, but even Betty the inquisitive dared say no more after she had been severely snubbed by Mary-Lou for asking, "Is there anything wrong with Margot and the others?" That, however, did not prevent her from discussing it with her own crowd when they were left alone for a short while and the upshot was that they all decided that there must be bad news from Freudesheim and had better leave the three to Mary-Lou and their own chums. In fact, by the time evening had come and Abendessen was over, it was all round the Senior school that Mrs. Maynard was very ill and the triplets had gone home to be close at hand in case they were wanted, and the other three had gone with them to stand by them in case of need. Though it was rather odd that the Head made no mention of it at Prayers!

Far from being at Freudesheim, however, they were all in the prefects' room with a Mary-Lou who was the complete Head Girl for once and, therefore, rather alarming. No one had ever seen her quite like this before.

She looked coldly at them before she said, "And now, I want to know the meaning of this morning's disgraceful scene. Rosamund! you're as likely as anyone to be able to tell me a plain, straight story. Begin, please, and don't leave anything out."

Rosamund, blushing wildly, told it with a good many halts and stumblings. She did not know nearly everything and Mary-Lou had to question one or two of the others before she had it all. Then she turned to Emerence.

"What is this clock? Where is it?"

"It's in my bag," Emerence said in subdued tones.

"I'd better see it. Go and fetch it, please."

While Emerence was gone, she turned, again to Rosamund, "Is that all you or anyone else can tell me, do you think, Rosamund?"

"I—yes, I think so," Rosamund replied. "It's all I know myself."

"Right! Then you can trot off. It's evidently no affair of yours and you've come into it more or less by accident. Sorry about that, but it couldn't be helped. Anyhow, no one blames you for anything. By the way, don't say a word to anyone else about this, will you? I must," Mary-Lou said gravely, "make up my mind about whether I can really deal with it myself or whether it must go to the Head. I hope it won't come to that, but I can't say yet. If it does, Mrs. Maynard would have to know about it and no one wants that to happen."

Margot reddened and shot a quick, horrified glance at Mary-Lou. Her sisters also sent appealing looks to where the Head Girl was sitting. It was wasted effort at the moment. She meant to get to the bottom of everything before she pronounced judgement. Rosamund quietly went off to seek some hidey-hole where she remained hidden until bedtime.

By this time, Emerence had returned with her bag. She set it on the table and took out the box containing the clock. She lifted the pretty toy out and handed it to Mary-Lou. That young woman stared at it with startled eyes. She had expected nothing like this and the sight rocked her clean out of her icy mood.

"What on earth did they rook you for this?" she demanded in her usual clarion tones. "Emerence! You must have taken leave of your senses when you squandered on a thing like this! What were you thinking of?"

"I wanted to give Margot something she really liked," Emerence muttered.

"My good girl, couldn't you have been satisfied with something considerably less? Besides, why on earth do you want to do that now?"

Emerence lost her head. "It's because I'm leaving at the end of the term." she explained. "It's really a good-bye present." Then she caught her hand to her mouth. "Oh, my word! Dad said I wasn't to say anything about it yet! I quite forgot!"

But the news had reached Margot and cut right through her sullen defiance. She gave a low cry of dismay. "Emmy! You're not leaving?"

Having let the cat out of the bag, Emerence decided that she might as well own up fully. "Margot, I'm dreadfully sorry, but I am. Dad wrote telling me. And he sent a cheque so that I could buy leaving presents for my friends. That's why I wanted to buy you the clock when you loved it so."

Mary-Lou's eyebrows could go no higher. They had already disappeared beneath her curls. In fact it was fully ten seconds before she got her breath. Then she said, "It strikes me there's a good deal for you folk to tell me. Sit down, Emerence, No, leave the clock where it is. I can't decide about that for the moment. I rather think this must go either to the Head or Dr. Jack. I don't for one moment believe that Margot will be allowed to keep it. It's far too valuable."

Emerence's face fell, but Margot was too much taken up with the news that she was to lose her bosom friend to pay any heed to Mary-Lou's last dictum. She sat staring at Emerence, consternation in her eyes. Emmy was leaving! She would be going back to Australia and they might never meet her again! It was a stunning blow.

Pity softened Mary-Lou's eyes as she saw the expression on the younger girl's face. All the same, this must be dealt with and quickly. She rapped on the table.

"Margot! Wake up! Pay attention to me, please. I want to know what reason you have for hating Ted as you seem to do."

All her grievances came crowding in on Margot.

"Because I do! She's stealing my sister from me. And Con's being infected by Len and she's begun to have special pals. I don't want them to—they ought to be satisfied with me!"

Ted sat up with a bang, her eyes looking ready to drop out of her head. Len and Con kept theirs on the table and Emerence let her mouth fall open, which made her look like a stranded codfish!

"But you have Emerence," Mary-Lou pointed out, paying no attention to the others. "Do you expect them to think and say that you're not to be friends with her any more, but be satisfied with them?"

"It's quite different. Emmy and I have been pals for years."

"It's no different! It's precisely the same thing for any of you. If one can have a friend, so can the rest. However, we'll leave that alone for the moment. Tell me; how did you propose to force Ted to break with Len if Len wouldn't break with her?"

"I—I was going to threaten—to tell all the others—that she'd been expelled from three other schools if—if she wouldn't promise me faithfully she—she'd have no more to do with Len. I—I didn't think she'd—like that!" Margot faltered. Somehow it sounded so very much worse when she put it into words herself and yet, with Mary-Lou's grave blue eyes holding hers, she couldn't refuse to explain.

"I see." Mary-Lou leaned back in her chair and thought. She decided that Margot needed a shock. It was high time she stopped this sort of thing. "In other words," she said slowly, "you proposed to commit blackmail. That's a criminal offence, in case you didn't know it and one of the nastiest there is. Men and women are sent to prison for that sort of thing."

Margot gazed at her in silence.

Len said rather shakily, "I thought blackmail was demanding money by threats."

"That's one form of it. There are others—trying to force someone to do something they don't want to do by using threats is one. That's what Margot meant to do." Mary-Lou said drily. "Now I'll tell you four something. One of the chief reasons why the thing was kept quiet was that the Head thought there were plenty of young idiots in the school to think Ted had been very daring and rather clever if they knew some of the things she had done. She wasn't!" Mary-Lou was quite ruthless about this and Ted's face burned as she went on. "She was merely making a sickening nuisance of herself and behaving like a silly young ass. She wouldn't be warned, so she got what she asked for—and serve her right!" At which point, Ted wished she could slide under the table and keep out of sight for the rest of this devastating interview. Mary-Lou carried right on. "When all comes to all, you know, she hasn't really done anything worse than Emerence, with whom you're so chummy, did in her early days!"

It was Emerence's turn to wish she could vanish as she recalled some of those exploits and she reddened as furiously as Ted had done.

"In fact," Mary-Lou continued sweetly, "I don't see that there's much to choose between the pair of them. However, Emmy began to get sense quite a while back and she's pulled up enormously. And I think, Ted," she suddenly projected a brilliant smile at the bemused Ted, "that we may say that you're doing likewise. Good for you—both of you! Keep it up! And now, that's all I've got to say to you two at present, though I certainly want to know more about this cheque of yours, Emerence. You two may go. Leave the clock, Emmy. As I've said, I'm afraid it's something I must hand over to the Head or Uncle Jack to deal with. I haven't quite made up my mind which, but I rather think that's what it'll come to in the end."

Thankful to get away with whole skins, the pair left. Mary-Lou was left with the triplets. She regarded them in silence for a moment or two. It was easy enough to deal with both Ted and Emerence, but this was more complicated. Finally she spoke.

"Len, it's more than time that you stopped worrying over your sisters and left them to stand on their own feet. They're quite capable of looking after themselves. If you don't take care, you're going to turn into a fidgety, fussy old maid before you're thirty and a nice thing *that* will be! Have all the friends you want and then perhaps you'll be able to get it out of your head that Con and Margot need you on their tails every other minute of the day. Anyhow, it's your right, as I told you before, and it's time you looked after your own rights a little. That's all I have to say to *you*"

Len got up and trailed to the door, for this was clearly dismissal. Arrived there, she turned. "I suppose you're right, Mary-Lou," she said subduedly, "but I honestly didn't mean to be fussy and interfering."

Mary-Lou gave her an indulgent smile. "I don't suppose you did, but that's where you're heading unless you check it right now. However, I think this has been a pretty sharp warning. You can look out for signs of it recurring in the future and stamp on it at once."

Len slipped out and Mary-Lou turned to Con who was looking as she felt, thoroughly alarmed. "Con," she said gently, "I'm sure you meant well, but it's high time you stopped blurting out just what's uppermost in your mind. There's such a thing as tact and if you're born without it, you must try to acquire a little. It was all very well when you were a little girl, but you're that no longer. Grown-up people who do that sort of thing are often avoided like poison by others because they won't try to think before they speak and so often hurt their friends badly. You can see for yourself what's come of your latest efforts. Margot is in a nice mess and though most of it is her own fault, you're not entirely without blame. Things were bad and you made them worse. Go away, and in future, try to think before you speak."

Exit Con, her cheeks fierily red, for she felt that every word of this speech was deserved. No one could say that

Mary-Lou wasn't dealing as faithfully as in her lay with the whole lot.

Only Margot was left now. Mary-Lou looked at her as she sat there with a dazed expression and her heart sank. How could she possibly cope with things as serious as the youngest triplet's sins? Wisely, she decided that it really was beyond her. She waited a minute to pray inarticulately but earnestly for the best words. They came to her.

"Margot," she said, and her voice was very kind, "I don't think you've ever fully realised till now just how awful your way of thinking has been, though I'm sure you do know it—now. But this is something I can't tackle—not properly. I'm not going to report you to the Head—I'm not even going to tell you to report yourself. But until you either do that or go to Uncle Jack—not Auntie Joey; or not at present, at any rate—you'll never know another happy moment. I'm leaving it to you to decide what you'll do. That's all," She paused. Then, touched by the deep unhappiness she saw in the blue eyes, she added, "But if you'd like it, I'll come with you to the Head and help you out at first if that's what you decide to do. If you want to be happy again, it's the only thing that will do it. I mean that—honestly!"

Margot sat silent, but the dazed look had gone. Mary-Lou watched her anxiously. Which way would she decide?

Margot had a hard fight with her pride and jealousy. It lasted a short while, during which the Head Girl remained as silent as she. But she did her best to make the younger girl feel that she hadn't to stand alone, at least, not until the confession was over. The voiceless sympathy worked. Margot looked up suddenly. Her jaw was set and her eyes were bright again. She got up from her chair.

"Come with me to the door, anyhow," she said with a gulp. "I'm going *now*!"

Chapter 20

THE HEAD MAKES A DECISION

"AND I'm not to ask a single question—not one?" Joey looked at Miss Annersley over the small dark head of her very new daughter with pleading eyes.

"Not a single question," Miss Annersley returned firmly as she cuddled the young lady's equally new twin brother.

"I'm not sure that I like it, Hilda. Oh, I can see that things have been happening while I've been out of circulation! For one thing, Margot is sweeter and more subdued than I've ever known her to be before. Con seems to be trying to think before she speaks; and I can see that Len is leaving her sisters to look after themselves and is going all out for her friendships with Rosamund and Ted. I'm more than thankful for that last! What I want to know is what have you all been doing to bring about such a state of things in so short a time?"

Her friend shook her head. "I told you, not a single question! Jack knows all about it. Can't you trust him and me?"

"Oh, I can trust you all right. But for my own satisfaction, I must have more. Tell me if it's good or bad. If your idea is to save me from worrying, let me tell you that I'm far more likely to worry if you try to keep me in ignorance in this style!"

"Yes, I see that. I can't tell you much, Joey, or not yet. It *has* been bad—very bad. But good is coming out of it. I'm sure of that. I think the worst is all over now; but it's been a long pull and a hard pull and your triplets have had some very stiff lessons to learn—are learning and likely to be for some time, for that matter. But they've come to it of their own free will, thanks, in the main, I think, to

Mary-Lou. You can't call them babies any longer, my dear. They're growing up and doing it quickly. Now that's all I can say—except don't worry! Your girls have fine stuff in them and before they're done, I know you'll have reason to be proud of every one of them—and I mean that!"

Joey sighed. "Just one thing more, Hilda! What about Ted? Has she made good?"

Miss Annersley nodded. "Yes, she has. She's working hard, playing hard and between that and the real friendship I can see between her and Len and Rosamund, she simply has no time to think up outrageous pranks. What's more, she's improving in looks amazingly and that's having a good effect, too. But I'm afraid there'll never be much more than a cool friendship between her and her mother—if as much. Ted's a clever girl and she realises that her mother has very little affection for her. By the way, I understand that Mary-Lou, having heard the whole story, told her that she had been neither clever nor funny, but merely a sickening nuisance! So if Ted was under any misapprehension about that, it has been well and truly corrected. Now I must go! I expect half-a-dozen people are crying out for me!"

She went off and Joey, still not too satisfied, but with her mind easy about her triplets as it had not been since she had come home early in July with her new twins, also departed. A batch of proofs had arrived that morning and she wanted to look them over before she settled down to correcting them properly.

The Head was right when she said she was wanted. From the time she reached the school until she shut her bedroom door on the world and sank down in a chair for an hour's rest before going to bed, she was kept hard at it. Then her mind went back to that night when Mary-Lou had brought Margot to her to confess.

It had been a difficult interview, but by the time Margot had got to the end of her sorry tale—including the eaves-dropping—the Head had known where she stood.

"I certainly didn't spare her," she mused. "And from all I can gather, Mary-Lou expected that, for from what Margot says, it was her kindness and offer to stand by that finally persuaded her to come to me. What a blessing that girl has been to us, all through her school-life! Though," and she laughed to herself, "I admit I didn't think so much of it when she made that wild start and nearly gave herself brain-fever by trying to catch up with Clem. All through, she has been just what we want our girls to be. When the time comes for her to say goodbye to us finally, I shall have the joy of knowing that we are sending forth a girl who will bear the standard of the Chalet School right through her life."

Her thoughts went on with the days immediately following when Jack Maynard had to be called in to ask what should be done about the clock. He had insisted on hearing the whole story and his deep disgust at his daughter's doings had nearly broken Margot's heart. For a full fortnight he had refused to have anything to do with her. Margot adored her father and his coldness had made her realise more fully than ever how far she had fallen. He wanted to have the clock given back to Emerence, but the Head had coaxed him to change his mind.

"Let her keep it, Jack," she pleaded. "Emerence had no right to give her such a thing, but it's done now. Emerence is leaving and goodness knows when those two will meet again. Let them have what comfort they can out of the clock. Not," she had added with a flash of insight, "that Margot will get much pleasure out of it for the present. It will remind her too much of all that has happened. To return it will hurt Emerence badly and she doesn't deserve it. I've told her all I think of her for suppressing that cheque when she knows the school rules as well as anyone."

So Margot was allowed to keep it and it was in her bedroom at Freudesheim. But the Head was quite right. It would be many a long day before the girl could rejoice in it again, and it served as a reminder to her of all that had happened at the time. But Margot was changing and changing fast. Her feet were on the right road and she would do her best to keep them there. When the day came that it was her turn to leave school and fare forth into grown-up life, she admitted to Miss Annersley that the little clock had helped her time and again to stop short when she had been going to go wrong.

Tired out from her busy day, the Head undressed, said her prayers with a special thought for Margot and Ted, opened her windows and then lay down. Before sleep finally came, she made up her mind about a project very dear to her heart. She must discuss it with Madge Russell and Joey, but she felt sure that she knew what they would say.

"I shan't say anything to her until the time comes," she thought drowsily. "And it shall be for the school only. After all, it's to the school that it matters most. The girls who are leaders can make or mar a school. Thank God, so far all our leaders have led the right way; but, apart from Joey herself, Mary-Lou most of all." Then she really did stop thinking, mainly because she was so drowsy, and fell asleep to slumber peacefully until the morning.

Chapter 21

CHEERS FOR MARY-LOU!

"HEIGH-HO! This is our last Sports Day as members of the Chalet School!" And Vi Lucy heaved a deep sigh.

"Well, that's no reason for trying to blow us all down into the valley!" Hilary snapped at her. "Stop grousing and bring your weighty mind to bear on the problem of how we're to find any more seats for the visitors. Apart from the Head's drawing-room, I don't believe there's a chair, stool or form left in the place and Burnie told me she didn't think we had enough, even so. Any ideas on the subject?"

"None whatsoever! I suppose the school will sit on rugs as usual? Have we got everything Auntie Joey can spare?"

"I expect so. Mary-Lou had a string of half-a-dozen hard at it before Frühstück, carrying over everything she could spare."

"Then the only other thing I can think of is to use the trestle tables and perch all the lightweights on them."

"And how do you propose to manage that may I ask? You can't very well ask people if they weigh less than — well, nine stone? Most of them would look on it as a deep and deadly insult."

"Ye-es, that certainly might happen. Then the only other thing that I can see is to collect up all the rugs and mats we can find and spread them in front of the chairs. Sure to be plenty of people who won't mind sitting on the ground for once. Any Old Girls, for instance."

"Well, I suppose it's the best we can do," Hilary assented, going off to find the games mistress and explain to her.

Vi remained where she was and here Mary-Lou found her when she came flying along to order all the Juniors into the house to go and change before Mittagessen.

"Hello!" she said, pausing a moment. "You seem to be taking things very easily."

"I've slogged the whole morning," Vi said with dignity.

"Well, come and help me round up the kids. Matey wants to make sure that they're all changed and ready before Mittagessen. Where's Hilary?"

"Gone to tell Burnie that if there aren't enough seats, we must use rugs and mats. OK. I'll come. Is Aunty Joey bringing the new babies along, do you know?"

"She is not! She's coming along after her rest, I believe. I rather thought she'd have been here this morning, but she didn't turn up and I didn't see her when I went over for chairs earlier on. Thank goodness none of the visitors turn up till fourteen o'clock.

"And thank goodness the rain ceased at the end of the afternoon yesterday! I had horrid visions of having to cut at least half the sports! But it's been so hot this morning that everywhere has dried up nicely and certainly the whole place looks really fresh and clean after the downpour." Vi cast a complacent look round as she followed Mary-Lou to the tennis courts where most of the sports would take place. All the nets had been removed, thus throwing the six courts into one big area which was surrounded now by the long rows of seats—a very mixed bag of them, too.

"Thank goodness indeed!" Mary-Lou agreed fervently. "Hello! There are Loyola de Manselle and Nest Owen. Latch on to them and send them in while I hunt up the rest!"

After that, they parted and from then until after Mittagessen all the prefects were kept busy. But once the meal was ended and they had cleared they had time, as the Head Girl said, to breathe freely.

It had been decided to invite the visitors to come for the afternoon session and during the morning, such unspectacular events as throwing the cricket-ball, some of the short sprints and both the long and high jumps had been got out of the way. What was left would, they all hoped, provide their audience with thrills at least.

"It's to be hoped that a third of them haven't to be treated for hysterics!" Lesley Malcolm said darkly. "Thank goodness we've cut out the flower-pot race. We've had it so often, it must be palling on people."

"Anyhow, it's always been a gift to Verity Carey," Vi put in. "Verity, how do you do it? You just seem to float from pot to pot. I never saw anything like it!"

Verity, a tiny girl and "sister-by-marriage" to Mary-Lou, since her father had married that young lady's mother, merely smiled sweetly and said nothing.

"Can you wonder?" Mary-Lou herself said. "There's nothing of her and never was. I'm eight solid inches taller than she is!"

The bell rang at that moment, so conversation had to cease and they all marched to Hall where they stood in their lines, wondering what was going to happen now. They couldn't take their usual half-hour's rest, since every deck-chair was beside the courts.

They were not left to wonder long. The top door opened and the Head, very stately in her blue silk dress and big hat to match, appeared.

"Just a minute, girls! We are going to send you out to the courts and you are to sit down and keep as quiet as you can for the next twenty minutes. The interval for refreshments will come at sixteen o'clock. All those helping in the visitors' marquee must be there at least ten minutes before then. There will be drinks for you in the other and also biscuits. Abendessen will come half-an-hour earlier in the garden and you can make up for it then. Juniors, remember what I said to you this morning and don't raise the whole Platz with yelling. That is all. Turn! Forward—march!"

Led by the prefects for once, the school passed out through the double doors at the bottom of Hall and marched smartly to the far end of the tennis courts where they sat down on the rugs spread for them. For twenty minutes they rested there with the prefects to see that they kept quiet as the Head had commanded. The staff came strolling out in twos and threes to take up their positions nearby. The Head, with Mdlle, Miss Wilson from St. Mildred's and Rosalie Dene went up to the other end and then the first visitors arrived.

It was a full and busy afternoon. The sports were as good as usual and the girls showed that if they worked hard in school, they also played hard. Mary-Lou won the long distance race, her lengthy legs eating up the distance. Margot took the high jump, Len and Con won the three-legged race by a very comfortable margin, and Ted showed what she could do in the way of rope-climbing. As Margot said with a giggle, she must be first cousin to a monkey for nothing else could have climbed at that rate!

Next came the open obstacle race which had been concocted by the prefects and a nice time they gave the competitors!

Besides climbing a tree and wriggling through three nets, they had to skip for twenty yards, hop on one foot for another twenty—whereby, five people were out of it—turn ten cartwheels, thread a dozen needles, add up an appalling sum of francs and centimes and get the answer right—this eliminated another four—roll over and over for a short distance and finally throw somersaults up to the rope which was held by two of the younger doctors from the Sanatorium. In the end, if fell to Verity Carey, who got through the nets faster than anyone else and, for a wonder, got the right answer to the sum first time.

The blindfold race was the usual yell, to quote Mary-Lou and was won by no one, for no one contrived to get anywhere near the tape. Finally, they came to what Mary-Lou described as the cream of the day. This was the idea Vi Lucy had said she had and it was funny, to say the least of it.

Ten girls were left in the finals, the heats having been run off earlier in the week, and they ranged from Mary-Lou herself to small Ailie Russell of Lower IVb. The competitors stood on their marks and a big bundle, well tied up, was put in front of each. When the pistol banged, they all squatted down and began to undo the knots with frantic haste. Then it was seen that each bundle held a collection of weird garments and the audience simply screamed with laughter at the sight of Mary-Lou trying to pull on a pair of Dutch breeches meant for a twelve-year-old over her long legs. Slim as she was, she filled them more than comfortably and her loud groan of, "Ow! I'll have to crawl or bust them!" was to be heard all over. The next article was a Georgian polonaise followed by a large shawl and a tiny mobcap which she perched carefully on top of her rampant curls. An enormous umbrella completed the collection and she opened it and then set off at a snail's pace in case she really did burst her seams!

Verity had to get into a voluminous skirt that trailed all round her feet, a pair of gum boots so large that, when she set off, she could merely shuffle in them, and, as a finishing touch, a pair of wings and a halo! The rest were equally weird and the sight of all these extraordinarily clad creatures shuffling, waddling, mincing and, in the case of Con, who had found an old-fashioned hobble skirt so tight that she dared not try to walk, jumping along, can be better imagined than described. Joey laid her head on her husband's shoulder and wept gently. The most serious-minded person there held her sides and shouted. Vi had certainly succeeded in livening up the sports on this occasion!

The race finally fell to Emerence Hope who had found a Father Christmas outfit in her bundle, complete with wig, beard and sack crammed with hay. She arrived at the tape crimson and perspiring, but Ricki Fry who was in full mandarin's dress and had had to race fanning herself the whole way as well as carrying a huge Chinese umbrella, tripped up over her petticoat; otherwise, the race had looked like being hers.

Only the tug-o'-war, a House event, was left then and Joey, remembering her new babies, had to slip away before then, so she missed seeing St. Clare's beat everyone hollow. But she managed to turn up for the prize-giving, looking as trig and fresh as if she had spent the entire afternoon resting.

The highlight of the term came on the following Monday evening at Prayers. As many of the girls would be leaving at seven the next morning, these were the end of term Prayers. When the little services were over and the Catholics had come to Hall to join the school to hear the Head's good wishes for their holidays, there was a little pause and then Joey appeared on the dais. The girls quite frankly gaped. This was a new departure.

Miss Annersley had come forward to the lectern once more and all eyes were turned on her as she spoke. "Girls! This year, we are awarding a new prize. It has never been given before, but I hope that, in the future, we may be able to give it again and again. It has been said that what a school is must largely depend on its leaders among the girls themselves. We have had many girls who have been fine leaders, but I think you will agree that one of the finest we have had has been Mary-Lou Trelawney who leaves us tomorrow to become a member of St. Mildred's next term."

"Mary-Lou!" She faced Mary-Lou who was staring with her mouth open. "It is with the very greatest pleasure that we present you with this—hardly prize, for there has been no competition—but reward for all you have done for the school during your time here. We are grateful for your help and our best wishes go with you into the future."

She stopped there and waited. But Mary-Lou was so overcome that Hilary and Vi had to pull her to her feet and push her towards the dais before she got there. Finally, she was standing beside the Head and Joey who was offering her a case, stoutly made of leather. Joey opened it before she put it into her hands and inside was a very complete first-aid outfit.

"For your use when you're trotting round eastern countries, pursuing archaeology," Joey said with a grin as the bemused Mary-Lou accepted it. She turned to the girls, but her own Margot was before her.

Springing to her feet, Margot cried, "She jolly well deserves it! Everyone! Cheers for Mary-Lou, the best Head Girl we've ever known!"

The cheers came—in such volume that the Head afterwards remarked that she only wondered someone from the Sanatorium didn't ring up to ask what was happening.

Mary-Lou stood stockstill, going alternately red and white. Then, still holding the case, she turned to the school and the shouts died down. Crimson and overcome to the point of tears in her eyes, Mary-Lou spoke.

"It's far, far more than I could ever deserve. I've only done what I thought I ought, and not always that. If you want to thank anyone, you ought to thank the school for it's the school that's shown me how to manage. Thank you all, awfully, both for this lovely thing and for cheering me. But I don't deserve it, honestly, I don't!"

Then she raced off the dais and hid herself as much as she could among her peers while once more the school let itself go in cheers for Mary-Lou.